Chasing the Devil's Tail

David Fulmer

Poisoned Pen Press

Copyright © 2001 by David Fulmer

First Edition 2001

10 9 8 7 6 5 4 3 2 1

Library of Congress Catalog Card Number: 2001091227

ISBN: 1-890208-84-1 Hardcover
ISBN: 1-890208-94-9 Trade Paperback

Poisoned Pen Press
6962 E. First Ave. Ste. 103
Scottsdale, AZ 85251
www.poisonedpenpress.com
info@poisonedpenpress.com

Printed in the United States of America

Thanks are due.

To my agent Laura Langlie, for never giving up the fight. To my publisher Robert Rosenwald and my editor Barbara Peters, for making it real. To Steve Loehrer and Barbara Saunders, brother and sister in all but blood, for staying in my corner. To Barbara Bent, for having her heart in the right place. To my parents, Thurston and Flora Prizzi Fulmer, and my sister, Karen Mertz, for tending to the roots of the tree.

This is for Talia, the flower on its highest branch.

You best be careful if you go chasin' the devil's tail, cause you just might catch it.

— *Attributed to Jelly Roll Morton*

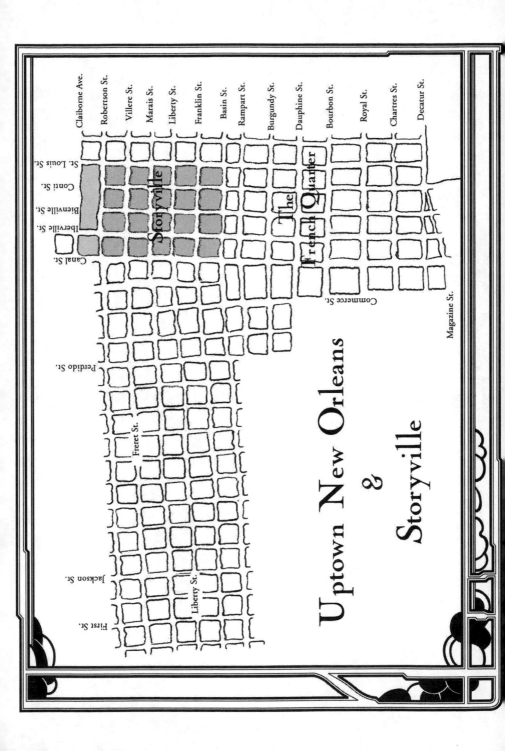

Uptown New Orleans & Storyville

Chasing the Devil's Tail

Prologue

Mayoralty of New Orleans
City Hall
January 29, 1897
No. 13,032, Council Series

Section 1.

Be it ordained by the Common Council of
the City of New Orleans, that from the first
of October, 1897, it shall be unlawful for
any public prostitute or woman notoriously
abandoned to lewdness to occupy, inhabit,
live or sleep in any house, room or closet
situated without the following limits: South
side of Custom-house Street from Basin
to Robertson Street, east side of Robertson
Street from Customhouse to St. Louis,
from Robertson to Basin Street.

It was after three A.M. when the trouble started.

Valentin St. Cyr was working the floor that night. He
never caught the fine lines of the spat, but it had something
to do with a certain pimp and some citizen's sister or daughter. The offended brother or father walked in off the street,
stepped up to the bar, put a foot on the brass rail and ordered
a glass of rye whiskey. He surveyed the room until he spotted the pimp, a ratty Creole named Littlejohn, standing not
fifteen feet away.

Ferdinand LeMenthe, taking a few minutes away from
the grand piano in Hilma Burt's parlor next door, glanced
up from his seat at the bar to see a dapper-looking white

man waving him out of the way with the blue-black muzzle of a Colt .22.

Valentin saw the whole thing from the other side of the room, but it happened so fast there was nothing he could have done, even if he had been willing to risk taking a bullet for a piece of shit like Littlejohn. In one instant, the pistol appeared and he heard a sharp bang and saw LeMenthe jump back as the shot whistled by to catch the pimp neatly at the base of the skull.

The music wound down in three jagged notes and the card players froze in mid-deal. All heads turned to watch the pimp crumple against the bar and then raise one hand as if asking for a moment's pause while he ordered a drink. His eyes fluttered and he fell forward stiffly, landing on the floor with a face-down thud.

The dapper fellow peered complacently over the end of the bar, laid the smoking pistol down and picked up his glass of whiskey. Valentin stepped to his side, slid the weapon out of reach, and sent for the coppers. Someone threw a rug over Littlejohn. The music started up again, the rounders went back to their hands, and the revelry resumed.

It lasted until New Orleans Police Lieutenant J. Picot arrived and promptly cleared the room. The fellows in the band called it a night, put up their horns, and stepped down yawning from the low stage. The gamblers pocketed their winnings, the suckers counted their losses, and they all pushed back from the tables. There was a scraping of chairs, a shuffling of feet and a babble of low laughter and goodnights. St. Cyr and LeMenthe tagged onto the tail of the crowd heading for the street.

"Hold it up, there!" Picot called. The two men turned to see the policeman standing over Littlejohn's body, crooking a fat sausage of a finger. Valentin walked back to the bar.

"You, too, piano man," Picot said, and LeMenthe joined him.

Picot regarded both characters with annoyance, then fixed a hard eye on the private detective. "Ain't you hired to prevent this kind of thing?" he said. "Ain't that what Mr. Tom Anderson pays you for?" He glanced at LeMenthe, taking in the piano player's light skin and wavy locks and fine tailored suit. "And what are you doin' in the middle of this?" he asked.

LeMenthe, a young man who almost never stopped talking, opened his mouth to explain. But Picot wasn't really interested. He said, "Shut it, now," and LeMenthe's mouth closed. He returned his attention to the Creole detective St. Cyr. "I want to know right now what in hell happened here," he demanded. "I want to know where is the man what shot Littlejohn."

Valentin said reasonably, "I believe you just chased him outdoors."

Picot stared for a moment, then looked at LeMenthe, who was trying not to smile. "Go," he said and the piano player went. Picot leaned his head toward St. Cyr as if indulging a secret. "I don't like you," he said. "And I don't care to see you again any time soon."

"That suits me fine," Valentin said and turned away.

He walked with LeMenthe to the door of Hilma Burt's mansion and then went home.

Within the hour, one of Picot's patrolmen found the fellow who shot Littlejohn the pimp, strolling calmly along St. Louis Street, enjoying the sights. He surrendered without resistance.

One

We have been visited by a sad
affliction. Several coons armed with
pieces of brass have banded
together for what personal good we
are unable to say, except that it be
for two dollars a week and glue,
but we are able to swear that if
their object was to inflict torture
upon the suffering community,
they are doing right well.

—*The Mascot*

Valentin heard the horn while he was still two blocks from
Jackson Square. It was quicksilver shooting from a Gatling
gun, exactly the kind of rainbows of loud brass, he imagined, that would announce the New Orleans version of the
Second Coming. As he stepped from Chartres Street into
the square, he saw a familiar profile juking across the open
bandstand, looking from that distance like a country preacher
cajoling his congregation.

They hadn't run up on each other in a few weeks, so when
Buddy saw Valentin step from the crowd, he broke into a
wicked grin and went careening over the rough boards,
blowing steam from the bell of his horn. He finished the
rowdy version of "Careless Love" with a shower of staccato
notes, then hopped down from the bandstand to cut a rolling

path through the crowd. Men clapped his back and women gave him sloe eyes, but he didn't notice, rushing up to Valentin, happy as a kid.

"Tino!" he shouted and threw arms that were all gawky angles around his friend.

⚮

They sat in the shade of a live oak. The day was hazy with heat and from that distance, the scene around the bandstand looked like an unfinished painting. Another band was playing, and Buddy was half-listening to the raggedy waltz, his fingers absently tapping out his own choice of notes on the valves of his horn.

Valentin took the moment to study Bolden with sidelong glances, taking in the almond-shaped eyes, the nose thin like an Egyptian, and the mouth with the lower lip full and the upper one peaked in the middle, as if they had been placed on him already fit for a horn. His hair, as always, was cut very short and parted with a razor. The one oddity was his clothes, now all dirty and in disarray. He had always been particular.

The band on the stand reached the end of the song and Buddy turned on him with a sudden frown. "What brings you out in the light of day?" There was a brittle edge to his voice.

Valentin let it pass, leaning back against the trunk of the tree and twiddling a blade of grass between his fingers. "Annie Robie," he said.

At the mention of the name, the dark cloud that was over Buddy's face lifted and he smiled again. "She sent you round?" he said, "Is that right?"

The band started up again and the strains of the slow waltz drifted from the hazy distance.

"Were you at Cassie Maples' last night?" Valentin asked.

The smile widened, all white teeth. "I was, yes."

"What time did you leave?"

Buddy served up a curious look. "I don't know. Musta been round one o'clock."

Valentin hesitated for a moment, then said, "They found Annie this morning, Buddy. She's dead."

Buddy blinked as if he didn't understand, his smile collapsing inward. "Did you say dead?" Valentin nodded. "How?"

"Miss Cassie found her in her room. It was like she went to sleep and never woke up."

Buddy shook his head slowly. "She was up and about. She took me to the door," he said. Valentin saw him struggle with the somber news, then sigh and say, "She was just a young girl," as if that mattered.

∾

They sat in the shade of the tree for another ten minutes, as Buddy lapsed deeper into silence, answering Valentin's questions shortly, then not at all. Finally, he got to his feet and walked away, not a word or a gesture or a look back, a tall figure in a stained cotton shirt and white linen trousers, horn dangling from one hand, wavering off into the pool of afternoon heat that hung over the park.

A few minutes later, Valentin stood up, brushed the Louisiana dust from his trousers and made his way out of the park, wondering why he had even bothered to come there.

∾

It had started early that morning. Too early.

He had been lying half-asleep, curled around a coffee-colored dove named Justine, when he heard the shuffle of footsteps in the hallway outside the door.

His right eyelid twitched and his hand stretched directly to the inside pocket of the linen suit jacket that hung from a chair beside the bed. He folded his fingers around the mother-of-pearl handle of his Iver Johnson revolver and drew the pistol down under the sheets, all without moving a muscle on his left side. Justine didn't stir, flat wearied from their tussling atop the cotton coverlet, her dark curls splayed across the pillow and one of her arms was flung palm-up over the side of the bed.

The rustle of movement in the hall grew busier and there came the hesitant tapping of a feminine hand on the door. "Mr. St. Cyr?" Though muffled, the name was pronounced the American way, *saint-sear*. The door creaked open a few inches. "Beg your pardon." The voice was a brown whisper.

Valentin relaxed his grip on the pistol, pushed himself to a sitting position and said, "Come in." One of Justine's dark eyes opened halfway. He made a small sound and she sighed and dug deeper into the sheets.

The door opened another few inches and the face of Antonia Gonzales appeared like the rising of an ochre moon. Miss Antonia slipped into the room and crossed through the gray morning shadows on feet that were light for so ample a woman. She bent down to whisper in his ear. He yawned, rubbed a hand over his eyes, and nodded.

～

The madam led him around the corner from Bienville and onto Franklin Street as the first true light of day poked through the mist off the river. They made a small parade on the deserted street, Miss Antonia in a shirtwaist of pale pastel buttoned at the neck and a silk moiré skirt that draped down to the wooden boards of the banquette, Valentin natty in a tight-fitting Cassimere suit of gray checks.

Though the hour was early, it was April and humid. All over the cobbled avenues, puddles of rainwater had collected skeins of green scum that gave up a sour stench. The two citizens of the swamp that was 1907 New Orleans marched west, taking bare notice. By noon this Sunday, the city would sweat enough to raise the Mississippi and the streets of cobble and dirt would grow rank, as dead animals, human waste, and kitchen slops steamed in the sun, attended by clouds of green flies. But from the hallowed pews of St. Ignatius

Church to the lice-ridden, dime-a-trick cribs that lined Robertson and Claiborne streets from Canal to St. Louis, only a fool would bother to complain.

They continued on to Franklin Street at an even pace, though the madam took two steps for every one of Valentin's and twisted her plump fingers in a constant fidgety roil. Valentin noticed, but wouldn't be hurried. Still, in the space of fifteen minutes they had crossed Gravier Street, leaving behind the stately brick façades, ornate colonnades, stained-glass transoms, and galleries adorned with potted ferns, to enter a dank, shadowy neighborhood of narrow dirt streets lined with houses that had weathered to a bleak gray, half their windowpanes stuffed with newspaper, their balustrades teetering on the galleries like loose teeth. The banquettes here were empty and the streets were quiet, but Valentin now glanced into every doorway and down every alley until they reached the corner of South Franklin and Perdido.

They stopped before a narrow two-story house of dull gray clapboard. He turned with a questioning look to Miss Antonia, who waved one fluttering hand, a pudgy brown bird, at a second floor balcony. He looked up at the wrought iron railing, once sturdy, now rotting away in the damp air, the French doors with their rusted hinges, and the dirty, cracked windows that stared back at him. He gestured for the madam to precede him up the wooden steps to the gallery.

∾

Cassie Maples, short and fat, her skin as black as an African night, pushed the door to the second floor room wide and stepped back.

Valentin went inside. It was a small room, not much bigger than a crib, just enough space for a divan, a wash basin, a folding screen in one corner with a Japanese design of peacocks on flowered branches, and a sampler on the wall. The French doors were closed and locked, odd for an already-sticky April and considering the sweaty business conducted within those walls. The divan was draped with a faded silk shawl, and stretched upon the shawl was the body of a young girl.

But that was all. He frowned vaguely and ran an irritable hand over his face. He hadn't gotten his sleep out, not nearly. Then he made the ten block walk with Miss Antonia all fussy at his side to be greeted by the body of a dead whore in a cramped upstairs room in a rundown sporting house. He wondered why the madam hadn't just gone ahead and called the coppers. He couldn't raise the poor girl from the dead nor make the corpse vanish into thin air, so he wasn't going to be much good at all.

He was about to mutter some excuse and take his leave, but he saw the two women standing in the doorway, watching him anxiously. He let out a quiet sigh and made himself step across the room to view the body.

She was naked except for a Liberty dime on a thin lace of leather around one ankle and a silver crucifix on a chain hanging from her neck. Her skin, deep black, had taken on a gray pallor. Her arms and legs were willowy and her breasts were round and firm, perfect circles. Her hands were folded between her legs, as if in blushing modesty. Her hair was jet black, cut short and pulled back severely from her forehead.

He studied her face, carved from soft ebony, a young face that had reached its final age. She was actually quite pretty, rare for what was called a "soiled dove" in the lingo of the penny newspapers. Valentin was relieved, as always, that the eyes were closed.

The rose was the first thing he had noticed when he stepped into the room, but it was the last thing he paused to regard. And the one thing he touched, lifting and replacing it with gentle fingers. A black rose in full bloom, stem attached, laid carefully across her torso, with the petals just touching the point of her heart.

He took another look around the room, saw nothing else unusual, turned away and walked into the hall. He closed the door behind him. The two madams searched his face.

"May I trouble you for a cup of coffee?" he said.

⁓

Miss Maples' girls had been sent away for the morning and the house was quiet. In the spare light, Valentin surveyed the usual trappings: Persian rugs, tasseled lamps, textured fabric full of blood-red swirls on the walls, heavy furniture covered in brocade, a tiered chandelier overhead. But he wasn't fooled. The hard light of day would reveal that the furnishings were all shabby secondhand goods and that the chandelier was missing half its pieces. There would be small dunes of ancient dust in the corners and ragged stains on the mangy upholstery. Footsteps would send an army of cockroaches and who knew what other vermin skittering along the baseboards.

He sat down gingerly on a café chair. The remains of the night's incense did not mask a damp, sour odor, evidence of a roof that leaked; and even from across the room he could tell that the maid—all sharp bone and nappy hair, homely and gap-toothed and looking as timid as a country mouse—had gone without a bath for more than a few days.

But he nodded politely, so startling the girl that when she stepped up with the china cup and saucer, her hands shook.

The two madams sat stiffly on the edge of a horsehair couch that was threatening to burst along its seams. Shafts of pale, dusty sunlight drifted through the tall, narrow streetside windows over Valentin's shoulder and across the thick rug. He sipped his coffee, feeling awake for the first time this day.

Cassie Maples paused in her fretting over the dreadful business upstairs to study the visitor. So this was the dangerous fellow Miss Antonia had whispered about. She looked him frankly up and down. He was on the short side and put together like a banty prizefighter. She noticed the frayed cuffs of the suit jacket, a shirt collar gone yellow with wear, a haircut of no recent vintage. She caught the distant set of his eyes and the way he settled in his chair, lazy and tense at the same time. A pint of Cherokee blood there, she guessed. Indeed, the man displayed a Creole that was odd even for New Orleans: light-olive Dago skin and curly African hair hanging down to his collar in back. A jagged nose like an Arab and eyes the gray-green color of the Mississippi. Though mustaches and beards were the fashion of the day, this one went clean-shaven. He was one of those types who missed being handsome, but would catch a woman's eye anyway, something about the way he—

"What has Miss Antonia told you about me?" The visitor interrupted her thoughts. His voice was slow and even, with a rough, almost hoarse edge to it. His gaze had settled on her.

"Only that you were a copper," the darker woman said, her hands now assuming a nervous flutter. "Before, I mean. But that now you are a Pinkerton man and you help out over in the District."

Valentin nodded. "That's right, except I'm no Pinkerton. I work on my own. I provide protection and fix disputes. Handle confidential matters, investigations and whatnot." He tilted his head toward Miss Antonia. "And I help my friends. When I can," he added, letting her know he hadn't crawled out of bed to spend his Sunday with her dead Ethiopian girl.

He sipped his coffee with its bitter hint of chicory. Miss Maples was staring at him anxiously and Miss Antonia narrowly, so he softened his tone. "I understand you want to keep this quiet," he said. The black-skinned madam let out a grateful sigh, but her frown returned when he said, "That's not possible. You'll have to call in the coppers. But we do have a little time. You can tell me about the young lady upstairs."

Miss Maples clasped her hands in her lap. "Her name," she began, "is Annie Robie."

As the madam recounted it—and as she had herself heard it late one night from the dead girl's own mouth—Annie Robie was descended from slave stock, her grandparents recognized as property of the family of the same name of the Mississippi Delta town of Leland, which was where she grew up, pretty and long-legged, with her mother's black-on-black skin and her father's high, West African cheekbones and slanted eyes.

She had been swept up one dizzy Delta night by a handsome Negro with pomaded hair, a gambler and moonshiner wandering far from his Georgia home and carrying a two-dollar Sears & Roebuck guitar, like many of the young men did nowadays. She was delivered two weeks later on Cassie Maples' doorstep with nothing but the rough cotton dress on her back. The guitar player had gotten all he wanted and had run off and left her as soon as they reached New Orleans. She was wandering along the riverbank when a local sporting woman found her, took pity, and carried her to Cassie Maples' South Franklin address directly.

To Miss Maples, because like all the bordellos in New Orleans, she catered with an eye to color. It was a matter of specialty, and Cassie Maples' back-of-town door was open to the deep browns and "Ethiopians," as some called the true black-skinned girls like Annie Robie.

She was nineteen, the madam explained, and except for when she went off for a few days with some fancy man, she had been a regular for two years, first as a maid to the working girls, later as a full-fledged member of the house, paying her fifty cents a night for the use of the room.

She was well liked and she did not cause trouble. She did not drink whiskey in excess, was never a hophead, and did not get into brawls with other girls and cause the police to be called.

"What about her male guests?" Valentin inquired.

"Only the better class of Negro gentlemen," Miss Maples replied with quiet pride.

"Creoles of Color?" The madam nodded. "White men?" She hesitated, glanced at Miss Antonia. "Now and again, yes," she said in a low voice.

Nothing odd had been heard or seen last evening. Miss Maples had gone off to bed, and the maid, making late rounds, had found Annie lying in that posture, complete with black rose. The maid ran to rouse the madam.

"If it wa'nt for that rose, I would have thought she was just sleeping," Miss Maples told him, her voice trembling.

Valentin drank off his coffee and stood up to stretch his back. The madam dabbed her eyes with one hand and gestured tragically with the other. The maid scurried from the shadows to replace his cup, bringing a gamy cloud of sweat. She shook some more, rattling the china, then ran back to her corner and faded into the furnishings. Valentin glanced at his pocket watch, replaced it and said, "Did Annie have any special friends?"

Miss Maples pondered. "Well, there was that fellow that brought her down here in the beginning. I believe his name was McTier or McTell, something like that." She saw the strange look the detective gave her at the mention of the name. "But I haven't seen him around in a year or more," she finished.

Valentin stared down at the worn carpet, seeing a handsome Negro with pomaded hair stretched out on a sawdust floor, blood bubbling from the hole in his chest. "That would be Eddie McTier," he said. "And he had no part in this. He was shot dead in a card game over in Algiers some months ago." The news was delivered in such an odd, muted way that the two women exchanged a glance that produced a question mark.

"What now, Mr. Valentin?" Antonia Gonzales said.

It took him a moment to raise his head and meet her gaze. "Now you can call the coppers," he said. "But don't worry, they won't cause you any trouble. They'll have a look around and write a report and ask after her next of kin. Then the girl will become an entry on a page which will go into a file and be forgotten." The women stared, astonished twins, at the muttered oration. "When they get here, send them up to the room," he said. "I'll be waiting." He turned for the stairs.

~

A half-hour later, a horse-drawn New Orleans Police wagon turned the corner at Gravier and pulled up to the banquette. Lieutenant J. Picot stepped with a grunt of irritation from the seat of the wagon and raised heavy-lidded eyes to the balcony. St. Cyr, the *private detective*, leaned there, one languid hand on the railing. Picot muttered something under his breath and motioned the two blue-uniformed patrolmen to follow him inside.

The copper quite filled the doorway of the room. He glanced over at Annie Robie's body and then his eyes, dusty marbles, turned on St. Cyr. "You are going to have to go easier on these girls," he said, smirking. He stepped across the room, stood over the divan, and shook his head. "No, she's a bit dark for your blood, ain't she?" Valentin didn't bother to answer.

The policeman raised both of the girl's eyelids, felt for lumps about the head and looked for finger marks around her throat, all the while yawning with disinterest. Finally, he picked up the rose, frowned, and glanced at the Creole detective. "What's this about?" Valentin gave a shrug. Picot peered at the tiny thorn pricks on Annie's breast, then tossed the flower aside.

He spoke over his shoulder to the patrolmen, who stood on either side of the door with their tall, round-topped helmets stuck in the crooks of their arms. "Carry her downtown," he said. "Maybe we'll have them take another look at the morgue, and maybe not." He yawned again. "Nigger sluts is one thing this city has in surplus." The two patrolmen walked out of the room.

"And what do you have to do with this?" Picot asked St. Cyr.

"Nothing," Valentin said. "A favor for a friend."

"Well, just so you know, there won't be no investigating here," the policeman said. "Not by me, not by you, not by nobody." He waited, but Valentin wouldn't rise to the bait. "We got more important things to do. And more important people to serve." He drew himself up and took a last look at Annie Robie. "Kinda pretty," he said. "But, by Jesus, she's black, ain't she?"

The rose was kicked aside when the policemen stepped up to wrap the body in a sheet of muslin. After they carried it away, Valentin picked up the flower and laid it on the divan. He went downstairs.

Picot had spoken briefly and with a barely veiled disgust to Cassie Maples and now closed his leather-bound notebook with a sharp snap. He threw a last cold glance at the Creole detective, who had just reached the bottom of the stairs and left to see the body downtown.

Valentin stood at the parlor window, watching the police wagon roll off, sipping the fresh cup of chicory coffee that the homely maid had pushed into his left hand even as he held a lukewarm one in his right.

Miss Antonia and Cassie Maples were whispering near the front door. He didn't have to hear to know what it was about. There had been a death in the house and a remedy was required immediately. The madams were discussing which hoodoo woman should be called in to rid the premises of whatever foul spirits were lingering.

Valentin set his coffee cup aside. The maid hurried from a corner to snatch it up and replace it. When he shook his head, the girl dropped her eyes and turned away, but he caught her by a dry, rough hand. Country. Country, and in grave need of a bath. "What's your name?" he asked, so startling her that she said it twice.

"Sally. Sally." Her eyes blinked crazily.

Valentin let go of the trembling hand. "You got any idea what happened to Annie?" he asked her. Sally shook her nappy head. "You remember the last man to see her?" he said, holding his breath.

The girl managed to find her voice. "She was up and about after that last one left," she squeaked. "She walk him to the door and then come back in. She was downstairs for maybe a half-hour after. Then I didn't see her no more."

"That so?"

"Yessir."

Valentin lowered his voice. "You know the man? That last one?" The girl's eyes grew wide. "You can tell me," he said and bowed his head like a priest at confession. Still, it took a few moments for Sally to decide to go ahead and whisper the name. Valentin raised his head and looked at her sharply. "You're sure?"

"Oh, yessir, I'm sure." He could barely hear her. "Miss Maples and the girls get all excited when he come in. Yessir, it was King Bolden, all right."

આ

Valentin walked out of the park and onto the quiet, sultry Sunday streets.

King Bolden.

Kid Bolden.

Buddy Bolden.

Charles Bolden, Jr.

The names were like stepping stones that wound back to the morning-bright avenues that fanned out from the intersection of First and Liberty. That was when they were kids, students at St. Frances de Sales School for Colored on Second Street. They had been best friends all through their childhood and until they were young men, until things changed for both of them.

Even then, in those long ago days, amid the grinding, grating, clanging, banging noise of the city, Buddy heard things. He would stop in the midst of their frantic play and pose suddenly, his ear cocked to the wind. "Do you hear that?" he'd say. "You hear?"

To Valentin it was just a wash of city noise bursting around his head, but Buddy caught something there. Even when it was quiet, when the darkness fell and the streets went still and their mothers had not yet stepped out on their galleries to call sweetly for them to come home, he would hold a finger to the night and whisper, "You hear, Tino? You *hear?*" Valentin tried, but only Buddy heard.

Later on, he became a family man who attended church socials and a cornetist of no particular distinction. He gave lessons to young boys who would rather have been playing baseball. His horn announced, in stately tones, births and confirmations and weddings and funerals, all the momentous occasions of life in the Uptown neighborhoods.

But then he got hired for a job with a band that worked a Rampart Street saloon, a dank, sweaty, bucket-of-blood patronized by no-good rounders, cheap whores and assorted minor criminals who didn't give a good goddamn what he played, as long as it was loud. Which suited him just fine; he was sick to death of polite music and polite audiences. And so he began spending long nights in that smoky back-of-town beer hall, turning New Orleans music upside-down.

He left the standard styles in the dust and stumbled onto his own sound, a crazy quilt that was sort of like ragtime, sort of like the gutbucket music that some now called "blues," with touches of the old quadrille and schottische dances, and fat chunks of loud and happy church music thrown in for good measure. All of it blasted out at maximum volume in a frenzy of motion, like a one-man drunken parade.

Within a year, he was filling the Rampart Street saloons every night and people all over the city were talking. A local newspaperman, after venturing a trip back-of-town to witness the spectacle, reported that what Bolden played was musical "chatter," using the French *jaser* to dramatize his disdain. It stuck; and soon everybody back-of-town knew what it meant when a band went to jassing a tune.

But nobody jassed like Buddy, especially late at night, when he'd find himself a gutbucket moan, blowing his horn so deep blue it was almost black, and so hot it was like the pit of a hot coal; either that, or in one of his famous rants, rushing up and down the stage like he was about to run right out of his mind, tearing jagged holes in the night, loud enough and rough enough, some swore, to rattle the bones of the most recently deceased in St. Louis Cemetery No. 2.

Though a nickname was an honor reserved for veterans, people started calling him "Kid" Bolden. Then he did what no other New Orleans musician, veteran or otherwise, would dream of doing: he put his own name on his band. No Pickwick or Eagle or Excelsior for him; that wouldn't do at all. It was the Kid Bolden Band. Then it was "King Bolden," and for the better part of two years, he was the true king of New Orleans music. And then it began to fall apart.

No one could say for sure whether it was the Raleigh Rye that flowed through the streets like an amber river, or the hop or cocaine they sold at the apothecary, or the sweet, beckoning lips and heavy breasts and wide-spread legs of those lowdown whores, some evil hoodoo woman or even Satan himself that got to him. But whatever it was, his crazy business went into the street, and people were whispering to Valentin, back after a long time away, telling him how his mulatto boy Buddy Bolden was breaking into frantic pieces in front of uptown New Orleans and that maybe he just ought to look into it.

Valentin did, and discovered that Buddy had just stopped minding his manners altogether and was pushing his insides to the outside, right through the silver bell of his cornet. He did whatever he wanted, drank too much, fucked any woman he could get his hands on and hit the pipe when the yen came upon him. Meanwhile, he remained loving to his wife and daughter and kind to his friends.

But soon the cracks turned into gaping holes and Valentin heard regular reports of his fits and tantrums and blue funks. There were brawls in the music halls, spats with the fellows in his band, shouting fights that erupted from the windows of his house and echoed up and down First Street. The whispered word was that King Bolden was flat losing his mind.

Valentin saw it happening, but there was nothing he could do. Buddy, always headstrong, was a fast train careening down the track, all engine and no engineer, and God help anyone who got in the way. Anyway, Valentin had been gone too long, and things just weren't the same anymore.

❧

The evening found him on the narrow balcony outside the rooms he let over Gaspare's Tobacco Store at the bottom of Magazine Street, a few blocks from the river. He sipped lemonade laced with rye whiskey as the darkness fell, bringing a cooling breeze. The Mississippi flowed by in the twilight, but he was conjuring the image of Annie Robie laid out on that divan. It was one of those things he should have gotten used to in his line of work, but never had.

Someone should write one of those mournful songs about her, he mused, a "blues" like all the guitar players were making up. Eddie McTier might have done it, but his singing days were over; Valentin had seen to that; and what an odd happenstance that he should be called to the scene of Annie's death just months after sending her man McTier down that last lonely road.

Now she was gone, and she'd soon be forgotten. Once the hoodoo woman cleared the haunted air, Cassie Maples would have no trouble finding someone to take her room. Come next Saturday night, the rounders would fill the lamp-lit parlor, drinking Raleigh Rye, listening to the Victrola, playing cards or dice, and waiting for a turn at whatever new dark-skinned girl lay across the divan with the faded silk shawl.

He looked south down Magazine, and as he watched the moonbeams flicker off the surface of the river, something familiar began to take shape, rising like an unformed ghost into the New Orleans night. For a moment, his gaze was fixed on nothing. Then he took a step back and shook his head and the shape fluttered away as if chased by a gust of wind off the water.

He poured what was left in his glass over the railing and heard it splash off into the gutter below. He went inside, through his front room to the bedroom in the back. He unbuckled the stiletto in its sheath from his ankle, took his whalebone sap from his back pocket and put both atop the dresser, then drew his pistol from the pocket of his jacket and slipped it under his pillow. He stripped down to his undershirt and drawers and crawled beneath a cotton sheet worn soft and thin. The window overlooking the tiny back lot and the alleyway was open, and mosquitoes buzzed around the electric lamp overhead, but he left the baire folded up over the headboard. He reached under the mattress for a volume of O. Henry that he kept hidden there. He had read only a few lines before his thoughts turned back to Annie.

He wondered if she had made plans for her Sunday, to go to church, to walk along the river, to sit with her face to a hazy Louisiana sun. He wondered if, in her last minutes, she had lost herself in wistful homesick thoughts of her kin back on the Delta. Did she recall Eddie McTier, her first sly corrupter? Or did she think about Buddy Bolden, her last man, with his black eyes full of a wild, white light?

Valentin rose up on one elbow. *Bolden.* Miss Maples had mentioned the late Mr. McTier, whom she hadn't seen in months, but not Bolden, a regular visitor. That news had been whispered by the homely girl in the filthy maid's outfit. He lay back, staring at the cracks in the ceiling plaster. Why not volunteer that bit of information? Because it pointed to King Bolden and Cassie Maples and all the others would want to protect him. Crazy or sane, he belonged to them.

They would have little regard for a history winding back to sun-dappled mornings on the corner of First and Liberty. Maybe Valentin and Buddy were friends once, but all the madams and the rounders and the sporting girls saw was a Creole fancy man who talked like a professor and passed so easily for white that he could be in the employ of Tom Anderson himself.

Valentin still knew Buddy better than any of them, but it didn't signify; and it wouldn't matter at all that his first instinct would be to protect him, too.

Two

I also want to call your attention to the enclosed clipping in reference to the restricted district: "They have begun this work as a result of the experience they have had in rescuing girls at the station. Who, it is said, have been on the point of one of the immoral houses, deceived into thinking they were respectable boarding houses."

This I believe is a lie and I believe they should be called down. Hoping you are well and are enjoying the best of health, I am,

Sincerely yours,
Tom Anderson

Valentin woke to the clatter of hack wheels on the cobbles of Magazine Street and the whistles of steamboats rolling up the river. He went into his toilet and washed and shaved, dressed in a round-collared white shirt and light trousers and visited the outhouse under the back stairs.

He walked six blocks north to find the District moving in slow eddies on this Monday morning. Doors were locked and shutters drawn at every address and only a handful of pedestrians and the occasional delivery boy were about. It was sedate; take away the bleats and rattles and rumbles of the trains moving in and out of Union Station and he might have been strolling to early morning market in some sleepy backwoods Louisiana hamlet.

But it was the main thoroughfare of one of the world's most notorious red-light quarters. As he waited to let a streetcar pass, Valentin gazed at the familiar scape "down the line." In the distance, he could make out the white walls and iron gates of St. Louis Cemetery No. 1, the somber keystone between the District and the French Quarter, occupied mostly by former residents of those neighborhoods. Across Conti Street, Storyville proper began with five of the grander bordellos in a stately row, divided only by a small firehouse. On the next closest corner, at Bienville, was Toro's Saloon, a popular watering hole for the District's musicians, rounders, and sporting girls. Then came the heart of the District, eight grand mansions leading down to Mahogany Hall. Finally, directly across the street from where he stood, taking up nearly half the block, was Anderson's Café.

All was quiet at this hour, but, of course, the calm wouldn't last. Around midday, a train would pull into the station and an eager out-of-towner would step off with a gleam in his eye and a strut in his gait. Up and down the street, doors and windows would be opening, gay notes would tinkle from a piano or Victrola, painted faces would offer up the first artificial smiles of the day. Our gentleman would pick a likely address from the copy of *The Blue Book* that a ragged kid had pushed into his hand back at the station. Stepping over a threshold, he would be greeted like an old friend by the madam and directed to pick from the bevy of ladies, all skilled, he was assured, in the most exotic arts of Eros. A small glass of Raleigh Rye—good for easing a new sport's jitters—brought a Liberty dollar, four times the price of any saloon. But it was no matter, why worry with the mood so merry?

The girl (schooled in Paris, the madam testified, though the girl's voice had an East Texas twang) led him up the stairwell and down the hall to her room. Once inside, the business moved along briskly. The girl undid his drawers and examined him frankly for telltale signs of the gleet. Then she reached for the washcloth that had been soaking in the bedside pan of potassium permanganate. She washed his member thoroughly, with motions that suggested more the cleaning of a kitchen vegetable than a prelude to amours. In what seemed a bare second, she settled herself on the narrow bed, pulled up her bloomers and spread her thighs wide. He threw himself on her, his heart pounding like a hammer, and in what seemed another second, it was all over. The girl bustled him out of her room and into the hands of the madam, who just as brusquely shepherded him downstairs and out the front door. Unless of course, he had more money to spend. The chicken had been plucked and sent packing, and the whole matter hadn't taken ten minutes, start to finish.

So the gears turned and the noise and motion cascaded through the week to a Saturday night crescendo of rye whiskey, loud music, rough laughter and fevered loins. There was always a bit of trouble, of course: fights would erupt, knives and pistols would flash and a corpse or two might be carried off. Later, the take was split. Sunday would be peaceful. Another calm Monday morning would come around and it would start all over again.

$\sim$

Valentin crossed Basin Street and passed beneath the colonnade of the largest building on the line and the grandest in twenty city blocks. He knocked on one of the double doors and momentarily an eye peered out from a clear spot in the frosted glass. He heard the bolt slide back and the right-side door opened wide. He slipped inside. The door closed and a colored man in waiter garb nodded blankly and walked away.

He had stepped across the threshold from the grime of the street into a mirage. Along one wall of the wide, high-ceilinged room, a marble-topped bar boasted copper fittings that looked like they'd come from The Maine. The floor was white tile, crisscrossed by runners of rich red carpeting. Spittoons of burnished brass gleamed at every six feet of bar space. Chandeliers like those in the opera house hung from gold-plated chains and a mirror ran the length of the wall along the back of the bar. There were mountain ranges of bottles in all shapes and all colors of the rainbow, and the bottles of Raleigh Rye, the District's common elixir, were lined up in brown regiments. Tall windows with shutters opened a crack allowed the morning sun to tint the room with a pale yellow light.

Valentin crossed the room to find the proprietor of all this grandeur seated at one of the round tables in his customary three-piece suit with watch and chain, studying a copy of *The Mascot*, Storyville's weekly penny paper, devoted mostly to reporting the most lurid scandals of the moment. He glanced over the top of his wire-rimmed reading glasses, laid his newspaper aside, and gestured to the opposite chair.

The face of Tom Anderson, "The King of Storyville," round, pink and adorned by a grand mustache—once blond, now gone to gray—and with eyes that glittered either a jovial or an icy blue, was the most famous visage around Uptown, surely all of New Orleans, probably the entire state. The papers had started calling the District "Anderson County" years ago, and he lorded over that piece of real estate like it was a private fiefdom. Little of consequence went on within those twenty blocks without his knowledge or blessing.

But he had stretched his fleshy arms beyond the District and into the realm of legitimate politics. With his Café as his headquarters, he got himself elected to the Louisiana State Senate and then appointed to the powerful Ways and Means Committee and the Committee for the Affairs of New Orleans. All this, even as he stood neck-deep in the sinful wallow that was Storyville. Never one to draw too fine a moral line, he was known to the police as a dependable stool pigeon as a young sport. He was now, next to the governor, the most powerful man in Louisiana. He hobnobbed with statesmen and celebrities. Gentleman Jim Corbett and John L. Sullivan had been his guests, and he headed the welcoming committee when President Roosevelt visited the city.

Still, the honors did not turn his head, and his duty to the place where he had made his fortune and now based his power never swayed. He kept all his friends close at hand, senators and scoundrels, madams of French houses and gentlemen with distinguished titles, monarchs and magnates and petty thieves and pimps and prostitutes of white and every shade of brown, confidantes and employees and favored customers. If he was the King of Storyville, they were his subjects.

Included in their number was Valentin St. Cyr, now sipping the fresh cup of coffee which Anderson had himself fetched from behind the bar. The two men chatted for a few minutes, chuckling over a cartoon drawing in *The Mascot*, and trading news on the bad boys who were mucking-up Storyville and the new girls who were rumored to be worth a visit. The King of Storyville went to the bar again, returned with the enameled coffee pot and refilled their cups. He sat down, laid his reading glasses aside, laced his fingers together and inquired directly into the shooting of Littlejohn.

"I don't believe you'll find anyone mourning him." Valentin glanced at the spot not ten paces away where the pimp had breathed his last. "The papers didn't even mention it."

"I can do without the gunplay," Mr. Tom said. "This isn't Algiers."

Valentin caught the comment, but let it pass. "It was a bit of bad luck," he said. "It could have happened anywhere."

"But it didn't happen anywhere, it happened here." Anderson's tone was snappish. "On your watch."

Valentin didn't take offense. Rounders were shot down all the time in Storyville and they both knew it. As long as no one who mattered got hurt, the occasional gunshot could give a room a certain racy reputation. No, there was something else bothering this white man.

"What's Picot think he's up to, throwing his weight about like that?" Anderson said.

"It was after three o'clock," Valentin told him. "It was time to close up anyhow. I doubt he would have done the same at midnight."

"I don't like him."

"I don't care for him myself," Valentin said. "But Uptown's his beat."

"For now," Anderson said in a distracted voice. He shifted in his chair and Valentin watched curiously as his face grew serious, almost mournful.

"I have a job for you," Anderson murmured. "A sad business. It concerns an old acquaintance." He tapped his temple. "The poor man had a collapse and his mind was affected. He's being committed to an institution. A very sad business." He allowed a few seconds of silence, then said, "You'll escort him to Jackson, to the State Hospital. Discretion is the order of the day. The gentleman is not without reputation in the community." His sharp gaze fastened on the detective as he brushed his copy of *The Mascot* with thick fingers. "Wouldn't do to have such news getting into the wrong hands." With a muted sigh, he drew an envelope from an inside pocket and handed it across the table. Valentin pocketed it directly.

"Please come see me when you get back," Anderson murmured. The Creole detective stood up and started for the door, his steps echoing on the tiles. "Valentin?" The detective stopped. Anderson had replaced his reading glasses and was paging idly through his newspaper. "I heard something about a girl found dead, where was it, Miss Antonia's?"

"It was in a Perdido Street house. Cassie Maples'."

"I see." Anderson said, without looking up. "How did she die?"

"I don't know. In her sleep, it seems."

"And what's this business about a black rose?"

Valentin allowed himself a small smile. He might have guessed that Tom Anderson would be on to every detail. "Probably some hoodoo charm," he said.

Anderson pursed his lips, musing. "Died in her sleep," he said. "You know, if she got herself cut up or shot, I never would have thought twice about it." He shrugged and opened his newspaper. "Remember to come see me when you get back," he said, and returned to his reading.

Valentin stood under the colonnade outside the Café. He looked south over the city. Clouds were coming up over the Gulf, which meant rain by afternoon.

A streetcar was passing and he hopped on, more to have a place to sit down than a need to go anywhere. The car was empty except for one black-shawled old woman. He took a seat far to the rear, slipped the knife from the sheath on his ankle and quickly slit the envelope open. It contained five new twenty-dollar gold pieces, each embossed with an American eagle. Far too much for this one assignment, it was a retainer, an unofficial salary. He had received such a payment the first time Anderson secured his services (a matter of minor blackmail, resolved with a promise of violence, delivered in a casual whisper), and the detective had understood immediately. Tom Anderson would have regular use for someone with his unique resumé, just as he depended on Billy Struve for information, just as he occasionally employed a dimwitted thug after gentler persuasions failed. It was another trapping of the King of Storyville's position; and the three high-toned madams with whom the detective had like arrangements shared this conceit. He also sensed that the first, too-generous payment was some kind of back-handed reward for a certain incident with a certain police sergeant.

Valentin found in the envelope one one-way and one round-trip train ticket to Jackson, and a folded sheet of cream-colored paper. On the paper, a flowing hand had inscribed:

Thomas Dupre
St. Ignatius Church
103 Orleans Street
11 o'clock A.M. precisely

For a startled moment, he forgot about the one hundred dollars gold in plain view of whatever rapscallion happened to board the car. He knew the name; indeed, most of New Orleans knew Thomas Dupre as pastor emeritus of St. Ignatius Catholic Church, for twenty-odd years pious shepherd of the flock, now retired five years. As the car rolled west down Basin Street, Valentin put the paper away, pocketed the tickets and the money and sat back, musing on the odd turn to his day.

∽

At a few minutes before eleven, he appeared at the side door of St. Ignatius and was ushered down a dim corridor and into the sanctuary by a white man a few years his senior who sniffed an introduction: John Rice, clerk of the parish. Rice was tall, with a narrow, pinched face. His beard and mustache were trimmed to delicate edges, spectacles perched on the bridge of his long, thin nose and he spoke in a high, clipped voice. His shirt with its too-tight collar was immaculate and his tweed trousers had been pressed razor-sharp.

He left the visitor alone and Valentin found himself sitting in a church for the first time since his father's funeral service sixteen years ago. The light through the stained glass was thick with dust and the air heavy with incense and the prayers of the penitent. As the deep, echoing silence lingered on, his mind began to wander.

An oval frame encased a photograph of his mother, a slim woman of mixed African-Cherokee-French blood, maid to a wealthy downtown family, and his father, a short, muscular immigrant from Sicily who worked on the New Orleans docks. In the photograph, their wedding portrait, they are standing side-by-side, his mother beautiful, with milk-coffee skin and long hair in dark ringlets, her blouse pinned at the neck with an onyx brooch; and his father holding himself with stiff formality in a too-tight wool suit, swarthy, with a curled and waxed mustache swooping over his shyly smiling face.

That image faded and in the next picture, his father is hanging from a rope that is attached to the limb of an oak tree on the banks of Lake Pontchartrain, murdered by men he did not know; and there, far behind in one corner, his mother's face shatters in grief and horror as she collapses to the ground...

Thankfully, at that moment, the door to the sanctuary opened.

Valentin stood up and watched as John Rice led a frail and stooped old man across the apse by one arm. One step behind was a nun in black habit, her head bent and hands clasped before her. As the little group approached, Valentin recognized Father Thomas Dupre from photographs in the newspapers. The priest was now over seventy, a small, doddering man with thin white hair combed back from a high forehead. His face was deathly pale and his eyes looked dazed behind tiny rimless spectacles. A signal passed and the nun backed away, crossing herself. Looking grim, Rice handed the detective a black Stetson hat and a packet of official-looking papers that was bound with a purple ribbon. He did not speak at all.

Valentin took the old man's arm and escorted him past the confessionals, through the chapel door, down the corridor, and out the side door of the church. A carriage waited with a blank-faced Negro in suit and cap at the reins. Valentin placed the Stetson on the Father's head, pulled the brim low in front, then helped his charge take an unsteady step into the seat. He nodded to the driver and the Negro snapped the reins. They rode all the way to Union Station in silence, the old man's pale blue eyes fixed inward. At one point he looked up, then reached out with a shaking hand, as if bestowing a blessing on the world he was leaving behind.

At the station, Valentin led the priest past the cars emblazoned with stars to the white-only coaches at the rear of the train, away from the grinding noise and gritty smoke of the engine. Segregation laws had been back in force for thirteen years, but Valentin could pass. It was always a bit of a gamble, however; his olive skin wouldn't mean a great deal if some drunken cracker at a backwoods station looked too closely and pointed a finger. It had happened before and he had been lucky to get away. But now he had a pistol in his pocket and white man or colored, priest or no priest as a witness, he was ready to use it.

At the first stop outside the city the car all but emptied of passengers. The train pulled out of the station. Father Dupre still did not speak to his escort, barely noticed him, as the flat Louisiana countryside rolled by. Valentin wondered if the old man had any idea where they were going. He glanced at the priest, mystified by the whole business. He had seen victims of afflictions of the brain shuffling about the streets of the city, all shaking hands and dead, vacant eyes, babbling nonsense. He had seen half-witted beggars with their wooden faces and blind stares. And once he had witnessed a lunatic suddenly go amok in the middle of a busy downtown intersection, stumbling into the path of wagons, screaming at pedestrians and raging madly against unseen demons until the police arrived to beat him to the cobbled street and carry him off. Father Dupre showed no such signs; Valentin saw nothing but a gentleman enfeebled by old age. It made him wonder why the priest was being sent off to the Hospital for the Insane at Jackson.

Which also made him wonder why Anderson created the drama of giving him the note, rather than just explaining that his charge was Father Dupre. Because he assumed Valentin wouldn't know the old gentleman? No, more likely he didn't want to answer the questions that the detective would have surely posed. Finally, why him? Why did Mr. Rice, or whoever was in charge at St. Ignatius, give this job to Tom Anderson? Wasn't that dealing with the devil himself? The only answer could be that Rice knew it would keep the matter quiet. Which meant they were making Father Thomas Dupre disappear.

He thought about it for a few moments more, and then shrugged it off. So what if they were? It was white people's business and none of his affair.

The train pulled into the Jackson station at two o'clock and Valentin escorted the priest out of the car. There was a double-seated hack with a mulatto driver dressed all in white waiting by the platform and they rode a dirt road between drooping live oaks and weeping willows that led outside the town to the grounds of Jackson State Hospital for the Insane.

When they reached the gate, Father Dupre stirred. He gazed at the complex of drab brick buildings that rose up behind a tall black iron fence. Valentin heard him sigh and saw him shake his head, as if in resignation. They stepped down from the hack. A guard greeted them and took a moment to look over the papers. Then came the only light turn in this melancholy business. The good Father, in his confusion, somehow forgot that insanity was also an issue of race and began to shuffle off in the direction of the colored wards, located closest to the gate. The guard smiled as Valentin went after his charge and gently turned him around. The guard led them up a stone walk to the main building. A doctor, a nurse, and a man in a suit appeared in the lobby and the patient was handed over with a minimum of fuss. It was all quite efficient. They paid no attention to Valentin. Before they finished, the staff members stepped aside to whisper over some detail and Valentin felt a tug at his sleeve. He turned to find Father Dupre fixing him with an intense, pleading look.

The old man went searching for words. "Will you hear my confession?" he whispered urgently. Valentin, caught off-guard, found himself staring dumbly into the pale, bleak eyes. "They are sending me to Hell for my sins!" Now he was pressing something into Valentin's hand. Valentin felt a pebbled snake of rosary beads between his fingers. "I have no more use for this," he said in a voice as dry as winter leaves. The eyes blazed for another instant behind the priest's eyeglasses. "Why will no one hear my confession?" he muttered fiercely. "Is it too late?" Then, just as abruptly, he let go of Valentin's sleeve and fell back, his face going slack.

A few moments later, he allowed himself to be escorted down the long corridor of hospital gray that led to the wards. Valentin watched until he and the nurse and the doctor disappeared around a corner.

～

He brooded in silence during the hack ride back into town, seeing the hopeless look in Dupre's eyes before him. He felt that somehow he had just buried a man as surely as if he had thrown dirt over his face and a haunting shadow came creeping back. So dark was his mood that he did not remember the rosary the Father had handed him until he was on the platform waiting for the 3:10 to New Orleans. He dug into his pocket. The beads were tied-up in a frantic knot. And as he untangled it, rose petals fell away, all in shreds, and colored a deep, dusty black.

When the train pulled into Union Station, Valentin sat without moving, staring across Basin Street. A misty rain was falling over the city. The sight of the two women in the second story windows of Emma Johnson's French Studio, sucking their thumbs as lewd notice of the specialty of the house, did not even register; even when three drummers at the other end of the car began to point their fingers and squeal like little boys at the crude display.

He got up, walked out on the platform and turned toward the corner of Basin and Iberville and Anderson's Café. He had gone a dozen steps when he stopped and pointed his shoes in the other direction, toward Orleans Street and St. Ignatius Church.

A caretaker ushered him into the church office. John Rice looked up in surprise from his desk to see Anderson's man standing there with droplets of rain glistening in his dark hair.

"Mr...."

"St. Cyr."

The parish clerk blinked rapidly. "Is something wrong?"

"No, it went well," Valentin said. He produced the rosary and held it dangling before the bespectacled gaze. "Father Dupre's," he explained.

Rice frowned and began to reach for the beads, then withdrew his hand. "A gift?" he said.

Valentin shook his head. "I don't think so. He was trying to tell me something."

The parish clerk sat back. "Tell you what?"

"It was something about hearing his confession. Then he gave me the rosary."

John Rice shook his head sadly. "Poor Father," he said. "Poor man."

Valentin offered the rosary across the desk. "You should have this."

Rice accepted the beads and sat pensively as the detective stepped out, closing the door behind him.

⁓

It was a pleasant enough evening for New Orleans, warm and windy and now just a leftover sprinkling of rain. Valentin decided to take a roundabout way back to the District, a route that would carry him through Jackson Square. The walk would clear his head, perhaps help to dispel his mood. He looked around to get his bearings, then headed for the alleyway behind the church that cut through to Canal Street.

The shadows were deep beneath the overhang of the tall building and it was cooler there. Valentin slowed his steps even more. As he dug through his pockets for a cigarette, he glanced about, then stared, forgetting about his smoke. A small plot of dirt emptied into an alleyway, fenced on three sides with stakes and clapboards. Pushed into one corner was a trash bin that was stuffed with discarded church papers. There was also a wreath, half-bare, left behind from some recent service. About the skeleton frame of wood and wire hung the ragged remnants of three dozen black roses.

～

A half-hour later, he walked into the Café to deliver his report. Standing at the end of the long bar, Anderson listened carefully and when he heard mention of Dupre's last cryptic words, shook his head slightly. He noticed how St. Cyr's voice had trailed off. A quiet fellow with something more to say. "What is it?" he prompted him.

Valentin chose his words. "There were petals from a black rose stuck in that rosary he gave me. Like the one in the girl's room over on Perdido." Then he related his visit to the church and coming upon the wreath in the alleyway.

"Who told you to go back there?" Anderson inquired crossly. "The poor old fellow gave you a gift. You should have let it go at that." He leaned against the bar, entwined his fingers. "His mind is gone. It's a terrible tragedy. A lesson to be learned. But best laid to rest." He was ending the discussion right there.

Or so he thought. "But what about those roses?" Valentin said.

Anderson made a dismissive gesture. "Half the funerals in New Orleans use them." Valentin looked troubled and the white man said, "What? You think an old priest had something to do with some Negro girl on Perdido Street?"

"No, not that." Valentin retreated and tried another tack. "What exactly was the nature of the Father's illness?"

Anderson's heavy chin took a set and his eyebrows knit in annoyance. "Something in the mind, but I don't know the details. It's none of my affair. The church prefers to handle these matters privately. I'm sure you can understand that." Valentin sensed that he had reached a line and dropped the subject. Anderson's tone became brisk. "I need you to work the floor this week."

Their business was finished. Valentin murmured a quick thanks and walked away. The door opened just as he reached it and Billy Struve stepped nimbly inside. The young man, his blond hair parted in the middle and slicked-down, gave Valentin a glance with his sharp green eyes. The detective hurried past. Struve, once a police reporter, was now Anderson's junior partner and chief spy, and his ears were open for any tidbit of news about the District. Valentin did not want any of his business turning up as a bit of gossip in *The Mascot* or, worse, in Bas Bleu's column in *The Sun*. Struve opened his mouth, ready as always with a question, but Valentin slipped out the door and into the warm spring evening.

Three

Before the negative was shattered, the subject's face had been scratched out by, it is said, Bellocq's brother, a Catholic priest, for reasons known only to himself and, presumably, his God.

— *Al Rose, "Storyville"*

The late afternoon light came through the window and onto a purple dress that hung on the wall like a storefront display. The door opened with barely a sound and the woman on the dirty, mussed bed looked around and smiled. She was happy to see the visitor slip inside, close the door and cross the floor to stand over her. A few murmured words and all in a nervous rush, her visitor reached for the silk sash and pulled it away. The kimono fell open on lumps of soft white tit hanging down, a fat roll of a belly, her thing down there.

The woman laughed, a dry, rheumy sound, as the kimono slipped to the floor to spread out in a silk swirl of cherry blossoms on dark branches. She slipped off the bed, went down on stiff knees and started fussing with buttons. *This whatchu want, honey?*

Her tongue was a wet tickle. She was doing it when she felt the sash from the kimono drape down on her shoulders, the soft silk sliding this way and that. She looked up, smiling, and at that moment the hands crossed in a jerking motion. The woman's eyes went wide as the silk wound tight, then tighter. Now there was another quick, trembling pull on the sash and her face passed from white to pink. But she didn't resist at all.

It was just a rough game; they'd done it before. She didn't think to fight back until it was too late and her tongue came out all wide and red, till she started spitting-up white, till she was kicking, bare feet sliding on the wood floor slippery with her own piss and then she went to flailing with her fat white arms, but they were too weak and in another half-minute, the last of the light in her eyes went out. The body was lowered to the floor. The whole house was quiet as a nervous hand pushed the black rose into the woman's palm and folded her dry white fingers around its thorny stem.

∼

E.J. Bellocq made his way down Iberville Street as the soft sepia evening descended. He dragged a tripod along under one arm, gripped his bulky black Bantam Special camera tight to his other side, and kept his eyes fastened fiercely on the banquette ten paces ahead. He didn't—wouldn't—look left or right. Across the street, on this corner and that, young sports stared, pointed and laughed. A glance would be open invitation to these louts. The Frenchman wouldn't tolerate it, even if he had the time. He had a paid appointment to photograph a sporting woman named Gran Tillman who worked in a house on Bienville, Lizzie Taylor's. She had told him to come by at seven o'clock, no sooner and no later. She was a woman of means these days and not to be kept waiting, or so she said. Bellocq hurried as fast as his legs would shuffle him along, looking like a crippled insect on the Saturday evening street.

Ernest J. Bellocq was one of the District's more grotesque citizens, a pale, almost translucent creature of French descent. He stood a little over five feet tall, but his head was as large as a pumpkin because of a medical condition called hydrocephalia. He had a broken little body and bent legs so that he walked like a duck. A contortion of bone and muscle clutched his throat, so that he also talked like a duck, and a French duck at that.

Bellocq was not a happy gnome, like some storybook character. He did not have a kind heart or pleasant disposition. He was not eager to please. He was a churlish and unfriendly man. He was ugly and misshapen and in poor health and the butt of cruel taunts by those who knew no better. Those few who knew him well enough called him Papá.

To earn his living, he took photographs for the Foundation Company of New Orleans shipbuilders. He recorded with mechanical precision the components of ocean vessels weighing tens of thousands of tons and made formal portraits of the stuffy and respectable white men who ran the firm that built them. In his off hours, he took photographs of the prostitutes of the District.

There was a certain windowless room in a certain house on a certain New Orleans street that was lined, wall-to-wall, ceiling-to-floor, with a catalogue of "French" photographs, mostly crude studies that captured women and couples in every conceivable coupling. All for sale, of course; when there was cash money involved, there was not much that man, woman or beast could not be persuaded or forced to do.

But E.J. Bellocq's photographs would not be found in this collection; his forte was something quite apart. With crabbed hands and milky blue eyes and a soul that was twisted with private torments, he revealed small stories on 8x10 inch plates treated with silver salts. The portraits of Papá Bellocq were also not in the florid, romantic style of the day. His subjects were not beautiful. They were for the most part hollow-eyed, vacant-looking women, even if barely beyond childhood. But Bellocq saw things in their faces and their bodies, and captured them on film.

He caught subjects as they teetered like clumsy dancers between chastity and sin, smiling their vague smiles, hearing promises. On others, he found desperate, haunted looks, as if they sensed their lives beginning to dim and go out like flickering candles. And some displayed no expression at all, their faces blank as stone as they leaned against a white wall or lay naked on a bed, their fates already drawn in the scars that brutal lovers left scrawled across their pallid breasts. The broken and crippled Bellocq trapped the faces beneath their fleeting masks, caught the dying light in their empty eyes, fixed in silver crystals the looks of forever saying good-bye to something.

≈

He arrived at Lizzie Taylor's one minute before seven-thirty. He had to ask three times before the stupid girl at the door understood him. She then informed him that Miz Tillman hadn't been seen all day. Bellocq chattered a string of angry syllables in a squirrel voice, as one of the girls would later remember it. Despite the young lady's protests (Miss Taylor was not in the house), he pushed his way inside and clambered up the steps, camera and tripod banging along behind. It took him all of five minutes to struggle like some tottering mechanical toy to the upper floor. He stomped from one room to the next, pushing open doors and generally raising a row all over the house. And so it was Papá Bellocq, the photographer of prostitutes, who opened the door at the end of the hall and came upon the body of Gran Tillman. She was lying on the floor, half-hidden behind a dressing screen. She was naked, her skin a pale, sickly yellow. The silk sash from a kimono was wrapped around her neck and in her right hand she held a black rose.

≈

A street urchin came to fetch Valentin at the Café. He walked into the room at eight-thirty. His eyes took in everything: Picot standing there, hands on hips, looking like he had digested something that didn't agree with him; Papá Bellocq hugging the wall, his big eyes stark with fear; the two uniformed patrolmen standing by, one of them holding an electric lamp. Then he saw the body of the white woman, the sash and the tattered kimono, a puddle of urine and a black rose. And hanging on the wall, looking out of place in that tawdry room, a dress, a gown really, deep purple sateen, with swaths of fabric, lace and bows. Valentin stared at it for a moment, then turned his attention back to the body.

"You aren't here by any choice of mine," Picot said by way of greeting. Valentin kept his eyes on the victim, avoiding Picot's glare in the process. The police detective made a sound in his throat. "Someone downtown got a call from your friend Mr. Anderson. And here you are." Valentin didn't comment and the copper gave up. "Looks like maybe we have a repeat killer, don't it?" He pointed. "This business with the rose mean anything to you?" Valentin said no, nothing. "What about that?" he said, jerking a thumb at the dress.

Valentin shrugged and on the edge of his vision, saw Bellocq open his mouth. He made the slightest shake of his head and the little Frenchman remained silent. Picot glanced between the two men with narrowed eyes. "The crip says this is how he found her." He smiled lewdly. "Says he was just coming here to make her photograph."

"I've seen his work," Valentin said. "What he says is reasonable."

"Well, I don't think it's *reasonable*," Picot hissed in sudden irritation. "We got nothing but what he says to go on, do we? That ain't enough for me. So we're just going to take him on downtown."

Bellocq's eyes grew wider still, like blue china saucers, and he gaped at St. Cyr in a mute plea. Valentin stepped around the body on the floor and murmured something to Picot. The copper listened and, after a grudging moment, nodded once, curtly. Valentin waved the Frenchman toward the door and Bellocq scuttled out like some frantic metallic crab. The two men waited as he made his noisy way along the hall and down the stairs. After the clattering faded away, Picot said, "Well, Mr. detective, why don't you have a look and tell me what we got here?" As usual, there was a sneer lurking.

Valentin took the lamp from the policeman's hand and knelt over the body of Gran Tillman. Picot yawned and leaned languidly against the wall, but Valentin could feel the copper's stare boring into his back.

She was a short, plain woman with liverish skin. Her face was round, her mouth full-lipped and filled with crooked teeth, her nose short and squat. Her body was just as round, except for where the flesh was already sagging. At thirty-five or so, Gran Tillman was a senior citizen in Storyville years. Indeed, her dead face looked weary and somehow not ungrateful for the long rest that was now hers.

Picot fidgeted impatiently and muttered as Valentin lifted the black rose from the palm of her hand, noting the absence of the iron grip of death. It slipped away easily, leaving thorn marks on her pink palm. He had only half-listened to Picot, but he got the message: though the sash was in plain view and there was a reddish tinge about the woman's neck (not to mention the amber puddle that had soaked into the floorboards), the policeman was going to report it as a death by undetermined causes. After another few minutes and a half-dozen curt words directed at St. Cyr's bent back, Picot called for a wagon to carry the body downtown. He gave the Creole detective a hard glance. "If you're all through, you can go," he said.

Valentin stood up and turned to leave, stopping to study the purple sateen gown, so out of place in those shoddy digs. He had just reached the doorway when he thought of something. "That other girl," he said.

Picot frowned absently as he stared down at Gran Tillman's body. "What? What girl?"

"From Cassie Maples'."

"Yeah, what about her?"

"Was a cause of death established?"

"Oh. Yeah, it was." Picot sounded bored. "'phyxiated. Probably with a pillow or something like that."

"Then it was murder."

"No tellin'," the copper said, barely listening.

Valentin frowned. "There weren't any signs of a struggle."

"Then it *wasn't* no murder," Picot snapped irritably. Valentin took a step into the hallway, dropping the subject. "But it's funny you should mention it," he heard Picot say. There was a deliberate note in the copper's voice and Valentin stepped back into the doorway. "I found out who was the last man she saw that night." The copper's lips stretched in a smile that the rest of his face didn't join. "It was that horn player Bolden." He laid his cold penny eyes on St. Cyr. "Friend of yours, ain't he?"

⌒

Just before the policeman left with the body, Lizzie Taylor, the madam of the house, appeared downstairs. Though she wrung her hands and could barely stifle her wails of grief over the poor woman's death, she was genuinely appalled that Picot wanted the house shut down for the night. "Tonight?" she kept saying between sobs, "The whole house?" But Picot was firm and in the manner of a wake, Miss Taylor led her girls across Iberville Street to Fewclothes' Cabaret, where they all got properly drunk in Gran Tillman's sainted memory.

⌒

Valentin hurried down Conti Street to Antonia Gonzales'. He found Justine dancing in the parlor with another girl while three well-dressed sports watched and whispered amongst themselves. He pulled her into the foyer and she pressed against him, grinning eagerly, a tan imp.

He held her at arm's length. "Listen to me," he said. "Be careful. Please. No strangers."

Justine's eyebrows went up and she smiled a little girl smile. "Are you jealous over me now?"

He said, "I mean it!" and the smile disappeared. "And tell the other girls. They ought not to be careless." He turned for the door.

"Valentin?" She was watching him, waiting. He moved a hand and she ran to get her shawl.

Four

> To tell a landlady from a boarder,
> their names have been printed in
> capital letters.
>   The star on the side of a landlady's
> name indicates a first-class house
> where the finest of women and
> nothing but wine is sold.
>   The No. 69 is the sign of a French
> house. The Jew will be known by a "J."
>   Wishing you a good time while you
> are making your rounds,
> —*The Blue Book*

Valentin was drinking his second cup of coffee when he heard a whistle from the street. He stepped out onto the balcony and leaned over the railing. Looking up at him from the shadow of the building was the same kid who had fetched him the night before, a pug nosed, pale-eyed, dirt-white product of one of the church orphanages and everyone on the street, where he spent his days, called him Beansoup.

"Mr. St. Cyr?" Beansoup called up. "Mr. Anderson says can you please come to see him at the Café."

"When?" Valentin said.

Beansoup wiped the back of his dirty hand across his mouth. "He says now. He's says for me to wait and bring you along."

ҩ

He walked a step or two behind Beansoup, who moved at a rapid, pitched-forward pace, his too-large, cracked leather shoes just skimming the banquette. An empty cloth newspaper sack hung from one of his bony shoulders and the pockets of his dirty white shirt and baggy britches bulged with a collection of litter. They passed by a green grocer and Beansoup, seeing the merchant turn his back, snatched two fat purple plums from the stand. He flipped one to Valentin as he bit into the other.

"How's the newspaper trade?" Valentin asked, polishing the plum on his vest.

Beansoup shot him a look. "It's for kids, is what."

"Yes, but you know that's how Mr. Anderson got his start," Valentin said. "Hawking papers on the street. Look where he is now."

Beansoup's eyes flashed with a sudden cunning. "Anderson got his start ratting to the po-lice," he corrected the detective, chewing noisily. "And he still got all them copper friends. And that's how he operates. I'm gonna do better'n'at. I got my own damn plan."

"What kind of plan?" Valentin said.

The kid wiped a bead of snot from his lip. "I'm goin' to be a fancy man," he announced.

Valentin stifled a laugh. "A fancy man?"

Beansoup nodded busily as they turned onto Basin Street. "I know all them fellows. I run their errands. Go to the apothecary when they need somethin'. Deliver their confident'al messages around town, whatever else." He looked up at the detective and closed one eye. "You seen 'em in them fine suits, all them rings and such?"

"I have, yes," Valentin said.

"All of 'em wear them fine new suits," Beansoup went on earnestly. "New derby hats. Diamonds in their garters. They always got plenty money. But not one of 'em got a proper position."

Valentin played his part. "They all have women taking care of them."

Beansoup winked and pointed a finger. "That's right. That's what I'm gonna do. Get a woman take care of me."

Valentin nodded soberly. "I see."

The boy spat the plum pit into the gutter. Then he reached into a grimy pocket and pulled out a handful of printed cards. "See this here?" Valentin looked. "Grace O'Leary" was inscribed across the top card in flowery script. "I stand on the corner. Fellow lookin' for a girl, I send him round to Grace. She been payin' me twenty-five cents every time."

"Sounds like a fair shake," Valentin said.

"Yeah, well, I'm gonna raise my price," Beansoup confided. "Pretty soon, she'll be buying me clothes and smokes, whatever I want."

"And she'll agree to that?"

The boy sniffed. "She'll agree or I'll give her a slap or two." He smacked a flat palm on his scrawny chest. "I know how to handle a goddamn whore."

Valentin was about to warn him against raising a hand to any Storyville woman when the kid suddenly began bawling out a song about his "big fat mama wit' d'meat shakin' off d'bone," screeched away in a flat, nasal gutbucket voice. People passing on the banquette turned to stare and some of them started laughing. Beansoup stopped just as suddenly as he had started and said, "Honeyboy."

Valentin felt his hearing return. "What?"

Beansoup was all earnest again. "Honeyboy. That's my moniker." He peered at the detective. "Whatcha think?"

Valentin made a show of thinking it over. "I'm sure it suits you," he said. They stepped under the colonnade at Anderson's Café and he laid a hand on Beansoup's shoulder.

He dug into his vest pocket with the other hand and produced a silver Liberty quarter, which he pressed into the boy's palm. Then he tilted his head toward the door.

"I suppose this is about the murder last night," he murmured.

Beansoup studied the coin. "Yeah, I spose it is." He yawned and looked away down the street. Valentin dug deeper, produced another quarter. He dropped it into the cupped palm, right next to the first one.

"Some people been talkin' already," Beansoup said, his eyes fixed on the two coins, "'bout how maybe that wa'nt just a lady gettin kilt like usual."

"And?"

"And Mr. Tom's a little vexed about it, that's all," the boy said with an off-handed shrug.

Valentin pondered the information as Beansoup rolled the coins about his palm. Then he reached for the door handle. "What was it?" he said. "Your moniker?"

The boy looked up and smiled with a mouth full of brown crooked teeth. "Honeyboy."

"I'll remember," Valentin said and stepped inside.

∿

The Café was dark, the curtains drawn like it was still the dead of night. The only thing moving was the tall Negro sweeping the floor in a slow rhythm. Tom Anderson looked up from his table and waved a beckoning hand. Valentin walked along the bar and took a seat. Anderson had a thick sheaf of papers before him, filled with tiny print that was very official looking. He put his pen down, laced his fingers together and furrowed his brow gravely. "Another murder?" he said.

Valentin gave a brief nod. "It was up Bienville at Lizzie Taylor's," he said, though Anderson surely knew all this.

"And another black rose?" The blue eyes rested on Valentin's face.

"That's correct."

Anderson mulled it over, frowning, then said, "What's the word on the street?"

"I've heard nothing at all," Valentin said.

The white man sat back. "Well, what do you think about it?"

"Those black roses are the main thing," Valentin said. "Looks like it's the same one who killed the girl on Perdido Street."

"Is that all?"

Valentin hesitated. "Well, there's the business with Father Dupre."

"That again?" Anderson all but rolled his eyes.

"It happened at the same time," Valentin said. "That girl died early Sunday morning. Come noon Monday, the Father was on a train to the bughouse. And he had a black rose in his possession. And now we have another murder—"

"Yes, yes, and another black rose," Anderson broke in. "So where's the connection?"

"Maybe Dupre knew something," Valentin said. "Maybe he heard something at confession."

The King of Storyville was already shaking his head. "That first girl, she was working way over in darktown, isn't that right?"

"Yes, but all sorts of men visit those houses," Valentin said.

"I know who visits those houses," Anderson retorted sharply, "and I know who doesn't." He picked up his pen, put it down again. "Dupre was retired. He couldn't have heard confession from anyone. This other murder..." He raised his hands, palms up. "Well, how in the world would he know anything about that? He was under lock-and-key at Jackson. You took him there yourself."

Valentin knew better than to push it any further. He nodded briefly and the King of Storyville said, "So someone has murdered two sporting gals. Someone with a crazy notion, these black roses..." He touched his bushy mustache ruminatively and shifted in his chair. "But let's not make something out of nothing here. That first girl wasn't working in the District at all. This other one, well, who knows what kind of business goes on at a house like Lizzie Taylor's?" He tapped a finger on the tabletop. "You keep your eyes and ears open. But most likely there's nothing to it."

"Nobody should say anything about the roses," Valentin said.

"Yes, yes, we'll keep all of it quiet," Anderson said. "God knows, we can't have word getting around there's a killer on the loose. Let's just hope this fellow's adventures are over." With that, he glanced at the papers on the table and said, "Now, if you'll excuse me, I have this awful state business to attend to."

Valentin stood up to leave. He had taken only a few steps when Anderson called out King Bolden's name. He turned around. "What about him?"

"Did you know he was taken to jail last night? Some sort of brawl, as I heard it. At one of those saloons where his band plays, I think maybe it was Mangetta's. I believe they locked him up." He picked up his pen and returned his attention to his stack of papers.

～

Valentin walked away from the Café and disappeared around the corner onto Iberville. From the doorway of an abandoned crib across the street, a tall man in a derby hat watched him go. He waited a few moments, then stepped onto the banquette and sauntered up the street, shadowing the Creole detective.

～

Tom Anderson tried to concentrate on the paragraphs of type on the page before him, a rambling bill of particulars about a proposed water line for St. John's Parish. He stared at the words for a few seconds more, trying to make sense of the sentence, then gave up and laid his pen aside. He sipped his coffee. Cold. He stared at the empty chair across the table and fell into a brooding mood.

As he expected, St. Cyr was on the money. The news about the back-of-town Negro girl had barely passed Billy Struve's busy lips on Sunday afternoon when the message arrived from the parish clerk at St. Ignatius concerning poor old Father Dupre.

Anderson had noted the curious timing, of course, but it gave him little pause. He pushed aside the matter of the girl's death—she was a Negro, after all—and moved directly to assist in the other matter. Though he was not himself a religious man, he respected the church as a power not to be dismissed, even though it had never been so potent as to stamp out the District's sinful trade or to remove belief in the *voudun* from the hearts of God's children there.

It was a standoff with a long history, and in his well-oiled style, Tom Anderson made sure it remained cordial, extending a helping hand with problems of a public or private nature that no amount of prayer could resolve. So a telephone bell tinkled or a message was delivered at his door. He came to know Father Dupre as a pious and kindly old rooster and his clerk John Rice as an officious bully. Over the years, Anderson had offered assistance to the church with the tact and discretion that was his signature.

Those instances had dwindled as the years went by and when a call did come, it was always from the parish clerk. Then he read in *The Sun* that the Father was turning his duties over to a younger man. He heard nothing more until he was petitioned over this last delicate business. When the request arrived, he thought immediately of Valentin St. Cyr.

The front door opened and closed and he looked up, expecting the detective—the *Creole* detective—to come barging back in to annoy him with another question, another suspicion. But it was only a delivery boy. Anderson picked up his pen, but didn't put it to paper, as his thoughts began another circle. He mused upon having to remind himself that St. Cyr was a colored man; and color was a brick wall. But this was New Orleans and nothing was ever that simple.

Sometimes it made Anderson weary just thinking about it. Ask any white man on the street and he would tell you there were four social levels in Crescent City society: the "Americans" of Anglo-Saxon blood, the descendants of French aristocracy, and the like; Creoles of mixed French and Spanish blood; a huge step down by law to the Creoles of Color, which included anyone with a single drop of African blood, such octoroons, quadroons and mulattos of the fairest complexions; finally, on the bottom rung, the Negroes, the most direct, most black-skinned products of slavery.

The caste system contained sub-divisions that defied any sane man's logic and memory, so that anyone in the City of New Orleans who actually tried to explain it ended up sounding like a madman. But at least it was so muddled that it allowed a few like St. Cyr to dance about all sides of the color line—a benefit to Mr. Tom Anderson.

He sighed quietly. If he paid proper respect to the petrified notions of superiority, no one with a trace of African blood would be allowed anywhere near his affairs. But, by God, St. Cyr had worked for him for almost five years now, and there was no one in New Orleans who matched him in matters of discreet security. Anderson shook his head grimly, imagining what would happen if he gave any one of the local crew of dirt-white toughs the free hand St. Cyr enjoyed. Those dunces would be likely to beat a man half to death when a simple word or two would do. Hopeless thugs, for the most part. He had owned yard dogs with more sense than all of them put together. But St. Cyr was another breed entirely and Tom Anderson afforded him so much deference that the detective could voice doubts about eminent white men like Father Dupre without a second thought.

The King of Storyville knew about St. Cyr, knew of his father and mother and his police career, about his friendship with that maniac King Bolden. He would have to hold such information on anyone he allowed so close.

Maybe he had given him too much free rein; but the man had earned it, and surely never abused the privilege. So if there was, by chance, something peculiar to the deaths of the two sporting girls, St. Cyr would take care of it. Though he would have to lose those notions about Dupre, that helpless old man of God.

Anderson ran a lazy hand over the pages before him and shoved his thoughts toward practicality. It was not his habit to create problems out of whole cloth. With two thousand soiled doves working the houses and streets, two dying mysteriously was no reason for alarm. God rest their souls, but it was a fact of life.

Most likely, the sad business would flicker away and be forgotten. The bodies of Annie Robie and Gran Tillman would go down into the cold ground or into paupers' biers; old Father Dupre would fade into infirmity in his own private grave behind the stone walls at Jackson; and business in Anderson County would go on without a pause.

The State Senator picked up his pen and returned to his work.

Five

New Orleans Parish Prison was a harsh, blank, three-story gravestone that stretched along Royal Street from St. Louis to Conti, a scofflaw's nightmare that began the moment his disobedient shoes were dragged up to the gray and somber edifice.

The ugly, glowering block of granite housed courtrooms, municipal offices, a police precinct and, in the basement, a gruesome excuse for a jail, all connected by echoing corridors and stairwells. If Hell could fit in a city block, Valentin had reflected, it would have the exact appearance of this building; and should he ever again be tempted by the fruits of crime, he need only poke his nose down the west side of the French Quarter, catch a glimpse of a single bleak cornerstone of the building, and he would be cured.

So it was only fitting that as he was arriving there late that afternoon, J. Picot was coming down the broad stone steps. The policeman stopped in his tracks and looked St. Cyr up and down, his lips curling. "Now what?" When the Creole detective didn't answer directly, Picot's grimace turned into a thin smile. "You here about Bolden? I heard they brought him in last night. Everybody heard. He was yellin' and screamin', fightin' with the officers. They had to put him down."

"Put him down how?" Valentin asked.

Picot made a lazy mime of swinging a club. "Knocked him cold, I hear. But I wasn't there," he added with a tone of regret. He fastened a hard eye on St. Cyr. "What, you goin' his bail now?"

Valentin shrugged. The copper shook his head. "I wouldn't waste my money. They need to throw away the key on that one. Nothin' but a rowdy. We get more calls when that band of his is playing somewhere. It makes people crazy. There oughta be a law." Picot's expression turned sardonic. "But while you're inside, go ahead ask him about that Negro girl over to Cassie Maples'," he said.

Valentin glanced at him sharply, but the copper had turned abruptly and was walking down the steps. "Watch yourself round here," he snickered over his shoulder. "You wouldn't want to find yourself locked up with him." That would mean locked up in the colored section, as they both knew. Picot strolled off.

⁓

The fellow who had caused all the ruckus presented such a picture staring out from the dim shadows of the cell that Valentin almost smiled. Buddy looked exactly like he did when they were kids and caught in some mischief: baffled by the fuss, but mostly indignant at being nabbed at all. Valentin stepped closer and noticed his right eye, slightly swollen, and purple-blue tinge of bruises here and there on his head. Behind him on a pallet on the stone floor, a lump of putrid-smelling humanity lay snoring up a storm. Up and down the narrow corridor echoed sounds and smells more akin to Audubon Zoo.

"Buddy?" Valentin said.

"My horn," Bolden murmured in a tragic voice. "They took my horn."

"What happened?" Valentin said.

The prisoner turned away and began pacing behind the bars. "I don't know. One minute we were playing. The next thing I know there's all this noise and the coppers came in and they carried me away."

"You scuffled with them."

Bolden stopped his pacing. "Did I?" He looked confused. "Well, they took my horn," he repeated. Valentin noticed the hands fidgeting about, and it occurred to him that it had been years since he had seen Buddy without a silver cornet either dangling from his fingers or stuck to his lips.

"Where's Nora?" he was saying. "Is she coming to get me out?"

"She can't get you out. They're going to hold you."

Buddy's face twisted up with a finicky disgust. Valentin understood. King Bolden had abruptly become a common criminal, stuck in Parish Prison, just another no-account nigger tramp like the rest of them up and down the line of cells. He blinked tensely. "For how long?"

"Probably two days."

"Two days!"

"It's nothing," Valentin said. "They'll take you out with a gang to clean up the Market." Bolden's face fell further. "You want me to go see her?" Buddy shrugged and muttered something. "It's only for the two days," Valentin said. "Then I'll come collect you."

King Bolden slumped against the steel bars. "What did they do with my horn?" he said.

~

Valentin stepped out into a cloudy evening. The streets around him moved in lazy slow-motion with citizens on end-of-the-day errands, sports getting an early line on the night's action, the odd drunkard drifting along on a cloud of cheap whiskey. As he stood on the corner of Canal and Marais, lost in his thoughts, the first thick drops of a Louisiana thundershower splattered on the banquette.

He bent his head, jammed his hands in his pockets and turned down Canal, walking into the approaching storm. He went at a hard pace, his shoes slapping water, putting distance between himself and that grim hulk of a jailhouse. He made his way south by ducking into doorways and under colonnades, stopping here and there for a few moments as the rain turned streets into shallow lagoons, then moving on. By the time he had reached Basin Street, he was half-soaked. He found a dry spot in the doorway of Cairo Club, closed for the night, and drew a thin cigar from his vest pocket. He struck a lucifer on the brick wall and smoked as he watched the hard rain sweep over Storyville.

In the space of a week, he had stood over the corpses of Littlejohn and two sporting girls, both of whom had been left with a black rose. He had taken a strange trip to Jackson with an old priest. And now he had seen King Bolden locked up in Parish Prison.

He guessed that the first three killings would add up to nothing. The Angel of Death stayed busy on these streets of New Orleans, and homicide was only part of his gruesome harvest; there were ravaging diseases and bizarre accidents and slow suicides to add to the tally, as evidenced by two cemeteries—St. Louis No. 1 and No. 2—so full of victims that they were buried atop each other, stacked like cordwood. Around those parts, slipping gently into the Bosom of God took some doing.

So he could forget about the pimp, and Annie Robie and Gran Tillman wouldn't be far behind. Even with Bolden and the priest to muddy the waters, there was nothing to make a fuss over. Old men's wits failed; and Bolden in jail was not exactly a surprise, either. Even Buddy knowing Annie Robie was no great mystery. Back-of-town was nothing if not a small village, so why wouldn't he know such a young, pretty girl?

The black roses were curious, but more than likely a coincidence, like Anderson claimed. Valentin had thought about visiting the local floral shops and ask about anything suspicious, then dismissed the idea. There were only two flowers, after all. It would be a waste of time. Odd things happened daily in Storyville. Once the sun went down, it was all a cheap carnival, layer on layer of illusion pasted on scarlet streets. That was the District, a thousand strange players shoved together on one crowded stage.

He let out a plume of smoke and turned his thoughts back to Bolden, now sitting in that dank cell. He could not remember Buddy even getting into schoolboy fights. No, young Charles Bolden didn't roughhouse much at all; and when he began with his music, he stayed off the streets and out of trouble altogether.

But the person he'd left at Parish Prison was not the Buddy Bolden he'd known back those long years ago. That fellow had been replaced by this raw, desperate character who too often had the eyes of a stranger.

Standing under the dripping eave, he shook his head at his own dramatics. He admitted what his thoughts had been teasing: that he would love the random pieces to assemble into a mystery, something beside the callow fringes of the flesh trade to engage him. And a chance to tangle with an evil and put something right.

He pitched the butt of the cigarillo into the gutter, watched the rushing water carry it away, then took out his pocket watch, glanced at it, and put it back. He stood under the overhang for another long minute, pondering what to do next, where to go. The rain was getting lighter. It would move on soon.

He had said something to Buddy about paying a visit to Nora. But he knew he could just as easily step onto the banquette, walk south, make a few turns and be back at his rooms before darkness fell. Bolden would never know the difference and he could put an end to his day.

More minutes passed and then he stepped to the corner and climbed aboard the streetcar heading west.

The car came to a stop and he stepped down. The rain had passed, leaving white tatters that snaked off the cobblestones like thin ghosts. The last rays of evening sun were peeking through the high distant clouds, casting the city streets in a soft mist the color of a seashell.

He stood on the corner, remembering. Across the way was the shave and barbering parlor at First and Liberty. Now run by Mr. Louis Jones, it was Nate Joseph's when Valentin was a kid, and was known as much as an informal social club and musicians' employment office as a barbering parlor.

But a barbering parlor it was, of course. He saw himself, a small boy, his tiny hand in his father's thick one, walking up to the double doors early on a Saturday afternoon. Inside, the solemn wink of greeting from Nate to his father. Being lifted onto the child's seat that crossed from arm to arm. The barber throwing the cape like a matador, the billow a white sail that seemed to fill the tiny room before settling over him, right down to his shoes. Then stopping to pour his father a glass of brandy before he got to the business at hand. His father's face was reflected in the glass, watching with a lazy but critical eye the career of the scissors. And if young Valentin sat still and did not fuss, a piece of caramel candy to enjoy on the way home.

Later, he and Buddy stood outside, looking through the glass at the fancy men preening for a Saturday night's action, getting their shaves, haircuts, manicures, and shoeshines. It was a ritual as stylized as Mass, and for the two boys, a glance beyond their childhood world into something strange and wild.

The men: Creoles of every shade, redheads with dark freckles on russet skin, tans and high yellows and black, black, African-looking sports. Now and then, one olive-skinned like Valentin. Their hair was pomaded or oiled shiny. There were diamonds on their fingers and garters and stuck on pins in their ties. Tiny envelopes with cocaine and cards of hop peeked from vest pockets. The shapes of spring knives or straight razors showed in their trousers, but pistols were checked at the door.

"Here, sir," old Nate would implore, his voice soft, soothing. "Let me take that for you," as if relieving the customer of a tiresome burden. And the oily blue-black weapon nestled with the others in a drawer beneath the mirror.

They took their turns dropping into a chair with its brass fittings and leather the color of old blood. They watched the world through cool, sleepy eyes like snakes, and like snakes they were always ready to strike. But they relaxed now, as the darkness fell and Nate pampered their heads and faces, one assistant tended to their manicures, and yet another shined their shoes.

Buddy and Valentin knew the cast of characters like some boys knew the players on a baseball club or the gamblers knew the horses at the Fairgrounds. So they noticed when suddenly one disappeared. Before long, they'd know why: in jail or dead, for the most part. But always there was another candidate to slip into the vacated place.

They were gawky kids, both growing too fast for their clothes. Buddy, brown-skinned, getting tall, Valentin shorter, his skin so light so people often thought he was plain Dago.

The two of them stood shoulder to shoulder, staring wide-eyed into that waiting room to the world of night. And the scenes beyond the glass were caught and held in time, like one of Papá Bellocq's photographs.

Still later, Valentin was sent off to Chicago just as Buddy's widowed mother was taking up with Manuel Hall, a plasterer by day and musician by night. It was Hall who taught Buddy the rudiments of the horn, but student quickly outstripped teacher and Master Bolden left high school to play music and work day jobs. Along the way, he fathered a son by a local girl, both of whom he promptly forgot.

By the time Valentin came back from his wanderings, Buddy was a bit player in the cast at the Louis Jones Shaving Parlor, because it was there and at the other barber shops around uptown New Orleans that band leaders left word that they were hiring for this job or that.

But he was not yet spending his nights there, lazing with the sports. He had a pretty wife and new baby girl and half of a double shotgun down on First Street, just up the street from the house he grew up in. That all came later, when his horn and his good looks and his reputation turned him into one of the fancy men that a new crowd of young boys ogled through the tall windows.

That was right about the time that Valentin joined the New Orleans Police Department. They saw each other now and then, but Kid Bolden was now a regular rounder and him a copper; they were set apart by their choice of uniforms and, truth be told, embarrassed by each other. It was after Valentin quit the force over that rough business with his sergeant and began working the back-of-town streets that their paths crossed again. The friendship resumed, awkwardly at first, then with more comfort. But a distance remained, and they both knew it would never go away.

~

Valentin strolled by the shop, saw only a solitary barber sitting in a chair, reading a newspaper. It was early; people were still at their suppers.

He walked down two blocks to the corner of First Street and picked out one of the white clapboard shotgun houses that lined the streets in every direction, set apart from the others only by the number 2719. The street was quiet. He put a foot on the perron and knocked.

Nora Bolden opened the door. Her eyes flashed with surprise, then settled on him with an inscrutable calm. "Is he dead?" she said.

～

Nora asked if they could walk. She left Bernedette with the next-door neighbor and they strolled to the corner of Philip and Howard, then east in the general direction of downtown, away from the neighborhood.

Valentin figured that she did not want to happen upon Buddy's mother and sister, who lived around the corner on Howard Street. He recalled Buddy telling him that Nora never liked his family, she called them "funny." Though she was religious, he guessed she had a superstition about whatever had gotten hold of him. One person picked up a curse or some other *gris-gris*, the whole family suffered. It could be in the blood and it could go back generations.

She was a small, very pretty woman of medium-brown skin, a good mother and life-long member of St. John Fourth Baptist Church who now found herself in a common-law marriage with a madman.

As they walked, she began to recount her own version of the tale. Everything was good at first, though she fretted over Buddy leaving steady jobs playing in parades and at concerts and white folks' dances to work in filthy Rampart Street saloons. She recalled him all happy at getting to lead his own little band, how he heard himself called "Kid Bolden" for the first time and rushed home to tell her about it.

She allowed herself a small smile. It was not so long after that people on the street started to talk about The Bolden Band, kids peeked in the windows to see her husband, young women at church looked him up and down and wet their lips.

His star rose. The word spread that his band could play anything, from sweet and solemn spirituals to double-time rags to gutbucket blues that would milk blood from a rock. And the show he put on! People loved it that Kid Bolden didn't sit stuck to a chair like the others. He got up and moved, up and down the stage, using his horn like a magic wand and sometimes like something dirty. Nora watched as he began to change, as he got lost in all the fawning attention, as he fell prey to the free whiskey and the loose women.

But it was really always the music. Thomas Edison had invented the machine to make sound recordings on cylinders of wax and then play them back. It was a true wonder, and as soon as the first contraption arrived in New Orleans, Buddy herded his band to the back room of the music store on Canal Street and made a recording, a rushed mess that convinced him to tear that band apart, build another. And then a third and a fourth and each one moved him more out in front, like the engine on a fast train.

How it all got crazier then! People rushed to listen to his wild music, to stomp their feet and yell, to flail about like they were in the jungle somewhere. At Longshoreman's Hall on South Rampart or Odd Fellows Hall in Storyville or Masonic Hall across the river in Algiers, at the outdoor dances in Jackson and Johnson Parks, in dirty saloons and in pavilions built on pilings on the waters of Lake Pontchartrain. Anywhere Buddy's band played, a crowd gathered. And it wasn't just colored folk either; downtown Creoles and even some reckless young whites from proper Garden District families were coming round to see what all the fuss was about.

So his one or two late nights a week turned into five or six. And then "Kid" became "King." And the music changed, not just popular styles "jassed-up" or "ragged," like they called it; Buddy turned everything around, then inside out.

Nora didn't understand what he was playing at all. She didn't hear the music; it sounded like a mush of noise. She didn't understand why it made people so frantic. She didn't understand why it started young girls fighting over who would hold his coat and scarf (but never his horn; he never let anyone touch his horn). She didn't get all the rambunctious motion up on the bandstand. And, as the months passed, she realized that she didn't truly know the man who was her husband and father to her daughter anymore.

But he was part-time in that role anyway, staying with her, disappearing and turning up at his mother's house on Howard Street, then disappearing again and coming home days later as if it was the most natural thing in the world.

They started having spats. Buddy would be calm and sweet one moment, in a rage the next, stomping from one end of the shotgun house to the other, ranting nonsense and scaring the daylights out of Bernedette. Then he was quiet again, lying on the couch with a wet cloth across his face. He got headaches.

Nora knew about the drinking, suspected opium. She didn't mention the women, either, though she surely knew about all them, too. It had been going on for a year or more, Buddy tottering around his home life with his wife and child, then crashing off into uptown New Orleans like some animal released from a cage.

"And this time they took him to jail," she said, ending on a weary note.

Valentin looked at her. "This time?"

"Oh, I had to call the po-lice myself," she said. "Once when he came in all crazy and started breaking things. The other when he stood outside the house in the middle of the

night. Yelling like a crazy man. Woke up half the neighbors.
The coppers came out, got him settled down."

"Yelling about what?"

Nora frowned. "I don't know. It didn't make no sense.
When he woke up the next morning, it was like nothing
happened."

They reached Perdido and Nora turned around without
asking and headed back the way they came. They walked in
silence for a half-block.

"So, Mr. Valentin," she said finally. "What am I gonna
do wit' him?"

"Maybe what he needs is a doctor," Valentin said.

She let out a low laugh. "He went to a doctor."

"He did?"

"About a month ago."

"Who was it?"

"Rall's his name," Nora said. "White man." She caught
Valentin's look of surprise. "I believe one of the fellows in
the band sent him there," she explained.

"And did it help?"

Nora's pretty face fell. "No. He got worse."

She invited him for a glass of lemonade. They stood on
the back gallery, looking out over the tiny yard, a patch of
dirt and a few scrawny shrubs all silver in the falling night.
Valentin thought to ask for the doctor's address and Nora
wrote it down on a slip of paper. She handed it to him and
he folded it and put it in his vest pocket.

"I'll pay him a visit," Valentin said.

"Don't be expecting nothing," she said grimly. "Buddy
wouldn't tell me what he said, so I went round to his office
to talk to him." She shook her head. "The man was drunk.
Middle of the day and the man's drunk. The *doctor*. He was
some help."

"I'll talk to him, Nora."

Nora shrugged. Then: "When they gonna let him outta jail?" There was an edge to her voice.

"Day after tomorrow. I'll go collect him."

She put a hand on the porch railing and seemed to tense a little. Then she said, "That band of his is playing over in the District this week. Up on Marais Street. Nancy Hanks'."

"I know the place," Valentin said.

"You think maybe you could you keep an eye on him?" she said. "When he don't come home I worry." She was silent for a long moment and when she spoke up, her voice was shaky, like she was verging on tears. "I don't know who else to ask. I don't know what to do." She looked at him. "Guess I must be crazy, too, eh?"

Valentin had been preparing an excuse, but now he patted her shoulder and told her he'd do as she asked. He finished his lemonade and Nora walked him to the front door. "He scares me, Mr. Valentin," she said suddenly. Valentin, standing on the perron, watched her face. "It's not him."

"What's not him?"

"It ain't Buddy anymore," she said. "Half the time, I believe it's someone else walkin' around in his shoes. I'm tellin' you, it ain't him. It scares me." She dropped her eyes. "He scares me," she said and closed the door.

～

Valentin walked toward Tulane, where he could catch a streetcar back to Magazine Street. Three blocks away was the very house where he had grown up. He walked straight on. On either side of him were landmarks, all the places he and Buddy had haunted as children, but he didn't look up.

His steps slowed as he reached the corner of South Rampart Street. He felt the shadows all around and he heard echoes in the still night. As he waited there for the streetcar, leaning against the brick wall of Charles Schneider's blacksmith shop, the shadows took form and the tale unfolded all over again. This time, he couldn't stop it.

It began with an urban war between two immigrant Italian clans, the Matrangas and the Provenzanos, who battled over the rights to the handling of fruit shipments from Central America that arrived on the New Orleans docks. The Matrangas brought the crude, bare-fisted street justice of their Sicilian mountain homes to the fray. The more urbane Provenzanos countered by snuggling close with downtown politicians.

Not that they were the sorts to run from a fight. The pitched battles between the two families included beatings and stabbings and shootouts on the streets of the city, some in broad daylight. Respectable citizens grew frightened and angry. Blood being spilled back-of-town was one thing; these people carried their hot-headed disputes everywhere, including the streets around the French Market, where servants of the "Americans" of the Garden District did their shopping.

It so happened that at this particular moment, David Hennessy, a former New Orleans detective, wriggled his way into the office of Chief of Police after five years in exile over the suspicious shooting of a man who just happened to be a political rival. Hennessy, a personal friend of Allan Pinkerton himself, fell to the task of settling the Matranga-Provenzano feud as his first order of business. But he came to the matter with a jaundiced eye, because some distant kin of the Matrangas had murdered his cousin on the streets of Houston years before.

Hennessy's Irish backside had barely settled into his new chair when Tony Matranga was shot several times as he took his evening stroll down Conti Street. The Matranga *padrone* swore that his assailants were none other than Frank and Joe Provenzano, heads of the rival clan. Chief Hennessy stood by as the police did their duty and arrested the Provenzano brothers. But, on the second day of their trial, he stepped forward to offer the judge reason to dismiss the charges. He claimed he had investigated and had evidence that the Provenzanos were being framed.

But he never got to make his case. As he walked to his French Quarter home the evening before his scheduled appearance, a young boy ran past and whistled; a second later, a sawed-off shotgun roared from the shadows. Hennessy fell to the banquette, mortally wounded. A friend who rushed to the scene reported that Hennessy gasped out that "the Dagos" had been his attackers. Within a few hours, fourteen Sicilians, some members of the Matranga gang, some complete innocents, were rounded up as suspects. The next morning, all were charged with conspiring to assassinate Chief Hennessy.

The incident caused a mistrial to be declared for the Proven-zanos, and the Matranga case now took over the front pages of the daily papers. It was roundly deemed an open-and-shut matter, except for the bothersome fact that there was not a shred of evidence, not a single eyewitness, not a speck of circumstance that tied the Sicilians being held in Parish Prison to Chief Hennessy's murder. The judge weighed the facts, then directed the jury to find some of the defendants not guilty, while he ordered a mistrial on the others.

American New Orleans boiled over. The dirty guineas were going to get away with a horrendous crime! The next morning's newspapers carried hysterical screeds and a public notice of a mass meeting near Congo Square to "remedy the failure of justice in the Hennessy case." The announcement closed with the ominous line: "Come prepared for action."

By noon, the mob that gathered at the Henry Clay Statue on Canal Street numbered fifteen thousand angry whites, a number of them armed. Local politicians mounted the base of the statue to whip the crowd into a frenzy. They marched off to Parish Prison, where the Matranga defendants were awaiting release. Guards barred the front gate, but a phalanx of hoodlums broke down a rear door and charged inside.

They rushed through the prison corridors, hunting down the Sicilians, who had been released from their cells so they could hide. Eleven men were cornered and shot dead. Six more were dragged into the prison yard and hung, in what became the worst mass lynching in the history of an America that lynched like murderous clockwork.

The violence continued into the night as splinter gangs raged off into Italian neighborhoods. Valentin remembered his mother running into his bedroom and shoving him out their back door and down the alleyway to a kindly old quadroon couple who lived a few houses away.

He never forgot that night and the cold nausea of fear, the helpless terror that gripped him as he and his parents huddled in the dark kitchen. That night, the way he understood the world changed forever. It was Friday the 13th, in March of 1891. He was fifteen years old.

~

The streetcar rumbled to a stop and he climbed on. Staring out the rear window, he watched the streets of his old neighborhood grow narrow and then fade into darkness. The tall man in the derby hat remained behind.

~

Just before midnight, there was a knock on the door. Valentin's mother wailed and his father reached for an ax handle. But it was only Buddy. He had crawled out his bedroom window to come looking for his friend. As the night passed, they sat at the neighbors' kitchen table, talking like nothing was happening, though they could hear the shouts from the street, breaking glass, the random crack of gunfire.

But it faded into the background as Buddy told him about two local rounders getting into a big, drunken brawl outside Joe Maxie's Beer Parlor. The two of them whispered over one of the pretty neighborhood girls. And Buddy talked about Manuel Hall, the horn player who was coming round to see his mama. It was that night that Buddy announced that he was going to be a musician. They talked about it until dawn brought a gray quiet to the streets outside.

That wasn't quite the end of the story. A month later, as his father and mother strolled along the river, they were accosted by two drunken white men who loudly opined that only a nigger slut would bed down with a dirty dago. His father beat both men into the ground and might have murdered them if his mother hadn't been there to stop him. But the following day, a gang of six whites cornered him in the warehouse on the docks where he worked and the next time Valentin and his mother saw him, he was hanging at the end of a rope. None of his murderers was ever identified.

~

He got off the No. 12 streetcar and then rode the No. 34 down Canal Street to Magazine as the last details of the story broke off in jagged pieces and drifted away again. As always, the memories wearied him. They always slowed him, like a weight on his back.

He unlocked the street door and climbed the thirteen steps to the second floor. He undressed and slipped into his bed, ready for sleep to take him. Before he drifted off, he decided he would go round in the morning to see the doctor Nora had mentioned. His curiosity had the best of him. He wanted to know if there was anything more to it.

Six

DR. MILES'
No. 150
SPECIFIC MIXTURE
Guaranteed
A Sure Cure
for
Gonorrhea and
G...GLEET

After his coffee, Valentin caught a streetcar uptown to Villere Street, got off and walked north until the cobbles gave way to dirt. He found Dr. Rall's office in a broken-down, one-story clapboard house along a deserted alley, just as Nora had described it. He knocked, but there was no answer. He tried the door—unlocked. He turned the knob and stepped inside.

It was a typical boxcar flat. The first room held a desk, a half-dozen chairs lining opposite walls and a coat rack in one corner. There was a stack of old magazines on one of the chairs. A pair of sliding doors leading to the room beyond was shut tight. It was the doctor's reception area, but there was no nurse or secretary on the job, and no patients waiting, either. Valentin slid the double doors aside and stepped into an examining room, with white enameled cabinets on the walls to his left and right, a roll-top desk pushed against the back wall and a steel table in the center of the floor. All of it looked dusty and quite unused. On either side of the desk was a door, one to a toilet, the other to a closet. A third, arched doorway led to the back rooms of the house.

He heard a muted thump from the back of the house and then silence. He waited for a few moments, then went around the table and opened the closet door. In contained one ragged winter coat on a hangar and a stack of boxes as tall as a man. Each was pasted with a small sheet of paper with the florid inscription "Dr. Miles No. 150 Specific Mixture."

When he heard more sounds of movement from the back of the house, he quickly closed the closet door and stepped back to the center of the room.

The man shuffling unsteadily into the room wore a dirty white dress shirt with collar missing, baggy gray trousers spotted with dark stains, suspenders hanging down and some kind of slippers. He turned for the toilet and caught sight of the visitor. He started, then blinked groggily. He tried to say something, coughed and then tried again. His "Kin I help ya?" floated on stale, musty breath.

"Doctor Rall?" Valentin said.

The doctor's doughy face was peppered with white whiskers and his wisps of gray hair stuck out at angles. The milky blue eyes tried to focus. "Howdja git in here?" His voice was a raw rasp.

"Valentin St. Cyr," the visitor announced himself. "Your door was open."

The doctor's gaze strayed away and he mumbled something that sounded like "potion." When he repeated it, Valentin realized the word was "appointment."

"No, I don't have an appointment," he said. "I'm here to ask about someone you treated."

Dr. Rall drew back and took a step away as if to dismiss him. "'Specting a patient." He coughed as he shuffled toward the toilet.

"I am in the employ of Tom Anderson," Valentin announced. As expected, the man stopped and stared. "This will only take a minute."

Rall glanced at the toilet door, then cleared his throat. "Well..." He made his way to his cluttered desk and sat down heavily.

Valentin took the chair next to the desk.

"What's all this about?" the doctor asked as he began to flip unsteady fingers through a stack of files in the metal tray on his desk. When Valentin didn't answer, he said, "What was the patient's name?"

"Bolden," Valentin said and the doctor's fingers stopped. "Charles. They call him Buddy."

The fingers resumed their search, but it was for show, because they went directly to a file folder that was second from the top. "Here," Rall said and opened the folder. "Bolden, Charles." He patted his shirt pocket and came up with a pair of bifocals, which he opened and perched on his nose. "Yes, I treated him."

"For what condition?" Valentin asked.

Rall looked at the sheet before him, but he wasn't reading. "He was... having fits."

"Fits?"

"Behaving in a troublesome manner." The doctor didn't elaborate.

"Did you find a cause?" Valentin asked.

"A cause." The doctor coughed dryly and glanced at his visitor. "These kinds of cases, there's rarely a *cause*. Speaking medically, that is." The eyes ran up and down the paper, looking for something that wasn't there. "I believe I...uh, prescribed something for him. A mild sedative, probably. It's really all we can do. Then wait and hope to see improvement." He closed the folder and tried a smile of tobacco-stained teeth.

"What sedative?" Valentin asked.

"I don't recall," the doctor said. "Seems I lost my notes somewhere. Probably a paregoric solution. That's very common." Rall was fidgeting, plainly ill-at-ease. He placed the folder back on the stack and began to fuss about with the scraps of paper that lay about his desk like so many dead leaves. He would not meet the detective's gaze as his own kept drifting to the toilet door.

"Do you remember Nora Bolden?" Valentin said. Rall blinked a few times more. "His wife."

The doctor's attention returned. "Whose wife? Oh. What about her?"

"She came to see you."

"Did she?" It wasn't an act; he clearly didn't remember.

"It's not important," Valentin said.

The doctor ran a nervous hand over his face. "I really have to..." And he lurched suddenly out of his chair and disappeared into the toilet, locking the door behind him.

Valentin listened to hacking and coughing and the sound of water running. He got up to take a closer look around the premises. Whatever doctoring was done there, he noted, was done without the use of medical equipment. Everything, the tables, the cases filled with instruments, the lights on their stands, was covered with dust, and cobwebs stretched across every corner.

He turned his attention to the doctor's desk. The scraps of paper contained notes scrawled in what looked like a child's hand. Valentin glanced at the toilet door and pushed a finger through the mess. He stopped, staring, and plucked one slip from among the others. He read the single word printed there. He had just slipped the scrap into a pocket when the door to the toilet opened again.

The doctor looked much the better. He had splashed water on his face, straightened his collar, buttoned his trousers, and pulled up his suspenders. He had made a stab at putting his licks of white hair in order and had doused himself with an ungodly cologne that sent a heavy cloud of sweet magnolia before him. He sat down at his desk once more and turned to his visitor with eyes that held a hard shine. "Was there anything else?" The voice was now firm, in control.

Valentin shook his head. He thanked the doctor and let himself out.

As he walked to the streetcar stop on the corner of Villere and Canal, he dug into his pocket and extracted the card he had filched. He read again the single penciled word: "Tillman." He considered turning around, going back and confronting the nervous doctor about why the name of a recent murder victim was lying on his desk. And while he was at it, ask him why he bothered to write Bolden a prescription for paregoric when a child could buy it over the counter at any apothecary in the city.

Of course, Rall would lie to him. *What was that name? Tillman? Don't ring a bell, no.* As far as the prescription was concerned, what he gave Bolden was probably what he himself had taken in his toilet, something a tad stronger than paregoric. Valentin stopped to recall the contents of the closet, bottles of a local remedy for gonorrhea and the sores they called "gleet."

He suspected that Rall, like dozens of other "doctors" in New Orleans, wasn't an M.D. at all, but a medicine show refugee who had bestowed credentials on himself, the whole of his practice dispensing patent medicines as cure-alls and various kinds of dope as balms to injured spirits. It was quite common, merely a matter of supply meeting demand without the complications of the law. It was a Storyville tradition.

On a notion, Valentin turned around and walked back toward the doctor's address. He was a hundred feet from the alley when Rall appeared suddenly, charging onto the street. The doctor hurried down two doors to a workman's diner and went inside. Valentin sidled up to one of the windows and saw Rall standing at the end of the long wooden counter with the proprietor's telephone in hand, talking to someone, his face flushed, his free hand waving in the air. Valentin watched him for a few moments, knowing there was no way to get inside and not give himself away. But of course, he knew what the call was about. He stepped back from the window and walked away.

            ~

A few minutes before six that evening, they walked into Frank Mangetta's place on the corner of Marais and Bienville. Mangetta's was a regular joint, located halfway between Storyville and Uptown, where white, black, and Creole musicians drank and played, one of the few addresses in the District open to Negroes, but only those who brought serious talent. It was a cavernous space, a barroom attached to a grocery where imported provolone and prosciutto hung from hooks and tins of Sicilian olive oil were stacked waist-high. On the saloon side were high ceilings, hardwood floors buffed shiny, wide windows looking out onto the street, tables filling up the center of the floor and along the brick wall opposite the marble-topped bar. There was a tiny stage of bricks and lumber in one corner. Mangetta, a sometime musician himself, ran the place like a benign *padrone*. Everyone knew he was good for a drink or a meal when times were hard.

The saloon was early-evening empty, save for a few lonesome souls who didn't look up from their short glasses of Raleigh Rye and mugs of beer when King Bolden burst inside and began rushing about the room, peering into every corner and under every table. He was starting to get frantic when a voice called out, "You lookin' for this?"

From the doorway that led into the grocery, Frank Mangetta held up a cornet of silvered brass.

            ~

Valentin leaned against the bar, talking to Mangetta. Buddy sat at a corner table, holding the horn to his breast, his right hand fingers running the valves in and out, as he guzzled greedily from the mug of beer the barkeep had delivered. Mangetta explained that the dent in the bell happened when a copper tossed the horn into one of the columns of solid oak. King Bolden's famous cornet had tumbled to a floor slick with spilt beer and rye whiskey and the contents of the overturned spittoons. Mangetta himself recovered it after the brawl died down.

He whispered an account of that night's trouble. Buddy kept wandering off the bandstand, walking through the crowd, then went out the front door and into the middle of Marais Street, his horn loud enough to cause sports in rooms up and down both sides of Conti Street to lose their attentions. These gentlemen complained to the madams, who complained to the police, who arrived to warn Frank Mangetta to keep his entertainers indoors where they belonged. Buddy overheard the exchange and offered his own opinion on the matter, which included a comment about one of the officers' unnatural love for his mother. At which point the sergeant in charge jumped onto the low stage and dragged the bandleader down by the scruff of his neck. Bolden fought back, laughing and shouting like it was some kind of frolic, and soon six coppers and half the crowd in the saloon were in the middle of a fray. Buddy didn't stop flailing about until one of the blue coats cracked him on the side of his head with a nightstick.

"He went down like a tree," Mangetta told the detective, shaking his head in awe as they watched Buddy seat himself at a table. "I thought they killed him." He smiled. "But look at him there. King Bolden. Don't look much worse for the wear, eh?" He went off to serve some customers.

                                            ⌒

Valentin had taken a seat at the table. He sipped his beer as Bolden guzzled his, and the more he guzzled, the more he seemed to close up, like he was trying to shake the jailhouse off by fading into the dark brick wall behind him. Valentin thought about asking him straight out about Dr. Rall and his "prescription," but a glance told him it would be a waste of time. Buddy was gone, mumbling to himself as he fretted absently over his damaged horn. Valentin turned in his chair to survey the evening street. It was starting to rain again.

As he watched, a New Orleans Police wagon pulled up to the banquette. Two coppers stepped down from the seat, strolled in the door and crossed directly to the bar, where Mangetta was tapping a barrel of beer. Valentin's eyes narrowed as he studied them. They looked like brothers and they looked familiar. When Mangetta saw them, he stopped what he was doing and the three men went into the grocery.

The saloonkeeper and the two coppers reappeared a few minutes later. Mangetta saw them to the door and then stood glowering at them as they climbed back into the hack and rattled away. He walked over to the table, shaking his head.

"I know those two," Valentin said.

"Joe and Bill Collins," Mangetta said shortly. "Two of New Orleans' finest."

"Were they here about last night?"

Mangetta said, "I wish they were."

"How much, Frank?"

"Too much," Mangetta said. "But I need to stay in business." He leaned a hand on the back of his chair, drew a toothpick from his vest pocket and began sucking it noisily. Bolden didn't look up. "How's the beer, gentlemen?" the barkeep asked.

Valentin answered for both of them. "It's fine."

Mangetta bent his head and lowered his voice. "So, what's this I hear about some sporting girls getting killed? One, what, back-of-town at Cassie Maples'?"

"Yes, her name was Annie Robie," Valentin said.

Bolden, who had been staring at his reflection in the bell of his horn, raised his eyes.

"And another one Saturday night?" Mangetta said.

"That's when they found her," Valentin said.

Buddy's hand shot out abruptly and he knocked his empty glass across the table. Valentin and Mangetta stared at him and he stared back at them like he was suddenly hanging on every word. Valentin righted the glass. He spoke to the barkeep but kept an eye on Bolden.

"That one's name was Gran Tillman," he said and at the mention of the name, Buddy let out a sudden cracked laugh, and then just as suddenly fell silent. Mangetta gaped at him, his eyebrows arching in astonishment. He was about to say something, but at that moment, the door banged open and two drummers walked in and made for the bar. Mangetta gave Buddy a last puzzled glance and went off to serve the two men.

Valentin leaned over the table. "What is it?" he said. "What?"

"Gran Tillman," Bolden said in a loud, sloppy whisper. "Well, I guess you don't know. She and Annie...ha-ha...they were *friends*, the two of them. She was the one first took Annie in. She was the one found her on the street after that Georgia nigger put her out." His dark eyes glimmered. "You know. That fellow you shot down, Tino. Gran Tillman. She was the one took her to Cassie Maples'. She and Annie was friends. Oh, yes," he finished, "they were great friends, those two." Bolden glanced dully at his empty glass, then shook his head and reached out without asking to grab the detective's mug.

Valentin watched him drink it down in one long swallow. "Where were you Saturday?" he asked. "Before you went to play, I mean."

Buddy puzzled for a few seconds, then shrugged and said, "Don't remember."

～

He was emptying glasses of beer as fast as Mangetta brought them to the table, ignoring Valentin as he went back to whispering to himself. Valentin listened for a few minutes, trying to make sense of the mumblings, then gave up. He looked at his pocket watch. He didn't have to be to work, but he got up to leave anyway. He'd heard plenty enough. He went off to find Mangetta and the barkeep promised he would rouse Buddy in time to make the four-block walk up Marais to Nancy Hanks' Saloon, where the King Bolden Band had an engagement.

"But I can't be stayin' up there," Mangetta said. "I got a business to run."

"I'll go by later on," Valentin said. "Nora wants me to get him back home."

They two stood looking at Buddy, huddled over in the booth, muttering like the madman he was. "Look at him," Mangetta said with a sigh. "Well, can't say I ain't seen it coming."

Valentin gave the saloonkeeper a glance. "What do you mean?"

Mangetta drew another toothpick from his vest pocket and waved it about like a tiny baton. "Mr. Bolden there has got himself into a corner he can't get out of."

"How's that?" Valentin said.

"See, he never got schooled like them reading types, Robichaux and all them. And he can't make his horn do what he wants no more. He got all this stuff in his head, but his mouth can't keep up. He hears it but he can't play it. And we ain't talking about just any old horn player. That's King Bolden there. Ain't never been nobody like him. Ain't never been nobody done what he's done with a horn. I betcha twenty years from now, people'll still be talking about it." He stuck the toothpick between two teeth and hooked his thumbs in the sleeves of his vest. "But it don't matter, cause I think it's all over now. And that's what all this trouble is about. He just can't do it no more. He can't go no further. Everybody thinks he's playing just like before, but he's just banging his head on the wall. Ain't no wonder he's acting up. It'd drive me crazy, too."

Frank Mangetta took a last look at King Bolden and with a slow shake of his head, went back to the bar. A few minutes later, Valentin stepped out the door and walked away down Marais Street. Bolden didn't notice.

∼

Twilight fell on the rooftops. Valentin wandered about his rooms, picking up a book and reading a page, then putting it aside and wandering some more. At eight o'clock, he went downstairs and walked three doors over to Bechamin's to buy himself a sandwich. He ate standing on his tiny balcony, looking out over the river, trying to puzzle out the day. There was Bolden's dope-addicted, dope-prescribing doctor with the name of the murderer's second victim scrawled on a slip of paper. And later, Buddy's sudden, chortling revelation that the two dead women knew each other well, meaning that he knew them both.

As Valentin turned ninety degrees to study the Storyville streets in the distance, he had a sudden shock of recognition, a feeling of alien foreboding that came from nowhere and told him there would be trouble tonight.

∼

Martha Devereaux stared vacantly out the window at the dark alleyway as she dabbed a bit of perfume between her breasts. She looked down and smiled at the way the yellow silk lapels of the dressing gown lay against her dust-colored skin. It was nice. She thought about the sport who gave it to her. Her vague smile dipped to a vague frown when she heard the tap on the door. Visitors were supposed to be announced. What'd they hire the girl for, anyway? It wasn't like she was some common piece of trash in some back-of-town French house, after all. This was supposed to be done right. Soon as this one left, she was going to say something to Miss Jessie.

She went to the door and opened it, and when she saw who it was said, "Where'd you come from?" and turned away.

She heard the door close and was glancing over her shoulder to say, "What do you want?" when she caught the motion of a blade coming around in a shrieking arc. She tried to scream, but the blade, plunging through her tan flesh, through muscle and gristle, caught the sound halfway up her throat. There was the sudden numbing shock and then a horrible, burning pain and she felt the splash of her own hot blood on the side of her face, down her pretty dress, on the floorboards and the white walls of the room. Her fists clenched and her eyes went blind as the room tilted and the floor flew up to slam into her face and she was numb all over and then there was nothing at all.

A starless night had fallen and Valentin couldn't shake the feeling of something brewing. He walked to and fro around his front room, unable to sit still for more than a minute at a time. He finally couldn't stand it anymore and just before ten o'clock, he went out and caught a streetcar to the north end of Marais Street. From his seat by the window, he noticed that Storyville was strangely quiet this Tuesday night. A few minutes later, he found out why. What looked like half of Uptown was jammed into Nancy Hanks' Saloon, crowding the dark, smoky room to the wide-open windows. Bolden hadn't crossed over to play in Storyville but once or twice before; this was a lagniappe.

Valentin went in and made his way to the bar. He looked over the heads of the sports and their women to the low stage on the back wall. The King Bolden Band was running down a fast-paced version of "Funky Butt," always a favorite with the uptown crowd, full of the kind of dirty lines that Buddy liked to shout out when he wasn't at his horn. They were working hard. Willie Cornish, deep black, six-feet-four and three hundred pounds, was sliding his trombone in brump-brump-brump runs down the scale. Frank Lewis and Will Warner blew twin clarinets, twirling about each other as they traded off on the melody. Jeff Mumford, a handsome sport, flailed away on his guitar, trying to lay chunking rhythm over the noisy horns. Young Jimmy Johnson, the only one standing, pulled at the strings of his bass fiddle and sweated buckets. They were all there. Except for Bolden.

Valentin looked around the room. He knew Buddy would sometimes wander through the audience or even go sit down next to a pretty lady, playing all the while. Or sometimes he let the others play on while he went off to get a drink of homemade liquor from the cook in the kitchen. He could even be wandering about the alley out back in a hop haze, waiting for someone to come collect him. He could be anywhere nearby.

Could be, but wasn't. Valentin peered closer at the faces of the men on the stage and knew from their expressions that the namesake of the King Bolden Band hadn't shown up at all.

He ordered a glass of whiskey and stood around for a good half-hour, looking now and then toward the door, waiting for the walking commotion that would be Buddy arriving at last. Two quadroon girls sidled up, giddy with drink, half the buttons of their dresses undone. One rubbed her pelvis against his hipbone while the other ran a hand along his thigh, each whispering a buffet of delights in an ear. He sent them away politely and leaned on the bar, listening to the band play earnest but mechanical versions of all the songs that Bolden jassed so crazily. He heard people around him calling out to Miss Hanks, wondering why the name King Bolden was outside the door when there was no King Bolden up on the stage. But the room stayed crowded. They all knew he could burst in like a Louisiana hurricane at any second, blowing for Kingdom come.

Valentin drank off another short Raleigh Rye, then went outside onto the banquette to get some air. Inside, the music wound down and then stopped. Jeff Mumford stepped out the door a few minutes later, wiping his brow with a handkerchief. He saw the detective leaning against the building and walked over to join him. The two men shook hands.

"If you're lookin' for Buddy, I believe you're wasting your time, Mr. St. Cyr," the guitar player said. "I don't expect you'll see him tonight."

"Frank Mangetta was supposed to bring him by," Valentin said.

"Oh, yes," Mumford said. "Mr. Mangetta brought him by early. And Buddy went right to the bar and started drinkin' up a storm. I turn around and he's headin' out the door. Said he was goin' down the line. Said he had business down there, but that he'd be back. But I ain't gonna count on it."

"What business?"

"Somethin' goin' on with some woman," the guitar player said.

"In the District? What woman?"

Jeff Mumford wiped his brow again. "Some sportin' girl down at Jessie Brown's," he said.

Valentin gave him a puzzled look. "Those are all octoroons."

Mumford shrugged. "I guess that's right. But that's where he said he was goin'."

Valentin didn't like the sound of it at all. He lowered his voice. "When you say something going on..."

Mumford waved a hand, palm out, stepping away from the subject. "You're askin' the wrong fellow," he said. "What's he up to anymore? Gettin' in some kind of trouble. Gettin' himself thrown in jail. All I do know is what he ain't up to anymore, and that's playin' music."

"You sure he said Jessie Brown's?"

Mumford nodded and looked away for a moment. "And he said he has some woman down at Florence Mantley's, too," he half-whispered. "Another yella gal. So he said." Valentin, more than startled by the news, shook hands again with Mumford, then started to walk off. "But lookey here, you find him, don't bring him back," the guitar player called after him. "I don't believe we care to see him at all."

⮋

Valentin walked down Iberville, away from Florence Mantley's gallery, at an angry pace.

The madam had stood there, hands on her wide hips, looking at him like he was some kind of simpleton. King Bolden? Here? She shook her head. What would he be doing in her house, her eyes said, cooking in the kitchen with the other niggers?

He murmured something about a certain girl he might be friendly with...all the while Miss Mantley just frowned and shook her head side to side. He apologized and walked away, seething. Bolden, chasing after some Storyville girl? What had he been thinking? He decided right then that he wasn't about to waste his time going on to Jessie Brown's. Keeping an eye on Buddy was one thing, getting caught up in his crazy business and making a fool of himself was something else entirely. He was finished with that before he started.

It was at that very moment that he glanced down Basin Street and caught sight of Beansoup running his way, arms and legs flailing, dirty face all pink and streaming sweat, heading for the precinct station on Royal Street with the news about the woman in the upstairs room at Jessie Brown's.

⮋

One of the other girls found the body just before the midnight hour and her screams set off the whole house. Miss Jessie rushed up the stairs and down the hall. When she opened the door to the room and saw what it was, her mind went blank. She closed the door, grabbed the still-screaming girl and slapped her so hard she knocked her down, then chased the rest of them downstairs and sent a street urchin running for the police. She had put everyone out of the house and now sat in her parlor, staring at the wall, her face growing whiter by the minute. She heard the wagons rolling up to the banquette and then the coppers came swarming inside.

～

Picot was standing a few feet inside the door, waiting for St. Cyr to appear. As he surely would. When Valentin stepped into the foyer, Picot turned around and held out a hand, fingers extended, as if pointing one would not do the trick.

"No, you don't," he warned.

"Who was she?"

"Out," Picot ordered.

"I'd prefer that he stay," a heavy voice intoned.

Tom Anderson stood in the doorway. He was dressed in a tuxedo of ebony black. Behind him were two young men, Mississippi toughs in suits that were too tight for their hard bodies and holding derbies that were too small for their round heads. Anderson rested his eyes on Picot. Valentin stepped out of the way of that flat blade of a stare.

"Mr. Anderson," Picot said, flushing. "You see, the problem is, he has no official status here. This is definitely a, a…a police matter."

"I understand," Anderson said evenly. "But if you'll allow me to vouch for him, I'll certainly accept the responsibility."

Valentin was surprised to see Picot hesitate. The man was either a braver man or a bigger fool than he'd imagined. Anderson's cool eyes went ten degrees colder. "If you wish," he said, "I can send one of these gentlemen to headquarters to get written permission from Chief O'Connor."

But Picot was already backing up, grabbing blindly for Valentin's arm. "No, that won't be necessary," he mumbled.

"Thank you, sir. Thank you..." and he all but dragged Valentin to the stairwell.

When they reached the second floor hallway, Picot walked directly away from the Creole detective and went to the third doorway on the left, alley side. He disappeared inside, leaving the door wide open. This, Valentin understood, was all the invitation he was going to receive. He stepped into the room.

It was the copper's little revenge. Valentin gasped and took a step back. Picot stood amidst the bloody carnage like a jolly Mephistopheles and laughed.

⤨

Anderson had commandeered the dining room and now slid the doors closed and crossed to take a seat at the table where Picot and St. Cyr waited. Each of the men at the table had a tumbler of whiskey before him. The two dull-faced roughnecks stood by the doors on either end of the room, their thick arms crossed stiffly.

Anderson turned to the policeman. "Lieutenant Picot, I understand your position as regards your official capacity. But I would like to hear your opinion on this terrible matter. Unless you'd prefer to wait for one of your superiors." He was being solicitous, giving Picot a chance to redeem himself and the policeman gobbled the bait, dismissing the concerns with a wave of one hand and flipping open his leather-bound notebook with the other.

"The girl's name is Martha Devereaux," he recited. "An octo-roon about twenty-three years of age. I believe she had some minor arrests. Drunk and disorderly, that kind of thing. But nothing on her record for over a year."

"What happened up there?" Anderson inquired.

Picot said, "What happened is someone cut her throat. One large stab wound in the, uh, jugular vein there. She bled to death. Not a pretty scene. It come out like a gusher. There's blood all across the floor, halfway up the walls, she—"

"No one saw anything?" Anderson broke in. Picot shook his head. "Or heard anything?"

Valentin spoke up. "With that wound, she couldn't have made a sound. It was in the throat and she—"

"Yes, yes, but, my Lord," Anderson said. "It's Tuesday night. Business is slow. How could anyone go by unnoticed?"

"I suppose the fellow could have sneaked himself in," Picot said. "And out."

Anderson sighed heavily. "The weapon?"

"A large kitchen knife or maybe a hunting knife," Picot said. "It's gone."

Anderson glanced at Valentin, then said, "And did you find a black rose anywhere about?"

Picot swallowed. "Yes, sir. By her door there."

"I see," Anderson said. His gaze lingered on the policeman for a discomforting moment, then swiveled to Valentin. "Anything to add?"

The Creole detective considered carefully. "Only that repeat killers do just that. The same thing over and over. We have these three women dead, but all killed in a different manner."

"You saying it ain't the same one?" Picot said sharply. "Well, what about them roses, then?" When Valentin didn't respond, he let out a tense laugh. "What, there some kinda black rose killer's club out there?"

Anderson waited, his eyes on Valentin, as if to say, *Well, is there?* Valentin shrugged. "Just an observation."

"Any other notions?" Anderson said to no one in particular, then with exasperation, "Or any suspects?"

Picot's face relaxed then, and his eyes wandered to the Creole detective. "We might have one," he said. When Valentin looked at him, he smiled coldly, as if he knew something.

～

Picot went back upstairs. Anderson whispered to Jessie Brown, then headed for the door with his men in tow. He stopped, took Valentin by the arm and steered him to the far side of the parlor.

"That copper's a dunce," he muttered in a low voice and then pointed a finger. "You fix this thing, Valentin. I mean directly. Find this fellow and get rid of him. Shoot him in the head or break his neck and sink his carcass in the river. This has to stop. We're not talking about some nigger house back of town or some dive like Lizzie Taylor's anymore. This is right in the heart of the District!" He took a moment to calm himself, glancing off at his two men, who were standing with their thick arms dangling and their faces showing nothing. "What's this about a suspect?" he resumed in a quieter voice.

"I believe he means Bolden."

Tom Anderson stared down at the detective. "Bolden?"

Valentin shrugged. "That's what he thinks."

"Well?" Anderson said. "What about it?"

Valentin shook his head, dismissing the notion, and Anderson treated him to searching look. "Well, whoever it is, you'd better stop him," he growled.

～

Anderson and his toughs went out the door and Valentin went into the sitting room to find Miss Brown slumped on a café chair, drinking off what was left of the whiskey she'd broken out for the three men. She raised wet eyes to the detective. "Valentin," she said, "Who'd do such a thing?" She took another swig from the bottle. "Such a fine girl. Such a fine girl."

"I need to know something," Valentin said quietly. "I need to know if King Bolden was around here tonight."

The madam looked surprised, then fearful, and then her thin shoulders heaved. Valentin had his answer but he let her speak.

"He came round to the kitchen. He talked to the cook. He was asking after her."

"After who?" Valentin said.

The madam's voice was so low he could barely hear her. "After Martha," she said.

～

Tom Anderson, pulling away in his Winton motorcar, watched narrow-eyed as the Creole detective bolted out the front door of the house and hurried away down the banquette.

From the second floor window, Picot also watched, with the same smile he had delivered at the table, a look of grim satisfaction that lit up his dull, copper-colored eyes.

～

From her office just off the parlor, Antonia Gonzales saw him come into the foyer and stepped out to greet him. But he strode right past her and vaulted up the stairs. Had it been anyone else, she would have whistled for one of the floor men who lounged on the back gallery, waiting to be called. Instead, she gathered up her skirt and went after him.

He opened the door without knocking just as Justine was lying back on the bed, as a man who looked like a prosperous farmer in from some rice plantation stood over her. They both froze; the citizen with suspenders askew, just about to drop his drawers, Justine in the motion of pulling her chippie up over her hips, her knees hiked and legs falling open. Her eyes went wide and the white man's face began to flush in anger. "What is this?" he barked.

"She's my sister," Valentin told him and Justine put a hand over her mouth.

The farmer stood there trying to decide whether or not he was going to get nasty, but he was saved the consequence of a decision when Miss Antonia bustled into the room. She treated Valentin to a withering stare and then extended a bejeweled hand to the man.

"Let me take you down the hall," the madam said in a low voice. "Someone you'll really enjoy. Come on, now. Have

I ever given you a bad time?" And so she cajoled the citizen out the door. He acted like he wanted to salvage his pride with a word to Valentin, but the look on the detective's face changed his mind.

Justine put an arm behind her head, watching him steadily. She lowered her legs but left the hem of her chippie up, waiting to see what he would do next. Valentin crossed to the bed and sat down. With a gesture that was prim in a clumsy way, he pulled the thin fabric to cover her, and then folded his hands together. He was beginning to feel ashamed and he dropped his eyes to the floor. Justine sat up and put a hand on his arm. "What is it?" she said in a quiet voice.

"It's number three," he told her.

~

Miss Antonia found them sitting side by side on the bed. She studied Valentin from the doorway, hands on her heavy hips. "Valentin," she said at last, "this isn't like you."

Justine shook her head at the madam. The madam glanced between the two of them and said, "Oh, no..."

He related the bare facts, leaving out the part about the blood, what looked like fountains of it, flowing into a deep pool across the floorboards and splattered over the plaster walls. He didn't describe the raw, gaping slash in the girl's throat. He didn't tell them about her dull, cold flesh and doll look of her dead eyes. When he finished, Miss Antonia sighed deeply, then hesitated, her eyes shifting to Justine. "I'm sorry, but you have a..." She glanced at Valentin, then touched a finger to the watch that hung from a gold chain around her plump brown neck. "You have a gentleman caller."

Justine said, "Oh."

Valentin heard the words and the note of dismissal. He thought to ask her not to entertain anymore, not this evening. But the moment passed and he took a deep breath, drew himself up and got to his feet. He was halfway to the door when he heard her tell the madam, "I'm sorry. No more. Not tonight."

∼

He left Justine at Miss Antonia's and made the five-block walk back to Nancy Hanks' Saloon, reaching those doors a little after one o'clock. He looked over the heads of the crowd and up at the stage—no Bolden. He ordered a whiskey to calm his nerves, then another, brooding a half-hour away while the band played on.

They were working through "If You Don't Shake, Don't Get No Cake," a lively dance number that seemed to drag like a slow mule without Buddy out in front, when an echo rolled in from the street and the door was blown open by a blast of loud brass. Every head in the room turned and the band on the stage almost stopped cold. Buddy lurched inside, his horn at his mouth and his eyes whirling crazily. Applause and laughter rippled up from the crowd. The fellows in the band peered into the darkness, glaring. Buddy didn't dare get directly up on stage, so he began to move through the crowd, all the time the horn shouting out a wild trill, like it had a life of its own. The manic look on his face had the people at the tables and the dancers on the floor hollering and after a half-dozen bars, Willie Cornish began to smile and Jeff Mumford laughed and suddenly the whole band seemed to shoot up about five feet into the air.

Valentin watched the crowd on the dance floor part like the Red Sea, and more people got to their feet to stomp the boards and Buddy took it as a signal to shift his gears, and went stalking up and down in front of the bandstand, his fingers punching out an electric code on the valves. The horn wailed louder and faster and then he went up the scale, up the scale to the B-flat octave and the others grabbed on for dear life as he took off.

The wooden floor was rumbling and the street windows were rattling and the women were yelling out his name, so

Buddy jumped on stage, weaving in and out and around the other players, smiling through his horn, dropping it for one beat to shout out something and they shifted keys up to C and halfway through the chorus, he ran over to the open window and jammed the bell of the cornet outside into the black, steamy New Orleans night. Valentin could barely hear Mumford shout out, "Man, whatchu doin'? What the hell you doin'?"

Buddy reeled around, his face all aglow, his eyes crazy with joy, his voice taking up where his horn left off. "I'm callin' my children," he shouted back, "I'm callin' my children home!"

~

Valentin never forgot that night. The band stayed on the stage for two hours, barely drawing breaths between songs. About halfway through, a woman who had worked herself into a lather began to undo the hooks on her dress and then walked right out of it and careened about the dance floor in her camisole. Then a voluptuous Creole girl went one better and threw everything off, stepping naked as the day she was born in the middle of the floor. Her body was so slick with sweat she looked like she was covered in oil and when Bolden saw he began to play to her, like a snake charmer, as she shimmied up to stand below the bell of his horn, her eyes closed, shiny flesh rippling in the low, hot lights.

Valentin watched as everyone else in the room disappeared and Buddy's stare fastened onto the girl, moving up her long legs, over her wide hips and heavy breasts to the face, the mouth open and nostrils flaring, framed by dark hair that whipped about in long wet strands. He saw the two of them entwine over five feet of air that was thick with sound, saw them wrap around each other in a hungry, invisible embrace.

The crowd fell deeper into the frenzy of motion and color and shouts and laughter, all to the rise and fall of King Bolden's music. Valentin looked from one side of the room to the other, stunned by the power of the hands and lungs of this one-man Louisiana hurricane. It was then that he saw, through a gap between two dancing bodies, the form of J. Picot standing in the doorway, regarding the scene with a cold sneer of an expression. Some bodies came together, blocking Valentin's view and when they split apart again, Picot was gone. After that, the night dissolved into a noisy, drunken revelry that ended sometime after four o'clock with Valentin St. Cyr and his old friend Buddy Bolden staggering out the door and onto the street.

∾

They made their way to the banks of the river and found a place to sit and share the bottle of Raleigh Rye that Nancy Hanks herself had shoved into Buddy's hands as they'd left the saloon. The first streaks of dawn were painting the sky out beyond Arabi as they flopped down on the rotting remains of the old riverboat dock at the bottom of Poydras Street. The noise and motion were gone, leaving an empty space around them.

Buddy swilled from the bottle, then waved it in the air. "Goddamn, what a night. What a *night*." He chortled weakly, took another long pull, then handed the whiskey to Valentin.

They drank in silence, passing the bottle and watching the colors where day and night combined in the mist that hung over the water. Minutes passed and Valentin sensed that Buddy was slipping away somewhere, but then he turned abruptly, closed one eye and gave him a quizzical look.

"So, what I want to know is, why the hell you been followin' me around?" he said. "I see you everywhere I go. What is it that's so damn important?"

"You know Martha Devereaux?" Valentin said. It came out louder and sharper than he'd intended.

Bolden stopped in the middle of raising the bottle. "What about her?"

"She was murdered last night." The bottle went up the rest of the way and an inch of it disappeared. "That's three girls killed now," Valentin went on, holding up fingers. "First Annie Robie. Then Gran Tillman. Now this one."

Bolden handed the bottle over. "I don't want to hear no more about it, thank you."

Valentin shook his head and turned away to watch an early-rising pelican's silent swooping glide over the green waters. He thought to begin snapping out the questions that were buzzing about his head, but instead he said, "I went to see Nora."

Buddy turned slowly to regard his friend. "What for?"

"To tell her you were in jail," Valentin said.

"You don't need to be upsetting my wife," Bolden snapped.

"She's already upset."

"What'd you go out there for?" The voice was harsh. "I don't go botherin' your little fair brown, what's her name?"

"Justine."

"Well, you don't see me goin' round Antonia Gonzales', makin' trouble with *Justine*. Tell you what. You stay outta my stuff and I'll stay outta yours." He made a rough gesture. "Now drink your whiskey."

Valentin raised the bottle, then lowered it. "Where were you around midnight?" he said.

Bolden turned to stare at him. "What the goddamn hell is this?"

"Were you anywhere around Basin Street?"

"Ain't none of your damn business where I was. Or what I was doin'."

"The way you been acting, maybe it is."

"What about the way I been acting?" He sounded suddenly weary of the whole exchange.

"There's somethin' affecting you."

Buddy didn't like the sound of that at all. He snatched the bottle back roughly and took a long swig. "Ain't nothin *affecting* me," he muttered.

It was now Valentin's turn to get angry. "Oh, no? All I hear is how you're goin' crazy. And I believe it. Half the time I see you, you're gettin' drunk. You don't show up to play with the band. You got yourself thrown in jail. It ain't good news." Bolden made a harsh gesture. "Goddamnit, what's wrong with you?"

Buddy lurched to his feet and planted an angry thumb in his own chest. "The only thing wrong with me is I happen to be the horn player who went and turned this whole goddamn city upside-down. That's right. Cause I don't play like nobody else, not like no John Robichaux, not like no Frankie Dusen, not like nobody. I got black folk, Creoles, white folk comin' out to hear. Comin' to hear King Bolden, and dancin' together like nobody's business." He weaved for a second, frowned darkly. "You want to know what's wrong with me? I scare the hell outta people, that's what."

Valentin shook his head at these dramatics. "The only people you're scaring is your wife. And your friends," he said.

Buddy gave him a cold look, raised the bottle and drained it in one swallow. He let it down, then banged it against his mouth again, in case there was a drop or two left. When he pulled it away, a trickle of red ran from his lip.

Valentin said, "Jesus Christ, Buddy."

Bolden reached with a fingertip, stared at the crimson smear and came up with an empty, lopsided smile. "It's only blood, Tino," he said. "Only blood." Then he smashed the bottle against the top of the nearest piling. He held fast to what remained by the neck, the jagged shards glinting in the first glimmering light of day. "So, do I scare you, too?" he asked his old friend.

His old friend didn't answer. Bolden laughed softly and tossed the broken bottle into the dirty brown waters of the Mississippi. Without another word, he walked away, going home.

Seven

thing
1er, but
;en the
should
3e to its
:h is the
. We had
recently
cases of
1ouses,
1ce also
that the
:he fatal
in veri-
)revious
· to were
  such
3 society
1r dear
them-
oring to
)w girls
1 to be
commit
.n such
ird case
1er our
s that of
vn girl
)son of
Street
·d in the
·riminal
Iudge A.
Louise
3lenville

Brutal Slaying
in the Tenderloin

Martha Devereaux, a colored woman 24 years of age, was brutally murdered on Tuesday night in the mansion of Jessie Brown on Iberville by party or parties unknown.

Her death is the third homicide of sporting girls in as many weeks without any clue to the identity of the perpetrator of the vile acts.

Chief O'Connor's office was not willing to provide comment in regards to the recent spate of deaths of sporting girls.

Miss Devereaux's body was carried to her home in Lafayette for burial.

Killer at Work in
Storyville?

The New Orleans Police had no comment on the recent deaths of three sporting girls in as many weeks.

Chief O'Connor's office offered no reply to questions about the possibility of the same killer at work in all three cases, though it seems obvious.

Mr. Tom Anderson also declined to offer an opinion of the tragic business, except to say that he is watching the situation closely.

One g(
follows a
it si no·
case that
follow sc
wake, bu
case how
occasion·
to report
two rou
and it ha
come to l
old maxi1
three is
fied. The·
cases we
read v
interest k
set man
girls fo
selves en
ferret ou
who cla
ladies cc
themsel·
ways. Th
to come
notice lat
a well l
Alice Th
1022 C(
who is ch
Second C
Court bei
M. Alvi1
Bless of l

Valentin folded the Late Edition of the Sunday *Sun* and laid it on the table. Tom Anderson loomed in his chair, eyes aglitter. "Watching the situation closely," he mimicked, his face going a deeper shade of red. "Now, don't I look like a perfect fool?"

"No one pays attention to these newspaper fellows," Valentin said.

"I pay attention!" Anderson slammed the table with his fist. "People all over this city pay attention! Important people. People I have business with." He glared, measuring the detective. "Now what do you have to report?"

Valentin cleared his throat. "I visited the house again this afternoon. Most of the girls have moved out, but I spoke to the ones who were still around. Nobody saw any suspicious characters. No strangers lurking around the time of the murder. The killer waited to slip in until all the girls were in rooms with customers and..." The King of Storyville's hard stare remained on him. "This fellow is sly," he limped on. "He doesn't leave much behind."

"What? He leaves his signature, doesn't he? Those goddamned black roses."

"Yes, but that's all."

"And that ain't enough, Mr. Private Detective?"

Valentin scratched his jaw nervously. "The truth of the matter is—"

"Is what?" Anderson snapped.

"That I made a mistake. I figured those first two murders happened because of some shady business with the victims. Robie and Tillman knew each other and I thought the two of them had crossed the wrong person." He tugged at his collar. "And Annie Robie was on Perdido Street and Tillman worked at Jessie Taylor's, so it didn't seem all so—"

"Important?" The King of Storyville was terse.

Valentin thought to remind the man across the table of his own dismissal of the first two murders, then decided against it.

"What about Bolden?" Anderson asked abruptly. "Have you questioned him?"

"I talked to him, yes."

"What did he say?"

"Nothing worth much of anything."

"Did he have an alibi?"

"He doesn't remember what he's doing from one minute to the next," Valentin said. "But I don't believe he's involved in this. He's not the type."

"Not the type?" Anderson's eyebrows arched. "You mean aside from the fact that he's a raving lunatic?" Valentin opened his mouth but the white man charged ahead. "Wait a moment! Isn't it true that during the time he was in jail, no women were assaulted? And the very evening he's released, there's another murder? And that he knew all three of these women?"

It sounded like Picot had been whispering in someone's ear. "You could say the same about another two or three dozen sports around here," Valentin countered.

"And what the hell is he doing with a white woman and an octoroon?" Anderson said. "We have laws against that kind of thing." He tapped rapid fingers on the table.

"I'll be keeping an eye on him," Valentin said. "But I've known him for a long time. He's troublesome, I'll grant that, but—"

"Troublesome isn't the word for it," Tom Anderson cut in again.

"He acts like a maniac, but he's no murderer," Valentin said. "He didn't kill these women."

The King of Storyville did not look convinced. "Then you damned well better find out who did," he said.

᠊᠊᠊

Bolden woke up in the white light of the afternoon and tasted blood. He lay still, his eyes on the ceiling, feeling his body come awake. His tongue probed until he found the ridge of the wound. *Cut my damn lip. Cut my goddamn lip.*

He looked down and plucked at his white shirt with his fingertips. He saw blood in a little pattern, a crimson Milky Way. He tried to remember what had happened, but nothing came to him. Last night was far away, hidden in a dark haze, like so many of his nights of late. He wondered where did they go? He thought about it some more, but nothing came. Yesterday was as blank as the white ceiling over his head.

He wanted a drink.

⌁

Valentin trudged home from Basin Street through quiet afternoon streets. When he got back, he threw himself across his bed and tried to sleep, but the angry buzz in his head went on and on and so he got up, went back outside and starting walking up and down Magazine Street.

He admitted to himself what he had told Anderson. He'd been stupid to toss aside those first two deaths just because one victim plied her trade in the Negro quarter and the other in a house on the District's fringe that employed low-class white women. There was a certain logic to it. Since Annie Robie and Gran Tillman were friends, there could have been some sordid business with the two of them that stirred the killer's wrath. Storyville was a wallow of such treachery. So some fellow who thought himself wronged murders Annie and then her confidante Gran Tillman, and the tale ends right there, the two deaths all but forgotten in the rush to the next weekend's pleasures. The black roses, symbols that had meaning only in the killer's mind, would disappear with the guilty party. The women would go down in the ground and a mystery would remain, for what little anyone cared.

But the homicide of Martha Devereaux had shattered that construction. Whether or not she was connected to the other two victims didn't signify. This was no longer part of the ordinary slaughter, the cost of doing business in a place like Storyville; and if there was any doubt, the murderer had underlined the point in poor Martha's blood.

He glanced at his reflection in a store window and stopped, startled to see that the face in the glass was smiling. The smile lingered and he felt a rush of guilty pleasure as he walked along at a quicker pace. Because now it was Valentin St. Cyr's job to bring the murderer down. The game had begun.

∼

At four o'clock the next afternoon, he mounted the rickety steps of Cassie Maples' brick house at the corner of South Franklin and Perdido. The door opened and the maid Sally stood there, her eyes twitching in perpetual confusion. She didn't seem to know what to do, and even took a startled step back when Valentin smiled at her. "Is Miss Maples in?" he inquired. Sally stared at him, didn't move. "Tell her it's Valentin St. Cyr," he said gently.

Sally found her senses, bobbed her head up and down and stood back so he could step inside. She closed the door and all but ran to the back of the house.

Valentin stepped into the parlor to find two fat black-skinned girls, both in worn day dresses, slouched at a café table, smoking and talking quietly. They looked up and stretched their mouths into smiles, but he shook his head and they went back to their conversation.

Cassie Maples hurried from the kitchen, and though she nodded politely in welcome, her eyes did a nervous flicker. Sally stood to one side of the kitchen doorway, watching as visitor and host exchanged greetings. "Mr. St. Cyr," the madam said. "Pleasure to see you again."

"I'm sorry to bother you," he said. "May we speak privately?"

∼

She led him into a small office that was little more than a closet off the dining room. A curtain-top desk took up one wall, with a swivel chair facing it. Two café chairs were placed opposite, just inside the door. A ceiling fan whispered overhead, barely stirring the thick air. Miss Maples sat down at the desk and gestured to one of the café chairs. "So you heard about that damn King Bolden, eh?" she stated directly. The startled detective had to hide his surprise. "He was here, all right," she went on. "Last night."

"What time was it?" Valentin said carefully.

"Musta been eight o'clock. It was already gettin' dark out."

"What happened?"

The madam drew herself up, all indignant. "He came up on the gallery, tried to come inside like somebody invited him." She crossed her fleshy arms. "I wouldn't allow it. Not after hearin' what happened on Saturday night. I told him don't come round no more. And I closed the door right in his face."

"Did he say what he wanted?"

Miss Maples snorted angrily. "He was mumblin' about Annie, said somethin' about wantin' to talk to her." Her eyes hardened. "That man is crazy. I had my Derringer pistol in my hand and I tell you, I was ready to use it."

Valentin sat back. "What did you say about Saturday night?"

She gave him a sly look, like she'd caught him trying to fool her. "Oh, I heard. How he knowed that poor girl got cut up," she said. "Just like he knowed Annie and Gran."

Valentin nodded slowly, reached for a thread. "That's something I did want to ask you about." He leaned forward, his hands on his knees. "Your maid out there told me about Bolden being here with Annie the night she died."

The madam's eyes flicked again. "I believe that's right."

"Did you see him leave?"

"Nossir, I didn't."

"Could somebody else have come in without you noticing?"

"That ain't likely," Miss Maples said. "Sally would have said so." The chair squeaked as she shifted her weight.

"Perhaps I could have a word with her," Valentin said.

"What? With who?"

"With Sally."

The madam's laugh had a rough edge. "What for? That girl can't remember what happened this morning, let alone back weeks ago."

"Please," Valentin insisted.

The madam kept her gaze on him. "All right, then," she said. She stood up and went to the door. She returned a few moments later with Sally at her heels. So close at her heels, in fact, that when the madam stopped inside the doorway, the girl bumped into her, bouncing like a pea off a pillow. Miss Maples glared in annoyance. Sally stepped back, now almost tripping over her own clumsy feet. It looked like a skit in a minstrel show. Valentin stood up.

"Sally, you remember Mr. St. Cyr?" Sally nodded. "He'd like to have a word with you." Valentin pulled the second café chair from the wall and placed it a few feet from his. Sally looked to Miss Maples, who nodded. The girl sat. Valentin turned to the madam and waited. Cassie Maples' mouth opened, then closed. "Excuse me," she said and stepped to the door. "If you need anything…"

"We'll be fine," Valentin said.

The madam made her exit, glancing back once, her face twisted up with concern.

Valentin sat down. Sally had folded her hands in her lap so tightly that her knuckles almost showed. A trickle of sour white sweat ran down the inside of her upper arm and dripped onto the thin cotton of her dress. Valentin noticed that her smell was not so strong; she had bathed at least once since he saw her last, and the dirty dress had gone through the wash. Even her hair appeared neater, done up in little bows, pickanniny style. But she was the same startled mouse he had encountered the night of Annie Robie's death.

He knew the type, backwoods girls who were the runts of the litter, judged too slow for school and too ugly for courting. They always looked the same, homely in the face and with bony bodies all askew, but with a sinewy length of muscle under tough hides. The only thing they knew how to do was work, and work they did. In the country, Sally would have carried firewood on her back, chopped cotton from dawn until dark, helped to slaughter the hogs. She had escaped that for the city, but here Miss Maples would drive her like a mule. She'd sling hot pots in the kitchen, tote huge baskets of laundry on her head and haul the occasional dead-drunk sport down the stairs and out the door. Valentin felt a twinge of pity for her. Such was her life, not so much above her grandparents' slavery. She would go through her days waiting for the next snap of anger or the next striking hand.

He gave her what he hoped was a calming smile. "I want to ask you about that night Annie died," he said, keeping his voice low so as not to give her a fright. She nodded and even seemed to relax a bit. "You told me that King Bolden was the last man to visit Annie."

She frowned, thinking hard. "Yessir, I did," she whispered.

"The last man you saw with her," he said. Sally blinked, not understanding. "I mean, if someone were to get in without you noticing..."

Now she understood. "Oh, I watch out, 'specially late," she blurted. For the briefest instant, there was something moving about behind her eyes, but then her face closed again.

"So there is nothing else you saw or heard that night? No one else about?"

Sally shook her head, whispered, "Nossir. Nothin. No one." And she dropped her gaze to the floor. After a moment, Valentin sat back, then stood up. She rolled her fearful eyes at him, cowering as if she had failed him and now awaited her punishment.

"Thank you for talking to me," he said quietly. Sally's mouth opened and she sighed her relief. "It's all right, you can go back to your chores," he told her.

She went to the door. She had just laid her hand on the knob when he said, "By the way, does a black rose have any meaning to you?"

She blinked slowly, looking as befuddled as before. "What kinda rose?"

"Black," he said. "Like was left with Annie when she died."

"Oh. I believe I seen ones like that at funerals," she said.

"That's all right, then," he said and motioned for her to leave.

Miss Maples was standing just outside the door. She treated Sally to a narrow-eyed stare, then turned to the detective, smiled too sweetly and said, "Will that be all for you, Mr. St. Cyr?"

"No," he said and watched the smile fade. "I'd like to see the back of the house."

"The back of the house," the madam repeated.

"Please," he said.

He followed her out of the office, through the dining room and into the kitchen, all under the silent eyes of the two sporting girls and the maid. Miss Maples opened the back door onto a wide gallery and he stepped outside. There was a small narrow yard that backed into an alleyway off Perdido Street. It was an easy egress. He knew the arrangement, of course; most houses in these neighborhoods had the same small yards, the same pattern of dirt alleyways. This far back-of-town was a blind maze where anyone could get lost.

He nodded to Miss Maples and went back inside. She followed him through the rooms toward the front door, looking more relieved at each step. Valentin understood. This was not Storyville, and the madam stayed in business at the whim of the precinct captain. Attention hinted at trouble and trouble could close her down. So she was at ease only when they had exchanged courtesies at her front door and he had walked out into the cloudy afternoon.

While he was waiting at the corner of Perdido and Gravier, he looked around and caught a flash of dark motion to his left. Sally was standing not fifty feet away, half-obscured in a recess of the corner building, waving a skittish arm at him. Valentin glanced back along the street in the direction of Miss Maples' house, then walked over to the maid.

"I don't want to get inta no trouble...," she mumbled.

"What is it?"

Her eyes bounced around the busy intersection. "Someone coulda maybe got in. That night Annie died. I don't think so, though. I was up, 'cept..."

"What?"

"There wa'nt no one in the kitchen," Sally said. "So I spose somebody coulda come in through the back...I was up, though...I don't know for sure..." The stuttered speech had taken all of ten seconds and she was ready to bolt.

"All right, then," Valentin said. "Thank you for the information."

"I don't want to be gettin' inta no trouble." Her voice was thin, shaking.

"You won't," Valentin said.

Sally tried a smile as she backed away, then turned and hurried up Gravier toward the alleyway, thin arms and legs milling, a tottery spider. She disappeared from the day-lit avenue and into the shadows, but he could feel the eyes in that black skittish face following him as he strolled away to Tulane Street where he could catch a streetcar back downtown.

She peeked once more around the fence at the end of the alleyway to make sure the detective went on his way. Then she scurried off toward the back of the house. Miss Maples would be in a fit if she caught her, maybe even mad enough to hit her with the switch, but she had gone ahead and done it anyway. She wanted to tell him something. He was polite. Nobody ever talked to her like that. So she wanted to tell him something.

~

He stepped off the car at Canal Street on the stroke of five and started off down Dauphine, along the back end of the Vieux Carre. It took another ten minutes to reach the milliner's storefront. He walked into the narrow, shadowed path that led around to the back of the building and knocked on the door. He waited, listening to the sounds of labored movement from inside. A muted voice squawked irritably.

"It's me, Papá," Valentin said.

The door opened. E.J. Bellocq glared at Valentin, rapped his cane on the floorboards and made another guttural noise that passed for a greeting. Valentin stepped inside and the Frenchman closed the door and locked it.

There was a library table in the center of the large, square, low-ceilinged room, and a roll-top desk shoved against one wall. Both were cluttered with camera gear, stacks of photographic plates, files and papers, an array of books and odd paraphernalia. A few chairs had haphazardly settled here and there and a selection of crutches and canes leaned into corners. Acrid chemicals had left their stains and their pungencies soaking into every surface.

The windows at the sides of the room were shaded with an opaque red fabric that kept out the light (along with the rest of the world, Valentin guessed). A small kitchen with a sink filled with dirty dishes and a sideboard lined with amber-colored bottles extended off this main room. The door to the toilet, which also served as the photographer's laboratory, stood open. A second door, leading to a bedroom, was closed. The air was thick with the smells of chemical potions, mildew, unwashed clothes, and the stale, dead scent of old candles.

He heard the arrhythmic shuffling of feet behind him and the little man moved to lean against the table and then wheeled around like a broken toy.

He had stopped staring at Ernest Bellocq years ago, and he now took in the globe of a head and the back curling under its weight, the spindled arms and legs, the huge, milky white eyes, the bowl of yellow hair that hung in a fringe over the forehead, the turtle mouth twisted-up in a more or less constant sulking grimace, without a second glance.

He fixed instead on the walls around him. Dozens of Bellocq's photographs, most of Storyville prostitutes, hung framed in open spaces and lay flat on every available surface. The Frenchman had created a haphazard museum of his images.

Valentin moved slowly along the perimeter of the room. Bellocq listed to one side as he settled on his metal cane, his wide, pale eyes blinking as he watched the detective review the collection. Valentin recognized some of the women in the photographs, but he often had to look twice because they appeared such different creatures when viewed through Bellocq's lens. He was at a loss to understand how the choleric little man could make his camera peer backward through the eyes of his subjects and look down into their empty souls. Even to a cynical type like Valentin, it was magic, a special kind of voodoo.

He happened upon a new print and stared at it for a long time. The girl—she looked vaguely familiar—was stretched on a divan for a camera that framed her from overhead. Her legs were scissored and her arms flowed away from her body like a ballerina's. She was naked, of course, the thighs and bosom plump, long hair in a single braid, the face young but the eyes blank, age-worn. She reminded Valentin of nothing so much as a bird plummeting from the sky, just as the arc of her flight was broken.

Bellocq watched Valentin closely. "So?"

"I do like this one," Valentin said and the French made a small sigh.

He pulled his eyes from the print. "You heard about this girl Martha Devereaux?" Bellocq muttered something, nodded. "You know her?"

The photographer glanced at him sideways. "No. I didn't know her at all. Poor miss."

"Terrible business, eh?"

The photographer allowed that it was as he turned away and began arranging a stack of photographs on his table. Valentin resumed his inspection of the prints on the wall. "I wanted to talk to you about the night you went to see Gran Tillman," he said over his shoulder.

The little man stopped his busy hands. "Talk about what?" His voice took on an edge. "You was up there. You saw what I saw, no?"

"You recall anything odd?"

Bellocq let out a sound that might have been a laugh. "The District," he muttered in his weird voice. "Everything is *odd*."

Valentin walked over to stand by the table. "Anyone about that you remember in particular?"

The response was a finger raised to one china blue eye. "Me, I remember every face. Always."

"And?"

The huge head shook once. "It was early. What, seven o'clock? Couple sports in the parlor, the usual ones, *complet*."

Valentin nodded as if it was what he expected, then turned around, crossed his arms and gazed blankly at the collage on the wall before him.

Bellocq stared at his visitor's back. "Am I suspected?" he asked and when Valentin didn't answer directly, said, "I didn't hurt no woman, Valentin."

Valentin half-turned toward the little Frenchman. "I never thought you did," he said.

Bellocq's wide eyes opened wider. "Then what you want? You come here to look at pictures of the naked girls?"

"I should have talked to you sooner."

"Why?" Bellocq said. "I couldn't tell you nothin' more." He once again busied himself with his papers.

"Why her?" Valentin asked.

Without looking up, Bellocq said, "Eh?"

"How did you come to ask Gran to pose for you?"

"I didn't, no," the photographer said. "She asked me. She want to pay." He shrugged. "You know, I don't care to do that kind of work. But the money..."

"How much money?"

"Twenty-five dollars."

Valentin looked at Papá Bellocq, who nodded slowly and said, "I tell her that, I thought she would say no. But she don't mind. She said, '*Bon*. Good.'"

"What was it you were about to tell Picot that night?"

Bellocq gave him a sly smile and waited. Valentin narrowed his eyes and conjured the room, corner to corner. "That dress," he said suddenly. "The purple one that was hanging on the wall."

"Ah..." Bellocq wagged a stubby finger. "That cost some money, too."

"She was going to wear it for the photograph?"

"I think so, yes. She want a proper portrait." The turtle mouth fell back into a frown. "Too bad. She didn't get it, did she, eh?"

Valentin dropped his gaze and began thumbing absently through another untidy pile of photographs, musing absently on the transaction between photographer and sporting girl, when he came upon a curious item. He picked it up and studied it, his brow furrowing. A heavy-breasted whore was posed at the foot of a four-poster bed in only stockings and garters. It was a classic Bellocq composition, but the whole of the woman's face had been scratched away by some frantic hand.

Valentin held up the print. "What happened here?"

The photographer glanced up, then produced what passed for a crooked smile. "My brother," he said. "Broke up the plate, too."

"Why?"

"He was angry." He waved a lofty hand in the air. "He's a priest, you know, and he took offense."

Valentin was astonished. "You have a brother who's a priest?"

"You didn't know that?" The Frenchman chortled darkly. "Yes, Father Bellocq. Oh, he's a good man, my brother. Good shepherd to his flock. He honors his vows, *non*?" His smile grew a little. "But he don't like what I do at all. He think what I make with these women, it's against God." Color rose to the round, protruding face and he held a hand to the heavens. "What I do is against God, eh?"

Valentin stared at the mutilated photograph until Bellocq reached out with crabbed fingers and took it away. "I tell him, what would we do if there wasn't all this kind of *mal...* this evil out here? We both wouldn't have no work." He gave up a gnome's laugh, all small teeth with wide spaces. "He didn't like that at all. So I think he won't be visitin' me again, not no time soon."

Valentin picked up another photograph, a simple study of a girl in a long white dress standing in a doorway. Bellocq had captured the moment when a fleeting look of hope met a dark fate, because it so happened the setting was the social disease ward at the "Ice House," the isolation hospital. Which signified that the subject might well be crossing the threshold into death's anteroom at that instant.

He heard the creator of this wonder say, "I got work to do."

He handed the print back and was heading for the door when he thought of something and stopped. "Your brother..."

Bellocq pursed his lips. "Yes?"

"He's a priest in New Orleans?"

"Metairie."

"Would he know Father Dupre?"

The photographer frowned. "From St. Ignatius? *Bien sur.* Who don't?"

"Has he ever talked about him?"

Bellocq, puzzled, said, "No. Why you want to know that?"

"I was curious," Valentin said. "It's nothing."

The photographer studied his visitor. "I hope that's right." He picked up the slashed-up photograph, dangled it in the air. "Them church people got no humor for some things."

Valentin opened the heavy door and early evening light slanted into the dusty room. He murmured a good-bye and from the shadows heard Bellocq say, "Whatever it is you lookin' for, I believe you lookin' in the wrong place, Mr. Valentin."

"Where, then?"

"I don't know. But not here." He held up the print in his hand. "This here's all I know about," he said.

Valentin stepped outside and the door closed behind him.

～

He followed the steps that Bellocq would have traveled, west on Dauphine, then north on Iberville. It must have taken the little Frenchman a good hour (he couldn't ride a bicycle or horse, of course, hated hacks and streetcars), but Valentin covered the distance in ten minutes, arriving at Lizzie Taylor's house at just before six o'clock.

All the way across town, he had the feeling there was someone dogging his steps. He glanced around and saw nothing. A half-block later, he turned to scan the street, hoping whoever it was would bolt in surprise and give himself away. But nothing happened. He wondered if it was his imagination. He took one last look around from Lizzie Taylor's gallery, then went inside.

Already the parlor was filling up, the girls at their freshest this early on, the rooms as clean as they would get all week. Which didn't say much; in the evening light, the whole of the house had a run-down look, and no amount of scrubbing would wash the stench of stale cigar smoke, cheap whiskey, cheaper perfume, and dirty sweat from the walls. Valentin went through the front rooms, noting the air of frivolity amongst the sporting girls and their first customers. If anyone was still mourning the death of Gran Tillman, he saw no sign of it. But then there was business to be conducted, money to be made.

He was ushered into the kitchen where Miss Taylor was having a cup of tea. She was an emaciated little woman who seemed always in some state of agitation, all nervous motion, her skin glowing red. Dressed in a worn gray Mother Hubbard, she looked up with a peevish frown when he entered, but after an exchange of greetings, gave him leave of the house.

He mounted the rickety staircase, thinking what a wonder it was that Bellocq had managed that task, and weaved through the traffic down the corridor to the room. He stepped inside and looked around. The bare bed, the café chair, the single clothes hanger on a nail were just as he had seen them last. The purple dress was gone.

He walked from wall to wall, peering down along the baseboards for any tiny item that might give someone away, but there was nothing to catch his eye. In fact, the floor looked like it had just been swept. No doubt it was the cleanest room in the house.

He stepped into the hallway, closed the door and went back down the steps. Miss Lizzie was putting fresh water on the stove. Valentin refused her offer of tea, but sat down at the table.

"What happened to the kimono Gran was wearing? Did the police take it?"

The madam swallowed. "Yes, but then I got it back in a paper sack."

"And?"

"It was burnt," Lizzie Taylor said.

He nodded. It was no surprise; hoodoo would have required it. He marveled for a moment at how badly the police (and the detective St. Cyr) were bungling, letting important evidence be destroyed. The more this day progressed, the more he wondered if Tom Anderson had the wrong man on the job after all.

"What about the dress?" he asked. "The purple one."

The madam look startled for an instant, then came up with a vague look. "I don't know what happened to it," she said.

She knew, of course, and so did Valentin. Such an expensive item would have been snatched away by one of the other girls at the first opportunity. So another piece went missing.

He asked about the activity around the house that day and got the answers he expected. It was mid-afternoon and everyone was out or still asleep when whoever had murdered Gran Tillman slipped inside. Later, there were all sorts in and out, street kids running errands, delivery boys bringing the liquor, the first of the dockworkers, teamsters and common laborers that made up the clientele of the house. Amidst the bustle, the evildoer could slip back out with bare notice.

"No one thought it was odd when Gran didn't come out?"

"Nossir."

"She doesn't show her face all afternoon and no one wonders why?"

Miss Lizzie got annoyed. "That ain't it at all," she snipped. "We didn't give it no thought because the last week or maybe two, all she did was loll about her room. She wasn't working no more."

Valentin said, "Ma'am?"

"She wasn't working no more. Said she was leaving. Giving up the life. Told me she wa'nt gonna be around past the middle of the month. Said I could go on get someone else to take her room."

"Where was she going?"

The madam shrugged her thin shoulders. "She didn't say. But she was leaving, all right." Her expression turned tragic. "Poor Gran. God rest her soul."

The madam couldn't tell him much more. She had been off the premises when the cripple Bellocq arrived to discover the body, so what little she could relate was secondhand. Her girls had been questioned up and down and could add nothing. Did Gran Tillman ever mention knowing Martha Devereaux? No one could recall. But dollar-a-trick whores working on the District's tawdry fringes were not generally acquainted with the pretty octoroons in Basin Street mansions.

That was all. The moment was passed and no one was likely to talk anymore about Gran's death. Superstition had stilled every tongue. Valentin shook his head in dismay; he was too late.

"How long was she with you?" he inquired, changing tack.

"Maybe a year, maybe less," the madam said.

"And before that?"

"She was around," Miss Taylor said.

"Around," Valentin said. "Around where?"

The madam tapped nervous fingernails on the sides of the teacup. "I believe she spent a few months with French Emma," she said.

Valentin was immediately alert. Emma Johnson was the proprietor of Storyville's best known French house, but she was better known for staging what was commonly called "the Circus," shows that involved crude displays of the wildest sexual acts. It was common for gossip in the local saloons to wind directly and with much gusto to whatever awful new debauchery had gone on at French Emma's the night before. The more cautious would hold their tongues, because the madam was also known as a dark queen of the voodoo.

"I don't take that kinda trade," Miss Taylor said, breaking into his thoughts.

"What was that?"

"Women with women. Children and such. *Animals*." Her red face was a mask of disgust. "I tell 'em, keep it outta here. They's plenty places around for that."

Valentin nodded, putting the information away. He stood up, shoved his chair under the table, and murmured a thank you.

"Poor Miss Gran," the madam said. "She almost got away."

"And she never said where she was going?"

"No, she didn't," Miss Lizzie said, growing petulant again. "I don't know nothin' more about it!" She pushed her teacup away with an angry motion. "How many more people I got to put up with over this?" she said. "First the po-lice, then that other man, then King Bolden, now you come round, how am I supposed—"

"Bolden?" Valentin interrupted. "What about Bolden?"

She jerked her head toward the back gallery. "He come round all drunk a couple nights ago. Come pounding on the door, but when I went and opened it, he just stood there. Just stood there starin', like he didn't have no idea where he was. I closed the door and when I went out again, he was gone."

"That's all?" The madam nodded. "What about this other man?"

"What's that?"

"You said the police, Bolden, and another man."

"Oh, him," she muttered. "I don't know. He didn't say his name. Said somethin' about bein' from City Hall and lookin' into these women bein' killed. Tall fellow. Wore a derby hat. Kept it on indoors."

"Did he ask you about me, by chance?"

The madam gave him a puzzled look. "You? No, he didn't say nothin' about you." Then, as he made ready to leave, she said, "He did ask about King Bolden, though."

~

He found the front door of Jessie Brown's South Basin mansion locked and a small sign tacked to the door announcing that the residents of the establishment had moved to an address on Bienville Street. He glanced at his pocket watch. It was almost seven o'clock and the banquettes would soon be filled with all sorts of rascals and giddy young men from decent families out on frolics. He thought about going home, since it seemed the trail could not get any colder. But what would he do? Read a book as he waited for the next murder and the next summons from Tom Anderson? Or for a call to bail King Bolden out of trouble one more time?

He walked along the narrow space between the houses and to the tiny backyard of the property. He raised his eyes to study the second story. Martha Devereaux's room was near the center, now closed up behind shutters. He looked over the back gallery, the tiny plot of dirt that passed for a back garden and the alleyway that ran along its edge. He sensed something in the air and for a moment thought he felt Bolden's presence hovering somewhere, as if Buddy had been there and gone. He let out a quiet laugh. The falling shadows were getting the best of him if he imagined he could sniff a suspect like some hound.

He went up the steps to the gallery and found the back door locked. He bent down and saw no light through the keyhole. With a quick glance down the line of galleries, he pulled his sap from his back pocket and tapped one of the panes of glass. A web of cracks spread to the frame. Another tap knocked a triangular shard onto the kitchen floor where it shattered with a tinkling sound. He jiggled another shard loose, then reached through and felt about until his fingers found the key. The bolt rattled and he opened the door and slipped inside.

The house was still. He took a step and a small battalion of roaches scattered across the floor and into the baseboards. He crossed the kitchen and walked through the downstairs rooms. All the furniture was covered in white sheets, an eerie sight. It would stay that way until a new tenant stepped up to sign a lease. But this house, so polluted with a ravaged girl's wandering spirit, might stay empty for a long time.

He stopped at the bottom of the stairwell and peered upward. The second floor was as dark as if it was the dead of night and the air from above was heavy and stale. He listened for any untoward sound. He put a hand into the pocket of his jacket to touch the grip of the pistol. At the same time, he felt the reassuring chafe of the sheath that held his stiletto at his ankle.

He started up. Boards creaked under his feet. It was deep in shadow at the top and he ran his hands around the corner of the wall until his fingers found the round knob of the lamp switch. He rolled it over, but there was no illumination from any of the crystal globes along the hallway. The electricity had been shut off. He found lucifers in his vest pocket, lit one and started along the narrow corridor, his shadow dancing before him.

The flame went out just as he reached Martha Devereaux's door. He lit another one and saw that the key had been left in the lock. He turned it, felt the bolt slide and just as he did, an echo rose up the stairwell from the lower floor. He started, then stood still, the fingers of one hand on the brass key, the fingers of the other holding the sputtering lucifer. He had heard a shuffling sound, then a quiet thump like a footfall.

The flame went out and he stood with his ears open, knowing that if he tried to listen too hard he would hear only the hiss of silence. He breathed out through his mouth, waiting for the sound to come again. He waited ten seconds, twenty. Nothing. He lit another lucifer, crept quickly to the head of the stairwell and listened. After a few moments more, what might have been a faint rustling reached his ears, but he couldn't be sure.

All was silent for a full minute and he walked back through the darkness. He stepped into the room where Martha Devereaux had met her gruesome end and crossed directly to pull open the middle window and push back the shutter. Fresh air wafted inside and an oblong of dusty light filled the center of the room. He backed into the corner to study the floor and walls.

She had been sprawled face-down on the floor, he recalled, her arms and legs extended, wearing a yellow silk robe that was soaked red. The rug—now gone—had been covered with blood, so much so that only a few patches of the fabric showed up. He now saw crimson splattered across the walls and a pink stain on the floorboards outlining where her bed had been.

That night, Picot had grunted a crude comment about Martha's position, opining that the murderer was on her— maybe *in* her, fore or aft, the copper had sniggered—when the attack came. Any man who paid for a fucking could have done it. Which, of course, made Picot's situation easier. Two thousand prostitutes servicing eight customers each on a busy night meant sixteen thousand possible suspects, so what could one poorly paid New Orleans police lieutenant do? But Picot was wrong, of course. The victim had known her killer.

She would have been standing up, just turning around, when the knife came; this he read by the blood splatter on the wall and floor. She had opened the door, he surmised, saw the visitor and turned away. The killer would have stepped inside, quickly closed the door and struck in a matter of a second or two. He imagined poor Martha, her eyes going wide in horror, grasping at the gaping wound, seeing the spouting of her own blood, trying to scream without a voice.

The murderer was done and gone just as quickly, out the door before Martha bled her life away, else there would be footprints. Valentin found that odd. Didn't most killers want to view the fruits of their vicious work? At least to make sure the job was done? Weren't most caught by something they left behind because they dallied at the scene? The only thing this one left was a black rose by the door—and not by mistake.

He stepped back further to lean in the open doorway, brooding. Jessie Brown had mentioned that King Bolden had been around that night, asking after the very woman who had died in this room. Which was all J. Picot needed to hear to make Bolden all the more suspect. But how, he wondered, could a Negro—and a brash Negro at that, known by sight to half of Uptown New Orleans—march through the downstairs rooms, mount the stairs and call on a sporting girl without being noticed? Because it hadn't happened that way, of course. The killer had slipped in and out unnoticed.

He looked back down the hallway and saw the small window at the far end, now clearer to the eye with the added illumination of Martha Devereaux's open door. He stepped down the corridor to find that the hardware on the window frame was turned to the unlocked position. The sash slid open with little pressure and he pushed wide the shutters. Light drifted inside, turning the brown darkness a pale amber and stirring the close air. He was now looking out on the narrow colonnade that fringed the house on both sides and the front. He poked his head outside into the cool evening and heard muted laughter and a cascade of notes from the piano in the house next door. Ten feet to the right he saw a sturdy cast-iron downspout that reached from the roof above all the way to the ground. It attached to the side of the house in a way that would make it easy for anyone except an old man or a cripple to reach the roof of the gallery by standing on the railing and pulling himself up with a single draw of arms. From there, it would be a few quick steps to the window and into the house—and that was how it was done.

As he closed and locked the window, he heard sound again, this time a heavy thump, then another. On quick feet, he slipped along the corridor, past Miss Devereaux's door and to the top of the stairwell in time to catch the shushing sound of hurried movement followed by a rattle.

There was someone in the house.

He bolted down the stairs to the landing and rushed toward the kitchen. Just as he passed into the dining room, he caught a dark blur of motion to his right and in that instant, he cursed his stupidity, even as he felt the blunt shock on the side of his skull. The blow knocked him off-kilter, his legs went askew, and he was suddenly tasting the dust on Jessie Brown's oak floor. Stars shot through blackness as he threw up a numb, clumsy arm and drew his legs in, but no second blow came. Beyond the roar of blood in his ears, he heard running feet and then a door slamming.

He didn't know how long he was out, probably only seconds. When he came to, he was looking at the doorway to the kitchen in dull surprise that he was still alive. He stayed still for a half-minute, and then pushed himself to his feet. The room tilted as he made his way to the kitchen. Head throbbing, he grabbed the doorjamb with one hand and put the fingers of his other behind his ear to feel a large lump and a trickle of blood. The door was standing wide open and pieces of glass that had lain just inside had been scattered, kicked aside by hurried footsteps. He shuffled onto the gallery and looked up and down the row of back lots. All was early evening still.

He sat on the top step for ten minutes, letting the cool air clear his head. Then he went inside, closed Martha Devereaux's room, and came back downstairs. He locked the door by reaching in through the pane he had broken. He paused to survey the back alley once more. A few houses down, an ancient colored man stood over a pile of burning trash, poking the flames with a long stick. Nothing else was moving.

He walked out of the District as the setting sun turned the sky from dark red to purple, trying to ignore the steady throbs of pain and the feeling of dismay that he had let himself get taken like that. Someone had followed him, lured him into a trap, and struck. But the attacker didn't try to finish the job; it was meant as a rough warning. Maybe it was the killer, but more likely someone like this fellow in the derby, or he wouldn't be around to think about it. He had been lucky, but he wouldn't slip like that again.

He stopped to touch the bloody knot behind his ear and fix his thoughts on what little more he knew.

Bolden had come knocking on Cassie Maples' door, drunk and ranting about the dead girl Annie Robie. Then he went to the house where Gran Tillman had stayed and repeated the performance. As if he was determined to fuel the talk on the street and make himself look guilty of something.

Valentin had learned that Annie Robie's friend Gran Tillman was giving up the sporting life when she was killed. That, the purchase of the purple dress, and paying Bellocq for a fancy photograph meant she was expecting plenty of money from somewhere. He had also discovered that Gran was a lover of women. Like so many of the sporting girls, she found comfort in the arms and pleasure between the legs of her scarlet sisters, even as—or because—she allowed men to defile her nightly. It was a fact that what *The Blue Book* and *The Mascot* called "Sisters of Sappho" staffed most of the French houses in the District.

Valentin didn't care who had frolicked with whom, unless Martha Devereaux and Annie Robie also dallied with women. That could point to murder out of hatred for a particular type. But it didn't seem likely that Martha Devereaux knew Annie Robie or Gran Tillman. To put it politely, they traveled in different circles. The only common thread was Bolden.

Another item was the mention of Emma Johnson. He was suspicious of anything or anyone touched by the claws of that vile witch.

On the subject of opportunity, he had confirmed what he had already guessed: that there would be a long list of those who could have committed the deeds, a list with Buddy Bolden near the top.

Now his thoughts came round to the beginning and a single question: Why? Why were the three women killed? He had small clues, but no meaning, no motive, and no pattern, and he couldn't abide occurrences that had no reason. Things could be explained, or so he believed; and if no explanation appeared, it meant he had overlooked something along the way. He turned south down Canal Street, first thinking about missing pieces, and then wondering where Bolden was this night.

∼

That night, King Bolden forgot about playing with the band and instead made his way to Common Street in Chinatown. As he moved down the narrow street to the little shop, he felt eyes copying him. He looked around and saw the Jew girl standing in a doorway just across the way, her black eyes pleading. He waved a rough, dismissive hand at her and went through the narrow door. When he came out a few minutes later, she was still standing there, still wearing the look of want. He glared at her, but when he turned to walk off along the broken-down banquette, she picked up her skirts and followed him.

Eight

Valentin worked the big room at Anderson's on Tuesday and Wednesday nights. Nothing unusual was reported and he spent the days mulling over the murders. He took some time to ask around on the streets and in the saloons about King Bolden, trying to ascertain his whereabouts during the missing hours on the night Martha Devereaux died. He came up with the usual story: *might have been here, thought I seen him there* and so on. The only person who knew where Buddy had roamed was Buddy himself, and he couldn't remember.

Though it had shrunk, the knot behind his ear continued to ache and Valentin could still place a rueful finger on it for a reminder of his bumbling. At least it was hidden under his dark curls, so he didn't have to explain it to Justine or anyone else.

By mid-week, he had turned over all the stones, except for the one he wanted to leave that way. As it was, he hedged until Thursday night, and it took a bit of will to walk down Basin Street and mount the steps at No. 335.

He announced himself and waited. A white woman with the face of a lizard appeared at the door. She looked him up and down with cold, hooded eyes.

"I'm calling on Miss Emma," Valentin said.

"She's inside."

"I'll wait here."

"Then you gonna be waitin' a long goddamn time," the woman said and closed the door in his face.

He took a step away, ready to leave. Then he turned back and raised the knocker again. The lizard-faced woman took her time opening the door and stood aside as he passed inside. She slithered around him and disappeared without another word through the door beneath the staircase, leaving him in a large foyer that was lit by gas lamps turned down low. He peered up the stairs into the dark crimson shadow of the second floor. A fellow looking for a good time might be drawn up those stairs like a moth to a flame, but Valentin was not fooled by the soft light and the demure promise of delights unseen. Emma Johnson's house was a mill for French sex, the servicing of customers so brief that each of her girls could entertain dozens a night, even more on holidays and during Carnival. Some were so busy they stayed in chairs for hours at a time as the men marched in for their minute of pleasure, then marched back out. But on this night, the upstairs business was slow. There was a more lurid entertainment on the ground floor.

On Valentin's right was a pair of heavy doors, solid oak with diamond-shaped panes of frosted glass that opened onto the main room of the house. He could detect figures moving about on the other side, like undersea creatures swimming through murky depths.

He had heard plenty about the big room that had been created by tearing down the wall to incorporate part of the house next door. He had heard talk about what went on there and still had a hard time believing some of it, though the witnesses swore it was all true. But he had never had cause to venture there, nor any wish to.

Though he had visited the madam's former address ten years earlier, when he was a copper walking a beat. A local newspaperman had picked up a rumor that French Emma was offering a virgin for sale and, fancying himself a crusader, went to her Gasquet Street mansion, posing as an eager customer. Once in the room with the young girl, the reporter pressed her into revealing that she had come to the house on the promise of five dollars, that she had no idea what the madam had planned for her. When the fellow started to leave without taking advantage of the child, French Emma was livid. "You're a fool!" she cried. "The girl's a virgin! You'll never get another chance like this!"

The reporter left, then returned with Officer St. Cyr at his side. Valentin took in the whole tableau in a glance: the room with a fancy bed all made up, the girl, thirteen at best, shaking with fright, the madam standing by in an indignant rage, like a miser watching a bag of gold being snatched away. He did his duty and made an arrest, but within a few hours the madam was back at the house. Her punishment was a tepid lecture from a local magistrate. Soon after, Valentin heard that the reporter had lost his job and taken to drink.

It was an early lesson in Storyville's homegrown code of law. Emma Johnson continued trafficking in virgins and whatever other diversions turned her a profit. Of course, since she had for years claimed powers, half the District swore that it was her voodoo that allowed her to flaunt the law. It was actually the money she stuffed into official pockets all over New Orleans.

The madam expanded her trade, moving into one Basin Street address, and then taking over the house next door, so that she now operated one of the largest palaces on the infamous street. She needed the room, as it turned out, to accommodate a new kind of entertainment.

Valentin wondered why Anderson let her stay in business, as she drew the wrath of do-gooders and was regularly held up as a symbol of the hopeless depravity of the District. When he posed the question, he was treated to a cool glance.

"Let's just say she has her value," Tom Anderson told him.

Valentin came to understand that there were wealthy men with a pronounced taste for Emma Johnson's bill of fare. But more to the point, the King of Storyville regarded her as a sacrificial goat. If he ever saw a need to placate the moralizers, he would close her down and chase her out of Storyville without a second thought— and, of course, with much self-righteous fanfare.

Valentin lingered in the foyer for another fifteen minutes. A dozen men, all well dressed, stepped inside from the broad gallery and slipped through the oak doors, letting out gurgles of rough laughter and clouds of cigar smoke each time.

By now, the madam knew he was on the premises, but was making him wait. He thought again about leaving, but after hesitating for another moment, he pulled open one of the double doors and stepped through.

The room was large, almost fifty feet wide and twenty feet deep, with high ceilings. There were chairs placed along three sides of the room and against the fourth, the back wall, was a low stage, framed in brocade draperies. All the shutters were closed tight and the lights turned off, except for a heavy electric lamp that cast a cone of light on the stage. Still, he could make out the shapes and smell the glowing cigars of dozens of men. Young girls, not one of them wearing a stitch of clothing, moved though the crowd, carrying trays of drinks. There was a murmuring of voices and laughter with an edge of excitement.

He wandered around, but the madam was nowhere in sight. He was making ready to leave when the light on the stage suddenly went out, throwing the room into total darkness and a jittery hush. Just as abruptly, the light flared again and all eyes turned to the low stage.

Then the crowd parted and a Negro girl of no more than fifteen, naked head-to-toe, came out a door on the back wall and led a spotted pony and dragged a wooden crate onto the stage. She looked like a child playing with toys as she brought the pony around sideways to the crowd and then shoved the box under his plump belly. She stepped away and there was a spattering of clapping hands and a buzz of voices, but the chatter died when a thin, black-haired whore, also stark naked, sidled from the shadows and onto the stage.

Hands on her thin hips, the harlot paraded around the pony for a few moments and then began running her hands over the beast from head to rump, now and then leering sidelong at the crowd. The men began to whistle and clap their hands. Valentin stared despite himself. He had heard about this, but he never thought he'd actually see it.

Now he watched as the woman began to caress the pony's thick belly with both hands, finally reaching between the heavy hind legs. She took the pink phallus in her fist and began to stroke it slowly. Valentin watched for another astonished moment then began edging away, feeling a skin-crawling sensation. As he reached the door, he glanced back despite himself and saw the woman had wriggled onto her back atop the wooden box and was wrapping her thin legs around the pony's rump. He turned away. His face felt hot and his stomach was churning.

He had just laid a hand on the brass door handle when he heard a rough voice say, "Where you off to?" He turned to see French Emma Johnson looming behind him in a dressing gown, her crossed-eyes fixed so that she looked like a gargoyle. "You're missing the show," she croaked.

"I'm not interested," Valentin said.

"No? I thought you were interested in all kinds of things."
The madam spoke deliberately as she waved a curt hand in
the direction of the foyer.

She closed the doors, shutting off the crude noise from
the big room. They moved to opposite corners. French
Emma fastened one cold eye on the detective while the other
wandered over his shoulder. Valentin stood stiffly, his arms
crossed before him. When he didn't speak up, she said, "What
do you want here?"

"I want to know if you have any information to offer
about these recent murders."

French Emma drew back. "And why would I tell you if I
did?"

"To maintain your position of respect in the community,"
Valentin retorted.

A smile almost crossed Emma Johnson's features and then
her face settled back into hard planes. "What information?"

"Gran Tillman," Valentin said.

"What about her? She worked for me for a short while.
That's all."

"What was her particular specialty?" Valentin said and
again Emma Johnson almost smiled at the formality of his
language.

"Her particular specialty was the dyke act," she informed
him. "She would perform with another woman for the
pleasure of our customers. And occasionally she would work
with Joe the Whipper." The madam's good eye glistened.
"He'd bend her over this here—"

"What else did you know about her?" Valentin broke in.

"Nothing," the madam said flatly. "She was here and then
she left. And now she's dead." She grimaced and her face
went rigid, as if already regretting what little she had told
him. He was about to pose another question when she said
abruptly, "I know why you're here. I know what this is all

about." She raised her sharp chin. "You're lookin' to save that nigger bastard Bolden."

Valentin was surprised. "What gives you that idea?" This time French Emma did smile, though coldly. He ignored it. "Do you know something about him?"

The madam crossed her arms. "I know all kinds of things. I got a skill." She stood like a statue, arms stiff, eyes like unmatched black stones.

"He ever come around here?" Valentin said.

French Emma smiled again, a chilling twist of her thin lips. "I don't allow niggers on the premises." Her eyes took him in. "That one, especially. He ever tries to come around here, I'll put somethin' on him he'd never shake loose." She glared. "You understand what I'm sayin'?"

Valentin didn't bother to answer. He wasn't about to play voodoo games. He was finished. He turned away and opened the heavy front door.

"You hear what I'm sayin'?" the madam repeated, her voice rising jaggedly. "You just let him come round here, I'll fix him!" Her shrill bray followed him onto the gallery "I mean to say, I'll fix him *good* this time!"

Valentin turned around and said, "This time?" But the door had slammed shut. He went slowly down the steps to the banquette. The madam's final words had been delivered with such venom that he felt a chill. My God, he thought as he made his way up the street, next they'll have me putting a dime around my ankle. He stuttered out a laugh at his own foolishness, but the sinister feeling didn't leave him until he turned the corner onto Magazine Street.

∼

Willie Cornish looked up from polishing his horn to see a fellow in a suit that was too tight for his heavy gut coming across the floor in his direction. Cornish knew he'd seen the fellow around somewhere, then suddenly remembered: a copper. He frowned, wondering what Bolden had done now.

The copper sidled up and pulled his lapel open a few inches to let Cornish see the gunmetal badge that was pinned to his suspender. "Lieutenant Picot, New Orleans Police Department," he announced. Cornish raised his eyebrows politely. "Bolden around?"

"No sir, I ain't seen him at all this evenin'," Cornish said in his deep rumble of a voice.

Picot's gaze wandered. "You expect him?"

"Couldn't say. Sometimes he comes, sometimes he don't."

"Oh? So what does he do with himself, out there roamin' about?"

Cornish laid his horn on the table. "I wouldn't have no idea."

The copper cast a lazy eye on the black-skinned man. "I wonder about that," he said. "What with all's been goin' on down in the District."

Cornish blinked slowly. "What…you mean with them sportin' gals?" Picot hooked a thumb under each lapel and said nothing. Cornish looked troubled. "You sayin' what? Bolden have somethin' to do with all that?"

"I don't know, my friend, but I'd sure be wonderin'," Picot said. He took another long look around the room, then nodded placidly, turned away, and strolled toward the street door.

Willie Cornish watched him go. "Oh, Jesus," he said under his breath. "Oh, my sweet Jesus."

A minute later, Jimmy Johnson came in through the alley door, dragging his bass fiddle in its case, banging everything in his path. He stopped when he saw the look on Willie's face.

"What's wrong with you?" the kid said.

"You ain't gonna believe it," Cornish said.

∾

Just before noon on Sunday, Valentin sat on a bench, watching Justine as she strolled the perimeter of Congo Square, talking happily with a quadroon girl from Grace Lloyd's on Conti Street. In their plain white dresses and high-buttoned shoes and their hair braided and pinned, they looked like daughters of respectable Creole families on an outing. From across the square, Justine caught his eye. She was standing by an Italian ice cart, gesturing. *Want one?* Valentin shook his head, but kept his eyes on her as she turned away and dug into her small purse for a nickel.

She had come from Mass as the tolling of church bells echoed down the streets. He wanted to loll the day away in his bed with her, but she had other ideas. She waited while he washed and dressed and then hurried him outside into the midday light.

It was a beautiful afternoon, the air dry for New Orleans, a breeze from the Gulf wafting the heat and the smell of the city away and a soft yellow sun poking out through high cottony clouds. The gray temper that had bewitched him over the past weeks had faded a bit and the shadows of the three dead women dimmed along with it.

He had waited all Friday and Saturday for a nudge on his arm and the whisper in his ear about another corpse and another black rose. But nothing had happened, and now he found himself basking in the New Orleans Sunday like some lazy dog, idly watching Justine and her friend as they continued their stroll around the square.

～

He had first met her in the summer before, in the heat of August. He had been frolicking upstairs with a quadroon girl at Mary Lee's mansion on Villere Street when a ruckus began in the next room, shouts and shrieks and the sounds of furniture being tossed about. When no one came up to settle the uproar, the girl insisted that he go see to it. She urged him in his ear then pushed him out of her and crossed her legs. She said she couldn't keep her mind on business with all the noise. He pulled on his trousers and undershirt and went out into the hallway. He stood at the next door, listening to a dull, mean, rumbling voice, then shrill syllables shouted back. He knocked.

A heavy-set white man with dark blond hair that stuck out in greasy spikes and a dirty brush mustache opened the door. He glared at Valentin with an inflamed eye. "What do you want?"

"I want the commotion to stop," Valentin said in a reasonable tone.

"Yeah and who the hell are you?" the man demanded.

"I'm the person responsible for keeping the peace around here," he lied and before the fellow could stop him, he stepped inside the room. He saw the night table was overturned and a porcelain lamp had been smashed into pieces. A framed painting and a sampler that had hung on the wall had crashed to the floor. A whiskey bottle lay on its side and the reek of liquor joined the odors of an unwashed male body, a bit of sweet perfume, and the earthy scent of a woman's sex. Backed into one corner was a short girl, skin the color of latte, with wide dark eyes that had a slight Asian slant, and a small, curved nose. Her loose curls hung down in tangled, sweaty strands. In one hand she gripped a sheet to cover her nakedness and in the other she held a knife. Though her face was streaked with tears and trickles of rouge, she looked grim, angry, and ready to use the blade.

"What's this all about?" Valentin asked, looking between them.

"She owes me," the man growled. "I hired her to work the revue down there at the Flying Horses. She's sposed to pay me back. I get what's between her legs whenever I want it. That's the deal. Now she says no."

Valentin looked at the girl, who said, "Never had no *deal*. I went with him once, counta he did somethin' for me. Now he wants it all the time." She wiped a hand across her face, smearing mascara. "He made me do it again," she said. "Now that's all."

The white man glowered. "It's all when I say so."

Valentin looked at him. "Maybe you should leave now."

"And maybe you should fuck yourself," the man said and then made the mistake of reaching out with one rough paw to push the interloper aside. In a blur of motion, Valentin's right hand went into his back pocket and whipped out with his whalebone sap to snap the blond man just above the ear. There was a flat crack, the pale eyes rolled up, and the fellow pitched sideways, his face first colliding with the wall, then hitting the floor. Justine looked down at the still body.

"What are you doing here?" Valentin asked her. "Ain't this Mae's room?"

"She let me have it," the girl said in a low voice. "So I could make some money. I quit that show. But he wouldn't leave me be. I don't know how he found me here." She kept her eyes on the supine form. "He ain't dead, is he?"

"No, he's not," Valentin said. "So you won't want to be here when he comes around." She nodded slowly. She didn't seem to know what to do next. "I'm in the next room," Valentin told her. "Come in there, if you like."

He was back in the room and in the bed when she knocked and stepped inside, closing the door behind her. She looked at Valentin and the girl. He whispered for the girl to move over and motioned for Justine to get into the bed. Later, when the girl left, she stayed on.

～

From the other side of the square, she caught his eye and smiled and waved.

～

She took a room with Miss Antonia and he visited her again. Each time, as he was pulling on his trousers, she said, "You comin' back?" It wasn't just a tired cadge for future business;

she wanted to know. She wanted him to come back and so he did, regularly.

He learned her story. She was from southwest Louisiana, a Creole of mixed African and Cherokee blood, the daughter of a drunken tenant farmer. He was a sorry excuse for a man who kept his wife pregnant until she died birthing a ninth baby, pounded his brood bloody, and occasionally raped Justine, his sixth child and the prettiest of his girls.

One summer night when she was fourteen, her oldest brother took one beating too many, stabbed the old man clean through the heart and dumped his body in a bayou. Justine ran away to Houston and took up dancing in a traveling show that was passing through. She soon found that men would pay plenty of money for what she had been giving away between the rows in the cornfields and in the back of farm wagons. And so she drifted from show to circus to show until she arrived in New Orleans and decided to stay put for a while. That night, her first night in a sporting house, she made the acquaintance of Valentin.

Now she earned her living entertaining men at Antonia Gonzales', white men with cash in their pockets. Valentin of course understood what she did there, but they never talked about it.

∿

The two girls looked over the Square at the Creole detective and Justine whispered something to her friend, something that caused them to laugh like schoolgirls.

∿

At first, she figured him for just another sport, the kind who would care for nobody and for nothing but his own pleasures. One of them who would come round to her room late at night, having lost his bankroll at cards, and pound her already weary hip bones until she cried out, even slap her if the mood struck him, then get up, take her money and walk out without a glance back.

She'd come across that type plenty. And Valentin St. Cyr seemed to fit the picture, with that flat expression and eyes cool and vacant, like he noticed little and minded less.

But he was the type of rounder she tended to latch onto, the kind who wanted one regular girl at his beck and call. It made her feel all worn-out and empty, living at the whim of some sport, but no way as used-up as those who took on one after the next, a dozen a night or so, until they ended up worn-out holes for any fellow with a Liberty dollar to dump his stuff into.

She thought he'd be like those others, but when she looked closer, she caught hints of something different. What she took for a hard front was stillness; and he wasn't cold; he just kept back from the world around him. She guessed this was because he was part Dago; she had seen the Italian men working in the gangs down on the docks and they were like that, stone-faced and quiet, keeping all to themselves. As she got to know him better, she came to notice the shadow behind his eyes. Something had happened to him. She knew the look, because things had happened to her, too.

When he let her visit his rooms one night, she saw books and was all the more curious. She even asked him if he was some kind of schoolmaster, to which he laughed, all embarrassed, and shook his head. Before she ran off from home, she had liked school, liked reading stories especially. But the mere fact that an adult male in the District read real books was enough to catch her interest and fix her eye more closely upon him. The other men, most who took her for a night at a time, passed through, and she barely remembered them at all. Only Mr. St. Cyr stayed on her mind.

∾

Valentin studied her as she watched the Razzy Dazzy Spasm Band playing their jugs and washboards and other made-up instruments for the strolling crowd. He saw her clap her hands and laugh with delight at the antics of the five white boys making music that clattered and banged and piped merrily across the square.

~

He found himself wanting her around. He liked the way she looked, short and lissome, milk-coffee skin, large dark eyes, full mouth, a nose small and curved like a Jewess and hair tied in an Indian braid and let down only for him. He liked her quietness, much unlike most of the sporting girls, those brash, braying types who delighted in raising a ruckus, in getting drunk and fighting.

He liked her smell. Most doves bothered only to cover their sheen of dirt and sweat with cheap perfume and went into a bath reluctantly. But Justine bathed often and earnestly, like she was working to wash something off her skin. Valentin guessed that it was the memory of the hands of her father, or perhaps the thought of the hands of the men who fondled her now.

He didn't dwell on what she did in her room those nights when she wasn't with him; he thought himself too much the rounder to let it vex him. He knew how she earned her money, but he told himself it didn't matter; the way she tussled with him beneath the sheets, with an eager energy that threw a rush of rose to her skin and lit up deep points of light in her eyes, made it all a bit better. He believed she was never that way with her other men.

But there was more that bound them. He had told her things that no one else knew.

~

They had frolicked until the sheets were wet with sweat and the humid air in the room was awash with the earthy smell of her body. She rolled on her side, her chest heaving. Valentin stretched his arms and legs wide, letting the night air from the window cool him. Her breathing became even again and she turned to look at him in the silver glow of the moonlight. She studied his face for a few moments and then said, "I don't know nothin' about you."

He gave her a half-smile, about to tell her there was nothing to know and that she should go to sleep. It was the middle of the night, after all. But she was watching him closely, waiting for him to tell her something. "Well, what do you want to know?" he said.

"Something about where you come from," she said. "About your family."

He thought he would just share the bare facts and be done with it. But he found himself recalling the whole tale, back into his childhood, from the first hateful sneer his olive skin had prompted from some white man on the street to his father's murder and the terrible black weeks that followed. He ended it by describing his mother's face, a mask of bitter sadness, as she watched the train carrying her son pull out, heading north and away from New Orleans.

"Away to where?" Justine asked.

Valentin blinked, saw the image fade. "What?"

"Away to where?"

"Chicago," he said. "To a Catholic school there. She wanted me somewhere where I'd be safe." He paused. "She was a little off the mark."

He learned literature, elocution, some mathematics and science from the strict nuns, and fighting and stealing from his classmates, all rough city boys. He fell in with a pack of Italian ruffians who drank whiskey and chewed tobacco and now and then burglarized lakeshore mansions. Justine shook her head over that, then smiled a little when he mentioned losing his virtue with a young Polish girl barely off the boat. "First time I saw a fellow killed was up there," he said, then told her about three thugs beating a small-change crook to death in a West Side alleyway.

"But what about your mama?" she asked him.

Letters came once every few weeks for the first year, ordinary news at first—too ordinary. As the months passed, the pages became mostly filled with scribbled ramblings, memories of her Cherokee and African grandparents shifting suddenly to a narrative of one of her visits to St. Louis Cemetery No. 1, where his young brother and sister were interred, victims of the 1880 visit of Bronze John, and where the cement on his father's bier was still gray.

"What about the summertime?" she asked him. "You didn't come home?"

He shook his head. "She wouldn't allow it. She wrote to me and said 'Don't come back to this place. I'll tell you when it's safe.' She promised she was going to get on a train and come visit. But she never did." After another moment, he said, in a quieter tone, "I guess...I didn't think so much about her after a while. I was chasing after girls and getting into trouble with those hoodlums up there. I was making plenty of money. I had some fine clothes. I was a regular little rascal..." His voice drifted off.

"And then?" Justine prompted him.

"Well, I figured I was going to be an A-1 criminal, a real Chicago crook, and then this one pal of mine went and crossed the wrong people. They caught him and cut him till he was dead. But before he died he started telling names."

"Your name?"

"I didn't wait to find out. I packed a satchel and got on the first train heading south."

"You came back?" He nodded. "How long were you away?"

"Two and a half years," he said. "I was eighteen."

He remembered walking up to the house on Liberty Street and finding a Negro family in residence. No, they said, they didn't know nothing about a Creole woman living there. He found the landlord of the property, who told him that one day a year or so ago, he went by the house and found it deserted, every bit of furniture still in place, food molding in the icebox, but empty of its tenant. He had waited a month and then rented the place to new boarders. He sold the furniture to the junkman.

Valentin walked up and down Liberty Street and finally happened on an old neighborhood crone who told him how one morning his mother had just up and gone away. She was wearing black and muttering prayers, another neighbor chimed in, as she wandered off in the direction of the river. He searched up and down the neighborhood, then the streets from the Quarter north and east. There was no trace of her. He checked the hospitals, the morgue, even the women's prison. There was no word and no record of her.

The next day, he went round to find Buddy, but he was off in Biloxi playing music. He visited St. Louis Cemetery No. 1, found the graves of his brother and sister and father. The flowers had long since wilted to dry ribbons.

"And that's how I knew she was either gone for good or dead," he murmured.

She watched his face. "So, what'd you do?"

"I left New Orleans. Went off, all over Louisiana, into East Texas, all around."

"And what did you do?"

"Just about everything," he said. "I worked in the fields a little bit, I was a teamster...and I helped out with a traveling show for a while." He glanced at her. "I stole a lot, too."

"You didn't rob no banks, did you?"

He gave her a thin smile and shook his head. "No. People get shot dead robbing banks. That wasn't for me. I broke into some rich folks' houses, stole jewelry, that sort of thing."

She leaned on one elbow. "Then how'd you end up being a copper?"

He was surprised. "You know about that?"

She nodded. "'Bout the first thing I heard. 'That's Mr. St. Cyr. He used to be a copper, you know.'"

"Well, I came back here and I needed work," he said. "It was a job and it wasn't the docks." He let out a small sigh. "And the truth is I thought maybe I could find out about those men killed my father. That's what I thought."

His police training included the rudiments of the law, investigative technique, the rights of the accused, practice with firearms. On the street he learned a different set of rules, such as the proper collection and distribution of money from the brothels, the apprehension of suspects without killing them on the spot. The goal in all situations was to maintain the give-and-take of the streets while leaving nary a bruise. He listened and learned. He became a good cop and he put his skills to trying to locate his father's murderers through official files.

"But there wasn't even a record of it," he said. "Nothing. Like it never happened."

He was a good cop, but he didn't last. He was on the force less than two years when he had to resign after drawing his gun on his sergeant. The man, half-drunk at mid-morning, was beating a whore who had refused to go down on her knees at his command. He knocked the unfortunate harlot unconscious in an alley off Robertson Street, then started to kick the helpless body in a drunken fury. Patrolman St. Cyr asked the sergeant to stop, but the older cop ignored him. When Valentin heard one of the girl's ribs snap, he drew out his police revolver, placed the muzzle inside the Irish ear, and pulled back the hammer.

If the whore, a pale, consumptive girl of seventeen, had survived, Valentin would have been brought up on charges. But she died and he was cleared. The sergeant was put behind a desk after a short suspension. Valentin's police career was over. He endured the cold stares, the turned backs and dark whispers for six weeks, then handed in his resignation. Three months later, the place they called Storyville was legally mandated.

"I heard about that, too," Justine told him when he finished. "About that girl that died."

It figured; he had never told anyone about the incident, but the news went down the line from house to house, and after he left the force, offers came for work around the District, enough to sustain him, which led to small jobs for Tom Anderson, the best friend the New Orleans Police Department could claim.

Anderson, like the others, found that he could be trusted with anything and he kept his fears so well hidden that he appeared fearless. He wished to be left alone, so he bothered only those he was paid to bother, and generally it was justified. He had occasion to knock a few misbehaving louts cold, cut several more and shoot one dead, that being Eddie McTier, a decent guitar player but poor card cheat and terrible shot with a Colt .44 pistol. He had left the Georgia fancy man on the floor of the Algiers saloon, bleeding his life out through a hole in his chest the size of a Liberty half.

"Was it hard?" Justine whispered. "Killing that fellow like that?"

"Not nearly as hard as I thought," he admitted. "Good thing, too, cause if I hadn't done it, I'd be the dead one." He paused. "I don't care much to gamble anymore, though."

He had reached the end. She continued to study him as if she was expecting more. Finally, he said, "What? What is it?"

"I want to ask did you grieve?" He gave her a curious look and she said, "Over your family, I mean. You lost all your family. Didn't you grieve over it?"

He had not expected the question, and he didn't know what to say, so he just gave a slight shake of his head. Justine watched his face go behind the blank wall she now knew well. She sighed and nestled her head against his chest.

He gazed out the window into the silver night, thinking about what she had asked. Had he grieved? He tried to remember.

At first it was a nightmare of tears and wailing, the house full of women from the neighborhood hovering around his mother as she tore at her face and shrieked curses, and then collapsed into helpless, hopeless anguish. There were long hours that she held on to him as if she would never let go.

He recalled the feeling that none of it was happening, from the time the police came to the door to take them to the scene, to the moment he watched his father's casket go into that marble bier, the iron grate closing with a grinding cry of metal against stone.

He held his broken heart together until the worst of it passed and by that time all he felt was a cold hatred at a world that had torn apart everything he had known. He shed few tears, and only in the deep of night when his mother couldn't hear, believing that if he did not stand firm, her mind would come unhinged and the last piece of his world would shatter. But she disappeared into silence anyway. She yelled at the neighbors to go away and take their pity with them. She walked through the empty house as if she was blind and deaf. It was in a lucid moment that she put him on that northbound train. She said it was to save his life, but he wondered if it was because she did not want him there to witness what would come next.

Looking back, it was a point on a map. Everywhere he had been, everything he had done, hearkened back to those few terrible weeks sixteen years ago. But for that horrible tragedy, everything would have been different. Everything. He thought back on the question again. The answer was: No, I did not grieve. I couldn't. I wouldn't.

He glanced down at her, wondering how he would ever explain it. The sad drama of his father's murder, the hard nights and days on the cold Chicago streets, and then coming back to find his mother gone, never to return, had all worked to wrap him in hard armor. Armor that he had carried along a maze of flat dirt roads that led to nowhere and back to

New Orleans. He knew now that Storyville's vulgar flesh trade, the way it cheapened life and broke people, had drawn that armor tighter and more rigid. But he had come to believe it was necessary. That way, he could tell himself that it meant nothing that the woman who lay beside him let strangers inside her sweet body. That way, he could shoot a man dead in an Algiers saloon and walk out without a glance back. That way, he could be relieved from caring about anything or anyone. If only it was that simple.

But just look what happened when the walls came down. Look at Buddy Bolden, falling into pieces, disintegrating by slow degrees, because he had no true defense against a harsh world.

His mind wandered for a few minutes. Justine's breathing deepened against his chest. "There's something else," he said.

"Hmm?"

"Something I'd better tell you." She opened sleepy eyes. "Valentin St. Cyr is not my true name."

She sat up, blinking slowly. "What is it?"

"Valentino Saracena," he said in a low voice, as if there was someone just outside the room who might hear.

She repeated it slowly. "Val-en-ti-no Sa-ra-ce-na. Something wrong with that?"

"No, there's nothing wrong with it," he murmured. "I felt that I had to change it if I was going to stay here. For all I knew, those fellows killed my father were still about." He smiled dimly. "And everybody knows a Dago never forgets an injury."

She watched him, trying to understand. He wanted to tell her the rest of it, to say, truly: I took another name like I was an actor in a play. But now all the others, my sister and brother, my father, my mother, and those murderers have all gone away, as if the show packed up and moved, leaving me behind. But he thought it would sound foolish and so didn't say anything more. She watched his face for a few minutes more, then drifted off to sleep.

❧

From across the square, Justine saw Valentin slouched on the bench, wearing that look that told her he was miles away. But a few seconds passed, his face cleared and he saw her and smiled.

❧

Valentin studied her profile and for a moment tried to imagine how he would feel if the Storyville killer chose her, if she were the one who had turned up smothered with a pillow or strangled with the sash of her own kimono or ripped open by a raw knife. He shook his head, dispelling the pictures he was seeing. Then he wondered if he would grieve over her.

❧

She was now finishing her round of the square, coming toward him with the octoroon girl. He stood up.

❧

On the other side of the street, the tall man watched the Creole stand up to greet the two women. The shorter of the two, and the prettier one, stretched to take his arm and kiss his cheek. St. Cyr smiled at her, his face opening for the briefest instant. The three of them walked off in the direction of Bayou St. John in the still, warm light of the Sunday afternoon. The tall man waited for a minute, then tilted his derby a few degrees and strolled along in their path.

Nine

Fair Lillian (Lulu) White, the diamond queen, says that she doesn't intend to go to the races anymore unless she is allowed on the grandstand. She says some people take her to be colored, but she says there's not a drop of Negro blood in her veins. She says that she is a West Indian and she was born in the West Indies. When a child, she was taken to New York by her father who was a Wall Street broker, and after his death she fell heir to 166 Customhouse.

—*The Mascot*

Jennie Hix loitered in the slate blue shadows of Common Street for three-quarters of an hour and then gave up. He wasn't gonna come…no surprise. Or maybe he'd already been and gone, got what he wanted and headed back Uptown. It was crazy for her to expect him to do anything on time, or at all, and so she stood there, all out of place, while curious Chinamen gave her curious glances.

She fidgeted at the mouth of the alley for another five minutes, then stepped into the narrow street and crossed to the door with the Chink writing on it. What if they said no? What if they talked Chinee so that she couldn't understand? Goddamn that damn King Bolden, he could get what he wanted anytime, so why should he care about her? She needed a pipe and now. She pushed the door open with a shaking hand, expecting the worst and wondering what she would do, how she would sleep, with nothing to smoke.

But in two minutes, she was back on the banquette, pulling her shawl over her shoulders, the package stashed snugly on her person. Now she could go home and sleep and to hell with King Bolden. She turned into an alleyway running off Common to Fulton Street. It was quicker that way and she'd be out of sight, though it wasn't but ten feet across and dark as a tomb.

She heard the footsteps behind her and thought it was Bolden come at last. She was about to turn around and cuss him out when an explosion went off in her head, a crushing blow that slammed a black veil over her eyes. She barely felt her knees hit the alley bricks when another blow came. There was a second of raging pain as her head shattered into pieces and then the blackness was all over her. The third blow was not needed. She was already dead when it landed.

A shaking hand dropped the single black rose into one of the tiny pools of blood that seeped onto the cobblestones.

～

Picot made damned sure that this time, by God, no St. Cyr got as much as a crack at it. He didn't like private security men, Pinkertons and whatnot. They made it look like the police department couldn't keep order. So St. Cyr was already on his list. Then he heard that the Creole had been a copper and someone at the precinct told him the story about how he pulled his weapon on his own sergeant over some crib whore, some piece of dirty white trash. It was not like the slut had any sort of a decent life. Unlike the sergeant, a fifteen-year veteran whose career was nearly ruined.

Now their paths crossed far too often. Which meant J. Picot was too often reminded of their shared secret. There was no doubt either way; the first time they ran up on each other, he knew. One of those things, like a sixth sense; and of all people, it had to be St. Cyr. The private detective had the advantage, though: he wasn't exactly hiding his Negro blood, he just didn't announce it to the world. People looking at him would think he was a Dago or a Spanish Creole. But the truth was that St. Cyr's mother was part African and that made him one, too.

This same part-African had served on the New Orleans Police force and now worked private security for some of the high-dollar houses around the District and had even got hired on by Tom Anderson, the King of Storyville himself.

When Picot first heard that bit of news, he had been sorely tempted to push a note under the door of the Café, exposing the deceit. But then he decided that Anderson probably knew, like he knew most everything else, but had gone on and employed the dago-nigger or whatever he was anyway. Also, Picot realized that if the Creole detective was as good as people said, he'd find the culprit who had turned rat and expose him. Which meant Lieutenant Picot was holding cards he couldn't play. So St. Cyr was the King of Storyville's pet snake, and a maniac like King Bolden walked the streets like he owned them, an affront to the New Orleans Police Department in general and J. Picot in particular.

Well, some things were going to change, Lieutenant Picot vowed, no matter who employed the services of that Creole reptile.

⌒

The jabbering fool of a Chink had come rushing into the station house on Canal Street a little after ten o'clock. The call came into the Precinct at the Criminal Courts Building at 10:15. Picot rushed his men to the scene, turning the corner onto Common Street at a quarter to eleven. He commandeered the alleyway and by quarter past the hour, the body had been wrapped and thrown in the back of the nearest wagon. Once the scene was swept clean, Picot strode through the crowd of Chink faces, hopped into one of the two police automobiles in the city and sped off.

By the time Valentin got word and arrived at the alleyway, it was almost three o'clock. The blood on the bricks had dried and whatever might have remained by way of evidence was long gone. Picot's work, he had no doubt. He walked the alleyway for ten minutes anyway, as sleepy Asian eyes watched him from dark doorways. Then he went home.

He tossed about on his bed with such agitation that Justine finally sent him to the divan in the front room. It felt like he had just fallen asleep when he heard the voice calling from the street. He looked at his pocket watch; it was eight o'clock. He stood up and stumbled to his balcony in his nightshirt.

Beansoup was looking back up at him, his shirt and trousers ragged and his pallid face scrunched up with the gravity of his errand. He surely didn't resemble any fancy man Valentin had ever seen. "What now?" Valentin said, though he figured he already knew.

"Mr. Anderson wants you," Beansoup announced solemnly.

Valentin rubbed his face and said, "Yes. Within the hour." The boy waited until he went inside then reappeared to toss a Liberty quarter over the railing. The coin tumbled through the air, shiny-bright in the morning light. Beansoup caught it with an expert snap of dirty fingers and ran away.

～

The two Mississippi roughnecks studied Valentin up and down as he stood by the front door waiting for Anderson to finish his business. The King of Storyville was at his regular table, whispering to a man whose shiny pate and drooping mustache identified him as William O'Connor, the Chief of Police himself. The two men stopped once to look across the room in the direction of the Creole detective, then went back to their whispers. Momentarily, Anderson stood up and walked to the bar. The two roughnecks moved aside to let Valentin join him.

As soon as Valentin got within earshot, the white man muttered, "Four dead." His voice was frigid. "Four weeks. Four dead bodies. Jesus Christ Almighty." He shook his head grimly. "So, tell me," Anderson said, now coldly deliberate, "Where was your friend King Bolden last night?"

"I don't know," Valentin said. "Playing with his band, I suppose."

Anderson's eyes flashed. "You *suppose?* The one suspect in this awful business and you don't know where he was at the time of the crime? Why is that? Do you have someone else in mind?"

"No, not yet," Valentin said. Out of the corner of his eye, he caught Chief O'Connor's stare.

"What do I pay you for?" the King of Storyville barked.

"I thought it—"

"You thought!" The slap of Anderson's flat palm on the marble-topped bar echoed through the room. "Let me tell you what *I* think. I think your friendship with that lunatic is affecting your judgment." He glared for another moment and then said, snappishly, "Perhaps you're not the man for this job."

"If you say so," Valentin said, keeping his tone neutral.

In the brief silence that followed, Anderson's blue eyes fixed on the detective. "You have other matters to attend to," he said. "Lulu White is fretting. She's afraid that one of her girls is next in line. I suggest you pay her a visit."

Valentin was puzzled. He'd heard nothing like that from the Basin Street madam. But he said, "All right."

"And you make damned sure you don't get in the way of the police." Anderson said, too loudly, "They want to put a stop to this awful business." He turned away and walked back to join Chief O'Connor at the table.

The two roughnecks and the Chief of Police watched as Valentin made his way to the door and stepped outside. Tom Anderson didn't look up at all.

∾

She was a short, rotund woman, medium-brown in color, with distinct African features, broad nose and high cheekbones. She wore fine clothes from New York and Paris and dripped with jewelry from her ears to her toes. She liked to wear wigs over her kinky black hair; she preferred varying shades of red. Her vanity was a legend around the District. Though her skin was the color of Delta mud, she denied African blood to anyone who would listen, creating instead a history of Jamaican gentry.

The truth was she had been born and raised in a sharecropper's shack outside Selma and had simply used her considerable wiles to become the most successful madam in New Orleans. Her mansion, Mahogany Hall, was the showpiece among the sporting houses of the District, catering to the carriage trade, with the most exotic women, octoroon, quadroon and white, staffing rooms furnished with the finest decor—including mirrors over every bed—and the likes of LeMenthe and Professor Tony Jackson at the parlor piano. Her name was set in stained glass over a front door of solid oak.

Lulu White was a born trader who now sailed on the veritable ocean of money that ran through Storyville, New Orleans.

In a given month, over a half-million dollars passed from the hands of sporting men and suckers into the pockets of the madams and pimps and crib girls, and from there into the private coffers of landlords, lawyers, and a multitude of city officials. Profits from the sale of beer, wine and liquor amounted to another hundred thousand dollars a week. Gamblers, dope pushers, musicians, and other fringe characters took in some thirty thousand in the same period. All told, one million dollars cash floated through the twenty blocks every month. And Lulu White claimed her share.

Other madams frittered their fortunes away in foolish investments. Some got into trouble trafficking in virgins and children. Some allowed pimps to infest their houses like money-eating rats. Some gave coppers, landlords, lawyers, and greedy officials leave to bleed them dry. Some stood by as drunken rowdies and those with depraved tastes ruined their good names. And some got fixed on morphine or rye whiskey or some no-good rounder and ended up on the streets.

Miss Lulu White fell prey to none of these dangers. She indulged no vice. She kept a dignified first-class house and plotted her business affairs like a scarlet Rockefeller. But she was not made of stone. She had one weakness: a particular fancy man by the name of George Killshaw, a slim, sharp-faced fellow who, though at least a quadroon, looked so truly white that he could pass even when Valentin got second looks. Lulu White treated Killshaw like a pampered pet, buying him clothes from the best stores, cocaine from the apothecary, and whiskey that came directly from Ireland. She turned her head to his pursuit of every new girl in the District. She loved him madly and her normally sharp eyes went blind when he was about.

But not so blind that she couldn't cast an appreciative gaze upon the Creole detective as he crossed the floor to greet her. He, in turn, smiled respectfully as she waved to him from the alcove just off the deserted parlor. She patted the cushion of the satin-covered love seat next to her. Valentin sat down. She shook a hand, jingling her vulgar jewelry, and a young Negro boy in white shirt and white linen trousers appeared with a coffee cup and an envelope, both of which he handed to the detective. Valentin pocketed the envelope, which was heavy with gold coins, with a small nod of thanks.

He sipped his coffee and waited. He was pleased that Killshaw wasn't lurking about. In fact, he recalled that he hadn't seen the fancy man about in some time.

"What a mystery is brewing out there," Miss White said in a most casual voice. Her gaze drifted to his face, then away again. "Someone is taking pleasure in killing our girls. And leaving a black rose behind."

Valentin glanced at his host. She laughed and laid a hand on his thigh. "Did you think I'd lost my touch? I still make it my business to know everyone else's. I have a very dependable source in the police department." Her smile faded and her expression grew somber. "I knew before that first poor girl's body was cold," she said. "I know about Gran Tillman and Martha Devereaux. And now he's taken one down in Chinatown." She began twirling a strand of her auburn wig around a finger that displayed two rings. "Or maybe this is not the same fellow."

"It's the same fellow," Valentin said.

"Yes, I believe you're right. If you ask me, I think he saw you pursuing him, so he moved." Valentin gave her a curious look and she shrugged her regal shoulders. "Who else? Our police couldn't find their shoes in a closet. This is Anderson County and you're his man."

Valentin sat back. "Maybe not." The madam waved an impatient hand and he said, "Did you tell him you were worried over this fellow attacking one of your girls?"

Lulu White raised her hennaed eyebrows. "I never said that! Some murderer come here? He wouldn't dare!" She treated him to a sly, laconic smile. "Mr. Tom has his own concerns."

Valentin allowed himself a smile in turn. "Chief O'Connor was at the Café when I went by this morning."

"And Anderson put on a show for him."

He thought about it a moment longer. "The coppers want me out of the way," he said.

"Of course they do," the madam said. "If it wasn't for Mr. Tom, you'd be out of the way for good." She let out a little laugh. "My God, Valentin, you're walking proof that they're bumblers. What do you expect?" She settled her round shoulders against the velvet cushions. "Now what's this about King Bolden?" she asked.

"It's nothing but talk," Valentin said. "He's someone to point fingers at."

"And you're sure he isn't involved?"

"I don't believe he is, no."

His tone was less than firm and the madam gave him a sidelong glance as she slowly stirred the coffee in her cup. "I'd like to help you," she said. "The police could make a terrible muddle of this. It would not be good for the District. So, anything I can do..."

"If there's information you could share. I'd appreciate that."

"Like what?"

"This last victim. Jennie Hix."

Miss White sighed sadly. "Yes, poor girl."

"I don't know her," Valentin said.

"It might help if I tell you she had a 'J' after her name," the madam said. In the code of the District and the listings in *The Blue Book*, "J" meant "Jewish," as "W" meant "White," "C" meant "Colored" and "Oct" meant octoroon. It was all rather straightforward, with the exception that "French" did not refer to women from a country in Europe.

"I'd like to see the body," Valentin said. "And the weapon, if it's been found."

"I think that can be arranged," Miss White said. "I'll send you a message later." Her gaze wandered away once more and she was silent for a long minute. "There's another matter

I want to discuss with you," she said, now plainly ill at ease. "It's George."

"What about him?" Valentin was careful to keep his voice neutral. In truth, he didn't like Killshaw at all. He thought him nothing but a skilled bloodsucker who had found the host of hosts in Miss Lulu White. He was one of those rounders known to have taken money from the likes of Emma Johnson for beating some sense into whores who had the audacity to try to escape the life. And then there was the night at The Big 25 when the two men had tangled. Valentin might have cut the fancy man a new profile had not the fat old bartender fired a pistol over their heads. Yes, George Killshaw was a sly, charming, handsome leech, but Lulu White adored him.

"I have a great interest in the moving pictures," she was saying. Valentin blinked, coming back to the present and puzzling over what seemed another change of subject.

"There's going to be plenty of money made in that business," the madam went on. "It's already begun. They fill theatres night after night in New York and Pittsburgh, places like that. They're setting up all kinds of studios to make the shows in Southern California. They say it's for the weather, that the sun shines every day. It's actually to avoid lawsuits by the Edison people, who are in the state of New Jersey and own the patents." She smiled slightly in admiration of such cunning. "I wanted to get into the business while it's still young. I believe it has a potential."

Valentin caught the look on the madam's face and could not help but surmise that she already saw herself bathed in flickering light, a bejeweled Grand Dame for all the world to worship. Valentin had heard about the moving pictures, had read accounts of audiences bolting from their seats as a speeding train bore down on them from a sheet of canvas. It all sounded like a cheap novelty to him, like something they'd put on at Carnival.

The madam sipped her coffee, cleared her throat. "I acted on my impressions," she went on. "I sent George to Los Angeles where these moving-picture people are settling to make inquiries and maybe an investment."

Valentin sensed what was coming. "How large of an investment?" he asked.

"One hundred and fifty thousand dollars."

Valentin didn't blink. He knew the answer but asked the next question anyway. "Was that in cash?"

"In cash, yes." He knew the rest of the story, too, but let her tell it to him. "I have not had any word from him and I'm concerned. So I'm wondering if perhaps you would be interested in traveling out there and seeing what you can find out."

For a moment, Valentin entertained the thought that this was a ploy to get him out of New Orleans and away from the murders for a good long time. But one look at Lulu White's carefully composed visage told him the madam was sincere. Her concern was a face-saving gesture. She knew, as he did, the likely fate of her fancy man and her money; and whatever lingering doubts he had went away when she said, "But it can wait until this other unfortunate business is resolved. Perhaps by that time, there'll be no reason for you to go west."

"I hope that's the case," Valentin said, meaning it.

~

The madam took his arm and walked him through the parlor. "All this about King Bolden," she said, dropping her voice to a dramatic whisper. "Voodoo, Valentin. The air is full of spirits. And a fellow like that is ripe for the picking."

Once again, he was astonished. The same woman who had the steely nerve to handle hundreds of thousands of dollars without blinking an eye also embraced the voodoo. But, then, if she had fallen prey to a confidence man like George Killshaw, her judgment wasn't near that perfect.

"It would be worth your while to pay a visit to someone." She glowered. "And I don't mean Emma Johnson. Someone with good intentions. Someone who can help you." It was a heavy hint, delivered just as they reached the foyer. He felt like a marionette whose strings had been rightly jerked.

"Anderson can't let this go on," she said curtly. "He's depending on you to fix it. But you'll need some help." Before he could reply, Lulu White said, "Please give my regards to your young lady," and closed the door behind him.

~

Walking home, he mused on the twists and turns, beginning with his visit to the scene of Jennie Hix's murder. Then came the summons by Tom Anderson and the scolding—delivered mostly for the benefit of the Chief of Police—in which he was dispatched to Lulu White, who offered her hand, but only if he would do her bidding and consult a voodoo woman.

He guessed that Jennie Hix had known Bolden. It seemed to be the prime qualification for becoming a murder victim. But Valentin didn't buy into the notion that Bolden himself was the killer; it was more like he was leading the lambs to the slaughter. Someone was trying hard to make Bolden look guilty. But why?

He switched his thoughts to Tom Anderson's little tirade. A little too much of a performance for that grand operator, even with the Chief of Police in the room. The King of Storyville was trying to communicate something.

On to Lulu White. Now, no matter how formidable a figure that madam cut around the District, no matter how much money she handed out, from the coppers on the street to the commissioners downtown, she was a colored woman and did not have the leverage to get him, of all people, into City Morgue to view the corpse in a murder case. That would require the hand of someone high up the ladder. Someone like Anderson. But why was the King of Storyville now hiding behind a madam?

Valentin mulled it over for a few moments more and then shifted his thoughts to the George Killshaw business. Though it was urgent enough to sway Miss Lulu's attention from the brutal slayings of the four scarlet ladies, it begged no thought at all. George was one fancy man Lulu White would never see again, and her one hundred fifty thousand dollars was gone right along with him. Somewhere beneath the California sun, he would be beginning a new life as a very wealthy white man.

Valentin arrived at the mention of voodoo. There was no way around it. The madam was firm: he would have to go seek out some likely party and waste his time with talk of curses, *gris-gris*, haints and powers beyond all knowing. He muttered a quiet curse, his own brand of hoodoo, as he turned the corner onto Canal Street.

∾

He tracked down Beansoup and sent him on an errand. Then he went home to get some sleep. Later in the afternoon, the ragged kid stood breathless at his door, telling how he had traveled all the way to the home of Willie Cornish at the Negro end of Ursulines Street. And then how the trombone player had growled out the answer to the question. Valentin wasn't at all surprised to learn that, once again, Bolden had not shown up to play with the band, this time at Masonic Hall. No one had seen him at all on the night of Jennie Hix's death.

∾

Valentin ate rice and beans in a workmen's café on Common Street, a block east of Fulton, where Chinatown began. After he paid his ten cents, he went out onto the darkening street. From where he stood, he could see the river, see the lights of the tugboats on their slow swim to the docks and hear their mournful horns.

Jennie Hix, the Jewish prostitute, would have walked this same banquette, coming south from Storyville. He wandered past laundries, restaurants and tiny grocery stores until he found the narrow alleyway where the girl's body had been found. He looked around. Diagonally across the street was a shop that was almost invisible unless someone was looking for it. He stepped closer to examine the tiny cove, with its narrow door and its one tall window with herbs and powders on display behind yellowed glass. Hanging from the door was a banner of rice paper decorated with a painting in red and black of two dragons entwined, their heads facing inward, eyes bloody, mouths wide open, tongues flailing, fangs like curved needles.

A tiny bell tinkled when Valentin pushed inside. He felt the eyes on him before he saw the old Chinaman. The old man stood stiffly behind the counter, his wrinkled chestnut of a face and wisps of gray hair framed in a small jungle of hanging herbs and shelves lined with ceramic jars and glass bottles. The parchment hands had stopped in the act of grinding something in a pestle made of alabaster. He muttered something under his breath.

"My grandfather wants to know are you lost," a child's voice said.

Valentin peered into the shadows to the right of the counter and detected a thin Chinese boy with a round, calm face. He was standing in a doorway that led to a back room, wearing a white shirt buttoned at the collar and loose black trousers. His feet were bare.

"My grandfather asks are you lost?" the boy repeated.

The detective's gaze moved to the grandfather, who was keeping his eyes averted. He bowed his head politely. "No, not lost. I'm here to ask a question." The boy translated in a voice just above a whisper. The old man said nothing and Valentin went on. "A girl came here last night. For opium."

A few words into the translation, the grandfather began to shake his head. "My grandfather says no opium here. Opium no good."

"A girl with dark hair. Dark eyes," Valentin said.

The old man chattered rapidly. "No," the grandson said. "No girl like that here."

"She was the one who was killed in the alleyway," Valentin said.

The grandfather's black opal eyes were fixed on the contents of the pestle. He whispered to the young boy. "He asks are you from the police?" Valentin shook his head. The old Chinaman said something that had a ring of finality about it. "No opium," the boy translated. "No Jew girl. No nigger man. Nothing."

The grandfather returned to his grinding. Valentin nodded a thank you and turned for the door.

He stepped onto the street and turned north once more. He now knew that the last moments of Jennie Hix's life had been spent in the same shop where King Bolden bought his opium.

～

The message came from Lulu White and at ten o'clock he walked down the alley that ran behind City Hall.

A cigarette glowed in the darkness. "Who's there?" a voice called out.

"The one you're expecting," Valentin said.

The cigarette was flicked away in a shower of tiny embers as a figure detached from the shadows. A moment later a door opened and white light poured into the alleyway. A mulatto wearing wire-rimmed glasses and dressed in a white apron covered with multi-colored stains was holding the door open. "You're goin' to make this fast, aintcha?" Valentin nodded. "C'mon this way, then," the attendant said and led him inside.

～

They walked along a narrow corridor with brick walls and wooden floor and electric lamps glowing overhead. Their footsteps echoed eerily in that narrow space. The attendant stopped at the first door and held it open. Valentin walked into the room.

"So, we meet again." Dr. Rall seemed to enjoy Valentin's startled look. But the smile could have been a product of rye whiskey, obvious at once from the smell of Raleigh Rye that mixed with his words and the way he swayed on his feet.

Valentin recovered and gave him a perfunctory nod. He took a moment to look around. The room was small, twelve by ten feet. Wooden shelves lined the walls, all filled with small bottles of chemicals and larger bottles containing body parts suspended in murky formaldehyde. The centerpiece was an enameled gurney with a body outlined under a sheet of muslin. The room reeked of acrid solutions, of the stale whiskey sweating sourly from the doctor, and what he recognized as the sweet, heavy odor of putrefying flesh. His eyes watered and he blinked to clear them.

"You ready?" Rall said. Valentin took off his coat and put it on a hook, then undid the top button on his collarless shirt. He nodded to Rall. The doctor pulled the cloth away and Valentin looked upon the corpse of Jennie Hix.

Her deep eye sockets, Semitic nose, and mouth painted in a cupid's bow proclaimed her one of the sporting girls who clustered in houses along the 900 block of Bienville, known as the Jew Colony. Her face was unmarked, save for creeping bruises, blue and purple and red and black. But the left side and the top of her head were all wrong, dented like a hard-boiled egg that had been bullied. Or like a doll that had been dropped and broken, a strange, unnatural sight. The curls of her thick black hair were still matted into the wounds and dried blood covered her ears and the back of her neck.

Valentin looked at the doctor, an excuse to avert his eyes for a moment. Rall was staring at the body while his left hand dove into his coat pocket to retrieve a flask. With a hypnotic motion, he pulled the cork and took a gentle swig. His eyes, bleary as ever, looked at the detective as he held the bottle in the air. Valentin shook his head and the doctor helped himself once again. "Awful, ain't it?" He replaced the bottle in his pocket. "What sort of crazy nigger would do a thing like that?" he mumbled.

"What sort of what?" Valentin said.

Rall blinked slowly. "I said, who'd do a thing like that?"

Valentin watched him for a moment, then said, "Do you have the weapon?"

"No, but I can guess what it was." The doctor clutched at the air. "Piece of pipe. Or wood, maybe. Probably pipe. Somethin' heavy, to cause them kind of contusions."

Valentin had surmised the same. Indeed, he wondered if it was the same piece of pipe that had put the lump on his own skull. "Three wounds?" he asked. Rall nodded. "Anything else?"

"No. No signs of struggle. No sexual battery." The recitation was quick, probably not much longer than the examination that had produced it.

Valentin studied the body of Jennie Hix, rubbing his forehead in concentration. "So a left-handed person would have come up from behind, swung the weapon and caught her here," he said, pointing to the left side of the prostitute's head, talking more to himself than the doctor. "Either a short person swinging upward or a taller one swinging from the hip. The wound goes upward, back to front." He straightened, but kept his eyes on the body and he moved around to get another angle.

"She would have gone to her knees," he murmured, noting red and purple bruises on her shins. "Second blow from above, to the top of the skull. That would knock her

to the ground, certainly unconscious. Maybe already dead."
He moved around to the other side of the body and saw a
patch of scrapes on her upper arm. "So she landed on her
right side. Third blow to the temple, while she was on the
ground. And if the second one didn't do it, that one would
have killed her."

Rall was staring at Valentin, even through the whiskey fog
appreciative of the detective's attentions. "That's probably it,
all right," he said. "Don't tell you who did it though..."

"No."

The doctor's gaze shifted. "Don't matter, does it?" he com-
mented.

∽

The attendant let Valentin out and stepped into the alley
behind him, closing the heavy door. Valentin was about to
walk away when he caught the attendant staring at him. He
stopped, let out a long breath, and leaned a shoulder against
the brick wall of the building. The mulatto dug in the pockets of his laboratory coat and produced a package of Dukes
and a box of lucifers. He offered the pack and Valentin
plucked a cigarette out, muttering a thank you. The attendant held a flame in cupped hands and two plumes of gray
smoke drifted into the night air. Valentin appreciated it; his
nerves needed a balm and the rough tobacco partially masked
the smells of the putrid fluids on the attendant's apron.

"What is it?" he said presently.

"What is what?" The attendant's voice was lazy.

"What is it you want to tell me?" The response was a
crooked smile. "All right, then, what is it you want to *sell*
me?" Valentin inquired and the attendant snickered, enjoying
the quip.

"Bet you been wonderin' what she was doing in Chinatown,"
the man said.

"I know what she was doing in Chinatown," Valentin
replied. The man's smile went away. "She was buying hop."

He blew another little cloud of smoke. "Let me guess. You found it on her. You might even have it in your pocket right now. I mean if you haven't already smoked it or sold it."

The mulatto crossed his arms. "I got it," he admitted, sounding a little miffed.

Valentin dug into his vest pocket and came up with a half-dollar. He held it out. "You can keep it," he said. "I just want to see the package."

The attendant glanced at him sharply, as if he couldn't believe his good luck. Then he grabbed the coin with one hand while the other dipped into a pocket to produce a little rectangle wrapped in decorative gold paper embossed with a design of two dragons entwined, their heads facing inward. Valentin felt two horse-pill-sized pieces of opium through the paper. That settled one question. He handed the package back to the attendant. "Where did you find it?"

The attendant leered. "It was hid down in her, uh, brassiere. You couldn't hardly see. She was big in there. She was a Jew, y'know, and them women is often—"

"I understand," Valentin said quickly. "Did anyone else see this?"

"I was in there all by myself." A wink. "Just me and her."

Valentin felt a hasty need to change the subject. "Doctor Rall," he said.

"What about him?"

"You tell me."

The attendant rolled his eyes. "He ain't nothin' but a goddamn drunk. And I believe he takes a needle now and again. Good thing I got to this one before him. Hell, I bet I'm a better doctor than he is."

"So, what is he doing here?"

"He's one of them they call after hours when we got a body like this one. No one worth a shit would come in late like that. For a dead whore, I mean."

Valentin sensed something more. "Is he the type to cooperate with the police?" he said.

The attendant nodded. "Yeah, that's right. Whatever the coppers want, Rall gives 'em. You know, 'wasn't no murder, it was a *suicide.*'" He mimed a scribbling motion. "He writes it down."

Valentin thought it over for a moment. "Three weeks ago," he said. "It was a Sunday morning. Early. They brought in a black-skinned girl."

The man shook his head. "Not in here, they didn't. The nigger corpses go round the other side."

"And who examines them?" Valentin asked.

"Whoever they call."

"Then it could have been Rall?"

The attendant nodded. "Yessir, it coulda been. But I can't tell you for sure. I don't work no mornings."

Valentin nodded. "Well, then, a week after that. A Saturday night. A white woman. You remember that one?"

"I think I do," the mulatto said. "Kinda fat, was she?"

"That's right. Rall get called on that one?"

The attendant thought about it, and then came up with a half-smile. "Yessir, I believe he did. The other one, too. The one got all cut up in that house on Basin Street. Rall did hers, too."

Valentin tossed the butt of his cigarette away. "Thank you for your help," he said.

"No, thank *you*, sir," the attendant said, clicking his tongue with familiarity.

Valentin walked out of the alley and onto the street. His progress was marked by J. Picot, who stood in a third floor window and watched until the detective reached Corondolet and crossed over. There another pair of eyes followed him, the eyes of a tall man who leaned in a darkened doorway. St. Cyr's footsteps faded away and the man stepped out and walked down the alley where the morgue attendant in the filthy apron was standing, his cigarette glowing in the darkness.

∽

Valentin was walking along, staring vacantly at the banquette, his coat slung over his shoulder, his shirt collar open, one thumb hooked in his trouser pocket. He turned right at the next street corner, lost in his thoughts, not really looking where he was going.

He heard a woman's voice yelling, "You get it the fuck outta here!" and then a harsh laugh. He glanced up to find himself on Robertson Street, but he walked on anyway. Cribs crowded the banquette and as he passed, he heard voices muttering orders, grunts like happy pigs, curses and laughter. Shadowy forms beckoned to him from shadowy doorways. "C'mere, daddy." The woman sounded weary. "You'll like what I got." A second, all but lifeless, called out, "Twenty-fi' cents. Do what you want. Twenty-fi' cents." He passed a silhouette through an open doorway, a man standing and a woman on her knees before him.

He was almost to Canal Street when a last voice spoke out of the darkness. "Well, look who's hangin' about down here."

Valentin glanced around. A white woman was perched in a wide window frame, sallow-skinned, short black hair in curls raggedly undone, circles of dark mascara around pale blue eyes, crooked teeth with gaps between. She was naked under a worn and torn kimono. One leg hung outside, swinging in a lazy arc. It reminded Valentin of a stationary version of one of the waffle carts that rolled the New Orleans streets, dispensing tawdry sugared confections.

It was also a perfect Storyville tableau; the crib girl could perch there all but naked, offering entry to any opening in her body for small change, but always sideways, because the law said facing the street was a "wanton display" and could bring a fine.

Valentin kept his eyes from the places in the garment that exposed the woman's pale body. "Alice Kane," he said finally. "I haven't seen you since you were up with Bertha Sullivan."

The crib girl spat on the sidewalk. "Bertha can kiss my ass, for sure." She fixed an eye on the detective. "And what are you doin' out here, Mr. Valentin?" she said. "I heard you got yourself stuck onto some young brown one uptown."

Valentin smiled and said, "I guess I got lost," and turned to move on.

"You caught him yet?" Alice asked. Valentin stopped and gave her a look. "Maybe you ought to pay your quarter and come inside," she said, then chortled at her pun. The laugh descended into a rheumy cough. "Maybe you oughta just do that," she said, her eyes watering.

"A dollar, if I can I get you to cover up a bit."

Alice Kane laughed again and held out a bony hand. Valentin dug into a vest pocket and produced a dollar coin. The crib girl took it and with slow fingers made it disappear between her legs. "If you want change, you can help yourself." She let herself down from the window and motioned him inside.

It was an eight-by-ten foot room, with rough-hewn clapboard walls and a single candle for light. A narrow iron bed with a stained mattress was pushed to the wall just inside the door. Next to it was a washstand that held a basin, a few rags and the usual bottle of purple permanganate of potash. There were thick spider webs in the corners and shiny black water bugs scurried along the baseboards. It smelled bad, all close and gamy, a mixture of sweat and sex and a heavy, too-sweet perfume, so that he had to hold his breath for a moment.

Alice Kane sat down on the stained mattress, the sash of the kimono tied loosely around her middle. Valentin leaned against the wall, his face half-hidden in flickering shadow.

The woman reached under the bed and came up with a bottle of Raleigh Rye.

"Drink?" she said, offering the bottle. Valentin shook his head. "Don't blame you," the woman said. "No tellin' what I had in my mouth." She laughed again, then became suddenly serious. "I asked have you caught the one been killin' them girls?" she said.

Valentin tilted his head slightly. "Why, you worried?"

The crib girl crossed her legs and studied her broken fingernails. "Funny, ain't it, how they all come outta houses?"

"How so?" Valentin said, suddenly impatient. It was late, and after the scene at the morgue, he was more than weary.

"No streetwalkers," Alice Kane was saying. "Nobody outta no crib."

"Yes, so?"

"You think women is gonna be gettin' murdered, it's gonna be round here," the crib girl said. "We ain't got no madams mindin' us. We ain't got no pimps stavin' off trouble." She attempted an expression of wide-eyed innocence and came up looking like a carnival doll. "Just us little lambs out here, all by ourselves. If you wanted to do somethin' right now, who'd stop you? You get your hands around my throat or make one little cut with a straight razor or you pull out that pistol you got in your pocket and...no more Alice. But all them that's getting killed, they all bitches outta one house or another."

"Do you know something?" He was abrupt.

"You asked was I worried," Alice said. "I'm tellin' you I ain't, because whoever's doin' this is doin' it for a reason. Not just to be killin' women. This ain't no Jack the Ripper cuttin'-up whatever whore he can grab aholt of. This man's got himself a plan." The crib girl nodded, agreeing with herself.

"Do you know something?" he asked her again.

She slouched on the mattress, propping on one elbow. "Naw, I don't know nothin'. I'm just sayin' what I think. And what I think right now is that you ought to put that coat down and shed them trousers and come and get some. Y'already give me a whole dollar." Valentin leaned away from the wall and stepped toward the door. Alice reached out a languid arm, but her hand fastened on his thigh like a claw. "Maybe you like some suckin'-off instead," she offered. Valentin peeled her bony fingers from his leg. "No? How come, Mr. Valentin? You get all you need from that little brown one? Is that it?" She sat up, letting her kimono fall open once more. "Well, you go ahead. You don't know what you're missin'. I ain't lost nothin' since I got run out of Bertha's. But you go on ahead."

He stepped through the doorway and onto the street. The air was fresher there, but only slightly. Alice's voice called from the shadows of her crib. "Hey, now, you watch her, Mr. Valentin," she said. "I believe she's in a house, ain't she?"

～

Instead of heading south to Magazine, he rounded the block and made a beeline down Conti to Antonia Gonzalez'. When he strode into the parlor, the girls got up to greet him, then sat back down when they saw who it was. The madam stepped up. "Valentin," she said, "what is it?"

"Justine," Valentin said. "Is she...?" He pointed a finger toward the upstairs room.

"She's not here," the madam said. "She left. Must be an hour or so now."

"Where?" He was feeling uneasy.

"She didn't say."

"With someone?"

"No, I don't think so," Miss Antonia said. "I was working on the books and when I came out for a glass of brandy, she was gone." She caught the look on Valentin's face, turned to the girls who were lounging on the couches and went about questioning them. One said simply that Justine had left without a word. And yes, she had been alone. Valentin turned for the door. "If she comes back, send her to my place. And send someone with her."

"Yes, of course," Miss Antonia said.

He hired a hack and offered the driver a quarter extra to crack the whip. Once again he found himself scouring the streets, trying to catch sight of a familiar figure. After a half-hour, he directed the driver out of the District and twenty minutes later, they turned onto Magazine. In the light of the lamp outside Gaspare's front door, he saw her waiting.

≈

He went into the bath and scrubbed himself until his skin glowed red. After he dried off, he walked through the shadows cast by a candle to the bed. She had already slipped between the sheets. He lay down beside her and studied her face. "What?" she said.

"Please don't ever do that again."

"But you didn't come by. You said you would come by."

"I know. I was held up. But, please."

"I'm sorry."

He laid his head on his arm. They were quiet for a long time. Justine watched the flickering flame of the candle as Valentin studied the patterns it cast upon the wall.

"I don't want you going back," he said at last.

"Oh?" The statement flustered her and she tried to make light of it. "And how will I eat?"

"I'll take care of that."

She laughed, but her tone was tinny. "So you're a rich man now?"

"Just until this is over," he said in a terse voice.

She was silent for a few moments. "And what then?" she asked.

He didn't answer. He reached over and snuffed the candle.

Ten

Windin' boy, don't deny my name
Windin' boy, don't deny my name
Well, I'm a windin' boy, don't deny my name
I'll pick it up and shake it like Stavin' Chain
Windin' boy, don't deny my name

He took her to a proper café for breakfast, boudin, eggs, biscuits and coffee. Lost in his thoughts, he spoke barely a word while they ate. As they were finishing their coffee, she touched his hand. "Are you still cross with me cause of last night?" Valentin gave her a small smile and shook his head. "What, then?" She looked wary and a bit sad, as if the light of day was erasing what he had said in the candle-lit bedroom.

She watched a shadow cross his face and she was about to save him the trouble and offer to leave when he said, "I want you to go to Miss Antonia's and get your things. I'll come by later to collect you." She saw a blush rise to his olive cheeks. "So you can stay with me."

It was all quite a surprise. She only hesitated for a moment or two, and then she nodded.

∼

The cleaning woman ushered him into Hilma Burt's parlor just at noon and he found LeMenthe at the white grand. It was the piano man's habit to use the early hours of the day, when there were no girls working and no customers, to practice new tunes that he had written or stolen. The grand was the only one of its kind in New Orleans and he was possessive about it, so he was the last to play it at night and the first to play it in the morning.

Valentin almost greeted him by calling out his given name, then remembered his new moniker, "Jelly Roll Morton," an assembly of family appellation and street lingo. LeMenthe told his friends that he was a performer and a performer needed a stage name, but since the only true "professor" in the District was Tony Jackson, he couldn't claim that title. So "Jelly Roll" it was. Valentin figured there was more to the story, but it was none of his business. Who was he to question a fellow who wanted to change his name?

LeMenthe—*Morton*—waved a free hand from across the parlor. "Mr. Valentin. Listen to this here..."

As Valentin stepped up to the piano, Morton began a stately ragtime pattern, as crisp and clean as Scott Joplin himself might play it and he sang in a rough, high tenor.

> *I'm a windin' boy, don't deny my name*
> *Windin' boy, don't deny my name*
> *Well, I'm a windin' boy, don't deny my name*
> *I'll pick it up and shake it like Stavin' Chain*
> *Windin' boy, don't deny my name*

Valentin grinned crookedly. All the rounders and sporting girls would know that a "winding boy" was one who could fuck all night long. And most would recognize the name of Stavin' Chain, a black hero like John Henry, reputed to have the sexual strength of a plowhorse and the physical equipment to match. Morton flashed a smile—one gold tooth glinting—and sang on.

> *Mama, mama, look at little sis'*
> *Hey, mama, mama, at little sis'*
> *Mama, mama, look at sis'*
> *She's out there on the levee and she's shakin' her tits*
> *Windin' boy, don't deny my name*

Morton was a kid, only nineteen or twenty, but the lyrics were whiskey raw and Valentin let out a laugh. "Wait a minute, one more," the piano man called.

> *Sister, sister, dirty little sow*
> *Sister, sister, dirty little sow*
> *Sister, sister, little sow*
> *Tryin' to be a bad girl, but ya don't know how*
> *Windin' boy, don't deny my name*

He brought the song to an end with a descending cascade of notes. "Think they'll like it?" he said.

Valentin gave him a laconic smile. "I think so, yes."

The gold in Morton's mouth glittered some more. "Yeah, people love it down and dirty, don't they? 'Specially them gals. They sure do." He fell to playing about the keys with one finger as he watched the detective. "What brings you round this mornin'?"

"I want to visit your godmother," Valentin said.

Morton stopped his doodling. "Why?"

"I want to ask her some questions."

The piano man pursed his lips, considering, then began another pattern, a slow gutbucket. It sounded a lot like something Bolden would play. Valentin said, "Where's she living at, Ferd?" He collected a sharp look. "Sorry, I mean Jelly."

"Out on the lake. St. Charles Parish." Morton stopped playing again. "Now, you tell me exactly why you want to see her and I'll tell you where exactly she stays."

Valentin leaned against the piano. "Truth is, it's this business with these murders. I just want to see—"

"—if some voodoo woman can help you?" Morton said, grinning broadly now. Everyone who knew Valentin knew of his disgust with the subject. "That don't sound like you at all," he said. "What is it? Somebody callin' a tune?" He laughed softly, shaking his head as he resumed the pattern on the keys.

"How many people you seen murdered round here?" Morton asked him presently.

Valentin shrugged and said, "Plenty."

"Plenty is right." He gave an emphatic nod. "Just so happens I'm right now working up a little song about Aaron Harris. You know 'bout him? Horrible man. First he killed his own brother. Then his little sister, a sportin' girl. She displeased him and he cut her throat. His own sister. There was more after that, but he got away with them, too. You know why? Cause his woman, Madame Papaloos, she was *voudun.*" Valentin opened his mouth to steer the conversation back to the subject at hand, but Morton plunged on. "She knew all the tricks. She'd rearrange his furniture, mess up his house, so's the police never could hang nothing on him. She'd stick needles in beef tongues, so's no one could testify against him. It's a fact. That evil fellow that committed ten, twelve killings, didn't do one day of time." He shook his head in wonder.

Valentin had heard these stories and a hundred more like them. He was not impressed. Anyway, he didn't need reasons to visit the voodoo woman; he didn't have a choice. "What about it?" he said. "What about Miss Echo?"

"Well, yes, of course you can go see her."

"You'll call her? Make arrangements?"

Morton came down the scale, a trickle of dirty blue notes. "She's hoodoo, man. She'll know you're comin'."

He lowered his gaze and started to play hard then, the same pattern, full of ragged tones that echoed through the empty, sunlit room.

～

He collected Justine after one o'clock and they carried her possessions—two satchels full—back to Magazine. He was going to leave her there to stow her things, but then he changed his mind and asked if she wanted to go along. It would be quiet out by the lake.

They walked to Union Station and bought two second-class tickets on "Smoky Mary," the small-gauge rail that served as something akin to a circus train on the weekends, carrying bands and revelers to and from the lake resorts and dance halls. Justine was delighted to have an afternoon out of the city, though when Valentin told her where they were going, she looked startled. She was a good Catholic, better than he by far, but along with the cross around her neck, she wore a dime on a thong around her ankle. Now, calling directly on a hoodoo woman, even a good one, made her uneasy.

But, truth be told, voodoo held sway in the District every day and night except for Sunday. The queens employed charms and amulets, black cat bones and mojo hands, all to help the women that came to them and to harm their enemies. French Emma Johnson, that black-hearted witch, was said to be able to seal up a sporting girl so that she couldn't carry on her trade, to cause syphilis using the scrotum of a goat and the gleet with the blood of a wasp. The faithful claimed her curses could cause crippled, idiot babies and that she could drop a man in his tracks with one look of her crossed eyes. Valentin knew none of it was true, but it didn't matter. She and another dozen like her cast spells back and forth, vicious harpies fighting like cats. There were far fewer good voodoo queens like Eulalie Echo, who applied spells to protect the girls from the wicked spirits that haunted the air. People believed; even the most devout Catholics remembered to mutter prayers to Yaya, the snake god, and often those who practiced *voudun* daily were also the first to Mass come Sunday morning.

So Justine prudently clutched the cross that hung around her neck as the train rolled along Bayou St. John toward the shores of Lake Pontchartrain.

The ride took less than thirty minutes, and he spent the time telling her about the extra car that ran only on weekends, designated for drunks and rough-housers returning from their day on the lake, too rowdy for decent company. Railroad guards would drag the offending characters into the car like so much baggage and when they got back to Terminal Station, a mule-drawn Black Maria would be waiting to carry them off to Parish Prison.

As he was relating this tale, he saw out of the corner of his eye the man who sat at the back of their car, watching and listening a bit too intently. Since he had been on the case, Valentin had the feeling of someone lurking about, but he had written it off to the whole jittery mess with the murders.

Now he knew his instinct had been correct. He moved his head a few degrees and caught the round shape of a derby hat. He glanced casually at Justine for a few seconds, then turned to stare at the man. Their eyes locked for an instant and the fellow got up abruptly from his seat and made his way to the other end of the car.

At Milneburg, they stepped off the train and right into the middle of a mid-afternoon shower. They waited under the station eaves, eating ham sandwiches and drinking from bottles of Chero-Cola that he bought at the kiosk. He watched the crowd. The man from the train was nowhere in sight.

The storm passed, the sun peeked out and they walked along a gravel road that followed the edge of the lake for a little over a mile until they came upon a tidy bungalow propped up on pilings, just as Morton had described it. A woman was fussing about with potted herbs laid out along the banister of her gallery. She straightened and watched as Valentin and Justine started up the walkway. When they moved out of the glare of the sun and into the shade, she smiled and gestured for them to come onto the gallery, then fixed the Creole detective with a look of mock severity. "You should have come sooner," Eulalie Echo said.

He sat at her kitchen table, watching through the open side door as Justine walked across a narrow strip of gray sand, took off her shoes, hiked up her petticoats and waded into the water. The brilliance of the sun on the lake gave her form a shimmery, dreamy quality as she kicked with her feet and splashed with her hands.

Valentin turned to regard Eulalie Echo, godmother to Mr. Jelly Roll Morton, as she poured them both a glass of lemonade. She was a willowy woman in her fifties, dark-skinned, with high cheekbones, an aquiline nose, and kind green eyes. She was wearing a white Mother Hubbard and though her head was wrapped in a *tignon*, a rainbow of African dyes, he could see her long hair, going to gray, was braided Indian-style. Huge earrings, hoops of silver, dangled along her neck. She padded around a kitchen that was large and homey, with more pots of herbs covering every surface and filling the air with a rich, exotic aroma.

"How's that godson of mine?" she inquired, as if she hadn't spoken to him recently, probably within the hour.

"He's doing well, Miss Echo."

"Calling himself by another name, ain't he?" Her smile was impish.

"He is, yes," Valentin said.

There was a silence while the voodoo woman regarded her visitor thoughtfully. "If you want something, Valentin, go ahead and ask for it," she said. She put the pitcher back in the icebox and sat down across the table from him.

Valentin gazed out the open door. "I want to put a stop to these murders," he said.

"How many now?" Miss Echo asked him.

"Four."

The voodoo woman muttered something under her breath, then said, "What makes you think I can help you?"

He shrugged. "Lulu White claims it's a voodoo matter."

"She would," Eulalie said. "Matter-of-fact, most people uptown and half of them downtown would say so, too. But you, you don't believe any of it, Valentin." Her voice was gentle. "So, tell me, whatchu doin' here?"

He hesitated. He wanted to say: *I'm humoring a madam who takes all this foolishness as if it's gospel truth. To remain in her good graces. To remain in her employ.* Miss Echo was watching him with a half-smile, as if she could read these thoughts. "Maybe if..."

"Maybe if what?"

"If this person, the killer, is a believer in it, then—"

"Then I can offer you some kind of a clue?" She gave him a coy look. "Or you want me to just make a spell and get him to stop?"

Valentin thought about it. "The clue would do just fine."

Eulalie Echo let out a delighted laugh. She shook her head and turned to watch Justine, now up to her knees in the cool green water. "She's a pretty girl," she said, and then brought her attention back to Valentin. "You think it's silly, eh? Like things we say to scare little children." He started to reply, but she held up a hand. "You didn't come all this way to talk," she said sharply. "So you listen now. I'm going to give you a little lesson. I believe maybe you need it."

Valentin slouched back in his chair, making an effort to hide his irritation at having to sit still for a long-winded recitation of the virtues of voodoo. Miss Echo seemed to understand this and smiled again, knowingly.

"This thing came over from Africa, by way of the islands in the Caribbean," she began. "People there, including one of your great-*grandperes* believed it, just like the Baptists believe in Jesus. Back there, they believe everything has a spirit. People, animals, plants, everything." She rapped her knuckles on the wooden table.

Valentin fidgeted in his chair and made a little sound of exasperation. Eulalie Echo drew back, crossed her arms and arched her eyebrows at this rudeness. "All right, then, Mr. Valentin, you want to tell me about voodoo? Or how them back-of-town people say it now? *Hoodoo?* Go on. You tell me everything you know. Maybe I'll learn something myself."

She waited until he said, "I apologize," then clapped her hands together. "*Bon.* You're not so stupid after all. So I'll tell you now. And you see if maybe it can help you put a stop to that evil over there."

She got up and made a slow show of taking a bottle of rye whiskey down from a shelf and pouring two short glasses. One she placed in front of Valentin. The other she held between her thumb and forefinger, turning it round and round before her eyes, staring through the amber liquid. "So, you know how it all started?" she said. "You know who was the first? The original voodoo queen?"

"Marie Laveau," Justine said from the doorway. She was standing there in bare feet, the bottom six inches of her cotton dress soaked gray with lake water, her shoes and stockings dangling from her right hand.

Miss Echo smiled. "Come in, child," she said.

Justine crossed to the table, sat down, laid her shoes on the floor near her chair and placed her stockings inside. Eulalie Echo watched the younger woman with a smile.

"Who doesn't know Marie Laveau?" Valentin said with the same edge of impatience.

"Well, then, you know her true name?" Justine said. "Do you?" Valentin opened his mouth, closed it. He looked at Miss Echo, who was smiling, then back at Justine.

"Her given name was Marie Glampion," Justine told him. "She was a colored Creole woman and she did the hair of all the rich French ladies. She'd hear them talkin', about their husbands, about their back-door men, about the other rich ladies. And Marie, she listened until she knew everything them folks was doin' and with who and when and where. She came up to the big houses to work and she met their husbands, too. And she started makin' arrangements for the real pretty octoroon girls to go meet the men. So she had all their secrets. And she'd tell them she'd keep their business to herself, but they had to pay her. And they did."

Valentin listened, not a little astonished. How did this country girl know all this New Orleans history, harking back to the days of the Octoroon Balls, where the young French aristocrats made market for comely mistresses that they'd keep for the rest of their lives?

"But Miss Glampion, she was voodoo, except they called it *voudun*, the French way," Justine was saying. "And pretty soon everybody knew, whatever you want, you go see Marie Laveau. She really was a queen. She had power over about all of New Orleans. The rich French people and the down-town Creoles. The madams in the mansions all up and down Basin Street and all the girls and the sports from way back-of-town, too. Everybody." She lowered her voice dramatically. "People say she could lay on a curse just by looking at you one way. Or she could give protection so nobody could harm you. And some people say she could heal the sick and raise the dead."

Valentin broke his astonished gaze to glance at Miss Echo. The voodoo woman went on rocking slightly in her chair, her eyes closed, as if she was listening to a student's recitation.

Justine reached out, picked up Valentin's glass of rye and took a small sip. "Then, later on, after Marie died, there was a whole other woman...she took to callin' herself Marie Laveau, but her true name was...um..."

"Malvina Latour," Miss Echo said quietly.

"Yes. She was still alive when I was a little girl. Even out in the country we heard about her. Some people say she was Marie's daughter, other people say it was Marie comin' back from the grave and startin' over again with another name. She could do that, that's what they said. She was like a cat. She had nine lives."

Eulalie Echo laughed softly. Valentin and Justine looked around to see her amusement was directed at his slack-jawed gape. He was truly surprised. In the whole time he had known her, Justine had spoken at most a half-dozen words at a time. But now she sat across the table, her dark eyes wide open and her face infused with a strange light, all full of the story.

Miss Echo leaned her head toward the younger woman. "Go on," she said.

Justine chewed her thumbnail for a moment. "That second Marie Laveau, they say she was a real black voodoo woman. She could put a curse on as fast as you could blink. Or take one away, same way." A pause. "She'd have these..."

"...ceremonies," Miss Echo offered.

"In a house," Justine said, barely missing a beat. She looked at Miss Echo. "Somewhere out here, on the lake."

There was a nod of agreement from the older woman. "*Maison Blanche.* And it ain't a stone's throw from where we're sitting."

"She had these here parties," Justine went on. "Hoodoo parties. They'd build a big fire and have a band to play, a man beatin' on a drum and all them African horns and such. The girls, they'd go all crazy and take off their clothes and dance." Her small, tan face seemed to turn older and darker. "The men would come to drink and dance with the girls. And that Marie, she'd make her voodoo. And then they was all on the floor...or they'd go out the door onto the beach..." Her expression lightened and she giggled. "Everybody was naked, women laughing and screaming and thrashing all around, and that music'd be playing, and it'd go on all night long. And Miz Latour, she'd sit there in a rockin' chair, watchin' it all, like she was...the queen...the queen of..."

"...the underworld," Eulalie Echo said through tight lips.

There was a heavy silence; the two women seemed to have gone adrift in the tale. A few moments passed and Valentin said to Justine, "How do you know all this?"

She blinked, and sat back in her chair. "My mama told me some of it," she explained. "And then, after I come here, when it was slow late at night, if it was rainin' and there weren't no men comin' in...Miss Antonia or one of the old women, they'd start it up." She smiled. "We'd be like little girls, all in this one room, listenin' to someone tellin' about Marie Laveau." She treated Valentin to a shrewd glance. "You ain't the only one likes stories," she finished.

Valentin drained his glass and Eulalie rose to refill it. She half-filled a third glass and placed it in front of Justine. She sat back down. "What else you want to know, Valentin?" she said, delighting in the scene that had unfolded at her table. Justine was smiling, too, pleased at having astonished him so.

Valentin shook his head, regaining his bearings. "I want to know what all that has to do with someone killing women in Storyville," he said.

Miss Echo shook her head. "So impatient. So impatient," she said.

~

It was getting stuffy inside and Miss Echo asked if they'd like to go for a walk along the lake. Justine was pleased to be outdoors again, but Valentin had to hide his irritation at the slow pace of the afternoon. The only reason he had come in the first place was to placate Lulu White; he was the reluctant knight sent off by one dotty queen to pay respects to her dotty sister. The day was all but gone and he had yet to learn one thing he could use.

So they strolled down the shoreline, Justine holding the detective's arm as the voodoo woman walked ahead, poking at shells and stones with a long, twisted stick of oily driftwood.

"You want to tell this impatient man some more of the story?" she called over her shoulder.

"No ma'am," Justine said quietly and gripped his arm a little tighter. Valentin noticed her pensive frown and understood. Telling stories on characters long dead was one thing; talking on hoodoo women who were quite alive and well was another entirely.

"How 'bout you, Mr. Valentin?" Eulalie inquired.

"I'd like to hear anything you care to share, ma'am."

Miss Echo stopped and turned around, one eyebrow arching. "Well, then," she said and looked away from the lake and in the direction of the city. "Ain't much real voodoo left. Not like the old days. When I was a young girl..." She paused. "Those women, they made magic. Used them black cat bones, John the Conqueror root and mojo hands, all that. Old Marie, she could make an old man wind like a young buck and make a young fellow bark like a dog. I mean to say they made *magic*." She shook her head. "Now whatchu got? You got old Zozo LaBrique puttin' the dust on them doorsteps and that cross-eyed bitch sayin' she can seal girls up so they can't work." She shook her head again at the sorry state of affairs.

"Mama Latour, she ruined it," she went on grimly. "Used to be, people believe in the voodoo for what it was, 'stead of for what it could do. They had respect. Then it got turned into something else. A show. A bunch of sportin' girls gettin' naked for old white men whilst some colored boys beat on drums. I don't know what it is, but it ain't *voudun*." She sighed. "But we still fight the old fight, now and then." She looked at him. "And I believe that's what you got in the District right now. Some true voodoo. A real evil, evil spirit. That's what's causin' these awful things to happen."

Valentin, fortunately, did not roll his eyes, because Miss Echo was gazing directly at him "You been seeing the power of the dark side. That would be your killer. And the reason how come nobody can't catch him is somebody's givin' him protection."

"Who?" Valentin asked, keeping his voice deliberately patient.

Miss Echo looked away. "I couldn't say."

It meant she wouldn't say. But Valentin didn't need a name; he could guess who it was she was talking about. "All right, then, protection from who?" he said. "The police?"

"The police!" The woman laughed, but her eyes looked suddenly dark and distant. "No, not from the police. From you."

At his side, Justine crossed herself.

～

On the way back, they came across a stray dog and Justine ran on ahead, chasing it at the edge of the waves. The talk of voodoo was put aside for a moment as they watched her romp happily with the animal.

Miss Echo didn't say another word until they were in sight of her house. But when she did speak, she stopped him in his tracks. "That young Mr. Bolden," she said. "He was out here quite a lot, you know."

"Where?" Valentin said, caught unaware. "Out where?"

"He was around for some of the voodoo balls," she said. "Up to maybe a year or so ago. Him and one of them bands of his, they used to play at the park at Milneburg. And after, he went by."

"Who said anything about Bolden?" he asked.

Miss Echo gave him a sly smile. "People talk." People meaning her godson, who never stopped talking. She would know every gossipy snippet from the street.

"What was he doing there?" Valentin asked.

"He came for the music," the voodoo woman said. "All those African drums and the horns and flutes. He went to them things and the St. John's Eve parties and heard the music. I mean that crazy voodoo music. He got hold of it right quick." She looked out over the water. "I suspect it got

hold of him, too. That's why he plays the way he does now."
She continued on down the path.

"What got hold of him?"

"The *voodoo*, Valentin." Now it was she who sounded impatient. "That's what this is all about, ain't it?"

"I paid a visit to Emma Johnson," he said abruptly. Miss Echo stopped to stare at him. "She acted like she knows somethin' about Buddy, too," Valentin told her. "Maybe had some dealings with him. So she said. Or made a hint."

The voodoo woman shook her head. "She is a bad, bad person, that one. Bad as they get." She continued walking. "If she got hooks into him..." She sighed heavily.

Valentin pondered in silence for a few paces, then said, "What can you tell me about black roses?"

Miss Echo nodded. "Ah, yes. I heard about that, too."

"The killer leaves one after every murder," he explained. "Does that mean anything to you?"

"No," she said, "but it could mean somethin' to someone else. I'm tellin' you it ain't the same anymore. It's every person just makin' it up on their own. It just ain't the same."

They walked on. "How do you know?" he asked.

Miss Echo said, "Hmmm?"

"About Buddy. The music. About him bein' out there messing with the voodoo."

They turned up the walk to her gallery. "Oh, I was there, too," she said.

～

Before they left, she loaded Justine down with two sacks; one filled with herbs and roots that smelled to high heaven, the other packed with beans, okra, carrots, onions, cucumbers and chicory from her back garden. Valentin sensed that she wanted to offer him something, a *gris-gris* to ward off the evils he faced, but she just took his hand in both of hers and wished him good luck. She stood on her gallery, waving, as they walked away.

The train rolled out of the station and back toward the city. Justine picked happily through her prizes and announced as they approached Union Station that she planned to make use of the contents of the sacks and cook dinner that night. He could tell she was happy to be able to have something common to think about, after their afternoon with a voodoo woman.

As they stepped onto the platform he caught sight of the man in the derby loitering among the crowd of passengers. He turned away from Justine with a sudden movement and walked through the milling crowd. The fellow saw the Creole detective coming, looked first concerned, then startled. He took a few steps backward. Valentin was ten feet away when he made a sharp jag and beat a retreat, pushing people out of his way. He strode down the platform and through the station doors. He didn't look back and Valentin let him go.

When they got to his rooms, Justine spread her bounty on the tiny kitchen table and then hurried out to the balcony. She peered toward Decatur Street in the direction of the Vieux Carre until she spotted a wagon in the distance. She stepped back inside to get her purse.

Much of what passed for shopping outside the French Market was done by way of rope and bucket. The produce man pulled his wagon to the banquette and the lady of the house would call out her list from a balcony, then lower her bucket at the end of the rope. The entire transaction was carried out this way; then the peddler would move on to the next balcony, the next mistress of the house.

But Valentin had no bucket, no rope; he ate at cafés and from street carts for the most part. By way of kitchen ware, he had in his possession one pot and one frying pan and some random utensils, all items left behind by a previous tenant. Except for three stale biscuits, a few spoonfuls of flour and sugar, a tin of milk, a bit of butter and a large can of coffee, there was not a speck of food about.

Justine surveyed his empty cupboards with a look of exasperation and went downstairs to wait for the peddler's cart. Valentin stepped into the toilet, took off his shirt and splashed water on his face. A few minutes later, he walked out in his undershirt to see Justine heading for the kitchen with her arms full.

～

She stripped down to a ribbed vest of soft cotton, carefully draping her dress over a chair. She then rooted about until she discovered the sack with a bare dusting of flour remaining and lit his spindly gasoline stove to set about making a roux with water and a fat onion from Eulalie Echo's garden.

Valentin moved a straight-backed chair so that he could watch her. Making do with his one dull kitchen knife, in quick little movements she chopped and stirred and moved the pot and pan about and for the first time, the smells of cooking food wafted through the detective's rooms in a rich cloud of Creole perfume.

After ten minutes of busy motion, she stopped and looked over the stove. She turned and saw Valentin watching her with his gray eyes. He stood up. She stepped out of the kitchen, brushing her hands. There was a sheen of sweat on her forehead and a light patch of flour on one of her tan cheeks. She glanced over her shoulder one more time to check the progress of her work, then reached around to undo the hooks of her vest.

～

Later, after they had eaten, Valentin carried the two kitchen chairs out on the balcony and they sat watching a freighter steam up the river to dock, the lights ghostly in the purple night. He felt strangely peaceful; it was as if he and Justine were separated from the streets of New Orleans and the rest of the world, hidden away in a dark and private corner. But he knew that in a few moments, he would have to get up, get dressed, walk the eight blocks to Basin Street and spend the better part of the night in Anderson's raucous big room. He let out a quiet sigh. He realized he would be quite happy to stay right there in those drab little rooms, far from the bedlam of Storyville; and that wasn't like him at all.

"Dinner was all right, then?" Justine asked, interrupting his thoughts.

He smiled. "I have to tell you again? It was good."

She was silent, but he could almost hear her thinking. "I could do it again tomorrow," she said at last.

He looked at her. "I expect you to stay here, Justine," he said. She almost relaxed in her chair, then sat up. "What is it?"

"I'm gonna need a bucket and some rope," she said.

～

On a bandstand ten blocks to the north, Buddy sat on a low chair, a slouch hat pulled down over his eyes. Minutes passed and Mumford and Cornish exchanged a long look of annoyance. But Buddy just kept staring at a point on the dance floor just beyond the stage. The crowd stirred, watching him, waiting, but he didn't see them at all, didn't feel the impatience of their movements, didn't hear their mutterings.

Another minute passed and then, with a sudden motion, he swung the cornet out of his lap and rapped it, bell down, on the boards, a quick one-two-three-four. The fellows in the band scrambled, caught up just in time as it came around. From under the hat, King Bolden smiled his wolf smile and brought the horn to his lips.

It sounded like a man growling in pain, and it was so loud, like always, that the front row of the audience took a reflexive step back, but then the bodies surged forward again as if sucked in by a magnet. From beneath his cocked eyebrow, he saw them coming and so he slouched down deeper into his chair and blew harder.

Blew harder.

They began clapping then, shuffling their feet, shaking their hips and shoulders as he pelted them with hot brass that cut through flesh and went right down to the bone. Then someone shouted "King Bolden! King Bolden!" and he half-jumped to his feet, stepped to the edge of the low stage and leaned down, pushing wind like a locomotive pushing steam. The floor began to vibrate, a window rattled and a whiskey bottle danced off the rack over the bar and shattered in a shower of clear glass and amber liquid.

He felt the breath come from deep down, from his private parts and then up his backbone, through his lungs for an extra shove and then out his open throat and between his thick, muscled lips. It was savage kiss onto hot metal and he flicked his tongue and tasted blood. He gripped the horn so tight his knuckles hurt.

He knew there was a crowd out there, on the other side of the haze of bottle and pipe, but all he saw was a spiral of red flame that came roaring out of his horn, rose and fell in wild gyrations, and then made an electric arc that cut through the air. He knew this was it, the way it was supposed to be. All that mess with the whispers and the narrowed eyes and the backs turned was gone; and the whole room, the whole of New Orleans, the whole world was filled with his horn. He was home.

∿

The upstairs room in the house on Bienville glowed crimson from a bedside lamp. The woman sat on the side of the sagging mattress, holding the man's yancey in her hand. She squeezed and pulled expertly, looking for the telltale drip of viscous yellow. She looked up and winked at him, trying for coy. Then she reached for the vial and the cloth that stood beside the bottle of Raleigh Rye on the night table. She washed and dried him with a practiced hand.

She put bottle and cloth aside, wiped her hands together and lay back on the bed. She raised her knees and spread her legs, feeling a brief ache run through her weary flesh. In the red lamplight, the hard lines in her face softened, her rough, painted skin flowed away from her bones, the dark mound between her legs rose up like a warm, wet oasis. She made a little gesture with her fingertips and the man who had paid his dollar pushed his pants down so his suspenders dragged around his ankles. His knees found the edge of the bed and he fell into her. She felt him there, a nub of something moving. A half dozen gasps, a raw, throaty moan and it was over.

The man was gone, almost like he was never there at all. The woman pulled on her camisole, put the towel between her legs and held it there while she took a quick shot from the bottle. She got up and stepped to the window and, for a few minutes, her mind wandered away to something someone had said somewhere, a faint echo from some other time and place. Then the door opened and the next one walked in, looking quite pleased with himself, acting like something special. They all thought they were something special. She made her mouth smile.

～

The office was deep in shadow that was broken only by the light of a dim candle.

"So, Lieutenant," the white man behind the desk said. "Are you at liberty to discuss these unfortunate murders?"

"We don't know who killed them girls," Picot blurted, fidgeting with his hat. "Not for sure. There's plenty of talk, though."

"What kind of talk?"

The policeman hesitated for a moment, then said, "About some hoodoo, for one thing. And also about that horn player, crazy fellow named Bolden."

"That would be King Bolden?" the white man inquired.

Picot looked at him. "That's right."

"Do you think he's responsible?"

The policeman shrugged. "He's good a suspect as any."

"Then why hasn't he been arrested?"

"They don't have a case," Picot muttered. "Not yet."

"I understand he's quite the character."

Picot nodded with emphatic disgust. "He is that."

The man made a steeple of his hands and said, "And Valentin St. Cyr."

The policeman's face took a cold set. "What about him now?"

"You tell me."

"Ain't much to tell," Picot said. "He works for Mr. Anderson. Thinks he's somethin' round the District. Likes to poke his nose into places it don't belong."

"He's investigating these murders?"

Picot made an angry gesture. "He ain't got nothin' to do with that."

"I believe he does, Lieutenant."

Picot said, "Shit."

"Tom Anderson doesn't hire fools."

The policeman grunted something under his breath.

The man at the desk touched his mustache, ignoring the outburst. "St. Cyr's a colored man, isn't he?" he inquired absently.

Picot's lazy, dirt-tinted eyes blinked warily. He feigned surprise. "Colored man? Well, now...I wouldn't...I don't know about that."

The man at the desk smiled. "Let's not waste time. I know about his family. I know he is." He paused. "And I know it's something you and he have in common."

Picot sat frozen in his chair. He swallowed and his face paled.

"I don't wish to make difficulties for anyone," the man continued placidly. "We can keep that in confidence."

The policeman finally managed to say, "How'd you come to know?"

"I'm privy to certain information," the man said.

He allowed Picot a few minutes to mull it over and the copper's mind finally wound about and came up with a glimmer of realization. He said, "Oh."

"I believe he bears watching," the man said.

"What's that?"

"St. Cyr. I believe someone needs to keep a close eye on him. It would not do to have him beat our own Police Department at cracking the case."

"No..."

"And if this Bolden is the man, do we really want St. Cyr to be the first one on it? Aren't the two of them friends?"

Picot grimaced. "They are."

"Well, then," the white man said. "Seems it would be in everyone's interest to keep a close eye on Mr. St. Cyr."

Picot nodded slowly. "Yessir, it would be."

The slow nod continued and the man behind the desk let out a silent sigh; the copper was either a dunce or still so unnerved at having his secret revealed that he couldn't think straight.

"I've had a man working on it, watching his movements, but he's been recognized." He waited, but there was no reaction from the policeman. "I would do it myself, you see," he went on, "but St. Cyr could recognize me and...well, you can see how that would be a problem." Picot nodded again blankly, still not getting it. "I'd be grateful for some assistance in this matter. Very grateful."

The color slowly returned to Picot's face and he met the white man's gaze. "I could help out with that," he said.

The man sat back in his chair and folded his hands complacently. In the black distance, thunder rumbled.

❧

Sixty miles inland, thunder rolled through the dark, flashing clouds that were mounting the horizon as the orderly, a large, kindly Negro named Henry, bent over Father Dupre's bed, tucking the sheets, settling the pillow. The old man was struggling, trying to whisper something, but the voice was hoarse and broken.

Henry murmured softly as he patted the sheet that covered the bony chest. "There now, go on to sleep," he said. The priest clutched onto the Negro's forearm, dark yellow fingernails digging deep into brown flesh. He tried to speak again, but it came out a rough gasp. The hand dropped. "There now, go on to sleep," Henry repeated, low and soothing now, and the old man lay back and closed his eyes. The orderly looked up at the black crucifix on the wall over the bed. He crossed himself before he slipped away.

∽

It was late and Florence Mantley was tired. You'd think these fellows had no homes to go to, she mused as she climbed the stairs, her joints creaking. They'd likely sit around all night and into the next day if she didn't chase them outdoors.

She had shooed the last one; or at least she hoped so. But there was no telling with some of her girls these days. They'd try to fool her, letting a favorite fancy man stay on after closing, strictly against her rules. If the fellow was in such a swoon, she told them, let him pay for a room at a hotel. It just didn't do to have leeches lolling about her mansion like they belonged there.

She was keeping a special eye fixed on Ella Duchamp. The young lady was about some sort of business lately, acting a fool, disappearing for days and then all whispers and shifted eyes when she was in the house. The madam knew this was usually a sign that some sweet-talking fancy man or handsome pimp had got the hooks in. She wouldn't stand for that behavior and the girls knew it. Miss Mantley boasted the prettiest, most accomplished octoroons in New Orleans and she meant to keep her good reputation. So if Miss Ella Duchamp was up to anything, she could find herself another address.

But all seemed in order this night. The madam went door-to-door only to find one exhausted girl asleep in each room and no unwanted guests. She took an extra long look inside Miss Ella's room, in case her fellow was hiding until it was safe. But the girl was curled under the baire, quite alone. Miss Mantley closed the door, moved along the corridor to her room at the end of the hallway. She could now attend to a bit of rest for herself.

She stopped to look out the hallway window at the still, blue New Orleans night. As she turned to lay a hand on the doorknob, she caught a flicker of motion. She jerked around, already angry at the trespass, and glared when she saw who stood at the head of the stairs.

"You!" she muttered. "What in God's name are you doing here?"

To her surprise, the intruder didn't say a word, didn't flinch, but came stalking a fast clip along the corridor. Miss Florence, now rightly incensed, put her hands on her hips and glared. The intruder still didn't stop, but instead came faster and before she could move or speak, hard arms slammed her heavy bosom, she jerked backwards, there was a crashing sound of glass all around her, and she was suddenly falling into a nightmare. Wind roared in her ears and then a huge hand pounded her into the ground.

Lying there on the hard dirt, she could hear the cries of the girls coming out of their rooms. She tried to raise her head, but she couldn't move at all. A wrenching pain wracked her body in three great waves and then suddenly went away. She saw faces in the broken window frame above, but the features weren't clear and their shrieking voices grew faint. Her eyes rolled up and she saw dim stars, but then they were gone, too.

Eleven

Too white to be black
Too black to be white
    —Dr. John, The Voodoo King

The storm from the Gulf circled around in the middle of the
night and Valentin was roused from a troubled sleep by fat, greasy
raindrops pelting the bedroom window. Justine didn't stir at all;
but he'd learned that she could sleep through a hurricane. Valentin
closed his eyes, then opened them again to stare at the spider
web of cracks in the plaster in the ceiling, sensing a shadow lurking
just beyond the edge of his vision.

He couldn't say what it was; maybe it had to do with the
tall man tailing him, or it was something he had carried
away from the voodoo woman's house, or maybe it was
Bolden's constant, creeping presence on the fringe of the
terrible string of murders. Maybe it was the key, the one
critical piece that he was missing. Or maybe it was all of it
put together. All he knew for sure was that whatever it was
would be gone when he turned his head.

He was awake. He slipped out of the bed and out of the
room, closing the door behind him. He crossed his living room
and opened the French doors. In the gray dawn, the wind
was blowing west to east, so he could lean in the doorway
and watch the clouds rolling in without getting all soaked.

The lead-colored sky, the sheets of warm rain and the
pre-dawn silence suited his mood. He remembered that it
was at this same hour some six weeks before that he had

gone off to view the body of Annie Robie. It was about the same time of day, on the morning after the murder of Martha Devereaux, that he had watched Bolden stalk away from the rotting pier as the sky went from deep purple to pale pink. It was in this same dull light that he had wandered home from the alley where Jennie Hix had died.

Four dead women, no notion as to who was causing the mayhem, and no notion why. And the only suspect in sight was Buddy, stumbling into the middle of the chaos like he was being shoved by an unseen hand. Even Valentin had to admit that he was the perfect suspect. Too perfect, in fact: it was if the scene had been arranged with him in mind...

He heard his name called and it surprised him. Time had slipped away while he had been standing there. The sky was a lighter gray and the hard rain had settled down to a steady, all-day drizzle. She called him again and he went to the bedroom door.

The baire was folded back and she lay swaddled in the cotton sheet, her milk-coffee arms and legs stretched out languidly. Her eyes were open, but she looked very sleepy. She sat up, stretched her arms wide, pulling her breasts tight. "I'm hungry," she said.

~

He trotted a half-block in the rain and ducked under the colonnade at Bechamin's. He bought a can of hot latte, some rolls, salami and provolone. As a boy, he had loved his father's bread-and-cheese Italian breakfasts as much as he loved his mother's eggs and biscuits.

Mr. Bechamin was behind the counter and the old Creole gave the detective a curious look, as if he was surprised to see him out and about. Valentin didn't notice. He stepped back onto the banquette with the sack under his arm.

~

When they finished breakfast, he cleared the table. She washed the dishes while he watched the rivulets running down the window. After a few minutes, he became aware of her voice. He looked up to see her standing by the table.

"I'm sorry, what?"

"I said if you want, I can buy a percolator," she said. "To make the coffee here. So you won't have to go out for it."

He nodded vaguely, but he wasn't really listening. She went back to the sideboard, dried the cups, put them up and then turned around, one hand on the edge of the sink. Valentin was leaning with his elbows on the table, his face cupped in his hands looking at the rain with a faraway expression.

"Valentin?" she said. He looked up at her. "I don't know what to do now."

He leaned back in his chair, returning his attention to the present. "Well..." he said, "what do you usually do?"

"I usually ain't up at this hour," she said with a nervous laugh.

He regarded her thoughtfully for a moment, then got up and went to the cold locker. He opened the wooden door, reached inside and produced a small can, made for spices. He twisted off the top and picked out five Liberty dollars.

"You can go to the five-and-dime if you like," he said, handing her the coins. "I'm sure you need more than a coffee pot."

She nodded. "I'll go get dressed," she said. He smiled. She smiled. They were behaving like students rehearsing for a school play. She left the kitchen, then came back to stand in the doorway. Valentin looked up from his seat at the table. "I ain't ever been much of the homebody," she said.

"That's all right," he told her. "Neither have I."

≈

She put on a white shirtwaist and silk skirt. Umbrella in hand, she went out the door, but not before kissing his cheek quite soberly. After she left, he sat at the table, staring at nothing. He couldn't shake a vague sense that something was wrong, but on this gray morning, his foggy brain couldn't fix on it.

He got to his feet and wandered about until he found a worn copy of poems and stories by Stephen Crane on the window ledge behind the couch. He carried it back to the kitchen, settled again at the table, and started reading.

∽

She was back not twenty minutes later. He looked up and saw the stricken expression on her face and there was a sinking feeling in his gut. He knew exactly what she was going to say, but asked anyway. "What is it?"

"Another woman got killed last night." Her voice was hushed.

He closed the book. "Where?"

"Basin Street."

"Where on Basin Street?"

"Florence Mantley's." Now her voice shook a little.

Valentin suddenly remembered knocking on Miss Mantley's door the night when he'd gone chasing after Bolden. "Who was the girl?"

"It wasn't a girl. It was Miss Florence." She looked at him, wide-eyed. "He went and killed a madam. If it was the same one, I mean."

"It was the same one," he said.

∽

He rode the streetcar to Basin Street and stepped down on the corner opposite Florence Mantley's sporting house. The police were long gone, except for two patrolmen huddled by the front door, sharing a smoke. He figured that one of them had been guarding the back gallery, got bored and left his post to join his partner. He cut across the street in the drizzle and made his way around the side of the house without being noticed. As he had guessed, the back door was unguarded. He slipped onto the gallery and into the kitchen.

He found two of Miss Mantley's octoroons—one of whom he knew slightly—huddled over a bottle of port wine at the kitchen table. She told him that the other girls had been sent away, but that they had been ordered by the police to wait there in case there were more questions.

He sat down at the table and listened to the scarlet sisters relate the events of the prior night.

It was around three-thirty when they heard Miss Mantley's loud voice in the hall, followed by a shriek and a sudden crash of glass. The girls ran out of their rooms just in time to see a shadow flee down the stairs. (One thought it was a tall man, the other insisted it was a short little fellow.) They saw the shattered glass and ran to the smashed window. Miss Florence's broken body lay two stories below. Someone ran for the telephone.

When the police wagon arrived, a fat detective with greasy hair snatched up the black rose that the killer had dropped at the top of the stairs. This same copper then rounded up all the girls and told them to say nothing to nobody, that as far as anyone knew it was an accident. Miss Florence could have been drunk and stumbled and fell out the window, he said. The fact that Miss Florence didn't take a drink didn't seem to matter.

Valentin asked directly which one of the sporting girls in the house was friends with King Bolden. The two exchanged a glance and then the one he knew said, "That would be Ella Duchamp."

⌒

He hadn't failed to notice that he hadn't been called to the scene of the crime and that no message had arrived from Anderson demanding his presence at the Café. He went there anyway. The doorman, a white fellow with pale, cold eyes, went off and came back to tell him that Mr. Anderson was busy. He was not invited to stay. Valentin wasn't surprised.

He understood that he needn't wait for a summons from Tom Anderson.

When he got back to Magazine, he found Justine had made market and was preparing a midday meal of cold chicken. He ate listlessly and she knew him well enough to leave him to his thoughts. She sat down across the table to eat. When she finished, she picked up his book and began to read, slowly, moving her lips over each word, her eyebrows knitting together as she guessed at meanings. After another half hour of silence, she took his plate away. He got up and went into the bedroom. She heard the springs rattling and squeaking as he tossed about on the bed. He reappeared an hour later and started wandering from room to room, his eyes fixed on the floorboards. Justine kept her distance by busying herself with tidying up. When she finished, she settled at the kitchen table again, poured herself a small glass of wine and picked up the Crane book. When he walked into the kitchen a few minutes later, she raised her eyes from the page.

"Well, I guess he's beaten me," he said, sounding sullen.

She put the book down. "What's that mean?"

"It means I can't stop him. He wins. He can kill every woman in the District if he wants to."

She thought about it. "So you're going to give it up now?"

He glared at her for a second, his eyes flashing, as if she had slapped him. Then his hand shot out and cleared the table in one furious sweep. Glass shattered, sweet wine splattered and the book arched away like a bird shot from the sky, pages all aflutter. She jerked away and lurched out of her chair, hiding behind her arms and backing into the corner. Her face was a paling, rigid mask and her hands came up, palms out with fingers splayed in the stark, frigid posture of an animal trapped and ready to fight.

He saw the sharp, hard angles of her face. The only other time he had ever seen her looking like that was the day he had met her, and that stopped him cold. For ten seconds they stood motionless, as the rain rattled along the gray windowpanes.

It was Valentin who broke the stare, dropping his gaze to the mess on the floor. Another moment passed and he put his hands on the edge of the table to steady himself. Then he reached down to pick up the book, brushing the broken glass from the open pages, dabbing a finger at the stains from the wine. He laid it on the sideboard and picked up a dishcloth, bent down, and began to wipe at the purple splatter on the floor, collecting shards of glass as he went along.

Justine watched him move the table, replace the book, muck about with the rag. Her hands came down and she sagged into the corner. She watched him pick tiny crystal slivers from the floor with his fingertips. The hard lines on her face flowed together and disappeared.

She let him labor away for a minute longer, then kneeled down and took the cloth from his hand. "I'll help you," she said.

～

They finished cleaning up the mess and sat down at the table. Valentin poured new glasses of wine for both of them. Shamed by his behavior, he avoided her eyes.

She let him get settled. Then she said, "You know what my mama used to tell me back home? That if we was out on the bayou, you know, and we got lost? She said don't try to figure out where you are. Just go back to the place you got off the path. Where you went astray." She paused. He was brooding, but at least he was listening. "So maybe you need to go back to where you got off the path. Where you lost your way."

"That would be at the beginning," he said quietly.

"So that's where you start at. Go on and tell me about it." When it didn't get a rise from him, she said, "What, you think I'm too slow to understand?"

He shook his head. She watched him. His face had that gone-away look and she thought he was going to disappear back into his sulk. But then he started talking.

~

He had heard what she said, but said nothing at first. It felt odd, letting her know his business. Letting anyone know, for that matter. He was about to brush it all aside and change the subject. But then, quite abruptly, he began to tell her. "Five women have been murdered in the past six weeks." He stopped and glanced at her. She was leaning with one elbow on the table, her eyes narrowed, nodding. "Four in the District, one over on Perdido Street," he went on. "Four sporting girls, one madam. One Negro, one octoroon, one Jew, two white. Each one was killed in a different manner. But each time, the killer left a black rose at the scene."

"What'd that tell you?" she asked.

"Not a goddamn thing!" he snapped. He felt her cool gaze and sighed, retreating. "That it's the same party each time," he said.

"All right," she said.

"The first one was Annie Robie," he went on. "A Negro girl in the house over on Perdido Street. She was smothered with a pillow." He hesitated for a second, and then said, "As it turns out, Buddy Bolden was there late that night. He may have been her last visitor, in fact." He frowned. "And he's been back since." He told her about the scene that Miss Maples had related.

"That don't look good," Justine said.

"No, it doesn't." A niggling memory suddenly returned, an oddity that had come to him, a few words he had exchanged with Picot. "There was this one thing," he said. "There were no signs of a fight. No thrashing about." He scratched his jaw. "She was a healthy girl. She was being suffocated. Why wouldn't she fight it?"

"Maybe she couldn't," Justine said. "Maybe whoever killed her had some help."

Valentin stared at her. "If there was... if somebody held her down..."

"But that would mean there was two people killed her," she said.

"Two people," he said, then shook his head. He could follow that path later. "Next one was Gran Tillman," he continued. "White woman up in the District. She was strangled with the sash of her kimono. No witnesses there, either. Nothing at the scene."

"You mean nothin' but a black rose."

"That's right."

"King Bolden knew her, too?"

Valentin nodded. "He did. And she and Annie Robie were friends. That's what I thought it was all about. At first, I mean. Those two mixed up in some business."

"What business?"

"I don't know, but it seems Gran came into money right before she died. Or was expecting to. She bought herself a fancy dress and was going to pay Papá Bellocq to make her photograph. She told Lizzie Taylor she was leaving. Giving up the life."

"Where was she gettin the money for that?"

He stared at the wall, his eyes blank. "Well, what if... what if maybe it was blackmail? What if she knew who killed Annie? And so she decided she'd sell her silence. But the killer figured there was a better way to keep her quiet. A sure way."

"I guess that makes sense," Justine said.

He frowned sourly. "Yes, if that had been the end of it. But then we come to Martha Devereaux. And everything changes. As far as I can tell, Martha didn't know Annie or Gran Tillman. She was a good bit different from those other two. She traveled in better company."

Justine cleared her throat. "She was the one that was stabbed?"

"That's right. It was a horrible assault."

"And King Bolden knew her, too."

Valentin sighed. "He was down there asking after her the night she died." He saw Justine's look and grimaced. "I know. It looks bad. But it gets worse. He knew Jennie Hix, too. The one that was beaten to death down in Chinatown. I think she met him at an apothecary there." He scratched his jaw again. "I can't figure out what was a girl from the Jew Colony doing way down on Common Street."

Justine thought about it and said, "I know that sometimes if a girl's bad about the hop, the madam'll put the word out round the neighborhood, don't nobody sell nothin, to her. Else she won't be no good to none of the men. So maybe she had to go there."

Valentin wagged a finger in the air. "And that's where she met up with King Bolden." He took a sip of his wine and placed the glass carefully on the table.

"Florence Mantley was the last one," he said. "I figure it was just her bad luck. The killer was stalking one of the girls. She had just finished checking the rooms and she was at the end of the corridor. The window was right behind her. The killer came creeping along, looking for that gal, and she surprised him. A push and..." He made a sharp shoving motion with his hands and Justine blinked, startled. "She fell two stories," he went on. "It broke her neck. The killer ran off just as the girls came out of their rooms. That's as close as anyone's been to seeing him."

"Was that Ella Duchamp?"

"What?"

"You said 'looking for that gal.'" When he hesitated, she said, "Ella Duchamp was another one of his women?" He caught her look; she was thinking, *That makes five out of five. What more do you need?*

"There's no doubt about it," he admitted. "He's suspicious."

"I'd say he's more than suspicious."

He pondered in silence for a few moments. Then he said, "Why?"

"Pardon?"

"I don't know why. I still don't see a motive. A *why*."

"You ain't got any idea?"

He took another sip of wine. "Well, you'd think right away a fellow commits these kinds of acts, he hates sporting girls." He smiled dryly. "That's not Bolden at all."

"Maybe it's not what we—" She caught herself. "Maybe it's not what the girls do. Maybe it's that they're just out there for any man to visit. Easy to get to, you see."

"Then why weren't any crib girls or the streetwalkers on his list of victims?" he said. "Why only women who work in houses? Somebody down Robertson Street mentioned that and it's a damned good question."

She looked at him curiously. "You were on Robertson Street?"

He thought it better to avoid that, so he pretended not to hear. He put on his best thoughtful face and fought a wild urge to smile. There he sat, sifting the gruesome details of five brutal murders, and suddenly he was wriggling like a guilty husband, back from a round of sporting. Before he did smile, he plunged on. "Is it because they work in houses?" he said. "Is he maybe trying to take some kind of revenge?"

"Revenge for what?"

"An injury?" he guessed. "A slight?"

Justine said, "Well, you know there's always men bein' put out at Miss Antonia's. Never allowed back in." She raised one eyebrow. "Remember? That's how I came to meet you."

Valentin pressed the tips of his fingers together. "Never allowed back in," he said. "Yes, someone could take offense at that." Justine looked at him as something occurred to her. "What?" he said.

"Well, there's one kind of man ain't never allowed into a house," she said. "Not in the District. Not as a proper customer."

Valentin's eyes went flat. "A Negro."

"Unless he's a professor. Or a cook."

"He sure ain't neither one of them," Valentin sighed, thinking about Bolden playing the part of the perfect suspect like it was a vaudeville routine. "Anybody who took a look at this would say he's the guilty one, no question."

"Anybody but you," Justine said. He didn't respond and she said, "Is it cause of you two bein' friends?"

He stared at the tabletop. "I don't know, maybe it is," he said. "But it ain't that I just won't look at the truth. After all these years, I figured I knew him better than anybody."

"But that ain't so," she said.

He glanced at her, then lowered his eyes. How quick she was; right down to the bone. "I don't know, maybe not."

Justine sat back, surprised by his confession. She wanted to ask more, but then she saw the wary look in his eyes and let it go. She said, "Tell me this. Could he do it?"

"I told you, I don't believe he would do some—"

"I asked you *could* he do it."

"Could he?" Valentin said. "Yes. But I could do it, too. Just about anyone *could* do it." He smiled without humor. "LeMenthe says it's hoodoo at work," he said.

"And why is that so hard for you to take?" she asked him. "You went to church, when you went, I mean. What's the priest talk about? Prayers and blessings. Spirits. The Holy Ghost. Satan. Evil deeds. I don't see a difference."

With a gesture of frustration, he said, "Oh, yes, there's a priest involved in this mess, too."

"What?" She was surprised. "What priest?"

He told her about Father Dupre, about the trip to Jackson, his strange plea, the rosary, the wreath behind the church. She listened, fidgeting with discomfort. When he finished, she said, "You think he has something to do with it?"

"Another thing I don't know," Valentin sighed. "I can add to it a drunken doctor named Rall, who treated Bolden and did the autopsies on the bodies of Tillman and Devereaux and Jennie Hix."

"What else?"

"There's been a man following me," he said. "The same one was on the train to Milneburg. Tall white man. Wearing a derby hat."

Justine said, "I didn't get much of a look at him."

Valentin looked away. "Do you know anybody like that?"

"A tall white man?" She smiled quizzically. "I'm sure I do. More than one. Why? Who was he?"

"If I knew, I wouldn't be asking," he snapped and Justine stared at him. He waved a hand, half an apology, and fell to brooding again. Except for the patter of the last of the raindrops on the window ledge, it was quiet for long minutes.

Justine spoke up first. "Why do you say for sure it's a man?" she asked. "A woman could do it, too."

"You didn't see what I saw. What he did to those girls."

"I don't care what he did," she announced firmly. "You hear what I say. A woman could do it, too." He guessed she was right, it was possible. But then she hadn't looked upon the broken, bloodied bodies of Martha Devereaux and Jennie Hix.

The storm had passed through and now the afternoon sun cast a soft swath through the windowpanes and across the floor. He had reached the end of it. She settled back and regarded him closely for a moment. "Did it hurt your pride?"

"What?"

"What Mr. Anderson said. All them thinkin' you didn't do right."

He got up from his chair and started pacing slowly. "Yes, I suppose so," he said. "But it's more than that. There's someone out there killing women whenever he wants. It's a true wonder. Just slips in, does it and walks out. Which is another reason I think it can't be Bolden. This is either a clever, clever fellow or one of the luckiest people alive, and he ain't either of those." He stopped and glowered. "But I don't care how clever or how lucky he is. He can't get away with it forever. Sooner or later, he's going to get caught."

"And you want to be the one catches him, ain't that right?" Justine said.

He looked at her. "No," he said, "I have to be the one."

Twelve

MANTLEY
Died
On Friday morning, May 31, 1907
at three o'clock
Florence Mantley
aged 41 years, a native of Baton Rouge and
resident of this city for the past eight years.
Mr. Tom Anderson invites her friends
to attend her funeral at
Gasquet's Funeral Parlor,
To-morrow (Saturday), June 1,
At 3 o'clock precisely.
Gasquet's, 224 Gravier

The preparations for Florence Mantley's last day above ground began at dawn, just as a weak, watery sun rose through the mist over the Gulf. The night of mourning was over and it was time to move on to the journey's end. The last of the visitors had left the front room of Gasquet's and stepped out onto Gravier Street some hours ago, and now the lid was closed on the coffin of heavy, dark mahogany where she lay adorned in her finest gown, her favorite gems, and a wig of auburn curls.

～

When the noon bells tolled, Justine hurried out of the bed and went for a bath. By the time Valentin roused himself, she had her clothes laid out, had thrown eggs into the frying pan and pushed a tray of biscuits into the oven. He sat down at the table, crossed his arms, and announced that he wasn't going. He wasn't about to show his face, he told her, not after all that had happened. She argued with him, insisted that he had to go, because wasn't it true that the killer might appear to see what his bloody hand had wrought?

It took the better part of an hour of pacing and fuming for him to give in. Even then, he lolled about, complaining under his breath, making such a nuisance of himself that Justine said he was acting like it was *his* funeral.

But at two-thirty, he found himself stepping onto Magazine Street in his black suit to board a streetcar for uptown and Gasquet's Funeral Parlor. As they passed the busy Saturday banquettes, he reflected grumpily on the odd turns his life was taking. There he was, in the midst of a string of murders, humiliated by the killer, being herded outdoors in dark suit and stiff collar, the very picture of a hen-pecked husband.

Justine turned her face to the streetcar window. He looked so fussy and unhappy that she wanted to laugh in spite of the grave business at hand.

By the time the car stopped at the intersection of South Franklin and Gravier, there were at least a hundred men and women, Negroes and Creoles and a smattering of whites, all dressed in dark gray or black, milling about the front entrance to Gasquet's. In an empty dirt lot at the side of the building, a marching band was waiting, the brass bells of the horns sparkling in the hot afternoon sun. At dirge-like intervals, the deep tentative thump of a bass drum punctuated the hushed murmuring voices. It was clear from the swelling crowd that Florence Mantley was a woman of some substance in the back-of-town neighborhoods on both sides of Canal Street.

Valentin and Justine joined the congregation. They saw the girls from Miss Antonia's huddled in a somber group and Justine walked over to talk to them. Valentin went along and waited by her side, his eyes scanning the crowd, noting the selection of local faces. He placed most of them as run-of-the-mill Saturday night sports and fancy men who had the respect to attend this solemn process, and tried to fix the others in his memory. But with his luck, the killer would be some common type who would disappear in this or any other crowd.

He didn't see Bolden about, but what would he be doing there? Even though he had first played music in parades like every other back-of-town musician, his horn was too wild for this sober task, so steeped in New Orleans tradition. In fact, brass bands herald every part of life, but none more extravagantly than the final passage into darkness. Uptown funerals were a sight to behold and a joy to hear; and in violent, disease-riddled New Orleans, the participants all got plenty of practice.

～

The first slow tones trebled from the bells of the horns and the bass drum began a steady rumble. Valentin looked up as a hearse with two white horses pulled around from the back of the building and headed up Dauphine at a stately pace, surrounded by a dozen octoroons, Miss Mantley's girls. Next came the madams of the tonier Storyville houses with their coteries, dappling the street in shades of brown, yellow and black. Valentin saw Antonia Gonzales, Lulu White, Lizzie Taylor, Countess Willie Piazza. A stone-faced Tom Anderson, host of the sad ceremony, walked along with Hilma Burt at his side. Then came two or three of the back-of-town madams, all shabbier than their Storyville sisters, including Cassie Maples with two of her Ethiopian girls and the homely maid Sally in an ill-fitting Sunday dress, clutching the madam's arm and looking startled by everything. Valentin nodded a grave greeting to all, spoke directly to no one, and was surprised when Anderson reached out and offered his hand.

But it was no polite gesture. The King of Storyville fixed the Creole detective with a blank stare, slipped a note into his palm, and then turned away. Valentin quickly recovered and stashed the paper in a vest pocket, feeling like half the crowd had witnessed the exchange. He went looking for Justine.

In the wake of the main body of the parade came the usual straggling mob of the curious, those with nothing else to do and eager for entertainment. This assembly represented a unique New Orleans brand of hellion, and their numbers would swell as the parade progressed, like a stream drawing flotsam from the banks.

He and Justine and the stragglers and this crowd—"the second line," as their number was called—fell into step as the funeral march began. The mood would remain somber for the entire twelve-block march to the cemetery as the band moved along in slow cadence, playing mournful hymns. It was a dark Mississippi of bodies, moving up the cobbled street past Charity Hospital and in the direction of the gates of "the City of the Dead," St. Louis Cemetery No. 2.

∽

The turgid army of second-liners stayed outside the walls, milling about on Robertson Street with their hilarity, while those attending to the grim business at hand moved silently down the narrow pathways that stretched between marble mausoleums with their oven-like biers stacked four-high into walls of brick eight feet deep.

No one was laid to rest below ground in New Orleans; the below-sea-level earth was so waterlogged that in earlier times caskets had been known to surface, sometimes float, even up-end and drop their ghastly cargoes into the light of day. So "the City of the Dead" resembled just that, a grid of tiny mansions and "fours" like tenement buildings, the dwellers all in the happy ranks of the deceased.

It was a show to the last. Even when the dear departed was not a person of means. In which case the coffin would be re-interred later in a more modest bier. But Florence Mantley could afford the best and so her remains would remain, encased for eternity in a fine marble tomb of classic Greek design.

The service was simple. A Catholic priest said prayers for the dead. The madam's friends and her staff of octoroons wept copiously into silk handkerchiefs. Eulalie Echo stood by, eyes closed in meditation, her presence an added comfort to Miss Mantley's departed soul. Grave-faced men lifted her coffin from the back of the hearse and carried it to a bier. The band played a slow spiritual. Justine watched the ceremony, lowering her gaze respectfully and whispering softly to herself. Valentin pulled at his damp collar and continued to study the faces in the crowd.

A soft murmur swept through the mourning as the gates to the bier closed with a grating sound that was quite final. The assembled mass snaked slowly back through the gates and onto St. Louis Street. As they drew near the gates, it seemed the pace of the steps on the paths increased, as if rushing to escape the Grim Reaper once more. As soon as the first of the feet stepped onto the cobbles, there was the sudden pounding of the bass drum, as sharp and loud as thunder, and then six brass horns and two clarinets and a saxophone split the day wide open. Now the parade could begin.

⌒

It was Bolden, crashing down the banquette from the Poydras Street saloon where he had started his afternoon. He was waving his cornet about like a sword and his eyes were bloodshot bright as he reeled drunkenly into the tangle of second-line bodies. The ruffians turned around, ready to fight, but when they saw who it was, a cheer went up. "Let him in! Let King Bolden in!" They were yelling. But when the marchers saw who was causing the commotion, they got their backs up and wouldn't budge.

He wasn't welcome. Since he started up his own bands, he had shown himself to be too busy, too drunk, too hung-over, or too full of himself to do his duty and join in the holiday and funeral parades. It was a disrespect that the first-line marchers took seriously.

So King Bolden got nothing as he came weaving up in their midst, his cornet blowing merrily. Their eyes spit messages as they played on, trying to ignore the man and his bullying horn. They changed the key, ragged the tune, raised the volume. But he kept charging ahead.

From a vantage point on the banquette on the north side of St. Louis, Valentin saw Buddy crash into the parade, saw the angry eddy of motion, sensed a brawl in the making. He grabbed Justine's hand and began edging his way around the crowd as it moved down the street.

But it was Bolden himself who calmed the waters. The first and second lines were snarling back and forth over the rattling drums, the marchers yelling "goddamn trash" at the second-liners and that bellicose group shouting back worse. Bottles and pieces of brick were starting to fly when Buddy lurched into the ten feet of space between the two and picked up the fast, happy version of "Just a Closer Walk with Thee" that the band was playing as it went by.

The black-clad first-line marchers continued to ignore him, turning their backs and tightening their ranks as they walked on. Bolden took no notice, zigzagging behind them on juking legs, delighting the second-liners and upsetting the marchers all the more. His horn flew above their heads like a bird flushed from the grass and his loud, dirty wave sound washed right over their tidy notes. Every time they tried to shift, he was one beat, one E-flat ahead. The rowdy noise of the crowd began to fall away as the skirmish began turning into a madman's show.

It was a Gatling gun against a wall of cannon, Bolden riddling the air with notes, the marchers firing back with their heavy brass, a momentary standoff of equal forces. Then one of the marchers, a clarinet player, succumbed to Bolden's rambunctious horn, broke ranks and started to follow it. Then a second and a third marcher fell out at the ends of the front line, caught up in his rowdy noise. And then the parade fell into a chaos that only Bolden could understand, horns and drums and bodies going off in a dozen directions.

The ranks reached the intersection and what remained of the front line tried to make a strategic turn down the crossing street. But they had taken only a few steps when someone realized that they no longer led the parade. One by one, they dropped their horns to their sides and looked around. The bass drum bumped one more time, then went silent. They turned, faces flushed. The music had gone on without them.

The jumble of bodies behind them closed, forming a huge, slow-rolling wheel. King Bolden was the hub, standing alone in the middle of the intersection while the parade orbited him. Valentin and Justine, standing just outside the circle, saw it all.

Bolden stood dead center, his horn pointed straight down at the cobblestones. A smile turned up the corners of his mouth. The motion of the crowd was slowing from a moving stream to a still pool. Streetcars rumbled on up Canal, but the hacks and surreys and two automobiles coming up on the intersection were all forced to a stop. Dogs jumped and yelped and small children raced around the legs of the men and the women, darting in and out to get a better view. Japanese fans and dark derby hats fluttered up little breaths of wind as parasols floated about like pond lilies.

Buddy now lifted the silver bell of his horn into the sultry air. He played one loud, pealing note, then stopped. He played another note, a fourth up the scale, this one quicker. Then the seventh, like the crack of a brass whip. Then he was hitting notes from all over the scale as he started to move, going round and round in a tight circle and tottering on the edge of balance.

He suddenly snapped out with his free hand and snatched a bottle of Raleigh Rye from some drunkard's grasp. A roar of laughter went up at the red-faced citizen's look of besotted surprise. King Bolden lurched on, played a fast, one-handed, downhill run of notes, took another quick swig from the bottle, played the same notes running up the scale.

He threw the bottle over his shoulder and it smashed onto the cobbles like the crash of a cymbal and he played off that, too, as he walked faster now, almost running. The machine gun of brass sprayed the crowd and they started getting a little crazy, the second-liners dancing on the banquette and in the gutters. Bolden went faster, made his circle wider, now bent a little at the waist as if the horn was flying off on its own and he was struggling to keep up.

Then came the moment when the two people who were standing in front of Valentin and Justine moved aside just as he was reeling by. Buddy saw his friend's face and stopped and stumbled back as if snapped by a rope, his horn still going blue blazes. He staggered a step to his left and Valentin moved to catch him before he fell, but he righted himself at the last second and the crowd nearby, witnessing the perilous balancing act, let out a whoop. The street tilted at a crazy angle and it was as noisy as a train wreck and King Bolden's face glowed, all full of black light. Every eye on the street was on him, every ear perked into the brass wind and voices were shouting out his name. "King Bolden! Oh, yes! King Bolden!"

He looked delirious as his horn danced on the hot air and another roar of laughter went up at the look on his crazy face. But what Valentin heard coming from the silver bell was too raw and piercing. He thought it sounded like a man crying out in torment and when the crowd before him shifted again, he caught his friend's eyes and saw a terrible, helpless pain, pleading for release.

∾

They sat on a perron as the parade moved on down the street and the horns and drums and shouts and laughs receded like a passing storm. Bolden had disappeared, too, a child's stick drawing staggering off into the echoing distance with the second-liners following in his ragged wake. Quite suddenly, it was another quiet, late Saturday afternoon in uptown New Orleans. Up and down Canal Street, the sounds of the rattling wheels of the streetcars and the clop of horseshoes on cobblestones could be heard again.

"I found out something," Justine told him presently. "Ella Duchamp, she's gone. Left town. Went off to Lafayette where her people are."

Valentin glanced at her, surprised again at her quick wits. He saw that she wore a troubled frown as she watched a last group of sporting girls straggle off. She looked so forlorn that he said, "What's wrong?"

"It's them girls from Miss Antonia's," she said after a moment. "The way they were looking at me."

"How's that?"

She stared into the distance. "Some of 'em were kinda sad, like they wish they coulda got out, too. But the other ones, the older ones, they was lookin' at me like...like 'you'll be back, young miss, don't you make no mistake about it.' Like that." She sighed. "I spose that's true, eh?"

Valentin said, "Not today, no," and she smiled wanly.

He went digging into his vest pocket for the note from Tom Anderson. He unfolded the paper and read the flowing scrawl: *Your services won't be required at the Café this evening. Please meet me tomorrow 9 a.m. at Miss Mantley's mansion.*

"You gotta go on to work?" Justine asked him.

He shook his head. So simple a message could have easily been whispered in his ear. So the delivery of the note was as telling as the words that were jotted on the paper. Anderson's stiff, silent greeting had been a show for the assembled crowd. He wanted it to be noted that he had accepted the private detective's hand, as a gentleman would, but that he had not spoken so much as a syllable to him. Valentin snickered darkly at his own foolishness; he had been roundly shamed in front of half of Storyville and hadn't even known it. He put the note away. "So what would you like to do?" he asked Justine.

She looked up and down the dirty street. "Go somewhere. Away from here. Up the bayou, maybe. Somewhere we can swim." She brightened. "Without no clothes."

~

The heavy banging on the door woke him from a dream about a parade of prostitutes walking through the gates of St. Louis Cemetery No. 2, a platoon of floozies, black, white and Creole, some in chippies, some in Mother Hubbards, some stark naked, their breasts bulging. A brass band marched along and though it seemed the whole thing was happening underwater, he could see a line of identical Buddy Boldens, each one wearing the same wild, hungry look as they manned the horns.

Then came a pounding like an angry drum and a rough male voice was calling his name. Justine woke up with a sharp cry; in one swift motion, he jumped out of bed and went for his pistol.

"Who is that?" She sat up, still half-asleep.

Valentin shushed her quiet, pulled on a pair of baggy trousers and went out of the bedroom as the pounding continued. He crossed to stand beside the front door. "What is it?" he barked.

"It's Willie Cornish," the voice rumbled. "Nora Bolden sent me."

Valentin opened the latch. Cornish, six-foot-three and black as pig iron, looked down at the detective. He appeared no happier to be there than Valentin was to have him. Valentin let the pistol drop to his side and opened the door the rest of the way. "What do you want, Willie? What time is it?"

"I'm—" he began, then: "'Bout one-thirty, I believe."

Valentin waved him inside and closed the door. "What's this about Nora?"

"She sent me round," Cornish said. "I mean, one of her neighbors telephoned at my sister's house. Said to tell me to go get Mr. Valentin and have him come to Buddy's."

"Now? What for?"

The big man shrugged his shoulders. "Whaddya think, what for? He's goin' crazy again."

"Valentin?"

The two men turned. Justine was standing in the bedroom doorway in her nightdress, looking like a sleepy child.

"It's about Buddy," he explained and turned back to Willie Cornish. Justine leaned against the jamb, listening. "The police been called?" Valentin inquired.

"I don't know 'bout that," Willie said. "The phone rang and this here woman's yellin' in my ear, sayin' Nora Bolden says please go get Mr. Valentin, have him come to the house right quick." The musician looked around. "You ain't got no telephone?"

"No, don't want one," Valentin said absently.

Cornish fidgeted. "Well?" he said. "You gonna go?"

Valentin thought about it for a moment, then nodded. "I'll go. Let me get dressed." He glanced at Willie. "You want to come along?"

"No, thank you, sir," the black man said with a frown. "I ain't goin' nowhere near him. I'm goin' home to bed." He glanced over at Justine and the expression on his face said he believed that's just where Valentin would be if he had any sense. He left without another word, closing the door behind him.

~

There were no streetcars running, but Valentin managed to catch a ride with a teamster who had chosen that odd hour to haul a load of nail kegs from the docks to a warehouse on Dryades. The driver, an ancient Negro, gave him a curious eye as they rolled north through the city. Down the streets to their right, the lights of Storyville glowed on like dozens of tiny fires.

He climbed down at the corner of First and Colonades and walked the remaining five blocks, all too aware that this could all be a waste of time and sleep, that when he reached the Bolden house more likely than not he would find that Buddy had either been hauled off to jail or was sleeping peacefully alongside his wife. And that he would face the two-mile walk back to Magazine in the dead of night.

But when he turned the corner onto First Street, he was met by the sight of what looked like half the neighborhood gathered around No. 2719. A mule-drawn police wagon was parked at an angle in the middle of the street. Valentin hurried his steps, then slowed as he moved closer and saw people milling about, talking and laughing. He heard the clink of bottles and the tootling of a harmonica. He made his way around the edge of the crowd of blacks and Creoles of Color and Italians. A New Orleans City patrolman lounged on either side of the perron at the Bolden front door. They were relaxed, enjoying the night air as they lazily twirled their nightsticks. Valentin glanced inside the house to see more people crammed into the front hall. "Is there a problem here?" he asked one of the coppers.

"Not anymore, St. Cyr," the other said.

He turned to find the patrolman, a white man his own age, wearing a sleepy smile beneath a waxed mustache. "You don't remember me?" the officer said. "Name's Whaley. We was in academy together."

Valentin placed the face, suddenly remembered the fellow as one of the few on the force who didn't join in shunning him and stayed halfway friendly after his run-in with the drunken sergeant. He was a jolly, sloppy sort, probably a bit too fond of the bottle, but a good beat cop, as Valentin recalled it. They shook hands.

"You out working this evening?" Whaley asked.

"No," Valentin said shortly. "What happened here?"

Whaley spit tobacco juice over his shoulder, hitting a bare patch of dirt six feet away. "Bolden comes home from Rampart Street, but instead of going to bed like a good fellow, he stands out here on the street, playing his trumpet and yelling and screaming. Woke up the whole neighborhood. We got a call. We was all ready to carry him downtown and lock him up, but by the time we got here, they had a damn ball going in the street." He laughed suddenly. "The same woman called in the complaint, she just came by and gave us hell for harassing law-abiding people trying to have a good time."

Valentin tilted his head toward the open front door. "He's inside?"

The patrolman nodded. "I believe they all in the kitchen."

～

He found Buddy at the kitchen table, holding court under the dim yellow glow of an electric light. The room was crowded, six or seven men and two women who looked like sporting girls. He was sitting in a straight-backed chair, his horn in his lap, drinking Raleigh Rye from a water glass. Bottles and glasses covered most of the tabletop. Nora was nowhere in sight.

He was in the middle of a story, something about a gentleman getting tossed off the gallery of a sporting horse and right into a pile of horse manure, when Valentin stepped into the room. He stopped in mid-sentence and his face lit up with drunken delight.

"Well, good God almighty, look who's out makin' the rounds!" he shouted. "Siddown, Tino. Have a drink." He waved his glass in the air.

Valentin shook his head slightly, and then gestured to the hallway behind him, his eyes flashing a message. Buddy's smile fell away and his neighbors got quiet. With a pronounced sigh, he drained his glass, stood up and walked out of the room. In the narrow hallway, he gave Valentin a cool look. Behind him, the chatter and laughter started up again.

Valentin saw the career of the day in Buddy's face. The first part of the afternoon in a saloon, then the wild performance at the funeral march, then the evening jassing for the sports and the sporting girls in some Rampart Street music hall (just as he and Justine frolicked under the stars in the cool, black waters of the bayou), then leading a crowd to a house party that included the better part of his First and Liberty neighborhood. The usual fight with Nora interrupted by the arrival of the police wagon. Buddy calming everything, then starting the party all over again as his wife carried Bernedette down the street to a neighbor's. But now his friend Valentin had appeared like a spell of cold rain.

Buddy crossed his arms and stared at the floor. "Whaddya want here?" he mumbled.

"Nora had somebody call when the coppers showed up," Valentin said. "She thought you were going to jail again."

Buddy looked up, exasperated. "It's just a social, is all. She ought not to worry. And you ought not to bother."

Valentin jerked a thumb at the two patrolmen standing just outside the door. "If they wanted, they could have taken you downtown anytime," he said. "Maybe you don't care, but it upsets her."

Buddy slid his bloodshot eyes at him. "What, is she payin' you, Mr. private detective?" Valentin didn't rise to the rough challenge. "Maybe you ought not be puttin' your nose where it don't belong. Maybe you could find somethin' else to occupy your time."

"You know, you're damn right," Valentin said. "Maybe I should just leave you on your own. And we'll see what happens."

It came out louder and harsher than he had intended, and the chatter in the kitchen behind them stopped abruptly. They both stood against the wall, not looking at each other, thinking their own thoughts. A young quadroon moved by, a neighborhood girl, giving them both a look as she went into the kitchen. Buddy watched her pass and smiled suddenly. "You ready to take that drink?" He looked happy again.

"I'm ready to go home," Valentin said and turned away.

"Hey, Tino," Buddy called out. "You wouldn't be so damn cranky if you got outdoors more."

Valentin stopped by the front door. "Is that right?"

The stiff, angry set of Buddy's eyes had gone away and he was now grinning like a fool. "You missed it," he said. "Funeral parade today."

"Oh, yes, for Florence Mantley," Valentin said, watching his friend's face. "That madam that got murdered in Storyville." Buddy stopped, looking confused, like he had forgotten what he had been talking about. "What about the funeral?" Valentin said.

"Oh." The bright expression crept back. "You shoulda seen me. I showed them damn marchers how."

"I saw," Valentin said.

Buddy's smile faded again. "You were there?"

"You knew Miss Florence?" Valentin asked.

He hesitated again. "I knew who she was."

"You hear what happened? Seems she caught someone creeping around the house. Surprised him. She was murdered on the spot. Pushed out the window."

Buddy nodded vaguely. "Uh-huh."

"You've been round her mansion, aintcha?"

Now Buddy's lip curled like he had just come upon something distasteful. "Me?"

"That's what I heard. You were looking for that octoroon girl. Miss Duchamp, ain't it?"

The horn player stared at his friend. He was about to say something when a renewed burst of laughter erupted from the kitchen. He glanced over his shoulder and when he turned back, his face had resumed its drunken giddiness. It was all making Valentin dizzy. "The parade," Buddy said. "You were there?" Valentin nodded. "How come I didn't see you?"

"It was a quite a crowd."

Buddy looked uncertain for a moment, then he laughed. "It was, wasn't it?" he said. "And did I show them damn marchers how?"

～

He watched Tino walk out the front door onto the dark street, then sagged against the wall and put fingers to his temple. His head was starting to hurt again. He heard someone call his name and he straightened and headed back to the kitchen, where his bottle and his audience waited.

Outside, Valentin asked one of the neighbors for a cigarette and leaned against the house to have a smoke before starting his long walk home. The crowd out front was thinning as the two patrolmen were urging the revelers to go to their homes and their beds.

The coppers were making ready to leave and the one named Whaley looked over and made a motion for Valentin to hop on the step-up at the back of the wagon. His partner glared, then pointedly ignored Valentin, who tossed the butt of the cigarette away, stepped over the banquette and climbed aboard. It was almost three o'clock when they pulled up at the corner of Common and Tulane, two blocks from his rooms. He and Whaley shook hands; the partner stared off over the river. Valentin had walked off only a few steps when Whaley jumped down from the seat as if he had forgotten something. They stood in the soft cone of light from the street lamp. "You want to watch out with that Bolden," the patrolman said in a low voice. "The word is out down to the precinct. Fellows saying he's gonna take a fall for them murders."

"Why?"

"Why not?" Whaley said. "Hell, somebody killed them women. People been talking, saying maybe it's him. I guess maybe's enough."

Valentin took a moment to glance casually back toward the wagon. Whaley's partner had turned his attention from the waters of the Mississippi to watch as the two men talked. "You could get yourself in a fix telling me this," Valentin whispered.

The cop snickered shortly. "Well, I wouldn't mind having you owe me a favor," he said. "I may be looking for a situation soon."

"So, that's it," Valentin said.

The patrolman shrugged. "You know how it is. Ain't nowhere to go if you ain't..."

Valentin understood; this simple fellow would never please the brass and never be mean enough or crooked enough to benefit from his badge. He'd walk a beat or ride a wagon until he retired. "You know if they actually got something on him?" he asked.

"It don't matter, does it?" Whaley said with a shrug. He looked away down the dark street. "But I believe I'd get shed of him if I was you. You get in the way, they'll just go ahead take both ya'll." The policeman stood by silently for a moment, as if waiting for his words to sink in. Then he waved a hand and strolled back to the wagon, leaving the Creole detective alone on the dark corner.

Thirteen

He could drink and he was a storyteller.
He couldn't go anywhere without making
a big splash. He could play, too. He took
up the ragtime, but he couldn't follow
through on it, he wasn't able.
— *Sidney Bechet*

Buddy heard glass exploding and his startled eyes flew open.
He lurched to his feet and a spike of white pain stabbed
him behind his eyes. The chair toppled backward and hit
the floor. He grabbed the edge of the table, blinking slowly,
trying to steady his trembling arms and shaking legs. There
were at least a dozen bottles on the table, some standing
upright, others on their sides, all empty or near so. Dead
soldiers. There was a dusting of ashes on everything and
burn marks in the paint where some careless fools had left
their butts. The room reeked of stale whiskey, stale cigarettes,
stale sweat.

He knelt down to right the chair and saw the shards of
the bottle that his outflung arm had knocked off the table.
He stopped to gaze, half-dazed, at the sharp, glinting glass
and at the brown trickle of whiskey that meandered across

the tiles to the corner. He heard a tolling of bells and stood slowly. He looked at the clock on the wall. It was not quite the stroke of noon. The tolling of bells. It was Sunday.

He picked up and put down four bottles before he found one with an inch of whiskey. He downed it in one swallow. The soft buzzing in his forehead let up a bit and he stood there, not wanting to move, trying to piece together the day and night before. The first image made him smile: a parade, a swirl of colors, people calling his name, his horn shouting louder and louder while he danced on the cobblestones. Then there were flashing moments from the low stage of a saloon, lights blazing red over his head like falling stars. Then he was back home with a crowd gathered round the table and Tino's face was in the doorway, a face that said he had done something. And after that, nothing.

He glanced down at his clothes. His shirt was stained with spilled drink and there were spots that looked like blood on his trousers. He thought maybe he should change, wash up and get himself into something fine, but the notion slipped away as quickly as it had arrived.

The bells tolled on. Nora and Bernedette would be making their way home from the service at St. John the Fourth. He thought about trying to clean up the mess on the table, then forgot about it and shuffled gingerly across the room, holding onto the table, sink, the corner of the sideboard, until he found his way to the door and out onto the gallery. The fresh air made him dizzy again and he grabbed the railing for a few seconds. Then he went down the rickety steps and across the backyard dirt and into the alleyway. It was better there, a dark, cool, silent place where he could hide.

～

Valentin found Florence Mantley's silent this Sunday morning, closed for good. A wreath was mounted on the door and bouquets of flowers—some filled with black roses, of course—were strewn about the gallery. He knocked on the heavy door until an old colored maid appeared. She didn't want to allow him in, but he mentioned Mr. Tom Anderson and she changed her mind. She ushered him inside and left him alone in the front parlor. She retreated to the kitchen, though every few minutes she peeked at him through the doorway.

He found a short glass vase filled with Richmond Straight Cuts on the mantle, took one and sat down on the overstuffed couch. The room, the house, and the street outside were quiet. He dug a lucifer from his vest pocket, flicked it against his thumb and sat back, blowing a gray plume into the air.

So Bolden had been all but pronounced guilty of the murders. Mostly, he suspected, because he was King Bolden. But maybe there was more. Sitting there in that silent room, he decided to put Bolden to the test and see how he fared.

Buddy would have to have a motive first and a means second. The motive could be the fact that he was at least half-crazy. True enough. Hadn't Valentin himself witnessed how he could go from calm and even-tempered to a spike of rage in a sudden second? Or the way he attacked his cornet, as if he could never play loud enough, fast enough, hard enough? As if there was something under his skin or down deep in his lungs or fixed somewhere in the tangle of his brain, crying to get out?

Put yourself in King Bolden's shoes, he reflected, and it all could make a horrible kind of sense.

You're a nobody, a commonplace fellow living an ordinary life. And then one morning you wake to find you're not that no-account person anymore, but a one-man miracle, a comet lighting up the back-of-town skies. People are telling you you're the best there is, the best ever. You can't buy your own whiskey no matter where you go, pretty girls tussle for as much as a word from your famous lips, and everyone you meet calls you "King." Best of all, they fill up the saloons and music halls, dance and shout to the tune of your horn, your music, you.

The colored boys especially, their eyes gazing up at you so proud they look like they're about to burst. Even white folks stand aside when you step by. You did it. What no other Negro ever did, at least not in this town. You did it. You're the one. King Bolden.

What a wild ride it would be, but it didn't last. It couldn't last. Buddy was too much of a madman and people were too fickle; and he had been so wrapped up in it that he never saw it coming. It all started to fall apart on him and he couldn't seem to fix it. It would be a cruel blade.

Valentin recalled Frank Mangetta's picture of Bolden, the one who broke all the rules, set a new pace, but ended up stuck in a trap of his own making, unable to move forward, unwilling to step aside for someone with a better lip and quicker fingers, someone less fond of Raleigh Rye and hop and the sweet flesh of the back-of-town whores. And what if some of those same women started thinking that maybe Mr. Bolden's day was done and he wasn't quite so special anymore...?

The cigarette had burned down. He got up, tossed the butt in the fireplace, and took a fresh one and another lucifer from the mantle. As he lit the cigarette, he noticed that his hands shook a bit. He started to pace the floor, letting himself think it: What if it's true? What if Buddy did those killings?

There was no telling how it might have started. Maybe he didn't mean to murder Annie Robie at all. A fit of rage and it was over. The victim's friend Gran Tillman would know, maybe try to turn a profit for her silence, so she would have to go, too. Who knows what Martha Devereaux did or said, but the demon rose up and took a knife to her. Jennie Hix crossed his path in Chinatown and lost her life. He was going after Ella Duchamp when he ran up on Florence Mantley.

If it was so, he wondered if Buddy had any notion what havoc he had wreaked; and he wondered, even more grimly, what it would take to stop him.

He blinked. What was he thinking? Buddy Bolden could not have murdered five women. It could not be true.

Of course, Valentin St. Cyr's "could not" would not make a bit of difference to the coppers. Buddy Bolden was a good-for-nothing, jassing Rampart Street nigger and so was capable of anything. He made a bad example. He had octoroons and maybe even white women sweet on him, and he got into houses that other Negroes couldn't even approach. Women were weak. He had charmed his way into their rooms and done his dastardly work. Add it all together and it was quite enough for the New Orleans Police Department. But it was not enough for Valentin, not nearly.

He tossed the cigarette and crossed to the windows. He pulled the curtain aside to gaze at the street. There was no sign of Anderson, just a few random souls late for Mass at St. Ignatius hurrying along the street. A hack passed, a clattering of hooves and wheels that echoed down the line. From the kitchen, he heard the maid start singing "Jesus Is Going to Make Up My Dying Bed" in an old, soft voice.

He thought some more. His gut told him there was something amiss in the equation, something very wrong about casting Bolden as a murderer. He resumed his slow pacing, brooding so intently on it that he did not hear the rattling cough of the automobile engine in the alley, nor the back door opening, nor the footsteps on the heavy Persian rug in the sitting room. He sensed a presence and looked up to see the King of Storyville standing in the arched doorway, wearing an off-white linen suit and holding a light tan derby in one hand.

Anderson stepped into the room and placed his hat on a chair. He reached inside his jacket and pulled out a dark cheroot, then patted his pockets until Valentin stirred, crossing to the end of the mantle for a lucifer. He struck a flame on the brick face of the fireplace and held it as the end of the cigar glowed an angry orange. Anderson nodded a thank you and blew a thin rail of smoke from beneath his thick mustache. His eyes roamed about the room. "She certainly ran an upright house," he said rumina-tively. "She was a credit to the District. It's a great loss."

"Yes, sir, it is," Valentin agreed.

"These terrible murders..." He took the cigar from between his lips, gazed at the spiral of smoke. "I heard King Bolden put on some kind of show out on the street yesterday," he said. "Some kind of show indeed."

Valentin wondered if Anderson expected him to comment, decided not.

"Chief O'Connor told me weeks ago that he was a suspect." The white man settled a cool gaze on Valentin. "But you don't believe he's involved, do you?"

Again, Valentin knew it wasn't a question and kept silent. Anderson gazed out the window and puffed his cigar. "I promised my friends in Mayor Behrman's office and the State House that I would resolve this situation. I assured those distinguished gentlemen that here in the District, we could keep our house clean. I convinced them that there was no reason to think about bringing in outside agencies. Outside agencies that might stay beyond their welcome, if you see my point." He now leaned a shoulder against the mantle and crossed one foot with the other in a posture that was too casual. He studied his cigar.

"You're a very smart fellow, Valentin. You should have understood my position. Or maybe you did and you just didn't care." He puffed reflectively and when he spoke again, his tone had a hard edge. "Five women murdered, King Bolden walks the street like he owns them, and you won't lift a finger to stop him."

"He's a scapegoat," Valentin said.

Anderson ignored the comment. "What happens when your murdering friend decides to wander outside the District, maybe over to the Vieux Carre or the Garden District? What then? What does that say about me? I'll tell you what it says. It says I can't police my own streets. It says I can't solve my own problems. I don't like that. I don't like that at all, goddamnit!" The voice had gone up to a thunderous pitch. He now straightened and drew a deep breath, calming himself.

"You're a colored man," he said flatly. "A Negro by blood and by law, no matter how many star coaches you ride in or how many books you read or how many white men you put down. By law and custom, you're a nigger, a darkey, as sure as if you just came out of a cotton field with a rag around your head. Or a Dago, which isn't much better. If those people knew your little secret..." He took a short puff on his cigar. "I knew it, but I engaged you anyway. I had such a regard for your talents." He looked at Valentin, sighing heavily. "This is a terrible disappointment," he said. He brooded for a few seconds more, then drew himself up, squaring his shoulders. *Here it comes.* Valentin thought.

"You are dismissed from my employ, Mr. St. Cyr," the King of Storyville said, his voice heavy as iron. "I can't abide your actions. Or lack of actions. You've had your head in the sand while those women were ravaged, one after another. You've betrayed my trust. Protecting that madman Bolden was more important to you than your duty to me and to the District." Anderson glared at him. "What, did you think it would end, that he would get his fill and stop?" he said. "Did you think he'd just go away and leave us all in peace?"

"I'm telling you it's not him," Valentin said in a low voice.

Again, Anderson didn't bother to respond. "I'm going to let you in on a bit of news," he said. "He is not long for these streets. Even if he gets away with these killings, he's finished. And it's been a long time coming. He's beyond control. He's a drunk and a hophead. He's got Negroes and Creoles and whites mixing together in those dance halls. He chases after white women himself. We have laws against that sort of thing. And there are plenty of people in this city who don't like him. People of influence. They don't like that music he plays and they don't like the way he carries on. He has no respect. He's bound for trouble."

The King of Storyville's pink face had once again grown red as he wound through this speech. He paused to puff his cheroot. Valentin stared past his now-former employer. Let him—let all of them—think what they wanted about him, and about Bolden. They were wrong. And he would live without this white man's money.

Anderson was watching him, as if reading his thoughts. "You can expect that your services will not be required by anyone in the District," he said, with what sounded like a touch of regret. He shook his head and his voice softened. "Listen to me, Valentin. I'll give you a last word of advice. Get out of the way. There are people in this city who would just as soon see you right alongside your friend Bolden, wherever he ends up."

He tossed what remained of his cigar into the cold fireplace and, with a last, long look at the Creole detective, walked out of the room. Valentin heard his footsteps proceed to the kitchen. Anderson exchanged some muffled words with the maid, and then the back door opened and closed.

Valentin stood there until he heard the distant sound of a motorcar stutter to a start and then chug-chug-chug down a side street, to the barking of the neighborhood dogs.

The unemployed Valentin St. Cyr reached for a third cigarette.

～

Justine had pulled the old curtains down and was washing the tall windows. In a thin cotton housedress that was tattered at the hem and the sleeves, a scarf tied over her head and rubbing at the glass with old pages from *The Sun* and ammonia from a bottle, she looked like she was playing the part of the maid in a stage play.

She smiled when she caught sight of him rounding the corner from Common Street. She stopped what she was doing to watch him approach and her smile faded. Even at that distance, she could see how troubled he looked, all but dragging his feet along the banquette. His appointment with Mr. Anderson had not gone so well. She had said prayers at Mass for him, but she could see from his bent back, the stiff set of his arms and his slow, stalking pace, that her prayers hadn't done much good.

∿

Pale light filled the room as he stood, arms crossed, relating most of Anderson's lecture, ending with the word that he was finished around the District. "He says I failed him."

Justine leaned against the windowsill.

"Oh, I failed all right, but not because I was protecting Buddy," he said. "I failed because I couldn't muddle through this mess and catch the true killer."

She was quiet for a few seconds. Then she said, "Does this mean I have to go back?"

He looked at her. "Back?"

"To Miss Antonia's."

He threw up his hands with a *"No!"* so sharp that it gave her a start. Then he muttered something she couldn't catch and stalked out of the room. She went back to cleaning in the kitchen. As she worked, she heard him in the other room and peeked out to see him stare at the floor, then throw himself down on the couch, then jump up and pace around some more. She was scrubbing at the sideboard when he stepped into the doorway.

"I can find work," he announced. "I can get along without Anderson and those damn madams. I can get along fine."

"I know that," she said. She watched his face. "What about King Bolden?"

"I was told that if I'm not careful, I'll go down with him."

She thought about that and said, "Then it's just as well it all turned out like this."

His eyes flashed and he started to say something, and for a moment she thought he was going to start throwing things again. But he just turned around and walked out. A moment later, she heard the front door slam and his footsteps echoing down the stairwell. She put her rag aside and went to the balcony. She watched him until he turned the corner at Canal Street, heading back toward the District.

～

Countess Willie V. Piazza took the Creole detective's arm and walked him through the parlor. At a mahogany table next to the street window, three men—two white, one who looked like a Mexican—sat talking in low voices. Their whispers stopped and they glanced coldly at Valentin as he and the Countess entered the room. He recognized one of the white men, Guy Molony, a murky, secretive rounder and sometime Pinkerton man. The other two were strangers. By habit, Valentin noted their features, pushed them into a drawer in his memory, all in the few seconds it took to reach the far side of the room.

Though Molony's partners were dressed in identical clean white shirts and cotton trousers, they were swarthy and rough-edged, like they belonged in some jungle outpost. Their faces glowed in fierce shades of red as they drank from glasses of whiskey. The white fellow's hair was cropped in short, spiky points and the Mexican's black curls were slick with oil. Molony, looking like a particularly dapper fancy man that day, turned away before Valentin could address him.

Valentin escorted Countess Piazza through an archway and into a sitting room cluttered with ornate bric-a-brac on little shelves. The madam released his arm and drew the sliding doors closed. She gestured to a French chair as she took a seat that resembled a throne. "What's Molony up to now?" Valentin asked as he sat down, an automatic response to intruders on his territory. Then he remembered it wasn't his territory anymore, at least not by Tom Anderson's reckoning.

The Countess arranged herself. "He's got a couple wild boys out there," she said with a sly smile. "They're mercenaries. Soldiers of fortune. Lee Christmas and Manuel something." She laughed lightly. "Molony tells me they're going to assemble an army and invade the country of Honduras." Valentin raised his eyebrows in polite surprise and the madam shrugged her round, elegant shoulders. "Who knows?" she said. "Perhaps I can some day say that a revolution was hatched right out there in my parlor."

The madam was clearly delighted at the idea. Valentin, who knew little of affairs outside the District, and cared less, said nothing. The doors slid open a few feet and one of the girls, a pretty quadroon like all the residents of the house, stepped into the room and bent to whisper in the Countess' ear.

Valentin watched his host as she spoke to the girl in a low voice, still baffled by her hospitality.

He had left his rooms, walked the eight blocks to Conti Street and went around to Antonia Gonzales'. At that door, he was told that the madam was indisposed, could he please call back another time? He then walked back to Basin Street to Lulu White's, where he received a similar message—the madam was said to be busy with a special customer—though the girl at the door whispered that Miss White expressed her regards. Tom Anderson's warning hadn't been an idle one, and so he mounted the gallery steps of Willie V. Piazza's mansion expecting yet another curt dismissal.

He was surprised, though, when the madam herself appeared and waved a quick hand, ushering him inside, though she did pause to cast a furtive glance up and down the street. Of all the women who had contracted his services, Countess Piazza was the one he would have thought most eager to be rid of him. While her taste for Continental conventions—including intrigue—demanded private security, Valentin knew she thought him the least of an array of evils, the best pick from a crude litter of thugs, hoodlums, and road tramps. She kept him always at arm's length; they had exchanged at most a few dozen words in all the months he had worked for her, most of them to explain that an appearance once a week was all that was required unless, of course, a situation arose.

But the only time he had ever been called to the house outside of his regular weekly visit was to dissuade an amorous Spanish prince from throwing himself from a second-story window. The prince was distraught because one of the Countess' lovelier quadroons would neither return his pledge of undying love nor accept his invitation to sail to Spain to become his mistress. The girl was Arkansas-born and didn't want to be so far from her kin. Valentin talked the broken-hearted prince down from the window ledge and sent him and his aggrieved Castilian heart away.

Countess Piazza rewarded the Creole detective with an extra twenty-dollar gold piece, but never said a word about the incident. She would expect the discreet touch.

Of course, she was not without her pretensions. Though her swarthy skin, long, fleshy nose, heavy eyebrows and coal black hair loudly proclaimed Italian blood, Willie Piazza was no more a countess than Valentin was a saint. But she was so convincing in the role that it never occurred to anyone around the District to question it; and no one close to her would presume to pry into her affairs, least of all her private security man. It remained a mystery and part of their bargain. If there was still a bargain for them to keep.

She waved the quadroon girl away and turned to Valentin with a sigh and a frown. "How did things ever come to this?"

she said and her tone, precise and cultured, held a tragic note. "Poor, dear Florence Mantley. Thrown from a window. May her soul rest in peace." Valentin nodded gravely. "And now you, Mr. St. Cyr," she went on. "It seems they've taken to killing the messenger."

Valentin gazed at the madam, a bit startled.

"You've paid a visit to Miss Antonia and Lulu White?" she went on, studying her fingernails. "And they sent you on your way?"

"Yes, they did."

"Did they tell you in person?"

"No, ma'am."

The Countess shook her head angrily. "Antonia called me up on the telephone. She got a message from Lulu White. Who got a message from Hilma Burt. Who informed her that Mr. Anderson preferred that we not retain the services of Mr. St. Cyr. The reason being that your mishandling of these murders is a black eye to all of us. And there was some mention of your friendship with King Bolden." Valentin nodded glumly. "Well, Hilma Burt and Lulu White and Antonia Gonzales don't run my business," the madam went on. "You won't get that sort of treatment at this address. I owe you that much."

He let out a sharp breath. "Those two should be ashamed," the Countess said. "Tom Anderson should be ashamed. And I'm appalled that I have to be a party to it." Her tone turned regretful. "But you understand that I can't conduct business without Anderson's blessing." She shook her head slowly, looking troubled. "Why he thinks you're at fault, I don't know."

"He says I let him down be—"

"You?" the madam broke in. "I don't see his friends in the police department cleaning up this mess. All those detectives, the pride of New Orleans, they don't have one idea about what to do, and somehow it becomes your fault? That's an odd bit of logic, I'd say."

Valentin said, "They believe King Bolden is the guilty party and that he's my responsibility."

The madam paused to regard him. "And what do you believe, Valentin?"

He stared down at the designs in the thick carpet, creeping vines entwined with creeping vines. "I know him," he said. "We grew up together. I don't think he has the nature." He grimaced. "I happen to know what it takes to kill a person."

Countess Piazza sat back. "Oh, yes. That fellow over in Algiers." Her black eyebrows knit together. "But people do change, don't they?" she mused. When Valentin didn't speak up, she added, "Friend or no friend, he is a disturbed man. That's a fact." She folded her hands in her lap. "What about the other part? Do you believe you're responsible for him?"

"I believe I'm his last chance," he said.

The madam nodded thoughtfully, then sighed once and extended ring-adorned fingers that held a small envelope. "This is something to help you along," she said. "I hope one day I will find you back in my employ. But for now..." She sighed again, deeply, then wished him luck and called for one of her girls to see him out.

❧

He was grateful for Countess Piazza's sentiments and the five gold pieces he had found in the envelope. But fifty dollars wouldn't last forever, and her kind thoughts wouldn't buy him as much as a ride on the No. 34 streetcar. Now, as he wandered north on Basin Street, eyes downcast, he tried to imagine how he would make up for the money he was going to lose. Maybe, after all of it was over, he'd end up down on the docks, just like his father.

His brooding was interrupted by a tug at his sleeve. LeMenthe—Mr. Jelly Roll Morton—had come along behind him without a word.

"How's tricks?" the piano player asked, eyeing him carefully.

"They could be better," Valentin replied.

Jelly Roll was trying to act cool and calm, but he was wearing a little nervous smile and he kept pulling his hands in and out of the pockets of his cotton trousers. "How was your visit with my godmother?" he said.

"It was...helpful," Valentin told him.

"I thought she'd put you right on them murders." Valentin made a noncommittal shrug and the piano man's brow furrowed. "It's just too damn bad about Bolden," he said.

Valentin blinked. Who said anything about Bolden?

"He shoulda never messed with that hoodoo," Morton pronounced, getting excited. "It got him good. He's just all full of bad *juju*."

"Maybe so," Valentin said, thinking that maybe Morton and all the rest of them were right. It was all the voodoo. He was ready to believe anything.

"You know what I say?" Morton muttered. "I say you better be damned careful if you go chasin' the devil's tail. Cause you just might catch it." With that, he turned and sauntered away.

Fourteen

Bas wants to know who is the one they have dubbed the "Black Rose Killer" in the spate of recent deaths in the Tenderloin?

It seems that the dastardly fellow leaves a black rose behind wherever he causes his mayhem, hence the name.

Someone knows who it is, but isn't saying.
—*The Sun*

Valentin felt curiously at ease for a fellow who faced Monday with an empty plate before him.

He had arrived back at his rooms the evening before to find that Beansoup had shown up at the door on an uninvited visit. Justine took pity on the boy and insisted that he stay for dinner. So they spent the evening sitting at the kitchen table and later on the balcony, he and Justine drinking wine and listening to Beansoup tell preposterous stories about his exploits. When it got late, she invited him to sleep on the couch and she made him a fine bed there. Valentin stood by, a silent witness to her continued nesting. With Beansoup tucked in and snoring softly, they went to the bedroom and frolicked before falling into a sound sleep.

That one evening with no talk of murders or crazy King Bolden or anything at all about Storyville had worked to lighten his spirits. What was done was done, and he was surprised to find himself feeling a certain relief. He shoved aside his guilt at leaving Bolden to his own devices. He had lost his livelihood defending that maniac, and that should be enough for old time's sake. It wasn't like they were the best of friends anymore; those days were long gone. He didn't even think much about what he was going to do next. For one day, he would attend to his own simple pleasures.

Even the weather was cooperating, the streets morning bright. Downstairs at the tobacco shop, he exchanged pleasantries with old Gaspare, bought himself a packet of Richmond Straight Cuts, and put a nickel on the counter for the morning edition of *The Sun*, like any other regular fellow. He had to smile at the picture he must have presented as he stepped onto the banquette.

He leaned against a lamppost to peruse his paper. He noted with appropriate interest that the murder trial of Leonard K. Thaw was still the big national story, with a debate over the sanity of the killer of millionaire Stanford White marking the headline. Further down the page was news of a war brewing in Nicaragua, items on the battle over railroad trusts, and a visit by the Ambassador from Japan. There was also notice of the passing of a prominent New Orleans attorney and a cartoon drawing of Teddy Roosevelt with huge mustache, teeth and glasses on a globe-sized head, perched upon a tiny pony. There was no mention of the Storyville murders, at least no front-page mention.

He almost didn't bother to go any further, but his curiosity led him on and there it was on page two, a story about the grand funeral of Miss Florence Mantley, late of Basin Street. It was a transparent piece that mourned the madam's passing and made only slight reference to the "undisclosed accident" that had caused her tragic death. It seemed Anderson and the police had managed to keep Miss Mantley off the killer's resumé, at least for the moment. Good luck to them, he mused vacantly.

Turning another page, his eye was caught by the column by the character who went by the moniker "Bas Bleu," known as the prime monger (and often creator) of gossip from the Uptown streets. The fellow, who through much subterfuge kept his identity unknown, feared no one, not Anderson, nor the Mayor, nor the Police Department, nor the criminal elements. He barked at the stuffy Americans on one side of Basin Street and the scarlet kings and queens on the other. His ear was to the wind and he would flaunt a rumor in the blink of an eye.

Bas led this day's charge with some banter about a certain prominent madam's recent dramatic weight gain. He turned his attention to a local businessman, "old Jew Myers," and a suspicious contract to sew uniforms for the police department. Then he plunged on to a screed about the "strange passing of Miss Florence Mantley, in the wake of the violent deaths of at least four sporting girls in the Tenderloin." Valentin straightened, feeling uneasy, and read on.

> *What is afoot in Anderson County? The good word has it that a certain obstacle has been removed from the case (with a 'good riddance' from Mr. Tom, Chief O'Connor, and the hoi-polloi of the demi-monde), and the police now have a clear path to ending this terrible string of crimes, which some are calling the "black rose murders." It seems this certain fellow had neither the nerve nor the wits to handle such serious business and has been put quite rightly in his place.*

Valentin stared at the print, feeling his breath grow short as a rush of blood rose to his face. He cursed, then let out a bitter laugh at the sheer audacity of the item. He read it

again, galled as much by the words on the page as what—
and who—was behind them. The nix was out on him and it
could have come only from one source: Anderson, no doubt
by way of Billy Struve. It was intended to get Uptown
whispering, to clear a path so that Buddy Bolden could be
lynched without a rope. It was so clever he had to admire it.
He crumpled the newspaper, pitched it directly into the
gutter and stalked away down Magazine Street.

∼

Justine had opened the door and stepped onto the balcony
just as he appeared on the banquette, so close that she could
almost read the newspaper over his shoulder. She saw him
lean his lazy body on the lamppost and read over the front
page. She saw him turn unhurriedly to the inside and peruse
another page, looking so at ease and she thought of calling
his name, surprising him, just to see the look on his face.
He turned another page and she saw him tense. He read for
a moment, then looked away, shook his head, and started
reading again, his posture going all stiff with anger.

A few moments later, he crumpled the paper, looking
like he wanted instead to tear it into pieces. He tossed it
into the gutter and stalked away, his head bent to the
banquette, as if there was something hanging onto his
coattails that neither his jerking steps nor the morning breeze
from the river could dislodge.

She watched him stop on the corner at Gravier, stare at
some point in the distance, then continue at a foot-dragging
pace, a man swimming upstream in a river of trouble. She
hurried down to the street, bought herself a copy of *The
Sun*, and scanned it until she found the article. Reading
slowly, she felt her heart sink. For a little while, she had
thought it was all over.

∼

For the next two days, he skulked about, barely uttering a
word to her. She kept busy with the rooms and did her best

to stay out of his way. He disappeared for long hours without explaining, and at night he made no move to her, but tossed about so much that she barely slept at all. Beansoup, however, had found Valentin's couch much to his liking, and Justine didn't have the heart to send him back out on the street. He wandered who knew where during the days, but he always found his way back to Magazine Street in time for dinner.

One afternoon, he showed up with a small Negro boy from the Colored Waifs Home named Louis something. Beansoup, it turned out, had bragged to his friends about the Creole detective and the Creole detective's friend King Bolden, and young Louis was eager to get a close-up look at the famous trumpet player. Disappointment showed in his button eyes when he found that King Bolden was not on the premises. Justine invited him to stay and eat, but he refused politely and went away.

⌒

Valentin walked up the steps to his rooms on Wednesday afternoon, just as a hard rain returned to pelt the streets. Justine was sitting on the couch, reading one of his books. After a few minutes, she caught him acting strangely, walking around, glancing at her with his eyebrows knit, then sitting down, getting up, and doing it all over again. Finally, catching another of his looks, she said, "What's the matter?"

"I was an *obstacle*," he said. She closed the book. He stood in the middle of the room, his arms crossed. "You should see the way they look at me on the street. Like I'm the one did those murders."

"But what do you care what them people think?"

He began pacing up and down. "That's not it. Don't you see? Now they'll say Bolden's guilty, but they couldn't hang charges on him because his pal St. Cyr got in the way."

"Well, there ain't nothin' you can do about that," she said quietly.

Valentin scowled and nodded briefly. "Maybe not. But before he's arrested, convicted and put to death, some evidence of his guilt would be in order."

She saw the sudden glimmer in his eye. "But, you're out of it now," she reminded him. "You said so yourself."

He stopped pacing and clapped his hands together in sudden animation. "Exactly! I don't work for Anderson anymore, and I sure don't have to worry about Picot and the coppers. I was an obstacle. They wanted me out of the way and they got their wish."

"But didn't Mr. Anderson say—"

"All he said was that I wasn't working for him," he told her. "He didn't tell me not—" He stopped and stared blankly at the wall for a moment, as a notion came and went. He shook his head. "I can do whatever I want. And what I want is to find out once and for all if Buddy had anything to do with those murders."

"How?"

He thought about it. "Maybe I'll ask him."

"Do what?"

"I'll ask him if he did it," he said. "It's the one thing I haven't done since this mess began. The one thing I guarantee nobody's done. Ask him if he killed those women and see what he says."

"Well, he's not going to admit to it," she said, and looked at him thoughtfully. "But what if he does? What if he says, 'Yes, I did it.' And then he tells you how, and when, and everything else? What if it has been him all along, Valentin? What'll you do then?"

"I'll turn him over to the coppers," Valentin said. "Or take care of it myself. Shoot him in the head and put him out of his misery."

"You could do that?"

"I could, yes," he said, looking starkly grim. "By God, after all this, if I find out it was him, I swear, I'll put him in his grave."

～

Magazine was getting noisy with the chatter of wagon wheels on cobblestones, the bleats of automobile horns trading with the whinnies of horses, the blue crackle of the streetcars, the early whistles of tugboats on the river. Morning light drifted through the windows.

Valentin made up a pot of coffee on the kitchen stove, chewing on a French roll while he waited for it to boil. He went back into the front room and woke Beansoup with a gentle shake. The boy sat up. He looked so comical with his hair sticking out at ridiculous angles and his befuddled expression that Valentin almost laughed.

Beansoup followed his host into the kitchen on stumbling bare feet and sat down at the table. Valentin put a cup of chicory coffee and a roll before the boy and then took the opposite chair. Beansoup slurped his coffee and gnawed hungrily at the roll, every now and again glancing over his shoulder, now wide awake and able to appreciate a peek at Justine in her nightdress.

Valentin brought his attention back around. "I need your help with something," he said and the kid stopped eating and began to grin.

～

After Beansoup had finished his breakfast (two more rolls, an apple and another cup of coffee), he pulled on his shoes and went out the door, intent on his errands, but not so intent that he didn't pause for a last glance at the crack in the bedroom door before he left.

Valentin went to the balcony and watched the skinny legs and arms disappear down Magazine, then went back into the bedroom, sat down on the mattress and ran a finger along Justine's cheek. She opened her eyes and smiled softly.

"Are you coming back to bed?" she murmured.

"No," he said, "I can't sleep."

"Why dontcha just let it be?" she said. "Let the police catch him. Whoever it is."

"No," he said. He saw the look on her face and went ahead and admitted the rest of it. "If the coppers beat me to the killer, I can't ever show my face around here again." She frowned, looking troubled and he said, "Have the kid stay here again tonight." She looked at him, surprised. "Well, he needs a place to lay his head," he said, "and it'll make me feel better."

They were silent, lost in their thoughts. He felt her hand on his arm. "You gonna be careful?" He nodded. "Real careful?" He smiled and nodded again. Her eyes wandered to the doorway. "Where's Beansoup?" she whispered. When Valentin explained that he had sent the kid off, she smiled, her eyes got smoky as she reached down, threw the coverlet aside, and pulled up the hem of her nightdress.

⌒

Late that afternoon, she stood in the doorway and watched him walk down the stairs. The street door opened and closed with a muted rattling of glass. She stepped back inside.

Beansoup sat stiffly on the couch, eyes wide with the vigilance that Valentin had told him was required for this task. Justine smiled; he looked like a startled mannequin, his bony limbs rigid, his eyes unblinking, his ears perked to the slightest untoward sound. She went to gather up the sewing she had begun, a new set of curtains to replace the yellowed and tattered ones that had hung in the street windows, probably for years.

⌒

It was nowhere close to the time that Buddy would get to Longshoreman's Hall, but Valentin wanted to be outside, moving, doing something. So he wandered, making his way along the north end of the Vieux Carre, down the streets that crisscrossed the one square mile that had composed the original city and now constituted Creole New Orleans. He passed through the cool shadows of elegant brick houses and under the ornate, wrought iron colonnades that hung over the banquettes.

His steps led him to the corner of Orleans Street, where he found himself gazing on the cuspate spire of St. Ignatius. He studied the church building long minutes, then crossed over and climbed the stone steps to heavy oak doors adorned with heavy oak crosses.

~

He walked through the silence of the chapel that was heavy with the smell of incense and stepped into the narrow corridor in the back corner. He spent a moment fixing his collar and cuffs. Then he knocked sharply two times and pushed the door open without waiting for an invitation.

John Rice looked up from his desk, a pen poised over a letter, his eyes widening in surprise behind his glasses. As Valentin closed the door behind him, he saw doubt flicker over the parish clerk's face.

But then Rice composed himself and said, "Mr...."

"St. Cyr," Valentin told him, though of course the parish clerk knew what it was.

Rice laid his pen aside. "Can I help you with something?" He did not make the offer of a seat.

"I stopped by to ask after Father Dupre," Valentin said.

The parish clerk made a show of pursing his lips with officious puzzlement. "You're inquiring on behalf of Mr. Anderson?" Rice said.

So it was going to be a fencing match. "Mr. Anderson will be pleased to learn any news about the Father's health," Valentin said as a parry, wondering if John Rice knew of his dismissal and would call him on it.

Perhaps not. The parish clerk patted his already neat hair and said, "Father Dupre is doing as well as can be expected under the circumstances. The staff at Jackson is taking excellent care of him." He took off his glasses, held the lenses in front of his face, and replaced them. His gaze wandered to the letter on his desk.

"Was the exact nature of Father's illness ever discovered?" Valentin inquired in a tone that was casual but concerned.

Rice considered, then said, with deliberation, "You may tell Mr. Anderson that the Father is in the best of hands. There's been some improvement, but these cases are very difficult." He produced a small, stiff smile. "Of course, we would all be most grateful if Mr. Anderson remembers Father Dupre in his prayers." He entwined his fingers and waited.

Valentin nodded briefly and made his exit. The parish clerk stared at the closed door, then reached directly for the walnut box on his desk that housed the telephone.

～

He walked out of the Quarter and into Storyville as darkness descended. He felt like he should be looking for something among the passing faces; or maybe there would be something, some key, lying on the banquette or floating in the humid air, and all he would have to do was see it and snatch it away.

He stopped when he reached the corner of Canal and Basin streets and looked back down-the-line. The piece to the puzzle had not appeared, maybe because everything he needed had been there for the taking all along. Maybe it was true that Buddy Bolden was the murderer of five innocent women. Maybe it was just that simple, and just that sad.

～

It was almost eight o'clock when he finally reached Rampart Street. The Longshoreman's Hall was lit up with electric lights strung all across the facade, casting a weak amber glow over the crowd at the front door, a raucous mob of sports and girls from the houses, gangs of college boys, out-of-town drummers in twos and threes, plus the usual assortment of sports, gamblers and local ne'er-do-wells. Above their chatter, the sound of a band jassing noisily came bubbling out the open doors of the building.

He stepped around the crowd and peered in through one of the tall windows. It was the King Bolden Band, all right, just like the signs next to the doors announced. But it was no surprise that there was no King Bolden on the stage, or that there was another horn player in his place. He could guess what it meant, and the only true surprise was it hadn't happened sooner.

He moved away from the window and into the street, watching for the familiar profile to come into view. Inside, the band wound down and the music stopped in a swell of applause and cheers. A few minutes later, Jeff Mumford and Jimmy Johnson stepped through the doors and found a place at the corner of the building to get a breath of air. Mumford, flexing his fingers, caught sight of the Creole detective and quickly averted his eyes. He worked his fingers for another half-minute, then straightened and walked over to where Valentin was standing.

The guitar player looked sheepish as he nodded a greeting. "You looking for Buddy?" Valentin nodded. "I might as well tell you. Willie said we're done with him."

"Does he know?" Valentin said.

The guitar player shook his head, looking genuinely regretful. "Nossir, I don't believe so. We just couldn't put up with it no more. Buddy, he's just...he's..." Mumford made a futile gesture, then gave Valentin an earnest look. "Can you tell him, Mr. St. Cyr? It'd be better that way." He offered his hand and then walked back to join Johnson. The two musicians went inside. Presently the band started up with "Sugaree."

～

If there was a night for Buddy to miss a show, this was it, but not five minutes later, Valentin saw the lank profile wavering out of the darkness up Rampart Street. Bolden reeled around the corner at Dryades and stopped dead in his tracks, his face breaking into a grin of delight as he took in the crowd milling on the banquette and spilling out into the cobbled street. Then he saw Valentin approaching him and let out a little laugh of surprise.

"Well, what the hell!" he said. "What are you doin' down here?"

Valentin blocked his path. "I want to talk to you."

Buddy waved his horn in the air. "Yeah, that's fine, but not now. I got to get inside, make some music for these folk."

Valentin held out both his hands. "Just hold up for a minute."

Buddy was about to brush by when the doors to the dance hall opened and the sound of a cornet came chattering out, carried along on a gurgling stream of rhythm. His head swung around and he frowned. "What the hell is that?" he said. "Who's playin' that horn?"

～

Longshoreman's Hall was a box of a building with a huge, open dance floor of rough pine flooring, ringed on three sides by a balcony that was crowded with tables. Beneath the balcony were more tables and, top and bottom, they were all packed with revelers. The two bars, one on each side of the door, were three deep with men shouting and grabbing for beer, champagne, and short glasses of Raleigh Rye. The floor was a bobbing pool of dancing couples, all sweated-up in the close air. On the stage, sounding loud and perky, was the Bolden Band: the regular fellows, minus Bolden, but plus another, a short brown man in a slouch hat, playing a golden cornet.

Buddy moved stiffly through the crowd of jigging bodies, getting jostled by elbows and shoulders and hips. It was dark, and nobody seemed to notice that it was King Bolden passing by. No one saw, and no one called his name. Valentin had followed him inside, but now he hung back, not wanting to witness what was about to happen.

Buddy, peering at the stage, saw the rotund man with the horn: Freddie Keppard, the only horn player in New Orleans that was in his class. Buddy pushed through the front line of the dancers, his cornet jiggling in his hand, trying to hold his smile.

As the tune wound down, Willie Cornish looked over the bell of his trombone and damn, if it wasn't Bolden coming through the crowd. In another second, Mumford saw him and so did the others, Freddie, too, and they all started looking off somewhere, as if the notes to the next number were written on the flaking wall paint.

The song ended and the fellows went to fiddling with their instruments. Buddy understood: they were making time for him to get up there, to tell Freddie thanks for sitting in, but King Bolden was here now, and ready to make some noise.

Willie watched him edge closer to the bandstand, waiting for an invitation. He turned away, blew the spit out of his horn, trying to get out of it. He felt the others watching out of the corners of their eyes and Keppard faded back, not wanting to get in the middle of something. Willie turned around as Bolden moved closer. The dance floor was clearing and finally some of the people noticed and started pointing and whispering. *Look, that's King Bolden there...*

Buddy looked up at Willie Cornish and made a move to step on stage and get going. But then Cornish held up a big hand, pink palm out, and said, "Wait a minute, now." Buddy stopped. There was movement behind him, and more whispers.

Cornish couldn't think of how else to put it, so he muttered brusquely, "Look here, we hired Freddie." Buddy gave him a blank look, so Cornish leaned down closer to his face and closer to his ear. "We don't need you no more, Buddy," he said in his low, gravelly voice. Buddy still didn't seem to understand, so he said, loud enough for the fellows on the stage and the dancers standing closest to hear, "You're out of it, y'understand? We can't be workin' with the likes of you. It's done. There ain't no Bolden Band no more."

He straightened quickly, took a half-step back, waiting for Bolden to go wild and start tearing the place apart, but Buddy just stared blankly, like he hadn't heard a word. The trombone player shrugged his big shoulders and turned away.

Buddy stood there, looking from one face to the next, his mouth working up and down. But they wouldn't return his stare, wouldn't pay him any attention at all. Cornish whipped an angry hand up to lead them into a slow-drag blues.

No one cared to dance. Most eyes in the room fell on Buddy, standing alone and very still in the middle of the dance floor. The song wound on, a deep, liquid-blue haze, and he brought the cornet to his lips at one point and a murmur like a small breeze passed through the crowd. But then he dropped it to his side and let it dangle. Voices were whispering now and the news went through the house in bare seconds. Not a few of these same people had been around when Kid Bolden first got up and started making people all crazy with his music, and now the last scene in the drama was being played out before their eyes.

Cornish waved his hand to bring the blues down short and stole a glance at Buddy, standing there like an empty sack. The room was still, like somebody had just been shot. Cornish shook his head, then turned around and counted out one-two-three, one-two-three, to start up "Goldenrod Rag."

At the fourth bar, a couple moved onto the dance floor, and then there was another, and then a dozen, and then it seemed the whole house descended, arms flailing gaily and feet stomping all merry on the rough boards. For a minute or so, they moved around Buddy in little eddies. Here and there, a reveler reeled by and gave a knowing glance, *That's right, that's King Bolden.* The band chugged along and it was Keppard up there now, and if it wasn't Buddy's soaring, staccato brass, he was tight and plenty loud.

They played on and Buddy seemed to grow smaller, shrinking away, until no one noticed him much at all. So that only a few people looked around when the light-skinned fellow slipped through the crowd, took his arm and led him away.

∽

Buddy had taken only a few stumbling steps down the banquette when the cornet dropped from his hand and clattered into the gutter. Valentin saw it fall and called his name, but Buddy walked stiffly down Rampart toward Dryades, never once looking back.

Valentin stopped to pick up the horn. There was a fresh dent in the brass to join all the old dirty ones. King Bolden had once preened the perfect silver curves, the silent sliding valves with their mother-of-pearl buttons, so the deep glow of polished brass reflected his strange circus world. And over the horizon of the bell, he could see all the tan and brown and black faces looking up at him. It was the very horn that had blasted New Orleans out of its slumber and set a whole city to jassing. But now it seemed lifeless, all dull gray and scratched and dinged, a forlorn and forgotten piece of metal, something for the junkman's horse-drawn wagon. Valentin thought to lay it down and let it be, but then he stuck it under his arm and followed Buddy into the night.

∽

They walked along the railroad tracks that ran through the yard behind Union Station. The night wind kicked up whorls of dust and gravel, and in the distance off to their left, Storyville rose like a vaudeville stage, all tawdry light, herky-jerky motion and tinny noise.

Buddy came upon a club car that had been pushed off on a siding and sat down heavily on the bottom step. He leaned back, gripped the railing and closed his eyes for a moment. He looked up when he heard Valentin come along and right away saw the horn. "Whatchu doin' with that?" he muttered tonelessly.

"You dropped it," Valentin said and held it out to him.

Buddy turned his head away. "I don't want the goddamn thing."

"You dropped it on the street," Valentin repeated. "In the gutter back there on Ramp—"

"Y'hear me?" Buddy yelled suddenly. "I said I don't *want* the goddamn thing!"

Valentin shrugged and tossed the horn on the second step. Buddy winced at the sound of brass clanking on steel. "Why dontcha just keep it?" His mouth twisted into a ghastly smile. "You ain't heard? Ain't no King Bolden Band no more."

"I heard," Valentin said. He watched Buddy's face, saw the awful, broken look, and tried to think of something else to say.

"And after what I done for them!" Bolden cried out. "They wouldn't one of them be nothin' if it wasn't for me. Willie Cornish, that fat fuck of a black-ass nigger, tellin' me there ain't no Bolden Band. Mumford acting like I ain't even there, and his own mama was a whore down—"

"I don't want to hear that," Valentin cut in.

Bolden stopped and gave him a hard look. "You see what they did? You see what they did to me?"

"I saw," Valentin said.

"Well, who the fuck's Willie Cornish to tell—"

"What do you care?" Valentin said. He was suddenly very tired of all of it.

Buddy's bloodshot eyes fixed on him. "What's that?"

"I said, what do you care?" He waved a hand back the way they'd come. "You don't give a goddamn about that band."

"Whatchu talkin' about?" Bolden said. "I started—"

"You don't!" Valentin cut him off again. "And you don't care about Nora or the baby, either."

"Don't you—"

"You don't give a good goddamn for anything, except getting drunk or smoking hop or chasing after some whore. Just whatever the hell pleases you. Ain't that right?"

Buddy stared at him, then let out a dull laugh. "You don't know nothin' about it," he said roughly.

"I know I'm about the only friend you got left!"

"You ain't no friend of mine," Buddy said in a low, mean voice.

Valentin felt a hot flush rising to his face. "Oh, no? Who do you think's been protecting you? Who you think kept the coppers from taking you down all this time?"

Buddy frowned in annoyance. "Whatchu talkin' about? Taking me down for what?"

"For those goddamn murders in Storyville!" Speaking the words made his stomach churn.

Buddy's mouth fell open. "What'd you say?"

Valentin let out a blunt, exasperated laugh. "That's right! You get it? The coppers and just about everybody else back-of-town think it was you murdered Annie. And Gran Tillman and Martha—"

Buddy lunged off the steel steps and grabbed a handful of Valentin's shirt in his fist. "You shut your goddamn mouth right now!" he snarled. Their feet went sliding on gravel and Valentin saw Buddy's black eyes were swimming with rage.

He clamped his left hand on Bolden's trembling wrist. "You knew every damn one of them!" he seethed. "You were seen at those houses. You got no alibis. That adds up to guilty!"

Buddy looked stunned for a moment and his grip weakened. He gaped at Valentin with some kind of terrible wonder. "They think... But I didn't...I didn't hurt nobody." Sudden blades of light shot from his eyes and his grip tightened again, choking now. "You goddamn son of a whore!" His voice almost broke. "I didn't hurt *nobody!*" He leaned close and Valentin could smell his breath, hot whiskey and yen pox and something bloody. "I didn't do none of that, you fucking dago fucking bastard!"

There was a second's frigid pause as Buddy wavered and Valentin took the second to slam him hard in the chest. He heard a hiss of breath and he slammed him again, knocking him sprawling into the side of the car. He thought it would stop then, that the shock would fix him where he stood. But Buddy came raging back, and clamped both his hands on Valentin's throat. He tried to wrench loose, but Bolden was bearing down with the same iron fingers that had worked that loud horn.

He couldn't breathe and he was standing outside of it, thinking: *he'll let go…he'll stop…* But Buddy didn't stop. He was trying to choke the life out of him. Valentin's brain was going blank as the Storyville lights began to dance like flames.

It happened with no thought at all. He dropped his right hand to his back pocket and came up with the whalebone sap, snapping it around to crack Buddy full force behind the ear. The iron clamp on his windpipe flinched. He swung again and Buddy staggered, grabbing for a hold on the side of the car, a sudden gush of blood down his collar. His black eyes went wild, and he rushed forward again. But Valentin saw him coming, dropped the sap and snatched the Iver Johnson from his pocket. He took one fast step back, stuck out his arm at full length, and shoved the short barrel into the flesh of Buddy's cheek, freezing him.

"I'll kill you, goddamn it!" he yelled, and his voice broke.

It lasted only seconds, but it seemed to go on forever. Valentin felt a cold rage and a colder fear, just like the moment before he shot a hole right through Eddie McTier's chest. His brain unlocked and a voice was whispering: *one pull and it will all be over.* He caught the harsh, knowing look on Bolden's face and he felt like his heart was breaking apart. The finger on the trigger relaxed.

Buddy jerked away from the barrel of the pistol and stumbled back. "You're gonna be sorry." His stare was hateful, and his wounded voice was full of venom. "I'm tellin' you you're gonna be *sorry* for what you done to me."

His crazy gaze shifted and he stalked off around the back of the car, stumbling over the first rail. He lurched out of sight and his curses were lost in the rumble of a train rolling through the back of the yard.

Valentin's hand shook as he lowered the pistol, put it back in his pocket and bent down to pick up the sap. He leaned a hand against the side of the car to catch his breath and try to keep his stomach from coming up. A minute passed. He went around to the back of the car, stopping to pick up the cornet. Bolden was not in sight. Valentin crossed over the tracks. "Buddy?" he called. He looked all around the yard, expecting to see the stark figure staggering about on the rough gravel. But there was nothing but long blue shadows and the clacking of the train moving off into the black Louisiana night.

He tucked the horn under his arm and began walking at a quicker pace. He crossed the next set of tracks, heading out of the yard in the direction of Storyville, calling, "Buddy! Buddy Bolden!"

～

The flat was quiet. Beansoup was curled in a ball on the couch, deep in sleep. In the bedroom, Justine dozed beneath the baire. The bells of St. John's had just tolled two times when the street door opened and closed. A figure stood motionless in the dark foyer at the bottom of the stairwell, poised, listening. One step up, then a second. The third step creaked, and the figure froze for five seconds. Then it was a few more swift silent steps to the second floor landing.

Beansoup heard a tapping on the door and opened one sleepy eye. Another tap-tap-tap and he sat up, blinking groggily in the dark. There was one more soft tap, and somebody whispering something. It was Mr. St. Cyr, home from his rounds. He untangled the sheet from around his legs, stumbled groggily to the door, and threw back the bolt.

The door burst open, hitting him full on, and a blow came hard across his forehead. He stumbled back blindly, tripping on the braided rug. He was already on the floor when the second blow came with a flash of light and a sharp pain that sent his head spinning in black circles. He cried out and slumped over on his side. Feet scrambled past his face and he tried to open his mouth, but he couldn't make any noise. He lifted his head, but the spinning made him dizzier and he fell back, unconscious.

Justine heard a noise from out in the front room that brought her half-awake. The apartment door opened with a bang, and then there was a thump, a strange heavy sound, followed by a muffled cry. It wasn't right at all and she wondered if she was dreaming. She pulled herself up from her sleep and was reaching for the baire just as the bedroom door was flung wide.

She saw the shadow and knew it wasn't him. Then she thought it was the kid, but before that had crossed her mind the shadow came at her. In a blur, the baire was ripped down and pulled around her. She caught the motion of something swinging round in an arc and tried to move away, but the blow caught her high on the head and knocked her back across the bed in a flash of red pain that made her ears ring. Another glancing blow on the shoulder knocked her the other way. A sudden spike of rage came out of her belly, a blood-red wave that drove her up off the bed, the baire still twisted around her. She threw herself against the shadow and her weight forced the body into the wall. She heard a sharp grunt and they tumbled down to the floor, arms, legs, and baire in a tangle. She was trying to fight, but the arm with the weapon came free and she couldn't cover up and there was another blast of bright pain on the back of her head and suddenly she couldn't move. She knew there was another blow coming, the one that would finish it. But before it landed, the shadowy form jerked away and there was a scrabbling of steps across the wood floor. Then the door slammed, and the only sound was a low moaning from the front room.

What seemed like hours passed before she got one hand to move, then the other. It took more hours for her to tug the ends of the baire from around her head and shoulders. She crawled to the doorway on all fours and saw the boy's body all crumpled into the corner. She heard his groans and tried to call out to him, but couldn't make her mouth work for all the blood. There was a terrible, numbing throb in her head, but she forced herself to stay up on her trembling hands and knees and crawl.

⮑

A mulatto workman, passing by just before dawn on his way to work at the French Market, found her body sprawled halfway out the street door. He ran to a call box, and in ten minutes, a horse-drawn police wagon came pounding down Magazine Street.

⮑

Wearied to the bone, Valentin gave up on trying to find Buddy sometime after three o'clock and made his way down Common Street to the river. He sat on a pier, watching the stars through the mist, trying to decide what to do next. Maybe nothing at all; the story would play out with or without him. Let Buddy lose what was left of his mind, let Picot have him, and he could go home to Justine and forget all of it.

He stopped, rubbing his forehead. It was too late for that; he was part of the story, too. He had been part of it all along.

Still, it wasn't until the first deep purple shades of dawn were tainting the black sky over the Gulf that he started home. He turned up Magazine and was almost to Gaspare's when he noticed that his street door was standing open. He took a step closer, saw the blood on the threshold and went racing up the stairs. He opened the door on the front room, ran through the bedroom and then rushed back down the stairwell and onto the street.

&

The copper behind the desk glanced up at the sweating, shaking, Dago-looking fellow. "What happened on Magazine Street?" the Dago demanded.

The officer examined him up and down for a moment, then said, "Two people was attacked. Young octoroon girl and that kid, what'd they call him…Beansoup." He cocked an eye at Valentin. "Do you know something—"

"What happened to them?"

"I believe they was carried over to Charity."

He swallowed, steadied himself. "Are they dead?"

The copper shrugged. "That I don't know."

&

He ran into the lobby of the colored ward of Charity Hospital at seven o'clock and had to pace up and down for twenty minutes before the doctor, a thin, serious-looking Creole, stepped up. "Sir?" he said politely.

"Justine Mancarre," Valentin said.

The doctor said, "She was the victim of an assault. She has some very serious injuries. Traumas to the head."

"But she's alive," Valentin said.

The doctor's eyes shifted away. Picot stepped up, looked at Valentin and said, without preamble, "Well, he's back at it, eh?" He turned to the doctor. "Either one of them die yet?" He said roughly.

The doctor looked at the two men, the copper with his lazy eyes and the other, the light-skinned Creole, with his face all rigid with fear. "They're both alive," he said and saw the Creole sag. "The young lady sustained the most serious injuries, but I expect they'll recover."

Valentin let out a breath and Picot sniffed and shrugged. "That's just as good," he said. "Means we got witnesses."

When the doctor stepped away, Picot turned around and said, "All right, let's get this over with. You know where he was last night?"

Valentin rubbed his eyes wearily. "I saw him at Long-shoreman's Hall...there was this...his band—"

"His band ain't no more," Picot said. "I heard all about it."

Valentin nodded; of course, Uptown news traveled fast. "We got into...into a scuffle...down in the train yard."

"A scuffle?" Picot smiled dimly.

"Then I lost track of him," Valentin said.

"So you got no idea what he was up to, say after two a.m.?" Picot's eyes wandered away. "Where he went? What he mighta been doin'?"

Valentin shook his head.

～

They stood over Justine's bed. She was all in white, her head bandaged round and round. Her eyes, half-closed, were dark liquid pools in a slow river of morphine. Aware of Picot's surly gaze, Valentin touched her hand, but she didn't respond. The Creole doctor came up behind them.

"When can I question her?" Picot demanded.

"Hard to tell," the doctor said. "Could be as soon as this afternoon. But it could be a few days."

"I'll be around," Picot said. Valentin just stared at her.

The doctor was studying the patient in kind. "Do you know who's responsible?"

Picot answered the doctor easily. "Yessir, I believe we do."

～

As they stepped up to the nurses' station in the White Ward, it suddenly dawned on Valentin that he didn't know Beansoup's true name. He'd been seeing him on the streets for years, the boy had slept under his roof and eaten at his table, and he had never bothered to ask his name. He felt a flush of shame.

"That would be Emile Carter," the nurse at the desk told them. "His condition is still serious, but he's stable," she said. "You can go up and look in on him if you want. Second floor."

Valentin climbed the stairs with Picot puffing along behind. They stopped in the doorway and looked inside. Stripped of his ragged street clothes and dirty mug all cleaned up, he looked like a different person. He looked like a child.

∽

The two men stepped out of the hospital as the first hard light of day eased its way into the sky over the Gulf. Without a word, they walked off in opposite directions.

Fifteen

That fast life, it just broke him up.
—*Peter Bocage*

Sunlight poured through the window in a brilliant fountain. Just beyond the sill, two women murmured, their voices like running water. With the jumbled rhythm of horseshoes on cobbles, the slap and jingle of reins and bridles, the steady roll of wagon wheels, and the cries of the street vendors, it was a band playing a quiet tune.

Buddy turned his head and looked through the gap in the curtains. The morning sun had cast everything on the street with a soft edge of golden yellow. He could smell coffee brewing and bread baking, beignets frying, the deep earth scents of the street vendors' fruits and vegetables and fresh meats, the musky odor of horses, and the exotic New Orleans filé that was in the air all the time but came on strongest the first of the day. He had always loved mornings. Though he couldn't remember the last time he had been up early enough to greet one.

He suddenly remembered waking up on a day like this long ago and knowing that a world filled to bursting with sound and light and motion waited outside. By the afternoon, the wet heat and the green flies would make the streets unbearable, but mornings stretched on so long that sometimes it seemed they would never end. He grinned, remembering the time...then, just as suddenly, a tiny blade of white light flashed behind his eyes and the thought fluttered away.

A cloud passed over and for a few moments the streets outside took on a gray cast like the shadows in one of that dwarf fellow's photographs. Then the color returned. He heard the door creak open and turned his head to see Nora standing there, looking wary.

"How you feelin' this mornin'?" It sounded like she was on the other side of a wall.

"Feelin' all right," he told her.

Bernedette's tiny brown face appeared from behind her mother's skirt. She stared at her father, blinking her wide, curious eyes, one small hand clutching the cotton folds of Nora's dress, the other trailing a ragged doll. Buddy was silent, gazing back at his child with a fearful wonder, seeing the face of an angel. He reached out his hand, but she shrunk back. Nora bent to whisper something in her ear. Bernedette entwined her feet and shook her head. Her mother put a hand on her back and sent her out the door and down the hall.

"Whatchu do that for?" Buddy muttered, turning his face away.

Nora saw the dried blood on the side of his head. "What happened to you?" He didn't answer. "Buddy? What happened last night?"

His eyes were fixed on a shaft of dusty sunlight that had fallen on the bed. A picture moved in his head, something with rough motion and dust kicked up in the air, doors opening and closing, the outlines of a wild struggle. It went away. "What about last night?" he asked her.

"It's nothing," she said. "You better let me clean you up." She took a step inside.

"No!" He glanced at her fearfully. "I'll do it."

"Are you sure you're all right?" He didn't answer and he didn't move. "You want breakfast?"

After a moment, he nodded. "That'd be fine."

Nora went to the door. "Mama's comin' by in a little while," she said.

Buddy smiled uncertainly, missing the hint. He made no move to get out of bed, to clean himself up. Nora stepped into the hallway and closed the door.

～

Ida Bass walked down First Street, a petulant frown settling on her face. The first thing she encountered when she stepped onto the banquette was two neighbor ladies who stopped whispering and put on that innocent why-good-mornin'-Miz-Ida-no-we-wasn't-talkin'-'bout-*you* look. Ida regarded the two of them steadily and said, "What's he done now?"

The women exchanged a glance and then dropped their voices to relate the tale. To the mother of Nora Bass (these days, she refused to call her daughter a Bolden), it sounded no different than before: Buddy coming home drunk and crazy in the middle of the night and raising Cain in front of his wife and child, raving like the maniac he was, terrifying his family and waking half the neighborhood. The police might have come, or maybe not. They might have carried him off to jail again. The women weren't sure about that.

It didn't matter to Ida Bass. It wouldn't make any difference. It was another chapter in the same old story. The Boldens and the Basses did not get on. In the convoluted caste system within the colored community, the Boldens were common in relation to the Bass family. Because the Creole of Color Basses had been free for decades before the War, while the dark-skinned Boldens would probably still be picking cotton on some plantation had not Mr. Lincoln set them free. And then there was Charles Bolden, Jr., the child Buddy had fathered and then forgotten, still appearing now and then when she and Nora made market, his grave little face a startling reminder of the vagrant father.

There was more to add to the rancor. Around the time of the marriage, one of Nora's distant cousins had whispered to another cousin a rumor of bad blood in the Bolden history, some sort of spirit sickness that went all the way back to Africa and infected the whole lot of them for generations. This cousin repeated what she heard to a neighbor and on and on, until the gossip landed on a Bolden's doorstep. After that, the battle lines were drawn.

Ida heard the rumor. She believed it then and believed it now. Didn't she see living proof just about every waking day?

And it had started out so well! Buddy was a musician, a respected vocation around New Orleans. He had been devoted to Nora and the baby and he went to church Sunday mornings and sometimes on Wednesday night. People spoke well of him and he made a good wage for a colored man. But earning a decent living playing for the better class of people and quietly attending to his family just wouldn't do for Mr. Charles Bolden. No, he had something else in mind. So he went about making himself crazy, playing jungle music for drunken niggers and their filthy whores down along Rampart Street, rotting his brain with Raleigh Rye and hot whiskey, using hop and cocaine for all she knew and, of course, running with those lowdown women who would hike their petticoats or go down on their knees for any man with a Liberty quarter in his trousers. Bringing Lord knows what kind of awful *gris-gris* into her daughter's home. It was a cheap, pitiful tragedy, the worst kind of hoodoo, and God damn Buddy Bolden for visiting it upon her flesh and blood.

She stopped on the corner and took a breath to calm herself. Peering down the block, she saw there was no crowd around the doorway of 2719, no police wagons in the street. It was quiet. *Thank you, Jesus.*

She sighed, pushing her dark thoughts aside. Truth be told, Ida Bass loved her son-in-law. More correctly, she loved the charming, handsome young man who had courted her daughter. The two of them had met at St. John the Fourth. He was a good-hearted fellow; he had been an attentive husband and father. But whatever bad juju had infected the family had caught up with him, too, and made him delirious. There wasn't a hoodoo woman in New Orleans who could fix him; it was too late for that. Ida suspected that Buddy would one day end up dead in some saloon or just go staggering off into his own crazy mind, never to be seen again. Either way, he'd leave his wife a widow and his daughter an orphan.

The one thing she didn't know, that no one dared tell a doting grandmother, was the talk going round about a suspect in the killings of those sporting girls down in the District. Though more tongues wagged every minute.

She stepped hesitantly to Nora and Buddy's perron. She lived in mortal fear that one day she would reach that door to find that her lunatic son-in-law had finally gone all the way insane and murdered her daughter and grandbaby in their beds. But Nora appeared at the door, weary and red-eyed, but otherwise fine. And Bernedette giggled happily when she saw her granma'm. She spoiled the child. Ida stepped inside and said, "Is he home?"

∽

Buddy heard the front door open, heard Nora's quiet voice, heard Ida cooing over her granddaughter. He got up and started to pace, listening to the voices in the other room. They were talking about him, he was sure of that. He saw it in the old woman's eyes every time she came round. How she hated him. And soon enough Nora would hate him, too, and so would his baby Bernedette. Nora's mama would see to that. It was never right between the two families, and the old bitch would fix him good.

Now the voices dropped down low so he couldn't hear at all. Why did they whisper? He stopped by the door, his eyes wide and ears poised. He could hear the tiniest slide of a valve off a note and he could catch a quarter-tone better than any gutbucket guitar player laying a straight razor to steel strings. So why couldn't he hear their voices?

He picked up the pitcher off the side table, poured a glass full and drank it in greedy swallows, half the water spilling down the front of his nightshirt. He sat down on the bed and waited. He felt his heart beating. A few minutes passed. Another babble of hushed voices in the front room. Then he heard fingers tapping.

"Buddy?" Nora opened the door.

Buddy looked up at her. "What is it? What are you doin' out there?"

"Mama's fixin' you something to eat."

He shook his head. "I don't want it."

Nora stepped into the room and stood over him, laying a hand on his shoulder. "You got to eat," she said. "You'll feel better."

Buddy stared at his wife, looking for a clue in her dark eyes. He thought he saw something there, a tiny shadow passing over her face. He watched her as she turned away and moved about the room, straightening this and that. She looked nervous. Something was wrong.

A few minutes later, Ida stepped into the doorway, holding a plate and some silver. She looked at Buddy's drawn face, his skittish eyes, the stubble of rough beard, the stain of dried blood. The close smell in the room made her hold her breath. Under it all was an odor like one of Bernedette's wet diapers. This from a man who used to spend hours fussing with his hair and clothes before he'd take a step outdoors.

She saw the way Nora stood away from her husband, watching him with a fretful expression and she thought: *You best fret, child.*

"Here you are, Buddy." Ida put a soothing tone to her voice as she held out the plate. Buddy shook his head slightly, so she set it down on the night table. "Don't you want to eat something?" She held a fork in her right hand.

Buddy glanced at the plate, smelled the fried eggs and grits. And something else, something that didn't belong. His eyes flicked; he understood. Ida stood there, holding the fork, tines out, a devil's implement. His eyes fixed on it. The sharp tines glistened and he felt a thrill of fear. He had a sudden urge to let out a wild laugh. They didn't know that he knew.

Nora said, "Buddy, what's wrong?"

He rose up, pointing a finger at his mother-in-law. "She's— She's tryin' to—" but the rest of the words wouldn't come.

Ida rolled her eyes in exasperation. Buddy had come half out of the bed, pointing a shaking finger and stuttering at her like some child throwing a tantrum. She dropped the fork onto the plate. It clattered and made a little spray of grits when it landed. What she wanted to do was call him down right then and there. But she knew that would only make it worse. She shook her head and turned away.

Buddy caught the look on his mother-in-law's face and saw her mask come away. She was turning for the door, leaving food meant to poison him. He knew. He knew. He knew.

A sudden bolt ran up his spine, sending a red flash into his brain. His hand swung out and grabbed hold of the handle of the water pitcher. He heard Nora scream as he swung his arm, bringing the pitcher sideways across Ida's head. She shrieked and fell against the wall as the pitcher shattered into a dozen pieces. There was a splatter of crimson over the old woman's hair as she grabbed and held fast to the doorjamb, going down, looking stunned, like she'd been pole-axed. Buddy now stood back, holding the handle of the pitcher, blinking in befuddlement.

Nora saw the glazed, empty look in Buddy's eyes. She ran to the door and all but dragged her mother out of the bedroom and down the hall.

Buddy sat down on the bed. He saw the pattern the grits and eggs and blood and water made on the wall and the floor. There were broken shards of ceramic lying about. He knew something was wrong. He wondered what had happened. Then he heard his wife calling out the window for somebody to help, somebody quick get the police. Her voice sounded like a wild horn reaching for some impossible note.

Quite suddenly, the room was filled with a quiet light as the walls fell away. Something broke and, for the first time in a long time, his head didn't hurt at all. The crushing weight was gone; he was as light as the breeze. He hadn't felt that way since he was a schoolboy.

He sighed deeply and smiled. It felt like it was over now.

∽

Picot stood in the doorway to St. Cyr's rooms. The Creole detective stood at the window, looking out onto Magazine Street.

The copper's eyes roamed around, taking in the mess in the room, complete with bloodstains.

"Look at this," he said. "Look at what he done. Two people in Charity."

Valentin kept staring out the window. "What do you want, Picot?" he said.

"I come to tell you there ain't no reason for you to finish the job on Bolden," Picot said. "We got him."

Valentin turned around. "Seems he come home this morning, actin' all crazy," Picot said. "Tore his own house up. But his wife got him settled, least she thought so." He went on, enjoying the beaten look on St. Cyr's face. "Her mama come over to help out, you know, to make him something to eat. But your friend Bolden, he gets it in his head that the old woman is tryin' to poison him." He laughed bluntly. "You know what he does? He jumps up out of bed, grabs hold of a water pitcher and hits her over the head. Broke the damn thing all to pieces and cut her up pretty good. Some neighbor called a wagon and they came and carried him over to Parish Prison. Again." Picot nodded emphatically. "Now, them detectives, they gonna get a confession outta him, I guarantee."

Valentin stood motionless as Picot backed out the door. "So, Mr. Detective, you can forget about it. This one's closed up good. And it's about damn time." He walked to the door, stopped and turned around. "Too bad about your sportin' girl and that boy," he said. "Never shoulda got this far. Never shoulda happened." His round shape disappeared down the stairwell.

❦

Valentin went back to Charity Hospital and sat by Justine's bedside until mid-afternoon, studying her bruised face, swathed all around in white.

He walked up the stone steps of Parish Prison at four o'clock, stepping out of an afternoon sopping with humidity into the cool stone corridors. He went down two sets of stairs to the detention center and stepped up to a tall desk to state his business to a uniformed copper with sallow skin, an enormous brush mustache and red, wet eyes that swam around Valentin's face.

Valentin requested permission to visit the prisoner, and when he supplied his name, the desk sergeant muttered raggedly under his breath. He took his time producing a visitor's card from a drawer, tossed it across the desk, and then embarked on a long-winded instruction about prison security that was meant to be insulting. Then he jerked a thumb and watched as Valentin was ushered through the metal door by a police guard, a heavy-set young man with dull eyes and red, tobacco-stuffed cheeks.

❦

Valentin followed the guard down the row of cells. His escort pointed a finger at the last cell, then stepped back, leaned against the opposite wall and crossed his arms.

Valentin's gaze roamed the shadows. There was a bed and a bucket, a tiny window up high and a bundle of sticks and rags shoved into the corner. Then the bundle moved and he realized it was Buddy. "Jesus Christ!" He glanced at the guard, who shook his head with rude disgust, as if to say, *These lunatic cases—that's what happens.*

Valentin put his hands on the bars. "Buddy," he called softly. There was only the slightest movement from the corner of the cell. "Buddy, it's Tino," he said. For a long moment, there was no response. Then Buddy turned in the general direction of the front of the cell. Valentin was startled by the stark, angled planes of his face, as if the bones beneath were trying to push out through the skin. There was a blank, becalmed, still-water look in his eyes.

"It's Tino," he repeated. Bolden stared back at him evenly, but with no hint of recognition. Valentin turned to the guard. "Can you let me in there with him?"

The guard made a self-important show of thinking about it as he worked over his chaw. Then he dropped a hand to his side and came up with a ring of keys. The bolt slid back with a clank that echoed down the corridor. The guard pulled the cell door open.

Buddy, sitting on the stone floor at the end of the iron bed, watched the visitor step inside with curious eyes.

"Buddy," Valentin said tentatively. Bolden looked at him but said nothing. "It's Tino. Valentin St. Cyr."

Buddy nodded vaguely, as if he was being introduced to someone he had met once or twice, but couldn't quite recall. Valentin lowered his voice even more, and Buddy suddenly leaned forward, his eyes wide, almost childlike. "Valentino Saracena. From St. Francis de Sales School."

Bolden considered the information, then stood up, smiled nervously, bobbed his head one time, and extended a clumsy hand. The two men greeted each other formally. The guard, catching sight of their clasped hands, said, "Hey, now, none of that," and they broke their grip. There was now something impish behind Buddy's eyes, like the two of them were schoolboys once again, caught at some prank.

"How are you feeling?" Valentin asked him.

"It's very dark in here," Buddy muttered vacantly.

"I need you to tell me something," Valentin said. Bolden cocked an eyebrow. "I need you to tell me about Annie Robie."

A flicker of recognition crossed his features. "I knew her, yessir," he said. "But she's dead now."

Valentin stole a glance at the guard, who was now staring at the wall at the end of the corridor as if Holy Scripture was carved there. He turned back to Buddy. "She's dead, that's right," he said. "And so is Gran Tillman. And Martha Devereaux."

"And Jennie...Jennie...uh..." Bolden said.

"Hix," Valentin said.

"Hix."

"And Florence Mantley."

Bolden nodded sagely. "Yes. She flew out the window."

"That's right," Valentin said. His voice was getting thick. "And then there were some people attacked. A woman named Justine Mancarre. The kid they call Beansoup. And your mother-in-law."

Buddy was watching Valentin steadily, nodding, but with no sign of understanding in his dark eyes. Those names didn't mean anything to him.

"You know why you're in here?" Valentin asked him.

There was a long moment's silence, and then, in a normal voice Bolden said, "Oh, yes, because it was me that did that. I did it to all of them."

Valentin felt a sudden, icy chill. "You did what?" he whispered. On the edge of his vision, he saw the guard waking up, moving closer to the cell door.

Bolden turned his face to the patch of light cast by the tiny window. "I killed them women," he repeated loudly, to no one in particular. As Valentin gaped, the guard looked frantically around for help. "All those poor girls…and that madam." He began talking faster, as his eyes flicked crazily about the cell. "Yes! Yes! All them sports and them pimps and gamblers, too. All them fellows in the band. I killed them all! I killed them all! Everybody's dead!" His voice had gone up a half-octave. Down the cellblock, the other prisoners shouted for him to shut up. Buddy's gaze was piercing as he turned to point a finger at Valentin. "You're dead," he announced. He looked at the guard. "And you're dead." Abruptly, his legs folded and he collapsed onto the bunk. His voice grew somber. "Nora's dead. Her mama's dead. And my little baby Bernedette." He drew in a deep, trembling breath. "And me. I'm the deadest one of all. Everybody's dead now. Everybody. Dead…dead…dead."

Valentin put a hand on the bars to steady himself. The guard snorted loudly, folded his arms and leaned against the wall once more, his jaw moving in slow circles. Buddy folded into himself like a flower in the dark of night. A slow minute passed.

"I'm going to go now," Valentin said.

The man on the bunk glanced up and for a brief instant, his eyes cleared and his face softened. The tiniest inkling of a smile lit up his features as he raised a hand in farewell. "Good-bye, fellow," he murmured.

Valentin gestured to the guard. The door was opened and he stepped into the corridor and walked away. The guard spit a languid stream of dirty red-brown on the floor as he swung his keys up to lock the cell. The bolt sliding back into place sounded like a blow from a hammer.

∽

At the City Attorney's office, he learned that Charles Bolden's criminal hearing was scheduled for Thursday, June the 4th. At that time, he was informed, it would be determined if there was evidence to bind the accused over for the assault on his mother-in-law. It would also be determined if there was sufficient evidence to hold the accused for the murder of one or more lewd and abandoned women in the District of New Orleans commonly known as Storyville.

⌒

As he stepped onto the banquette, he heard the rattling cough of an automobile engine coming along Royal Street. The motorcar pulled up, wheels sloshing in the filthy gutter. Two toughs sat like twin blocks of stone in the front seat of Anderson's yellow Winton, eyeing him coldly. The one in the shotgun seat reached around and opened the rear door. Valentin got in.

⌒

Anderson was sitting at his usual table, dressed in a light-gray three-piece suit, a long, gold watch chain across his paunch. As the Creole detective approached, he motioned for him to take the opposite chair. Ceiling fans whispered overhead.

"You spoke to Mr. Bolden?" the white man asked directly.

"I visited him," Valentin said, marveling at how fast the news had traveled.

The King of Storyville said, "And now do you believe he committed those murders?"

Valentin shook his head.

"What about the attack on your young lady and the boy?"

Valentin said nothing.

"And his mother-in-law?"

"That one, yes," he conceded.

"But you think he's innocent of the rest of it." Anderson's tone was curious, as if he was edifying himself on some arcane subject of interest.

Valentin knew he wasn't going to sway the man, but he went ahead and spoke up anyway. "I think he made himself a convenient suspect, is all. Someone to pin those crimes on."

Anderson pondered for a moment. "So the killer is still on the loose."

"Yes."

"What are you going to do about it?"

"Try to run him to ground."

"And if that's against my wishes?"

"I'm not in your employ, sir. I believe that allows me—"

"Allows you?" Anderson barked, and rapped his fist on the table. "You are *allowed* to do what I say! Are you forgetting who's in charge here? Have *you* lost your mind now? You go against me, and I'll make your life a misery, friend!"

He stared balefully at Valentin for another moment, then sat back and began absently fingering his watch chain. "But I hope it won't come to that," he said, his voice now matter-of-fact. "Let me present the situation. You go chasing after this supposed guilty party. In the meantime, King Bolden will go on trial for those murders. Justice will be swift. He will be convicted and sentenced to death and that sentence will be carried out. He will be hanged by his neck in the yard at Parish Prison." The blue eyes shifted. Anderson released the watch chain, leaned over the table, and made a conciliatory steeple with his fingers. "However, if you let the matter rest, I can promise you he will only be adjudged insane and remanded to Jackson. His life will be spared."

Valentin stared at Tom Anderson, stunned at the open threat. "That means guilty or not, he's marked down as murderer."

"Guilty or not, he's marked down as an insane person," Anderson said. "A sick man. Exactly what he is."

"There's still no proof that he killed any of those women," Valentin said thickly.

Anderson now laid his hands flat on the table. "We're not going to discuss it any more," he said. "You have a choice to make. Make it."

Valentin sat stiffly for a long minute, then rose from his chair and walked away.

Sixteen

Description of the Insane Person Named in the Within Warrant
Name: Chas. Bolden
Sex: Male
Age: 29
Color: Negro
Color Hair: Brown
Color Eyes: Brown
Occupation: Laborer
Single: Yes
Residence: Parish Prison and 2719 First Street
Nativity: La
Character of Disease: Insanity
Cause of Insanity: Alcohol
Is this his First Attack? Yes
How Long Been Insane? 1 mos.
Is Patient Dangerous to Himself or Others? To Others
Has Suicide Ever Been Attempted? No
Is There a Disposition to Destroy Clothing, Furniture, etc? Yes
Are the Patient's Habits Clean or Dirty: Filthy
What was the Patient's Natural Disposition? Quiet
Have Any Members of the Family Ever Been Insane? No
Has the Patient Ever Been Addicted to the Intemperate Use of Alcohol, Opium or Tobacco? Alcohol.
Has the Patient Ever had any Injury of Head, Epilepsy or Hereditary Disease? No
What is the Cause of this Attack? Alcohol
Has Any Medical Treatment Been Instituted? Yes
Any Restraint or Confinement been resorted to? Yes
If So, What Kind? Parish Prison, seven days
General Remarks: Received Thursday, June 4th, 1907 and on Friday, June 5th, 1907.
I delivered to Dr. Clarence Pearson, superintendent of the Insane Asylum at Jackson, La. the within named Interdicted Insane Person Charles Bolden. Returned same day.

> G.A. Putfark
> Deputy Sheriff

The double-seated hack creaked along the dirt road that meandered from the depot to the hospital on the outskirts of town.

The papers stated that the fellow in the rear seat of the wagon with his hands and legs manacled to an iron ring on the floor was Charles Bolden. Two uniformed guards, young white men with sunburned faces, slouched in the fore seat, enjoying the trip away from the hospital grounds.

It was mid-afternoon and the sun was high in a clear near-white sky. The two wagons far ahead, filled up with white inmates, kicked up a cloud of gray dust that drifted back down the road and the guard driving the hack cursed lightly and then slowed the team of mules to a languid, flopped-ear pace. When the first two hacks, led by Sheriff Putfark, rounded a turn in the road and fell out of sight, the guards exchanged a look.

"Well, whaddya think?" the driver said, starting to laugh a little.

"I think it's a mighty hot day," the other said.

The driver pulled up on one of the reins and steered the team off the road and into the shade of a pale oak. To the right, not fifty feet down a slope and through a stand of pine trees, a creek ran, green water flowing in slow eddies. "What about him?" the driver said, jerking his head at the back seat.

The other guard looked at the patient's eyes, placid pools full of dark, quiet shadows. "He won't be no trouble."

The driver began pulling off his high-topped shoes while the other guard grabbed the chain and gave it a hard tug. The links jangled. "He's good," the guard said.

The driver was already hopping down from the seat. The second guard kicked off his shoes and started after him.

The patient watched as the two men trotted through the low brush, pulling at the buttons of their uniform coats, then their trousers. The clothes fell to the wayside and the naked bodies, as pale as the bellies of fish, came out of the brush, arched through the air and collided with the still green surface of the water in one wide splash.

He stared in wonder as the two heads reappeared, throwing water in long silver sheets, making coarse music with their laughter. Above him, on a branch of the oak tree, a mockingbird began to warble. He looked up, listening with every bone, every muscle. The dark bird's song trilled up and down, up higher and down lower, and then began again.

The moment was still: the sun glowing hot, the smell of the dark earth, the sway of the deep-green leaves, the rippling of the silver-blue water, and a bird song that went on and on. Time did not move at all. But then the two men came out of the water, laughing and clapping their hands. The bird flew from the branch with one last shrill call and Buddy watched it go until it became invisible against the bleached afternoon sky. He sighed and tried to move his hands, but the weight, the hard iron weight of the chain, held them fast.

The men climbed the bank, laughing, shaking brilliant cords of water from their red arms and legs. They hurried into their uniforms and trotted to the side of the road, with their shirts and trousers all soaked damp. The guard looked up at the patient. He knew the expression, becalmed, composed, beholding something far away that no one else could see. "What'd I tell ya?" he said to the driver as they clambered back into the wagon. "This one ain't gonna be no trouble at all."

The driver snapped the reins and the hack lurched forward. Behind them, the road disappeared in Louisiana dust.

~

The week came and went without fanfare around the District, almost as if nothing so remarkable had transpired over the past two months, with the usual amount of drunkenness, debauchery and petty violence from the army of men who marched through the gilded doors of the mansions and slipped like furtive rodents into the creaking cribs.

But those who paid close attention noticed a lingering tension on the streets. Doors were locked and checked twice, the sporting girls and madams and floor men were more than watchful. But the days passed by without incident, and the extra caution was soon forgotten. After all, word had it that the killer had been King Bolden, of all people, and he was gone for good.

Any citizen who came down Rampart Street looking for the King Bolden Band was told that it was no more, but those same fellows jassed regularly at Longshoreman's Hall with Freddie Keppard on the horn. They went by the Crescent City Band.

The rumors on the street made their rounds, of course. The sporting girls clucked in dismay that such a fine man would come to such a terrible end; and the rounders, nodding over short glasses of Raleigh Rye, allowed how they knew it would end up like this, what with the way he acted and all. Those who had despised him all along, who were disgusted with his music and his antics, or had nursed bitter jealousies over his fame, pursed their lips, narrowed their eyes, drew up all prim and righteous and said: *Now, didn't I tell you so?*

It was rainy one day, bright and hot the next. Valentin waited uneasily through the long week, but nothing much happened. It was quiet, as if Bolden's departure had calmed the turgid Uptown waters. No women were assaulted. Indeed, Storyville seemed all too happy to accept that the nightmare was over and move along.

If Valentin held himself to blame, it appeared he was a minority of one. His mistakes had been either forgiven or forgotten. Messages came to his door, offers of a night's work here and there, entreaties from the madams. He ignored them, and instead spent the hours when he wasn't caring for

Justine pacing his front room or wandering the nearby streets, turning the case over again and again, searching in vain for the missing piece.

Beansoup was released from the hospital the Wednesday following the incident, and Justine on Friday. The boy went to a Catholic orphanage where the nuns fussed over him day and night. He was a pint-sized hero.

Valentin settled Justine in his bedroom to recover. He was solicitous with her, tending to her every need, feeding and bathing her, barely allowing her to raise her head from the pillow. After a few days, the soreness where she had taken the blows eased, but she still felt weak and often dizzy. A doctor visited every third day to check on her. He said her fractured skull seemed to be healing nicely.

She slept much of the time away and while she slept, he sat by the bed, long hour after long hour. At first, he would simply study her face, then turn to stare out the window, all in brooding silence. But then he found himself at odd moments murmuring to her, as if she was wide-awake and listening to every word.

It began with whispered apologies for not protecting her. She had been attacked while he was playing detective and he was ashamed. He guessed that it was his pride, that he was out to prove that he was right and everyone else was wrong. That he was better than they thought. And that his friend Buddy Bolden was not a murderer. He did not entertain the possibility that Bolden had attacked her and Beansoup—at least not aloud.

Because he didn't believe Buddy was guilty. There was plenty to point to him, but Valentin didn't buy any of it. There were too many pieces missing.

He told her he had always expected that Buddy would go out in a blaze of light, his heart exploding from too much of everything; either that, or shot dead by a jealous rounder or a woman he had wronged. But to see him voided of everything, a tattered, hollow shadow, edging along with silent steps, was one possibility he had never imagined. In his pride, he had betrayed every one of the people he cared about. But, of course, she didn't hear any of this.

~

The hack pulled to the gate of Jackson State Hospital. Valentin asked the driver to wait and stepped down.

The doctor, a white man about his own age, ushered him through a set of heavy doors. A large room stretched out before them, the ceiling arched like a cathedral, with hallways to the wards running off at right angles. Tall, barred windows made patterns of dusty yellow afternoon sunlight on the white tile floor.

Thirty-odd male patients shuffled aimlessly about or stood as still as stones beneath the domed ceiling, each one seemingly lost in a private world. The doctor touched Valentin's arm and pointed to a gaunt figure in a blue hospital robe who was shuffling absently along the far wall, one hand held out tentatively before him. As he moved along, he laid fingers on the wall molding, then the windowsill, then the next piece of molding. Valentin watched, feeling a tightening in his throat.

"He has to touch everything," the doctor said in a quiet voice. "He gets very upset if he misses anything."

"That's all?"

"Yes. He's very docile. Never any trouble. He sleeps a lot, of course. They all do."

"Can I speak to him?" Valentin said.

"I doubt he'll recognize you," the doctor said. "He doesn't recognize anyone. His wife came up just last week." He shook his head. "Nothing. He didn't even blink. She was very upset, but…" The two men watched Buddy for a moment.

"Do you know what caused this?" Valentin said.

"We give it the name dementia praecox. But the truth is we really don't know. There's too much pressure, and something in the mind bends until it breaks."

"Will he get any better?" Valentin said.

The doctor was about to launch into a well-practiced speech about always keeping hope, but after studying Valentin's face for a few seconds, he said, "Not likely, no." He glanced at the object under the Creole's arm. "Is that a gift?"

"It's his horn. He was a musician, you know and... I thought he might like to have it." The doctor looked dubious, but he nodded his permission.

Valentin walked across the room and stood by the wall. When the patient's gaze came to rest on the obstruction in his path, his feet stopped moving, his dark brow furrowed as he held his searching hand suspended in mid-air.

"Buddy," Valentin said, very softly. There was not the slightest flicker in the patient's expression. "It's Tino, Buddy." He slipped the horn from the coverlet and held it up before the dull eyes.

The black scarecrow before him took a slight, shuffling step to the side and moved past, his hand already stretching to caress the next piece of polished molding. Valentin felt no difference in the air around him. It was empty, as if no one had been there at all.

∽

The two men shook hands and the doctor went back to the ward. Just before the doors closed behind him, Valentin caught a last glimpse of King Bolden, patiently padding along the blank wall, touching every surface with that gentle hand.

He stopped outside and leaned against the building, his forehead in his hand, trying to grasp what he had just witnessed. Buddy didn't know him anymore. He didn't know anyone. He was gone.

He walked down the hill and back out the gate, ready to leave that place. The hack driver blinked awake, yawned and reached down to give him a hand up. At that moment, Valentin happened to glance back and saw the building that housed the White Wards, the very place where he had delivered Father Dupre. It seemed like it had been a long time ago, but he realized that it had only been a matter of weeks. Back when the whole terrible mess began.

"Sir?" The hack driver was waiting.

Valentin hesitated another moment. "I forgot something," he said and went back through the gate.

He found himself in the lobby, standing on the very spot where he had turned the priest over. Nurses and attendants bustled about on soft-soled shoes. An old Negro was mopping the tiled floor. He walked up to the man and spoke to him in a low voice. The Negro mumbled a name and he tilted his head politely in the direction of the staircase.

On the second floor, Valentin found the attendant named Henry pushing a tiny, enfeebled white man in a wheelchair. He stated his business and was directed to a room with two beds. On one of them, Father Dupre sat staring out the window. He looked small and lost inside his white hospital gown and his flesh seemed to have retreated from his bones. He blinked slowly and whispered to himself.

At the foot of the other bed was a dapper little Frenchman, dressed nattily in a white shirt and cotton trousers and sporting an impeccable mustache. He sat quite upright in an ornate wooden wheelchair, a book in his lap. He looked at Valentin with bright bird eyes. Valentin nodded a greeting and returned his attention to the priest. "Father Dupre?"

Dupre looked around, his eyes milky blue. After a moment, he said, "I know you," in a calm voice.

"Valentin St. Cyr. I escorted you here from the city." The priest nodded slowly, though he didn't seem to have heard. "How are you feeling, Father?" Valentin said.

The old man made a noncommittal motion with one thin hand. "You come from New Orleans?" he inquired presently.

"Yes, Father."

"You're familiar with St. Ignatius Church?"

"Yessir."

"Could you tell me, is someone tending my flock?" The voice took on a slightly fretful note.

"I'm sure they're in good hands," Valentin said.

Another long silence followed, but Valentin could see something working about behind the priest's eyes. He heard a deep sigh and then, "How I failed them. I pray to God to forgive me." The old eyes roamed beyond the window to the hospital grounds and rolling green fields. "That poor child," he said. "The black one. What happened to her?"

Valentin was startled. "She died, Father."

Dupre closed his eyes and sighed again, a deep, weary echo. "God rest her soul. God forgive her. God forgive us all." The priest's silence lasted a minute, then two. Valentin heard a low whistle and turned to see the Frenchman in the wheelchair curling a finger at him. Valentin stepped around the foot of Father Dupre's bed.

"He won't say nothin' now," the Frenchman whispered in an accented voice. "That's how he does when the others come by."

"What others?"

"Them nuns and such. People from his church. Some tall fellow wit' a mustache, he come by once a week. It's always the same t'ing. 'God forgive her. God forgive us all.' Then he won't say one more word. I'm tellin' you, he get that look, he's not gon' talk to no one, *comprenez vous?*"

Valentin nodded. He was still fixed on the priest's mention of Annie Robie. He'd been right. There had been a connection. But he didn't know what it meant.

The Frenchman gave him a quick smile. "Name's Beauchamp," he said and rapped his knuckles on the arm of his chair. "You take me down the kitchen. Time for my *au lait.*"

⌇

They went out of the ward and along the corridor until they reached a set of double doors near the top landing of the stairwell. Beauchamp pointed a finger and Valentin pushed him into the ward kitchen, a sunny room with tall windows. A fat mulatto woman at the sink turned around when she heard the doors swing open.

"Ah, Monsieur Beauchamp," she said with a rich laugh. "It's that time, ain't it? Comin' right up." She splashed milk in a copper pot and threw it on a burner. In two minutes, a steaming *café au lait* was placed in Monsieur Beauchamp's gnarled hands. Valentin declined the offer of a cup for himself.

"Like to get over by the window," Beauchamp said and Valentin started pushing.

"Sun side of the house," the Frenchman said when they reached the destination. The view was the back of the grounds, over the rice fields that stretched to the horizon. The old man sipped his *au lait* with satisfaction and Valentin began working on an excuse to get away. Between seeing Bolden like that and then the old priest talking about Annie Robie, he felt like he had been pushed through a wringer.

"You know what I think?" Beauchamp inquired abruptly. "Dupre's the best kinda priest there is. He don't say much of *nothin.*" He cackled and then gave Valentin a shrewd look. "Whatchu doin' visitin' him? I take you for a sportin' man."

Valentin shrugged. "Not exactly," he said.

"But you got business in the District?" Valentin admitted it with a nod of his head. "I can tell. I spent most of my young years down there."

Valentin wasn't much interested, but he said, "Is that right?"

"I was solicitor for a half dozen them sportin' houses." He smiled smugly. "I was quite the rounder, too."

Valentin slouched against the windowsill. How many times had he listened to Storyville old-timers rant on about the supposed golden years, the middle 1880s, when it was a wide-open town? Now, Valentin guessed, he would hear about how the young fellows these days...

"You young fellows these days, you don't remember the District before they made the law," Beauchamp was saying. "It was better, for sure. Big mansions. Beautiful ladies, but they cut you same as a man if you get outta line." He frowned with distaste. "That was 'fore they made it all *legal*."

Valentin stood there, getting impatient, wondering if he was expected to push the old man back to the ward, or if he could just leave him there by the window and go back to the waiting hack, back to New Orleans and away from that place.

"Old Dupre, he remind me of all that," Beauchamp told an inattentive Valentin. "Them priests, all them proper American people in the Garden District, all them church folk, no, *'specially* them church folk, they raised holy hell. Actin' like they was all religious and proper, and took offense cause it was gon' be a legal District." He laughed again. "Shit! They all owned houses, I mean sportin' houses, in some other part of town. You believe it? It's true. They knew they was gonna lose plenty of money if the houses went illegal everywhere but the District. Mansion full of sportin' girls, that's five hundred dollar a month, just rent." He kissed the tips of his old fingers. "Good-bye to all that. Yessir, they fought the District up and down the line."

Valentin shrugged and said, "Well, they lost."

"You think so, eh?" Beauchamp said. When Valentin didn't respond, the old man gave him a knowing look. "When I was a young sport, I never heeded no one neither," he said and before Valentin could respond, said, "You can take me back now. And you can go on and leave."

∾

Valentin stared blankly out the window as the train rolled south. He saw Buddy pacing along the walls of the ward, patient and unperturbed, a dead man with a heartbeat. Old Father Dupre, another dead man, whispering about poor Annie as he sat stone still on his bed like he was waiting for death to walk in. And the wizened old Frenchman with his stories, entertaining for a few minutes, but then it was the same old saw about the District before Alderman Story and the City Council got to work on it. Back when the whole of New Orleans was a city of sin. A time when...

He straightened in his seat. A thin, almost invisible thread dangled before him. In his mind, he reached out, plucked it between two fingers and gave a gentle tug. The thread was attached to a rope that was fixed to a trapdoor, and he grasped it in both hands and pulled, and in one crashing instant, it sprung wide open.

A rage of pictures and voices came tumbling out and brought him lurching to his feet so suddenly that he scared the wits out of the drummer who was dozing across the aisle. As the other passengers gaped, he stalked up and down the aisle, cursing to himself and making gestures like a madman, all the way to Union Station.

∾

He strode up Canal Street like a man in a fury. He was furious, all right, and the object of it was one Valentin St. Cyr, private detective. He felt like cracking his head against the brick wall of the nearest building. How could he have been so blind, so addle-brained? It had all been there, right from the beginning!

Where was it, Miss Antonia's?

Anderson knew where Annie Robie had died; he knew everything that went on in the District. And he wasn't simply mistaking one Basin Street mansion for another. He had moved the scene of the crime all the way from back-of-town to Storyville. Tom Anderson knew much more than he would—or could—tell him. It was the first clue, and Valentin had missed it by a mile.

He stopped again and began walking in circles on the banquette, looking as crazy as Bolden himself. It had been a gift, Anderson's way of telling him right from the start that the game was Valentin's to win or lose. He shook his head in amazement. It was a politician's maneuver, pure and simple: setting events in motion, but keeping a card up his sleeve while he held himself safe from any scandal.

Valentin would run down the killer because his old friend Buddy Bolden was the prime suspect. Or so the King of Storyville hoped. St. Cyr did not disappoint him.

But King Bolden had played his part far too well; he was crazy as a bug, a target so easy that he couldn't be ignored. So while he was sacrificed, the true killer waited in a house at the corner of a dark Uptown street.

⚬

Valentin stayed on the No. 12 streetcar until it stopped at the corner of First and Howard. He stepped down and the car rumbled away, the overhead wires shooting blue sparks against the falling night. He crossed over eight blocks, going east, and arrived at the corner of Gravier and South Franklin. He stopped, studying the narrow two-story house of gray-brown clapboard. He put a hand inside his coat and felt the hard weight of his pistol. The hand went up to adjust his collar. He ascended the steps. On the threshold were the remnants of a cross, drawn in salt.

Valentin stepped carefully around it and knocked on the door.

Cassie Maples stared at him in surprise. "Mr. St. Cyr," she said.

He took her aside as two of her black-skinned girls watched with curious eyes from the parlor. He stepped close and whispered in her ear. Miss Maples listened, then drew back frowning. He patted her plump arm and she shrugged, looking quite baffled, and pointed toward the back of the house.

~

Sally was standing by the kitchen sink, her back to the door. Behind her, she heard his voice call her name. She hung the drying rag over the spigot as her left hand dipped into the gray, soapy water to grasp the wooden handle of the big kitchen knife. The Creole came over to stand by the sideboard, watching her calmly. She could have lunged at him from where she stood, but he didn't look worried at all.

"You ain't gonna use that thing, so you better put it down," he said quietly. Then: "Sally!"

The girl's liverish eyes jumped. "Yessir?"

"Put the knife down." He spoke to her gently, as if she was a small child.

"No, sir," she said. "I can't do that. Not now." She looked vaguely troubled. "Whatchu want here, sir?"

"I know," he said. She stared at him, then shook her head stubbornly. "But I need you to tell me exactly how it all happened."

Sally watched him with a baffled calm.

"Sally?" he said. "You can tell me."

A deep sigh rose from her flat chest. "It wa'nt none of it my fault," she said.

Very deliberately, Valentin took one of the ladder-backed chairs from against the wall and carried it to her side. Sally didn't look at him and she didn't move. He left the chair and backed away. "Go on, sit down," he said.

After a silent moment, Sally slumped into the chair, suddenly shaking, as if she could barely control the movement of her arms and legs. The knife hung listless at her side, the tip almost touching the floorboards. Valentin crossed his arms and watched her. Sally's eyes were fixed on the floor halfway between them. He got the sense she was waiting for him to begin.

"I figure you were the one who let the Father into the house that night," he said, keeping his voice even. "Was it by the back door?" She nodded. "Maybe Miss Maples knew, maybe not."

A half-minute of silence went by. Then she said, "She didn't know."

"Didn't know at all, or didn't know it was a priest?"

"She thought it was just some white man didn't want nobody seein' him," the girl explained. "Like some old married man. But she don't know much of nothin'. Cause she drinks at night."

"Who brought him by?"

Sally hesitated another few seconds. "Big tall nigger name of Anthony. Drivin' a hack. Always wore this here suit."

"How did it start?"

"Annie went down there to the church," Sally said.

"Why?"

"Well..."

"Was it to pay the rent?"

Sally looked surprised. "Uh-huh. See, it was me who went most the time. But I had a fever this one day and Miss Maples sent Annie. And she met the priest." Her mouth tilted. "Annie said he started talkin' to her, askin' her about where she was from and all...and he said she should come back...she wasn't no Catholic, but he said she could come back anyway. And she did."

"And then he started coming here."

"Yessir. Guess they couldn't have no nigger gal at a white church. But the Father, he want to see Annie, so he come round here."

"Were the two of them...were they..."

Sally pursed her lips primly. "Oh, no, they wa'nt doin' none of that. Father Dupre was too old." She paused for a moment and her voice dropped. "But what I think is, he was in love with her."

"And it was always you who let him in?"

"Well...it got to be that we was like, uh..."

"Friends," Valentin said. "You and the Father got to be friends?" He saw another trace of a smile cross her moon face. "Did he bring you presents?" She nodded. "But then something happened," he said.

Sally's dark brow creased. "Annie saw that fine surrey and that nigger driver and them fine clothes. And she said she want some of that. This other woman, she told Annie she could get it if she want to."

"Gran Tillman."

"Yessir," the girl said. "Gran said Annie should tell Father Dupre she needed to get some money or she couldn't keep the secret no more. And that's what she did." She shook her head woefully. "I told her not to mess with it. But she wouldn't listen to me at all."

Valentin saw her gaze shift and turned his head to catch movement in the kitchen doorway. Miss Maples and the two girls had crept up and now stood crowded together like a trio of anxious birds, their mouths agape, watching and listening. Valentin waved a sharp hand and they disappeared in a silent flurry. He looked at Sally.

"So Annie and Gran had a plan to blackmail Father Dupre," he prompted her.

She looked away somewhere. "It was wrong what they did," she said.

"The night she died."

The black eyes came back to him, looking a little hard. "Yessir?"

"Did Father Dupre come here?"

"Yessir."

"Did Annie say something to him that night?"

"Yessir," Sally said. "She meant to get some money. So Annie did what Gran said and asked for it. But the Father had to go away, cause Annie had a caller come in late."

"King Bolden."

"That's right, yessir."

"But then he left, too."

"Well…yes…" The knife twitched in her hand and her eyes skittered to and fro.

"It was after that, wasn't it? That the trouble started."

The girl's eyes were cold stones. "It was him," she said, now sounding hateful. "That other man."

Valentin stared at her and another door in the back of his mind opened. "John Rice."

"Yessir."

"What happened?"

"Well, Annie was asleep. He come round the back and I…I let him in. He said for me to come with him. We went up to her room and he told me to take a pillow and push it over her face. He held on to her arms. I held there until… until he told me to stop."

"Then what?"

"Then he make her look like she was sleepin'."

"What about the rose?"

"He had it with him."

She paused and her shoulders sagged. She and been holding her secret a long time.

"Why didn't you tell someone?" he asked. Sally mumbled something. He leaned forward. "What was that again?" he said.

"Because he said I'd go to hell for sure if I did," she blurted. "That I'd burn in hell. Burn in hell for a thousand years." Her thin limbs shook and the knife blade rattled against the leg of the chair. "And the next night, that was Sunday, that woman come over from the District while Miss Maples was away." Now her eyes looked fearful again.

Valentin frowned. "What woman?"

"Miss Emma Johnson," Sally said in a muted voice.

Valentin nodded. It was almost perfect. "And she told you what?" he said. "That she'd put something on you if you didn't behave? Some kind of *juju*?" Her eyes fluttered and she nodded. "That would have been the end of it, except there was something Rice didn't count on," he continued. "Someone figured out what had happened. Gran Tillman."

"She was the one brought Annie to the house the first time. And she and Annie was...they was...you know...together sometimes." A strange look crossed the girl's features.

"So Gran started to make some noise of her own?"

"She told Mr. she want some money or she's gonna tell."

"So she had to go," Valentin murmured.

"Mr. came round. Said I was the only one who could do it. Said God would want me to." She gave him a pleading look. "He said I done right. That Gran was a bad woman. That she was going to make it bad for the Father."

"Did he tell you how to do it?"

Her features tightened. "He said just pull somethin' around her throat. It wouldn't hurt, and it'd be quiet. She'd just go to sleep. He gave another one of them black roses to leave behind. And then he brung a rose for every one."

Valentin wanted badly to call for a drink, but he knew he couldn't break the spell.

"That could have been the end of it, but then I started poking around," he said, mostly to himself. "Another problem. No telling what I might find. Maybe that a priest was seeing a young Ethiopian girl. In a sporting house. A house that the church owned. And that the girl turned up dead." Sally nodded miserably. "Rice paid you another visit."

"Well, no, he sent for me to come down to the church. He said we had to fix it."

"To get me off the trail."

"He asked me who come to see Annie."

"And you told him King Bolden." Valentin imagined John Rice's delight at this incredible stroke of luck. Bolden the madman, the corrupter of New Orleans' young people, falling right into his clutches.

"He say, we got to find another girl this King Bolden like." Sally's voice dropped to a conspiratorial whisper. "He say, that's the girl to get. I say, no, I can't do that no more, but he say I got to. Cause I already done that one and he knew 'bout it. He could tell on me." Her eyes flitted in animation. "I heard some of the whores say how King Bolden was sweet on this here octoroon girl named Martha down at Jessie Brown's."

Valentin gestured. "Is that the knife?"

"Yessir." She cleared her throat. "He said don't do her like I did Gran. He said just make like she's a hog you slaughterin'. That's what I did."

"That put King Bolden right in the middle of it," Valentin said. "But I kept coming around." He sat back. "Did Rice tell you to take care of me, too?" She nodded slowly. "So you followed me to Miss Brown's."

"Yessir."

"Why didn't you finish the job?"

Sally looked at him. "I didn't want to…" she began. "You was…I mean, I thought maybe I could make you go away."

"Then you went after another woman. The Jew girl in Chinatown."

"I followed King Bolden and saw him buyin' hop down there at the Chinaman's. I seen her, waiting for him." She paused. "So then that one night I followed her down the alley."

"And another one's dead. But the police still couldn't pin it on Bolden."

"Mr. say I should find just one more girl. And after that, it'll be over. I heard about that one down to Miss Mantley's.

I went there, but it was Miss Mantley saw me and..." She shrugged.

"Did Rice tell you to come to my rooms?"

"He told me to get your woman. But when I got there, I...I couldn't. I wouldn't." She sounded tired. "I'm sorry about that. They gonna be all right?"

"They'll be all right, yes."

"That gal of yours...she fought back."

Valentin stared at the floor, letting the stab of anger pass. "Sally?" She looked at him. "How did you get away with it? I mean without anybody knowing?"

A sudden bitter frown darkened her face. "Oh, that wa'nt hard. I run errands to the other houses, so I'm all over. But nobody sees me." Her mouth twisted up. "I'm a damn nothin', is what. Nobody sees me at all. Least, they didn't..."

Valentin noticed a strange glint in her eyes and understood. Fear had made her kill that one time, but it was more than that fear that made her repeat it. She had been the weakest of the weak, she was nothing to no one. But maybe she wasn't so powerless after all. She had struck terror in the hearts of all those haughty whores and madams. She had almost gotten away with five killings. She had the police and everyone else running crazy over her crimes. She was someone after all. She was the Black Rose Killer.

But then the light in her eyes dimmed as quickly as it had appeared. "What's gonna happen to me?" she asked in a small voice.

"You'll be arrested," Valentin said evenly. "You'll go on trial and hang for the murders of those women."

A tear welled in her eyes. After another moment, she brushed it away, looked and him and said, "How did you know?"

"I saw Father Dupre. He told me." She stared at him. "And he gave you God's forgiveness," he said.

"He did?" Another tear trickled down her dark cheek.

"He said, 'God forgive her. God forgive us all.'"

She let out a long breath. There was a grim pause. "And what about Mr.?" Now her voice was brittle.

"I'll take care of him."

When she raised her eyes, the cold glimmer was back. "Then I guess I'll see him in hell," she said.

∽

He hurried away from the house, but he had gone only one block when his steps slowed and then he stopped. There was no place he need rush to; it was all over now. He would make his way to St. Ignatius and confront John Rice. Then he could inform the police. But there was no rush. After that, there would be nothing more for him to do but go home and keep vigil at Justine's side.

He started walking again. He crossed over four streets to Freret, and found himself passing by the tidy brick facades of St. Frances de Sales School for White and St. Frances de Sales School for Colored, the latter the place where he had first met Buddy Bolden. He walked a bit farther on and, for the first time in fifteen years, rounded a corner and found himself standing on the banquette before the house where he had grown up, the home that his mother had deserted when she wandered off over the lonely dirt roads and barren fields and tenant farm shacks that painted the landscape all the way west to the setting sun.

The empty windows of the clapboard house stared back at him like blind eyes. The eggshell boards had chipped and gone gray and the low wooden steps to the front door had broken off in stunted pieces. It looked like it hadn't been occupied in years. He wondered why this house was one of the few for blocks around that stood deserted. Why had the families that had moved in gone away, leaving empty rooms behind? Because the air was haunted? Because his mother had left some hoodoo that the tenants could not erase? Because a ghost lingered there?

He stepped on the perron. The brass doorknob, now rusted to a dirty brown, rattled loosely in his fingers. The slightest push would open the door on whatever was left inside.

He caught himself. He knew that on the other side of that door were rooms that had once held life, but were now empty but for ancient dust. There would be no echoes and no shadows, nothing left of the home he once knew. The house was as blank and silent as a bier. He dropped his hand and walked away.

~

Miss Cassie and the two girls stood in the doorway, looking in at her like she was some critter locked in a cage, until she couldn't stand it anymore, and she ran out the back door, across the gallery and into the alleyway.

The thoughts churned dully as she half-ran, half-stumbled on.

They gonna hang me. Gonna put a rope around my neck just like they did that boy from Yazoo City. That one that had him a white girl. Hung him from a black tree in the dead of winter. His neck all stretched out like that. The ground was frozen.

No more: Sally! C'mere, girl! *No more:* get this and get that. *No more:* bring that nigger maid in here. I want to see you girls frolic a little.

Who, Sally? She's ugly as sin.

G'wan, bring her on in here.

No more takin' from what's left in the bottles after the night's over. No more finding me a little piece of hop, or a bit of cocaine that slipped under some gal's bed. No more puttin' my mouth on one of the girls when it's a slow night or when they just want some and there ain't no one else around.

That man. That evil, evil man. He said it would be over and everything'd be the same again. He lied. He knew all along what was gonna happen to me. He knew all along.

∾

Valentin walked three blocks down and turned the corner onto First Street. No. 2719 was a few doors down on the other side of the street and now he slowed his steps to regard the house. A light glowed dimly from a back room. A few neighborhood folks strolled by. It all seemed quite peaceful, the evening street moving like a gentle current. And why not? The madman had gone away.

Valentin knew he had stumbled onto the truth and found the guilty party. Buddy Bolden was innocent of everything except losing his mind. But Valentin felt no relief, just a nagging emptiness, a vacant sorrow for all the ghosts, living and dead.

∾

John Rice heard the timid tap on the door and said, "Come in," without looking up from his work. He heard the soft creak of hinges and footsteps. He sensed the visitor stepping inside. His brow furrowed with annoyance as he tried to finish the sentence.

As he placed the period, he caught a blur and looked up to see a flash of motion, a swishing arc as the blade came around with two bony, crusty black hands clasped on the handle. He was slammed in the back and a hot, ripping spike of pain went all the way through his chest. He bolted half out of the chair and a gush of blood and vomit spewed from his mouth and across his tidy desk. He tried to lurch away but one of those awful claws dug into his shoulder and pushed him down and, through the fountain of blood, he became most enraged that this nigger actually put hands on him.

His chest and back were searing as he tried to push himself out of his chair again, but the fire suddenly went out, leaving a numb haze of pain, and he felt terribly weak, too weak to move. Blood was soaking down the back of his shirt, and he wondered dully if it was the same knife she used on the whore.

The girl had backed away and the last embers of the rage that had lit up her eyes had burned out, leaving them flat and calm like an animal's, without mercy.

~

Valentin came up on Orleans Street and gazed at the steeple of St. Ignatius, posed against the inky night sky. He was thinking with grim pleasure about what he was going to say to Rice when he heard the side door bang open and saw a thin, dark figure bolt off into the shadows of night.

He groaned out a curse as he ran for the door. She'd done it. She'd beaten him again.

~

He rushed into the office and found the parish clerk half-sprawled over the desk, one hand gripping the back edge of the solid oak top, the other clutching at his chest as if he was trying to contain his very life from seeping away. Blood had flooded the desktop and splashed down the sides to settle on the seat and in a pool on the rich carpet. The knife had been slammed in below the shoulder blade with such force that only an inch of steel shank remained between John Rice's flesh and the hilt and the point protruded an inch out from his chest in front. Sally had learned some lessons about murder.

Rice's face had gone gray and his breath came in long, weak, burbling gasps.

"Can you talk?" Valentin said.

Rice shook his head and his gaze shifted to the oak telephone box on the desk. Valentin crossed his arms. The parish clerk's whole body shuddered. "Help...please..." It came out in strangled gasps. "... for ....for Father...Dupre..."

"It wasn't for Father Dupre," Valentin said. "You bought the houses. You collected the rent. Plenty of money and no one knew. But the Father got sweet on a young black girl. That just couldn't be. It would ruin everything." He leaned closer. "Five women dead. Could have been six." He brought his face closer to white man's, and caught the dry, husk smell. "You sent her after *my woman!*" he snarled.

Rice looked back at him, his eyes suddenly brimming with hate. Then the eyes rolled up and a trickle of blood ran from the corner of his mouth. Before another minute was out, his expression had frozen into a death mask.

Valentin did pick up the telephone then, and told the operator that he wanted to speak to Lieutenant J. Picot at Parish Prison precinct.

~

Picot rolled through the door like a charging boar and came to an abrupt stop, his eyes going wide. The two blue-coated patrolmen fanned out on either side of him and all three coppers gaped at the bloody tableau. One of the bluecoats crossed himself and murmured under his breath. "What the hell..." Picot said hoarsely. "What the hell...You did this?"

"No," Valentin said, "your friend here met up with the Black Rose Killer again."

Picot drew his eyes off the bloody corpse and stared at Valentin. "What was that again?" he said.

"You and Mr. Rice," Valentin said. "I believe you're acquainted."

The copper made to come around the desk, then caught himself and stopped short. "We better step outside," he said in an almost polite voice. He muttered instructions for one of his patrolmen to call downtown, and turned for the door.

On the stone steps, he produced two cigarettes from a packet. He offered one to Valentin, accompanied by a light. A rumble of thunder echoed over the west side of the city. "So?" the copper said.

"It wasn't Bolden," Valentin said.

"Who, then?"

Valentin turned his face away and blew a plume of smoke. "I believe you got some things to tell me first."

After a few seconds, Picot got it. "Come on, now," he growled. "I can't be divulging police business. Don't be askin' me to do that." Valentin smoked, looking over the cobbled street. "It's confidential," Picot hissed. The policeman waited until half their cigarettes were gone. "Rice called me in," he said in a tight voice. "Said I better watch the both of you. Said Bolden was guilty and that you was protecting him. Said it wouldn't do to have him gettin' away with it just because of Tom Anderson's man."

"But you never had a thing on him, did you?" Valentin said.

Picot didn't reply directly; answer enough. He cleared his throat again. "All right, then. Let's hear what you got to say."

Valentin explained as simply as possible. When he first mentioned Sally, Picot frowned and said, "Who? What maid?" and Valentin remembered what the girl had said; invisible, indeed. He took the copper through each of the murders and ended with the assault on Justine and Beansoup. All but the first committed by a dirt poor, unschooled, homely country girl who was scared out of her wits. But she had outsmarted everyone; or, rather, they had outsmarted themselves.

"All them killings to protect a priest?" Picot said.

"That wasn't it," Valentin said. "The church owns Cassie Maples' house. And probably a few more. Rice had bought them up with church money. He was collecting rent and putting some of it in his pocket. But you knew that, Lieutenant." The copper opened his mouth to protest, then closed it, and dropped his eyes. "So, you have a murder back-of-town and somebody starts looking too hard..."

As they talked, two police wagons filled with coppers came rattling up the street, followed by a hack carrying the parish coroner. A captain of detectives arrived and, mounting the steps, waved a sharp hand at Picot.

"Where is she now?" the policeman whispered as he turned to follow his superior inside.

"I don't know."

Picot looked startled, then angry, then he sighed and went inside, leaving Valentin alone on the night street. Some minutes passed and it started to rain.

～

She walked back uptown, staying to the side streets. She had washed the blood off in a rain barrel along the alleyway off Gravier Street.

She heard the sound of thunder, first far off and then closer. As she crossed Poydras, heavy drops splattered wetly on the cobblestones. The rain dappled the street and the wind came up, and New Orleans settled under the gentle hush of an evening shower.

She passed a dozen pedestrians before she reached Canal Street, and the few that bothered glanced at her then looked away absently, as if she was some stray dog, or not there at all. Black thoughts tumbled through her head. She was nothing before and she was less than nothing now. She had done bad things, terrible things, and people were going to hate her, and then she was going to die, her neck breaking as she choked at the end of a rope. Her mama would be so ashamed. She would cry out loud and say, *Why? Why, my baby? Didn't I raise you right?*

They would bury her back beyond some cornfield outside Yazoo and no one would put flowers on her grave because it would be haunted ground. And for a long, long time, little boys would talk about it, dare each other to go see.

She tried to feel sad, to mourn her own poor lost soul, but the tears wouldn't come out. She just felt sleepy. The rain fell harder, soaking the nap of her hair, soaking through her clothes, making her shiver. She wanted to go home. She wanted her mama.

She saw the streetcar coming down the line, all lit up inside, full of white folks on their way to enjoy themselves in the French Quarter. It was rolling along at a steady speed, the steel wheels grinding and the wires overhead crackling and spitting blue fire.

In the whole time she had been in New Orleans she had got to ride the streetcar maybe a couple dozen times. She wasn't worth the fare, so she walked. She thought about that as she took one careful step into a street that was slick with rain.

She began to run. The rain was coming into her face, pelting her eyes and cheeks with little darts. She ran harder, her dress sticking to her thighs and in between, and her old shoes felt wet and heavy like the river mud back home. As she came close to the tracks, she raised her eyes and saw the face of the conductor looking down at her, his mouth falling open and eyes going wide as she made the long, clumsy leap and disappeared under the car's heavy wheels.

Seventeen

Six white horses in a line
Six white horses in a line
Six white horses in a line
Gonna take me to my buryin' ground
　　　　　　—"One Kind Favor"

The King of Storyville was sitting at his usual table with a bottle of brandy, a half-full glass, and a second, empty glass before him. A gray afternoon peeked in through the shutters. He gazed moodily into the shimmering amber liquid until a shape appeared there. He looked up. The Creole detective was standing on the other side of the table, watching him, his mouth forming a tight line. He hadn't heard him come in.

"Is it over?" Anderson said. Valentin nodded. "Please, sit down." Valentin sat. The white man poured brandy into the second glass and placed it before him. The two of them drank in silence. Then Anderson said, "You know it had to happen this way."

"I don't know that," Valentin said flatly.

"Believe me, it did."

Valentin looked across the table. "You knew something right from the start."

The King of Storyville gave an absent shrug. "I guessed that Father Dupre was somehow connected to that girl at Cassie Maples.'"

Valentin emptied his brandy in one swallow and reached for the bottle without asking. "I received a visitor very late

Saturday night," Anderson went on. "Sunday morning, in fact. He woke me up."

"John Rice."

Anderson nodded. "He asked my assistance in a delicate matter. He wanted to get Father Dupre out of the city. He said the Father's afflictions had become a problem for the diocese. An embarrassment, if anyone got wind of it."

"Did he mention Annie?"

"He mentioned no one. He asked that I not pry further, that I trust his word on the matter." Anderson grimaced. "Trust his word." He smoothed his mustache. "And then, of course, I heard about this girl in the house back-of-town. So, I thought perhaps…"

Valentin said, "Heard from who?" Though he thought he knew.

"From Antonia Gonzales," Anderson said.

"You sent her to me?"

"In a manner of speaking. You were already in her mansion. With your young lady."

Valentin sat back, shaking his head. "You arranged all this and then ended up chasing me away," he said. He knew why the King of Storyville had played the game, but he wanted to hear it from the white man's lips.

Anderson's eyes wandered off for a moment. "I have a longstanding friendship with the police department. It's an important friendship for everyone. It simply wouldn't do to have my man crossing into their territory and causing them all manner of trouble. I had no choice but to let you stumble, then send you away."

"I was the goat."

"More like the wolf," Anderson said with a half-smile. "I knew that—"

"—that I would come back and try to solve the case."

Anderson nodded. "I was counting on your friendship with King Bolden…and your pride. I knew you wouldn't let go of it." He sipped his brandy, watching the Creole's stony expression. "I want you to know I'm sorry about Bolden. But he would have ended up in Jackson, or someplace worse, sooner or later."

"I would have picked later."

The King of Storyville pondered for a moment. "But you know that if it wasn't for him going there, you might never have caught the guilty party."

"I would have caught her," he said.

"I suppose so," Tom Anderson said, "but I couldn't wait."

The Creole detective made a rude gesture with one hand and Tom Anderson regarded him narrowly. "It wouldn't have made so much difference in the end, Valentin."

"I might have saved Buddy."

The King of Storyville lifted his glass, put it back down. "You did save him. You saved him from being railroaded for the murders. He would have hanged for that."

"He's locked up in an insane asylum."

"It's better than him being dead."

"Is it?"

"Maybe in a little while he'll be cured and he can get out of that place."

"You didn't see what I saw," Valentin said. "He'll never get out of that place."

Anderson was silent for a few moments. "Well, I'm sorry," he repeated.

Valentin turned a frigid stare on him. Anderson would brook such a look from few men, certainly no colored. But he let it pass and waited until St. Cyr's harsh eyes softened with an odd sadness and shifted away. "Storyville," he said in a bemused voice. He sighed out loud, shrugged his heavy shoulders, and moved on. "I want you to come back to work for me," he said.

Valentin's brow furrowed. "I'd like to think about it, if I may," he said.

The King of Storyville nodded benignly.

~

Justine Mancarre recovered from the injuries she suffered in the attack, though she continued to experience occasional bouts of dizziness and blurred vision in one eye. She remained in the apartment on Magazine Street.

Lulu White's fancy man George Killshaw was never seen or heard from again. Miss White's one hundred fifty thousand dollars cash went with him, but she eventually decided against dispatching Valentin to California to locate him.

Guy Molony, Manuel Bonillas, and Lee Christmas were successful in engineering the overthrow of the government of Honduras.

One month later, the Creole detective returned to the employ of Mr. Tom Anderson.

~

On a day painted with the coppery light of early autumn, Valentin stepped off the train at the Jackson station. One more time, he rode a hack along the road overhung with weeping French moss, arriving at the grounds of the hospital in the stillness of a late morning.

He was standing in the corridor as Buddy approached at his creeping pace, his fingers touching every bit of molding, every protuberance, every whorl in every appointment, just as before. Their eyes met for an instant, but Valentin saw no spark, no light at all, just silent pools that reflected nothing. He watched Buddy go on his shuffling way, feeling an urge to speak to him, to call his name, to tell him he was sorry. But instead he just stared at the lost soul who was once his—

"You a friend of his?" a voice said.

Valentin turned to see a Creole attendant, medium-brown, in white shirt and trousers, standing in the archway. "Is he getting any better?"

"No, but I think he's fine the way he is," the attendant said. "He don't cause us no trouble."

"But is that all he does?"

"Yeah, well, pretty much so, yessir." The attendant paused for a moment, then came up with a curious smile. "But you know there was this one thing happened," he said. "This been a few weeks back, it was a Sunday afternoon. We had this here orchestra from town playin' in the ward. While they was playin' their tunes, Mr. Bolden didn't pay no mind, he was just walkin' up and down like he do, there in the back of the room. But then those fellows stop playin', you know, and put their instruments down." The Creole lowered his voice secretively. "Well, I see Mr. Bolden walk up there to where their chairs is at, and he goes and picks up this horn." He laughed quietly. "I ain't never seen him do nothin' like that before, y'understand, so I'm watchin' him, wondering what is he up to...and he took that horn and carried it over to the window."

Valentin stared at the attendant, thinking: *I know this. I know this story from somewhere.*

The man said, "Well, he put it to his mouth and I say, my Lord, is he gonna *play* that thing?"

Valentin, now rapt, said, "Did he?"

"Well...I don't know if he played, but he made some kinda noise out of it," the Creole said. "And everybody looked around, you know, like who is makin' that ruckus?"

"Then what happened?"

"Well, one of the other 'tendants walked over there and took the horn away. Mr. Bolden didn't fuss, didn't do nothin'. He just looked out that window for a long time, and then he went away." The Creole shook his head. "I can't for the life of me figure out what he thought he was doin'."

They turned to watch Buddy creep away down the long, shadowy corridor. "He was calling his children," Valentin said. "He was calling his children home."

〜

Though he went to see Nora now and again, that day in October was the last visit Valentin paid to Jackson State Hospital for the Insane. He believed that King Bolden would never leave those grounds, would never come back from the still, silent, empty place he had made for himself.

He was correct. Twenty-four years later, Charles Buddy Bolden died quietly, in his sleep. He was buried in an unmarked grave near the hospital grounds.

Afterword

I drew on a variety of sources for this narrative. Three in particular are recommended. The first is *Storyville, New Orleans* by Al Rose (The University of Alabama Press, Tuscaloosa, AL) for its panorama of the District throughout its colorful history. The second is *In Search of Buddy Bolden, First Man of Jazz* by Donald M. Marquis (Louisiana State University Press, Baton Rouge). It is the only definitive study of this enigmatic genius. Finally, Richard Gambino's *Vendetta* (Doubleday, New York) documents the drama of the lynching of Italian prisoners in New Orleans' Parish Prison in 1891.

Additionally, I wish to thank Dr. Bill Meneray for the use of relevant materials from Special Collections department at the Tulane University Library, as well as those unnamed others who supplied additional threads to this tale.

—David Fulmer

To receive a free catalog of Poisoned Pen Press titles, please contact us in one of the following ways:

Phone: 1-800-421-3976
Facsimile: 1-480-949-1707
Email: info@poisonedpenpress.com
Website: www.poisonedpenpress.com

Poisoned Pen Press
6962 E. First Ave., Ste. 103
Scottsdale, AZ 85251